SHE'S UP TO NO GOOD

A NOVEL

SARA GOODMAN CONFINO

LAKE UNION

PUBLISHING

Published by Lake Union Publishing, Seattle

www.apub.com

Amazon, the Amazon logo, and Lake Union Publishing are trademarks of Amazon.com, Inc., or its affiliates.

ISBN-13: 9781542033619
ISBN-10: 1542033616

Cover design by Philip Pascuzzo

Printed in the United States of America

For my grandmother

CHAPTER ONE

"I met someone."

I didn't look up from my phone, my legs curled under me on the sofa as I scrolled real estate listings. "Oh! I meant to tell you; I did too. Remember that girl with the horrible, yappy dog? Her name is Vanessa. She's actually nice. I'm following her on Instagram now."

"No. I—" Brad stopped, cleared his throat, and tried again. "I mean I *met someone*, met someone."

This time I looked up, my eyes narrowing. "What does that mean?" He didn't respond. His shoulders were hunched, his face set in a pained grimace as if bracing for an attack. I glanced down at his left hand, saw his thumb worrying the white gold band that he had worn for the last four years, and felt something in my stomach drop. "Oh."

He sank into the chair opposite me. "Jenna—I—I'm sorry."

I exhaled audibly and nodded. "Well. Okay. It's done, though, right? We'll—we'll get some counseling, and we'll—we'll deal. People do . . . things . . . and they come through it."

His eyes widened. "No."

"What do you mean no? No, it's not over with . . . her? Or no you don't want . . . ?"

"I'm sorry."

I didn't realize my phone was still in my hand until I threw it across the sofa. "Stop saying that!" He winced, and I felt a wave of nausea wash over me, but I fought it back and got myself under control. "But—we were looking for a house."

"I know."

"And were going to start trying for a baby once we were in the house."

"I know."

"And you . . . you were . . . lying . . . when you said you wanted that?"

"Not . . . lying exactly. I do want kids. And I thought maybe it would help. Look, I wasn't trying to find someone else. It just happened. And it made me realize how unhappy we were."

"*I* was happy!"

He looked like he was going to argue, and I felt my hopes rise. Not that I *wanted* to fight, but if he was willing to, there was still a chance. I could get him to come around. But then he changed course. "Okay. I haven't been. We fight all the time. We barely ever have sex anymore. And I'm tired of having to pretend everything is perfect when it's not."

I took a deep breath. He wasn't *wrong* exactly. We had been fighting a lot. And sex? It couldn't have been *that* long, could it? No, I couldn't remember the last time we actually did it, but it couldn't have been more than—I stopped myself. If I had to calculate, it wasn't a good sign. But . . . that didn't mean we weren't happy. Maybe there were some cracks in the foundation, but it wasn't anything we couldn't fix.

"We can work on all of that. We can go talk to someone. We can— we can take a trip. Get away. Just the two of us. Reconnect. Put the baby stuff on hold for a little while. I mean, not too long. We're not getting any younger. But a little while. Until we're on more solid ground. We'll go back to that resort we went to on our honeymoon—we've been saying for years we should go back. We were so happy there. We'll go there, and we'll just . . . fix this."

Brad shook his head. "I don't *want* to work on fixing things anymore. It shouldn't be this hard. You and I were always better on paper than in person. And with Taylor, it's just . . . easy."

"*Taylor*? She's twenty-two, isn't she? You're leaving me for a cliché."

Brad jerked his head to the side to crack his neck, which made me cringe. He knew I couldn't stand when he did that and apparently didn't care anymore. "Don't you see? This is exactly what I'm talking about. You don't even care that *I'm* not happy. You just care about how you're going to look when you tell people."

I glared at him. How dare he act like I was shallow for not caring about his feelings when *he* was leaving *me* for a twenty-two-year-old?

My mouth dropped open to argue. To tell him that he was the one who didn't care about *my* feelings. But all that came out was a whisper.

"But we're married."

Brad leaned forward, his elbows on his knees, and began to speak, his tone earnest, but I only heard phrases over the roaring in my ears. *Unhappy for a while now . . . realized I was relieved when you weren't pregnant . . . fighting so much . . . not in love anymore . . . both deserve better.*

I interrupted him mid-sentence. I may not have comprehended much of what he said, but I had heard enough. "You won't even try?"

"I'm sorry."

"But—we just ordered a Peloton. It hasn't even come yet!"

He shook his head, rolling his eyes slightly. "You can have it."

"I don't care about the stupid Peloton!" He flinched. I looked up at him. "So, what? You're just . . . leaving?"

He cleared his throat again, and this time I felt my chest clench as I realized the next problem. "Tonight, yes. And you can stay as long as you need to until you figure out what you want to do. But—" I held up a hand and he stopped talking. I knew what was coming. The condo was his before we got married. I had never been on the deed. And as a middle school teacher, I knew it was way, way out of my price range. "I'll help you out as much as you need to get on your feet."

"I guess I need a lawyer to figure out how this works." I was trying to get a reaction. Brad was a lawyer, and that had to sting. But he nodded.

"I'm going to sell the condo. I'll give you half."

My mouth opened again, this time to tell him I didn't want it, but I shut it quickly. If he was going to blow up everything we had built and leave me single and homeless at thirty-four, I shouldn't walk away with just a ridiculously expensive exercise bike. I nodded almost imperceptibly.

He stood and walked to the door, where he picked up a duffle bag that I hadn't noticed him packing. "I'm sorry," he said one more time from the doorway, pulling off his wedding ring and leaving it on the little table where we put the mail. And then he was gone.

I dropped my head into my hands, tears of frustration at my own inadequacy beginning to fall. *How did this happen?* I asked myself. We had been together six years. *Six years!* And then just out of the blue . . . ?

But was *it out of the blue?* a tiny voice in my head asked. Now that I knew the context, he had been smiling at his phone a lot. In a way he didn't smile at me anymore—when had he stopped looking at me like that? I never even asked him what he was smiling about. But the truth was, I didn't care. I should have cared. I should have asked. I should

4

have realized something was wrong when *he* stopped wanting to have sex. Or maybe I should have cared when I stopped wanting to, which was a long time before he did.

But I hadn't.

I swore, breaking the silence of the room. It was too quiet. I looked around my home of the last five years, seeing it through fresh eyes now.

This condo . . . Well, it had always been a waystation. Even before we got married, the plan was to buy a house to start our family in. This was never a forever home.

And maybe that was where the trouble started. I was ready to move and try for a baby four years ago. But Brad found something wrong with every house. Or the timing was off with his job. And whenever I brought up a baby, he reminded me that he wanted us to be settled in a house first.

On the one hand, it was better that he was selling the condo. I wouldn't have to imagine him there with some fresh-out-of-college, doe-eyed blonde who laughed at every inane thing he said. But on the other hand, why hadn't he been willing to take that next step with me?

I took a deep breath. *I can do this.* Yes, I was hurt, but I had survived one hundred percent of the setbacks I had faced so far in life. This wouldn't be the one that destroyed me. I would take a couple of weeks to lick my wounds and then . . . Well, I'd just figure out a game plan. Because I had to.

But to do that, I needed to leave. Right then. Staying in the condo even just overnight would make it harder.

"This isn't my home," I said out loud, picking up my phone from the end of the sofa where I had thrown it.

I felt my shoulders droop as I unlocked it and saw the house I had been looking at when Brad dropped his bomb. It would have been such a perfect place to raise a family. I felt my imaginary future children popping like bubbles and dissipating into the air.

With a sigh, I swiped up to close the app and took another deep breath, looking one last time at the Washington, DC, skyline through the balcony door. Then I went to my contacts, pressed the call button, and cradled the phone to my ear.

"Hi, sweetie. What's up?"

My voice broke as I started to cry in earnest. "Can I come home for a little while, Mom?"

CHAPTER TWO

Six months later

My mother strode into the family room and planted herself directly in front of the television.

"Hey!" my dad and I said in identical tones.

"Mom, you're in the way."

She raised an eyebrow and moved a hand to her hip. "*I'm* in the way? Last I checked, this was my house." Dad picked up the remote from where it sat on the empty sofa cushion between us and turned off the TV, scooting infinitesimally away from me.

"Uh. Okay. Sorry?" I looked at my dad, silently asking him what was going on with Mom. He didn't respond. His fingernails were apparently fascinating.

"Jenna, it's Saturday night."

"Did you want to watch the movie with us?"

My mother blinked heavily and exhaled. "I want you to get out."

My stomach dropped. She was my mom. She wasn't supposed to kick me out, even if I was almost thirty-five and camping out indefinitely in my childhood bedroom. "Where am I supposed to go? I don't get paid over the summer."

"I don't mean you have to *move* out. I mean, yes, I do. You have to move out. But I don't mean tonight. I mean, you need to start *going* out and seeing people. And doing things. And not watching *Caddyshack* with your father on a Saturday night. Or else you're going to be living here until you're our age."

"It's *Groundhog Day*," my dad volunteered. "We watched *Caddyshack* last night. It's a Bill Murray-a-thon." Mom glared at him, and he stopped talking.

"I go out," I grumbled.

"Happy hour on the last day of school doesn't count."

"Where do you want me to go, Mom? My friends are all married. It's not like they're going out to bars. They're home. Most of them with their kids."

"And if you don't start going out, that's *never* going to be you."

I felt self-righteous tears pricking at my eyes. "That *was* me. I'm not even divorced yet."

"By choice. If you signed that separation agreement and let him file, you could be free in a couple of months instead of dragging it out for a year. And if you let him out sooner, he'd sell the condo, and then you *would* have money to move out, even over the summer."

I crossed my arms sulkily. Brad absolutely deserved to have to wait the full year of separation to file for divorce. I wasn't going to make it easier on him by saying our separation was mutual so he and Taylor could be together guilt-free sooner. Even if stalking on social media had proven that she wasn't actually a twenty-two-year-old blonde, I wasn't feeling particularly generous toward my replacement.

My mother wasn't deterred. "Also, those married friends have single friends. And you should be using online dating. Set up a Tinder account."

"Ew! Mom! That's mostly for sex!" My dad mimed smothering himself with a pillow.

"Match, then."

"That's for much older people."

"Jdate."

"People who are desperate to get married."

"Look, I don't care which one you use, but it's time to get out there and meet people. Have you even put on a bra or makeup since school ended?" My father found a piece of lint on the sofa that completely engrossed him. "I'm not saying you need to get remarried right now, but you need to do *something*. I get that you needed to hide for a little while, but enough is enough. You can't live in your childhood bedroom forever. You're not in high school. You're going to be thirty-five in a few weeks. It's time to get your act together."

I rose, stung, and stormed up the stairs without a word. I almost slammed my bedroom door, but that would only prove her point, so I shut it quietly instead and edged around the Peloton, which took up way too much space in the room but that I insisted on keeping. I had found Taylor on the app, and Taylor used hers daily. That didn't prove they were living together, but either they were or Brad had bought a second one, because he was on a four-month streak as well.

I sank onto the double bed that had seemed so big when I transitioned from my twin at fifteen but that now hurt my back because the mattress was twenty years old, and my spine was about to enter the second half of its thirties. *What am I going to do?*

The reality was that I had no desire to date anyone. Not that I actually missed Brad either. Truth be told, I didn't. He snored. He was frequently condescending. He belittled my job as less important than his. And he had terrible taste in music and movies.

Instead, I felt hollowed out. Like someone had taken a melon baller and scooped out all the pieces of who I actually was. Sure, I still looked like Jenna. But realizing my life was a total lie took a toll. I wasn't ready yet to reemerge, admit that I had lost, and start again. I just didn't have anything to give someone new. The well was empty.

It'd serve her right if I went on Tinder and brought a guy home, I thought, imagining the look on my mother's face when some random dude came walking into the kitchen in the morning, shirtless, to drink milk straight out of the carton. *You told me to try Tinder,* I'd tell her, shrugging. Not that my parents kept milk in the house. My mother used powdered creamer, and my father was lactose intolerant. But random one-night stands had to drink milk out of the carton while half-naked. Everyone knew that.

My work best friend did have a guy she wanted to set me up with. The thought filled me with dread, but maybe going on a date would get my mother off my back for a month or so. And that was all I needed. Another month. Maybe two. I'd feel more like myself then.

Hopefully.

CHAPTER THREE

I avoided my mother as much as I could for the next few days, which took a lot of careful listening at doors and sneaking into the kitchen at odd times to eat. If I was invisible, maybe she would forget I was there. Like that woman who lived in the walls of someone's house for years before they realized she existed.

But Thursday night, I heard the unmistakable arrival of my grandmother, followed by my father tapping quietly on my bedroom door. "Your grandma has that crazy look in her eye," he said when I let him in. "You know she and your mom are going to fight when she shows up like this. You can't leave me alone with them."

I sighed but agreed to come down. There was a good chance that my grandmother would take my side. Evelyn Gold's primary form of entertainment was antagonizing her two daughters, which frequently worked to her grandchildren's benefit. She could turn on us just as quickly but usually didn't if our mothers were present. If torturing her daughters was an art form, my grandmother's work belonged in the Louvre.

My grandma turned her gaze, as sharp as ever though she was almost eighty-nine, on me, her eldest granddaughter, as I slid into my seat at the dining room table. "The recluse is alive," she said, the corners of her lips twitching into a half smile. "I was sure I'd have to burn the house down to get you to come see me from the way Anna talks."

My mother's mouth tightened into a thin line. "She comes downstairs. She just doesn't leave the house."

"Who wants to leave the house these days? You've got everything you need inside with the Google and the Facebook. Besides, it's too humid." She winked at me. "You just stay in your cocoon until you're ready to come out."

"You're not helping, Mom."

"Not helping *you* maybe. Jenna, darling, am I helping?" My dad started to laugh, which he tried to hide behind a fake coughing fit when my mom glared at him. Grandma pursed her lips. "On second thought, don't answer that. I wouldn't want to get you in trouble."

My mom shook her head and changed the subject. "Have they set a date for the wedding yet?"

"Whose wedding?" I asked.

"Your cousin Lily. She's marrying that boy from the bog thing," Grandma said.

She meant my cousin's blog. I raised an eyebrow. "And she's actually having a wedding?"

"Sounds like it."

"Huh. Good luck finding anyone willing to be her bridesmaid."

Grandma waved a hand in the air. "Water under the bridge. That was all ages ago."

I opened my mouth to say, *It was just a couple of months ago,* but stopped myself. It wasn't. It was a year ago that my cousin had been a bridesmaid in five weddings over one summer and had blown up her life by writing a blog trashing the brides, which of course went viral. Lily always had a flair for the dramatic, which, to be fair, did run in the family. It couldn't *not* when you were descended from our grandmother. But it *had* been a year, hadn't it? Which meant I had been living in my childhood bedroom for . . . Oh no.

"Good for her," I murmured half-heartedly.

My grandmother looked at me sharply again, then reached over and patted my hand. "Brad wasn't the one," she said. "You'll see. I never liked him."

Couldn't you have told me that six years ago? I thought. But then Grandma turned her attention back to my mother.

"Sometime in the spring, I think. Staying local. Nothing big or fancy."

"I'm glad it worked out for her," Mom said. "Joan must be over the moon."

Grandma rolled her eyes, but there was a gleam of amusement in them. "Joan is already trying to plan some huge wedding. It's her last one, after all. She wants to go out with a bang."

A muscle tensed in my mother's jaw. I was the eldest of her three girls. Beth was thirty-one and had just had her second baby. But Lindsey was twenty-nine and showed no signs of settling down anytime soon. And a nearly thirty-year-old unmarried daughter paired with a soon-to-be-divorced nearly thirty-five-year-old daughter put her at a distinct disadvantage in the lifelong competition between the two sisters.

"But," Grandma continued, cutting into the chicken piccata on her plate. "I didn't come here to talk about Lily tonight." She speared a small piece with her fork. "I came to say goodbye."

I felt my blood turn to ice. Cancer. It had to be cancer. She didn't *look* sick. But she always looked the same. My breath came in shallow bursts as I heard an unfamiliar sound from across the table. I looked over to see my mother, deathly pale, holding a hand to her mouth. "Oh, Mom," she choked.

Grandma put her fork down and calmly dabbed at her mouth with her napkin, looking at the effect she'd had on us. "Such a fuss. I'll be back in a week or two. And I'll have my Apple phone thing with me."

"Wha—what are you talking about?"

"I'm going home. To Hereford. Tomorrow."

"You're . . . what?"

She nodded.

"Why?"

"I have some business to attend to."

"What business?"

"My own." She crossed her arms.

My mom looked at her mother warily. "How are you getting there?"

"Why, driving of course."

"Absolutely not."

Grandma perked up significantly at her daughter's declaration of war. "Absolutely yes. I've driven there a thousand times."

"Not in the last thirty years!"

"You don't know everything I've done. And I'd like to see you try to stop me."

"Mom. You're almost ninety. You can't drive from Maryland to Massachusetts."

"Watch me."

My mom opened her mouth to argue, but a voice stopped her. "I'll drive her."

The voice was mine.

"You?" Mom asked.

I found myself nodding.

Grandma leaned back in her chair, looking at me appraisingly. "Why?"

"I—" I didn't know the answer. I turned to my mother. "You said I needed to get out—"

"I meant on a date!"

"And . . . well . . . I've never been to Hereford."

"Yes, you have," they said in unison.

"I—I have?"

"We took you when you and Beth were kids," Mom said. "You loved the beach there."

I could suddenly picture standing on a rock jetty, watching a tiny snail crawl around a tide pool. "The rocks?"

Grandma nodded. "You'll know it when you see it. It's in your blood."

I wasn't so sure, but I continued. "And—well—it'd help everyone out. And it's not like I have anything better to do."

Grandma cocked her head at me. "Go pack. We leave at eight. I want to be there in time for dinner."

~

My mom knocked on my door as I was packing, then came and sat on the edge of my bed. "Grandma went home?" I asked.

"She did. I wish she wouldn't drive at night, but she refuses to Uber."

"Can she even work the app?"

"I think she can do a lot more than she lets on." My mom hesitated. "But she can't do as much as she thinks she can anymore either. Don't let her push herself too hard."

I scrunched up my face. "Has anyone ever successfully stopped Grandma from doing *anything*?"

"Once or twice." The ghost of a smile crossed her face. "But you need to keep an eye on her. Her heart isn't what it used to be. She messes up her pills sometimes. And she absolutely cannot drink. Her doctor was crystal clear about that." My mother now insisted on accompanying my grandma to the doctor, partially because of the mix-up that had occurred with her pills, but mostly because my grandmother was an inveterate liar. If my mom wasn't in the room, not only would Grandma spin any number of outrageous tales to the doctor, but my mom would never get a straight answer about her mother's health. I was surprised my grandmother tolerated that invasion of privacy. But it was the one sign that she was, in fact, slowing down somewhat. She would never admit it, but taking the wrong pills and the disorientation that followed had frightened her.

"Is she up to this?"

"I think she'll be okay with you there. Alone? No."

"Okay." I nodded, looking at the clothes strewn across the bed and draped over the Peloton. "What's the weather like there? I don't know what to pack."

This elicited a genuine smile. "Cooler than the beach here. Definitely bring a couple sweatshirts. Some long pants. It can get chilly at night. You'll want sneakers. There are hills in town, and a lot of the paths are pretty rocky." She paused. "Or at least they were. I haven't been in so long now. I'm sure a lot has changed."

"Why did you stop going?"

"Well, Sam's wife sold the cottage. We used to spend every summer there when Joan, Richie, and I were kids. But then when my grandfather died, he left the cottage to Sam, and when he died, Louise sold it. And with no place to stay and my grandparents gone . . ." She trailed off, shrugging. "That time we took you and Beth, everything just felt wrong. Your grandmother was—everything was different. And—I don't know. It was so far to drive when you were little, and it was just easier to take you to Ocean City."

"So, bathing suit, normal beach stuff, but some warmer clothes too?"

"Bathing suit if you want to lie on the beach, yes. You won't get in the water."

"Pollution?"

"What? No! It's gorgeous water. It's just *cold*."

I added two swimsuits to the pile, along with coverups. I didn't know if I'd actually get beach time, but if so, that made this whole crazy plan worth it.

"Bring real clothes too. I don't know if she has you staying anywhere near the beach. You could be in town, which is five miles from there." I added a couple of sundresses, a cardigan, some jeans, and a few shirts to the pile. "You should go to sleep," she cautioned. "It's a hard drive when you're doing the whole thing yourself."

I rolled my eyes. I had driven from Daytona to DC senior year of college when my idiot friends decided to drink hurricanes an hour before we had to check out of our hotel over spring break. But someone had to get us home, and I was the responsible one.

Yes, Brad had done most of the driving when we went places in the last half decade, but I knew I could do it. Besides, my grandmother couldn't possibly be more belligerent than three drunk college girls. And getting out of my parents' house, even if it was for a road trip with my grandma, would be a welcome reprieve for a few days.

CHAPTER FOUR

"We'll take my car," my grandmother said, giving my BMW the side eye over her comically oversized sunglasses. The car was the first thing I looked for in the settlement agreement Brad sent—it would be mine outright when I signed it.

I looked at my grandmother's dinged-up Lexus, parked crookedly in her driveway. "Why? Mine is newer. And I have Sirius."

"Well, I'm serious too. And I don't ride in German cars."

"What's wrong with German cars?"

She put a hand on her hip. "I can think of about six million things wrong with them, young lady. Now put the bags in my trunk. We need to get on the road."

My jaw dropped open. "You won't take my car because of the *Holocaust*?"

"Just because it didn't happen in your lifetime doesn't mean it didn't happen. It happened in mine, and I don't ride in the German cars. You don't like it? Don't come with me."

"I—" I stopped myself. This wasn't going well. And if it was a sign of what was to come, my grandmother *might* just be worse than a carful of drunk sorority girls. I took a deep breath. "Okay. Let me just grab my stuff. Does your car have Bluetooth at least?"

"Is that some kind of pirate? No, it's a normal car."

"I—uh—okay." I pulled my suitcases from the trunk and trans-
ferred them to the less offensive Japanese sedan, then took my grandmother's bags from the front step. "How did you get these down the
stairs?"

"How do you think? I carried them."

"How?" I asked, heaving the second one into the trunk. "I can
barely lift this."

"Maybe I'm stronger than you." I looked at her. She looked like a
cartoon insect, smiling behind the sunglasses. "I packed them downstairs. I'm quite resourceful, darling."

"Clearly." I held out my hand. "Keys?"

"Don't be silly. I'll drive the first shift. In fact, I can drive the whole
way. You can take a nap."

"Grandma. You're not driving the whole way. Why not just let me
do it?"

"Because I'm not dead yet. My car, my rules. I'm driving. At least
until the first stop." I shrugged and went to the passenger seat.

My grandmother climbed gingerly into the driver's side and buckled herself in with great effort. "They make these things so hard to do.
My whole life we never needed these. Now they give you a ticket if
you don't wear it, but they make it so hard to hook." I tried to make
it look hard to buckle mine, but it clicked easily. "There we are," she
said finally, then backed rapidly out of the driveway, running over the
curb and bouncing into the street with a loud thunk. "Did you say
something, dear?"

I gripped the door handle, eyes wide as she peeled off down the
street at nearly double the speed limit, weaving wildly. "Maybe I should
drive. You can navigate."

"Who needs to navigate? I know the way. Driven there a thousand
times. Maybe more."

"Yeah, but—that was a stop sign!"

"It's a suggestion. They put it in a few years ago. No one stops there."

"Do—do they make you take a test—at your age—when you renew your license?"

She waved her hand flippantly. "Oh, I don't have one of those."

"A *license?*"

"They took it when I had that mini-stroke thing a few years ago. So stupid. I'm fine."

"You don't have a license?"

"Why would I need a license? I know how to drive. And no one thinks I'm too young to drink."

"Grandma, pull over."

"Why? What's the matter with you?"

"PULL OVER NOW!"

She pulled to an extremely crooked stop, the front end of the car a foot from the curb, the back end at least four feet. "Whatever is the matter? We haven't even made it out of the neighborhood yet."

"Out. I'm driving."

"No, you're not."

"Grandma, if you don't get out of this car and let me drive, I'm calling the police myself."

"What are the police going to do? Put me in jail?"

"Yes," I said through gritted teeth. "And I'd rather not start our trip by bailing you out. So switch with me."

"So dramatic." She sighed, unbuckling her seatbelt and then fixing me with a withering look. "Don't tell your mother about the license."

What have I done? I thought, realizing that staying home with my parents might have been the better plan.

~

My grandmother gossiped about my cousins for the first half hour while we left the Maryland suburbs of Washington, DC, and merged onto I-95 North. I listened half-heartedly. I didn't really want to hear about how happily married two of them were and how happily engaged the third was. Not when I was about to become the lone divorcee.

There was a lull as signs for Baltimore appeared, and I changed the subject. "So why are we actually going to Massachusetts?"

She scowled at me. "I told you. That's my business."

"Okay, but like—I won't tell Mom. You can tell me."

"Why are you really getting divorced?"

I looked over at her, eyebrows raised. "Excuse me?"

"You want to ask questions about things that aren't your business? I'll do the same. So don't tell me it was because he found someone else. That's the symptom that sends you to the doctor, not the diagnosis."

I winced as I remembered Brad's voice. *We haven't been happy.* "Okay. We don't have to talk about why we're going."

"You don't get off that easy," Grandma said, taking off her enormous sunglasses and peering at me. I kept my eyes deliberately on the road. "Was the sex not good?"

"Grandma!"

"What?"

"I don't want to talk about *that* with you."

"I don't see why not. It's how you got here, after all. And believe it or not, it's how your mother got here too."

"Please stop."

"Your grandfather and I never had a problem in that area, thankfully. Not that I had a lot of experience before him. But I had some."

I imagined unhooking my seatbelt, opening the car door, and rolling into traffic. "Can we please talk about literally anything else?"

She let out a cackle of laughter. "You asked why we're going. You don't want to know the answer?"

"If the answer is you're going to find some guy who you slept with before Grandpa, I don't want to know anymore."

"I'm not going for Tony."

"Ew. He has a name. You actually—ew." I took my hand off the steering wheel to rub my temple.

"Of course he has a name. And there's an important lesson there for you. It's not like you only get one love of your life. I had two." She paused, and I could feel her shrewd eyes burning a hole in the side of my face. "Although I don't think you've had one yet."

I rolled my suddenly tight neck in a circle, wondering briefly if the reason Brad always cracked his when he got stressed was because *I* was the one making him crazy. "I loved Brad," I said quietly.

She shook her head. "Tell yourself that if it makes you feel better."

"What do you know about it? You weren't in our marriage!"

"You weren't either, or there wouldn't be someone else there now."

I held up a hand. "Can we just not talk for a little while? We've got a long drive—a long week—ahead of us, and I'm not trying to fight with you."

"Who's fighting?" I shot her a dirty look and she capitulated.

For approximately three miles.

"Tony's not really the start of the story," she said as we neared the Harbor Tunnel on 895. "My father is."

"Zayde." I nodded, using the Yiddish word for "grandpa," which my mother called him.

"His name was Joseph. Yusef, really. But he wanted to be American. He came here from Russia, you know. He was nineteen and was running away."

"What was he running away from?"

"A bad marriage."

I sighed loudly. "Okay, really? Is this whole trip actually a setup to get me over Brad? Because you're not very subtle about it."

"Who's being subtle? Not everything is about you, you know. And this trip isn't."

We were quiet for another mile, and I finally forced my shoulders to relax. "Fine," I said as we emerged into the light. "What was so bad about his marriage?"

"Oh, he wasn't married. His mother hired a matchmaker for him. And when they set up the *shidduch*, he followed the matchmaker to find the girl. He wasn't marrying her if he didn't like the looks of her. And he didn't. He said she looked like an old sack of potatoes."

I blinked at the rationale. "So he just ran away?"

"He pocketed the money his father gave him to buy a wedding suit, took the train across Europe, and bought a ticket on a ship to America instead."

"How did he settle in Hereford?"

"By accident. He took the train from New York to Boston, where a cousin was. But he fell asleep and missed his stop. When the line ended, he got out and walked from the station to the water and said that was where he wanted to live. And he did from then until the day he died."

"What about your mother?"

"She was from Rockport. A couple of towns over. Her parents came from Russia while my grandmother was pregnant with her." She paused. "I never knew my grandparents."

"How did they meet?"

"She was clerking for her father. She was older, twenty-five by then. He was twenty-four. Papa walked in, took one look at her, and knew she was the girl for him." She stopped talking, her lips pressed into a line that meant she wasn't going to elaborate further.

We rode in silence for another two miles, and I wished for my car, where I could put on music from my phone. My grandmother's face was turned to the window. I looked over at her, thinking for the first time that she looked older than the grandmother of my memory. Vain to a T, she religiously followed a skincare regimen that kept her looking

23

younger than many of her contemporaries. Not that she had that many contemporaries left. Most of her friends and all her siblings were now gone. She was the second-youngest of seven, but the baby of the family had died very young in some nebulous accident. And my grandfather had been gone for—wow, was it five years already? Loss takes a physical as well as an emotional toll, and the lines on my grandmother's face told that story.

I saw the sliver of my own face in the rearview mirror. No, there weren't lines yet, but that didn't mean I looked the same anymore either. Six months of learning to live with the fact that my life was never going to be perfect—that *I* was never going to be perfect—had done some damage. I may not have looked *older*, but something had changed. I didn't know how to quantify it except that I didn't like it.

I glanced back at my grandma, who was watching me through the same pair of eyes as mine, just hooded in wrinkled lids. "She wasn't in love with him, you know."

"Who?"

"My mother. She was in love with someone else. That's why she wasn't married at twenty-five."

"Then why—?"

"He wasn't Jewish, so her father wouldn't let her marry him. I think she married Papa to get away from her father's house."

"That's horrible."

"It's how it was back then." She shrugged. "You married Jewish, or your parents sat shiva for you. It's why I didn't marry Tony. He was Portuguese."

"And you just went along with that? That doesn't sound like you."

She let out a small bark of laughter. "You know me well. No. But it was for the best. In the end. My father did eventually come around on Tony—too late for us, but things work out the way they're supposed to. It wasn't his fault. He was a product of his time. Just like I am. Just like you are."

I shuddered. "Just tell me this Tony guy isn't actually my grandfather. I couldn't handle that."

My grandmother was indignant. "I wouldn't do something like that!"

"Are you telling the truth?"

"Of course I am! I would never lie."

"You lie all the time!"

"True." She grinned. "But I would never cheat." And with that, she began to tell me about the day she met the first love of her life.

CHAPTER FIVE

February 1950
Hereford, Massachusetts

Evelyn Bergman wasn't the smart sister. That was Helen. She wasn't the beautiful sister, Gertie. Nor was she the sophisticated one, Margaret, or the baby, Vivie. But no one remembered that she had four sisters when she walked by and flashed that wicked smile of hers, her brown eyes twinkling with a spark so full of humor and life that the recipient felt like he was the luckiest person in the world.

And she knew it too.

So when she first saw the boy leaning against the wall outside the drugstore, she didn't hesitate. Never mind that he wasn't alone. She had noticed him before. And that day she decided she wanted to get noticed in return.

"I'll be right back," she told Vivie and their friend Ruthie. Vivie was eighteen months younger than Evelyn. Ruthie was exactly halfway between their ages.

"Where are you going?" Their mother had tasked Vivie with keeping Evelyn in line; an impossible assignment, which she was destined to fail daily.

"I have a date tonight."

"With who?" Vivie squeaked. Gertie and Helen, at twenty-three and twenty-six, were married. Margaret was in college—Joseph insisted all of their children attend, though Miriam deemed it wasteful. But Joseph was equally firm on one other point: there would be no dating before college.

Evelyn inclined her head toward the two boys, who were in the process of lighting cigarettes from a shared pack against the wind. "The one on the left." She started across the street, then called back over her shoulder. "He just doesn't know it yet."

She stopped directly in front of her target, who lowered his cigarette to avoid blowing smoke in her face. "Can I bum one of those?"

Tony's breath caught when he looked at her. He knew who Evelyn was. You didn't live in Hereford and *not* know. But he'd never spoken to her, let alone been on the receiving end of that smile.

"Good girls don't smoke," his brother Felipe said.

Evelyn laughed merrily. "I don't think anyone has ever called me *good* before." She leveled her gaze back at Tony. "Now don't get me wrong. I'm not fast. And I've got two older brothers, so I know how to take care of myself fine. I'm just not one for following rules. Now, how about that smoke?"

Tony tapped one out of the package, lit it, and handed it to her. She held it but didn't put it to her lips and extended her right hand. "Evelyn Bergman."

"I know." Tony shook it. "You're the girl who crashed into the movie theater."

She laughed again. "My goodness, that was ten years ago. You've known who I was for ten years, and I don't know your name?"

"Tony," he said. She cocked her head to the side, asking a nonverbal question. "Antonio."

"Portuguese?" It wasn't a random guess. He wasn't Jewish, or she would know him already. And the Portuguese community in the coastal fishing towns was large. They had been there longer than the Jews, who

27

mostly fled the pogroms of Russia and more recently the Germans, and they were a dominant portion of the fishing industry. Felipe was dressed for the docks, though he didn't smell like he had been there yet that day.

Tony nodded, knowing that would be the end of it. Evelyn wasn't the only Bergman everyone in town knew. Joseph, in the more than thirty years since he had arrived in the sleepy seaside town, dirty and tired from his voyage, had established himself as a pillar of the community. He began by working for Mr. Klein in his dry goods store, first by stocking the shelves, then working the register as he gained Mr. Klein's trust. He was a fast learner, studying first English, then business, then how to charm the people of Hereford. And when Mr. Klein dropped from a heart attack one day, his widow sold Joseph the store—what he couldn't afford outright, she allowed him to pay off gradually.

Once he was a business owner, he met and wed Miriam, the daughter of a wholesaler with whom he did business, and set about populating the town with his seven offspring. He sat on the town council, the only Jew and the only immigrant to do so. He believed in the country he had made his own and appreciated a place where an immigrant could rise and be respected. He was honest and fair, respecting hard work above all else.

Except with any man courting one of his five daughters, in which case the young man needed to be Jewish and college educated in addition to hardworking. Joseph himself would only have passed two-thirds of that test, but religion was the area where he refused to budge on any form of assimilation. And the young men of the town learned that quickly when the elder Bergman girls came of age.

"Do you like Frank Sinatra?" Evelyn asked.

"I—yes?"

"Great. We'll see that movie with him and Gene Kelly tonight."

"We'll—what?"

"You're taking me on a date," she explained slowly.

"I am?" She nodded, and he couldn't stop himself from grinning.

"Don't get any ideas now. Remember, two brothers, and I always have a hat pin on me."

Tony placed his hand over his heart in a pledging motion. "I'll pick you up at seven?"

"Oh goodness, no. My father would murder you. I'll meet you there."

"Um . . . okay."

"Great," Evelyn said with a bright smile, then turned to walk away. She took two steps, stopped, and turned back, holding out her hand. "Wait. Here's your cigarette."

"You can have it."

Evelyn laughed. "Oh, I don't smoke." She placed it between his fingers. "I'll see you tonight, Tony."

"What was that?" Felipe asked as they watched her cross the street to the two girls who gaped at her brazen display.

"I think I just fell in love."

Felipe shook his head. "That's the kind of girl who ruins your life."

"Maybe. But she might be worth it."

CHAPTER SIX

"What does that mean, you crashed into the movie theater?" We were nearing the Delaware state line.

My grandmother chuckled. "I was infamous for that one. We lived at the top of a hill. It was—that house had some kind of magic to it. It didn't look that big, but it was like it took a deep breath and expanded when everyone was there. There were only two bathrooms for the nine of us. And on Fridays, you couldn't use the downstairs tub. Mama kept the fish for *Shabbos* dinner in there until it was time to kill it and cook it."

"She kept a *live fish* in the bathtub?"

"Every week." She shrugged. "We were used to it. And you'll never taste a fish that fresh."

"Okay," I said, my eyebrows raised. "But the movie theater?"

With a slight shake of her head to clear away the other path her thoughts had taken, she returned to the hill. "The movie theater was down the hill. They had only built it a few years earlier. Maybe in 1935? It was still pretty new. It was the old kind—not like these big ones today—with one screen and a balcony. Papa used to park his car on the street outside the house. I was seven and decided I was going to 'drive.' I got some friends, and we hopped in the car and were playing. But I must have knocked the brake off, and then I was really steering down the hill. Crashed right into the front doors."

"Were you hurt?"

"Nah. But they were showing *The Wizard of Oz*, and when people came running to see if I was okay, I said something about not being in Kansas anymore. That was the story that went all over town."

"What happened?"

"Mr. Ambrose owned the theater. He saw I wasn't hurt, so he marched me home by the ear and delivered me to my mother. Horrible old man. If he'd had a decent bone in his body, he would have taken me to Papa's store." She looked over at me. "I was Papa's favorite. I was never in trouble if he was there. Mama was a different story."

"What did she do to you?"

"Nothing. I hid under the bed until Papa got home. She got the broomstick to try to get me out, but she couldn't reach when I got into the corner. And he didn't care about the car."

"Explains a lot," I muttered.

She shrugged. "You can worry about the small stuff, or you can live your life. Papa believed in living."

I pulled the car toward the left as we neared the rest stop. "I could use a coffee."

"If you're getting tired, I can drive."

"Absolutely not."

"Because I crashed into a movie theater over eighty years ago?"

"Because you don't have a license!"

"You and my mother would have gotten along. No fun at all."

"I'm fun!" My grandmother raised an eyebrow, and I felt my shoulders slump. "Okay, maybe not these days. But normally I am."

"I'm sure you are, dear." She patted my arm. "No one said you weren't."

"You just—oh, never mind." I decided to make the coffee a venti.

After parking and helping my grandma undo her seatbelt, I stood on the sidewalk to wait, then realized she was struggling to get out of the car. I went to the passenger side and noticed a large scrape down the side. "Do you need help?"

If looks could kill, she would have been the only one left to drive the car. "I do not *need* anything."

"Of course not." I remembered my mother's warning and the fact that my grandmother had a bad hip. "My legs are really stiff after being in the car that long. I'm here if you just feel like taking my hand."

She peered up, checking for sarcasm in my response, but when she saw none, she put a spotted and wrinkled hand in mine and allowed me to heave her up. Once on her feet, she shrugged me off, but I kept my pace slow to match hers. *She was really going to try to do this alone,* I thought, shaking my head. My mother always told me to smother her with a pillow before she got as bad as Grandma, which I had thought was melodramatic, but if my mother turned into this? Yikes.

After a visit to the restroom, we waited in the Starbucks line together. "I hate that you can't use the app at rest stops," I complained.

"What's an app?"

"It's a . . . I don't know . . . a thing on your phone. And you can preorder at pretty much every other Starbucks."

"Why would you want to do that?"

"So you don't have to wait in line."

"If you don't want to wait, just go to the front of the line."

"You can't do that."

Her mouth curled into a grin. "*I* can." Shaking off my attempt to put a hand on her arm, she walked right up to the front of the line. "Excuse me," she said to the man standing there. He looked about thirty and was staring at his phone screen. "I'm almost ninety years old. Do you think I could go ahead of you?"

"I—um—yes, ma'am. Of course."

She reached up and patted his cheek. "Such a polite young man. Your grandma must be so proud of you." She turned back to me. "Come on. We need to get back on the road."

"Excuse me. I'm sorry," I said, mortified.

"It's fine," he said, gesturing to the waiting barista.

"A venti skinny caramel macchiato." I turned to my grandmother. "What do you want?"

"A coffee. Did you order food? I'd take one of those triangle things."

"What kind of coffee?"

"The coffee kind."

I shot an apologetic look at the people in line behind us. "Okay, what size?"

"What size are you getting?"

"Venti."

"Vanity? Really? I wasn't flirting with him. I just wanted some coffee."

"No, Grandma, a venti is a large."

"Then why didn't you say large?"

I looked in horror at the now significantly longer line behind us. "Okay, do you want a large?"

"What would I do with a large? I'd never sleep again."

"Oh, for the love of—what size coffee do you want?"

"A small, darling."

"Do you want anything with flavors or an espresso drink?"

"Hmmm, I don't know. What flavors are there?"

I threw my hands up, exasperated. "She'll have a tall drip and a blueberry scone."

"A drip sounds terrible. Get me what you're having." I rubbed at my neck but complied, then paid and half dragged my grandmother to the side to wait for our order.

I looked down at my phone and began composing a text to my mother.

But when I finished, I realized my grandmother was far too quiet and looked up to see she had wandered to the milk station. I took three steps toward her, then stopped as I watched her open her purse and dump the entire container of artificial sweeteners into her bag. I rushed over. "What are you doing?" I hissed.

She looked at me in surprise. "What? They're free."

"You're not supposed to take all of them!"

"Why not? They have more." Raising a hand, she called to the closest barista. "Miss! You're out of Sweet'N Low."

"I will *buy you* some Sweet'N Low. Just put it back."

"I'll do no such thing. You never know if they'll have it when you're traveling." The barista brought over a box of sweeteners and began restocking the station. "Thank you, dear." My grandmother waited until the barista had walked away, then looked at me triumphantly and dumped the new packets into her bag as well.

I heard my name, grabbed the tray with our coffees and the scone, and took my grandmother's arm, dragging her toward the door. "I cannot believe you just did that."

"You have a lot to learn." She plucked the smaller of the two coffees from the tray and took a sip. "I love when they put the caramel on top of the foam."

"I thought you didn't know what kind of coffee you wanted."

My grandmother just smiled.

CHAPTER SEVEN

April 1950
Hereford, Massachusetts

As her vivacious second-to-last child kissed her father goodbye and practically floated out the door, Miriam watched with the trained eyes of a mother who has already raised three older daughters, then she sighed heavily. Evelyn might have said she was going to the carnival with Ruthie, but it was obvious, both from the fact that Vivie was not accompanying her and from her demeanor, that she was lying. Evelyn had a boyfriend.

Drying her hands on her apron, Miriam walked to the door of the living room and cleared her throat so Joseph would look up from his newspaper. "She goes out a lot lately," Miriam said, nodding at the door.

"She's a happy girl. With many friends."

Miriam didn't reply. He had been so quick to assume wrongdoing with their older children, and yet, when it came to Evelyn, he was blind. So instead, she turned her attentions to Vivie, who was draped across the armchair in the corner of the living room, her nose in a book. "Why aren't you at the carnival?"

Vivie looked up guiltily, confirming Miriam's suspicions. "I . . . didn't want to go." Lying might come easily to Evelyn, but Vivie had yet to master that skill. Especially to their mother.

Turning a quarter of the way back to Joseph and speaking louder, so he couldn't pretend not to hear her, she spoke, ostensibly to Vivie. "She has to bring you next time. She can't go with Ruthie and not you."

"She said she didn't want to go," Joseph said in his heavily accented English from behind his newspaper. Miriam sighed again, returning to the kitchen and the seemingly unending stack of dishes, even with five of her seven children grown and out of the house.

It'll be a relief when the sixth goes, she thought, leaning heavily against the counter. Her back ached lately, and she felt every moment of her almost fifty-six years. It wasn't that she didn't love her headstrong, obstinate daughter—quite the opposite. But Evelyn was the most work of her children. The most worry. And always the most trouble.

So it was no surprise that she would be the one to fall in love while still in high school. Miriam thought Joseph was a fool for insisting their five daughters go to college. Bernie and Sam could use those degrees and make something of themselves instead of being shopkeepers. Not that she begrudged Joseph his store. He had made a comfortable life for them. They were respected in town and wanted for nothing. It was a much better life than she ever expected. But her sons—she *kvelled* thinking of them—they deserved so much more.

Daughters—what could they do, really, other than marry well? Yes, Helen and Gertie worked in the factories during the war, while first Bernie and then Sam went off to fight, but an actual career would be secondary. Yet Miriam did not argue, because she felt they would find better husbands in college than in town, which both Helen and Gertie had done.

Evelyn would, too, Miriam knew, providing this local boy didn't get in the way of that. When Vivie excused herself to go to bed, Miriam cornered her in the bedroom Vivie had shared with Margaret and Evelyn until Helen and Gertie left, vacating a room.

"Who is he?" she asked quietly, closing the door behind her.

"Who?"

Miriam sat on the bed and fixed her daughter with a knowing stare. "The boy Evelyn is seeing." Vivie's mouth dropped open, but she closed it quickly. "I know you know."

"Mama, please. She'll hate me."

"She won't. She needs you too much."

"I promised."

"And she keeps her promises?" Vivie's eyes welled up, and Miriam felt a wave of pity. It was hard living in Evelyn's shadow. "Is he Jewish?" she asked finally.

Vivie shook her head and Miriam hesitated. That was both better and worse. Joseph perhaps could have been swayed by a Jewish boy who had marriage potential. But when he learned this, he would be the one to insist it end. For once, Miriam would not have to be the heavy with Evelyn. He doted on her, and while Miriam understood why—even she wasn't immune to the girl's charm—it meant that Miriam was the one who had to put her foot down. The other children she could soothe when Joseph wouldn't let them curl their hair or wear lipstick or go to the movies on Shabbat or do so many of the things the other American children did. But Joseph never refused Evelyn, so Miriam had to. And Joseph, inexplicably and infuriatingly, argued with Miriam for Evelyn to receive the same privileges that he had denied their first five children.

"Your father will put a stop to that."

"You can't tell her I told you." Vivie's eyes were wide, and Miriam pulled her in to her bosom and held her. "Shh, *bubbelah*. I won't."

When Miriam returned to her bedroom, she retrieved a hatbox from the trunk in the corner and sat heavily on the bed with it.

Checking the clock on the nightstand, she gingerly lifted the top and removed the hat, revealing a stack of letters, tied in a faded ribbon, from oldest to newest. They were all sealed. Miriam held the stack to her chest, closing her eyes and feeling an overwhelming sense of sympathy for the daughter who thought she didn't love her.

Miriam loved Joseph for saving her from a life alone in her father's house. For giving her their seven children, each a miracle in their own right. For the six grandchildren she had from her three eldest, and the seventh on the way. For trusting her to run the household as she saw fit. For denying her nothing. For the life they had built together.

She loved him as much as she could, but her whole heart wasn't hers to give. And as long as a letter arrived each year on her birthday, she knew, even though she couldn't bring herself to read them, that Frank still loved her. Even though her father had sent him away. Even now, more than thirty years later.

For a moment, she wavered, remembering the heartbroken months she spent after Frank left. The despair she thought would swallow her whole. But she saw the photograph she kept on her dresser of Bernie, her firstborn, as a baby.

No, Miriam thought. Ending this dalliance was the right thing to do. Besides, nothing could crush Evelyn. She might be willful and spoiled and impossible. But she was strong. And stopping this now would only ensure that she recognized the right path when it presented itself.

And where would Miriam be now if she had married Frank? A sailor's wife with no family, no real home? She was better off where she was. And Evelyn would be too.

CHAPTER EIGHT

"What happened to Vivie?" I asked.

"What do you mean?"

"Well, I know she died young." When Grandma didn't reply, I looked at her. She was looking out the window, but I saw a muscle jump in the loose skin of her jaw. "How did she die?"

"It was an accident. She drowned."

"In the ocean?"

"It wasn't in the bathtub."

There was a note of pique in her voice, so I tried to go for a laugh. "The bathtub with the fish on Fridays?"

That elicited a small smile. But when she didn't keep playing with me, I realized I had touched a subject that wasn't open for discussion. There was no outlandish lie. No equivocation. Just short answers and silence. The most un-Grandma answer I had ever received. So I steered the conversation back to the story she had been telling me.

"Your mother was onto you and Tony, then?"

"She had her reasons. I didn't understand them until she was gone. But I took one look at Vivie when I got home and knew the jig was up. Mama had her so cowed. Vivie was . . . delicate. She couldn't handle yelling and Mama was a yeller. I just yelled back. Maybe that's why Mama didn't like me."

"I'm sure she liked you."

"Oh, she loved me, don't get me wrong. If she didn't, she wouldn't have bothered telling Papa. She would have let it go on and made it worse when he found out. I'm just not everyone's cup of tea." She chuckled. "Well, maybe everyone's but hers."

How do you get that level of confidence? I wondered. *I used to be brave, but never like that.* Not that I felt brave anymore.

"What did your father do when he found out?"

"Told me I couldn't see him anymore."

I rolled my eyes, changing lanes. "Because he wasn't Jewish? I've never understood that. Like honestly, who cares? It's just another reason to discriminate against people."

Grandma threw up her hands. "Do you know what year I met Tony?" I shook my head. "Nineteen-fifty." She looked at me expectantly, then sighed. "Do they teach you *anything* about history in schools these days?"

"Grandma, I'm literally a history teacher."

"And you don't know when the Holocaust was?"

I groaned internally. Everything was about the Holocaust with her generation. "It wasn't like he was German."

She didn't reply quickly, meaning I was about to get a lecture. "Papa came from a village in Russia. The Russian army used to come through and take boys when he was young. The boys never came back. His mother hid him by shaving her head to make wigs for him and his brother and dressing them as girls whenever they came through.

"He tried so hard to bring his family over. He sent money. His mother didn't come. Then after the war, he spent years trying to find his relatives, his friends. He never found anyone." She was staring straight ahead and had pulled her sunglasses back down over her eyes.

I was just opening my mouth to say something—I didn't know what exactly yet—when she continued. "I found them though." I shivered involuntarily at her tone. "When the Holocaust Museum opened,

I marched down there and met with their historians. I said I wanted to know.

"The village was in Poland by then, not Russia. Before the war, there were ten thousand Jews there. Seventy-three survived. The rest went to Treblinka. Everyone he ever knew—just . . . gone."

She wiped at an eye under her glasses. I had never seen my grandmother cry. Not even at my grandfather's funeral. "He knew. When he didn't find them, he knew." I found myself breathing rapidly and felt a sense of heaviness in my chest that I couldn't explain. I hadn't known any of these people. But I also hadn't known my family had lost anyone. We were all here, on all four grandparents' sides, before it happened. I thought we were untouched.

"When you experience that—well, you get a pass on some things," she concluded.

"You're not mad at him?"

"Darling, how could I be? I wouldn't have your mother, or you or Joan or your uncle, your sisters, or your cousins if he hadn't done what he did. And it was me who decided, in the end, to marry your grandfather. You think I would settle?"

I tried to picture her settling for anything. This ridiculous, indomitable woman. "Is that why you won't ride in a German car?"

"Who says I won't ride in a German car?"

I gritted my teeth. "You did. That's why we took your car."

"Oh. I lied. I just didn't think you'd let me drive yours." She grinned. "But if I was wrong, I'd be happy to take it for a spin when we get home."

CHAPTER NINE

April 1950
Hereford, Massachusetts

"Did you have fun last night?" Miriam asked, setting a plate in front of Evelyn at the breakfast table. On weekdays, she served the black pumpernickel bread that she made herself, slathered thick with butter. Joseph had urged her for the last few years to buy her weekday bread and use that time for herself. Miriam simply looked at him and continued kneading the dark dough seeded with caraway. When the house was full of children, there would be pumpernickel on the table on Sundays too, but now that it was just four of them, there was challah, left over from Shabbat.

Evelyn glanced up at her suspiciously. Miriam disapproved of most fun, but she saw nothing amiss in her mother's demeanor. "I did." She smiled as she bit into the soft challah. Miriam saw the smile from the corner of her eye, and the edge of her mouth turned down.

"Even though Ruthie didn't go?"

"What do you mean?"

"I called her mother this morning." Joseph lowered his newspaper. *I knew it*, Evelyn thought, even as she recognized she was in trouble. Her father claimed never to hear what was happening at the table while he read his newspaper. "Ruthie stayed home last night."

"I went with some girls from school," Evelyn lied smoothly. "Ruthie changed her mind at the last minute." She held up a hand to shield her mouth from her father but spoke loudly enough to ensure he heard. "She's on her monthlies." Joseph raised his newspaper quickly, and Evelyn's chin tipped up in satisfaction. Her mother wasn't catching her that easily.

"You went with that Portuguese boy from the docks," Miriam shot back, and Joseph's newspaper fell to the table with a thud as his hand slammed on top of it.

Evelyn looked from Miriam to her sister, who was whiter than the tablecloth her mother bleached twice weekly, then glared murderously at them both.

"Evelyn," Joseph boomed. "Explain."

She looked back at Vivie to try to gauge just how much her sister had divulged and saw a tear slip down her cheek. A wave of guilt washed over Evelyn at Vivie being caught in the middle. It wasn't her fault; their mother was a tyrant. She gave Vivie what she hoped was a reassuring look and turned to her father, her voice cool.

"I went on a date."

"You're not allowed to go on dates."

"Papa, it's 1950, not the dark ages in Russia. Everyone goes on dates."

"Your sister doesn't."

"Vivie is sixteen."

"Your older sisters didn't."

Evelyn tried not to laugh. Honestly, she did. But she felt her lips twitching into a smile, and then the laughter bubbled out. "Oh, Papa." She reached out to put her hand on his. "Yes, they did."

A cloud of anger crossed his face as he started sputtering, but Evelyn rose from the table and hugged him around the neck. "Papa, darling, don't get angry. It's nothing serious. It's not like I'm going to get pregnant or marry him." Miriam gasped. "I like him. He likes me. And you'd like him too."

Joseph ducked out of her grip, but the thunderous rage that had accompanied a similar conversation with Helen simply wasn't in him with Evelyn. She knew how to manage him, and even when he knew he was being managed, he was powerless to resist his favorite daughter.

"He's not Jewish?"

"No. He's not."

"And he works at the docks?"

"He's still in school. But his family owns boats, and he helps them sometimes."

Joseph shook his head. "No. If he was Jewish—but he's not. I forbid this. You will not see him."

Evelyn looked at him appraisingly, judging her best course of action. He wouldn't throw her out, that much she knew. But he could make it significantly harder to see Tony. And she had no intention of giving him up. So what he didn't know couldn't hurt him. He'd settle for a simple, "Okay, Papa, I won't," and there would be no follow-ups. She glanced at her mother out of her peripheral vision. That one would be a problem. Miriam was standing, arms crossed, watching her second-youngest daughter shrewdly. No, for Miriam, she would have to put on a show to be believed.

She could do that. Evelyn looked longingly at the bread on her plate, wishing she had gotten a couple more bites in first. She was hungry, and no one made bread like her mother. But this was more important than her stomach.

With a sudden motion, she swept her plate off the table, shattering it on the floor. Had it been her mother's good china, she would never have gone so far, but this was their daily set, easily replaced from Joseph's store. "I will never forgive you for this," she said, breathing raggedly. Then she turned and stared at her mother with genuinely

44

poisonous eyes. When Miriam opened her mouth to speak, Evelyn burst into fake tears and ran upstairs to her room, where she slammed the door behind her and locked it.

Then she knelt at the grate on the floor, which led directly to the dining room below her, where she could hear every word said at the table.

"I hope you've learned a lesson," Joseph was saying, presumably to Vivie.

"Yes, Papa," she whispered, barely loud enough for Evelyn to hear with her ear to the floor.

"She's a good girl," Miriam said. "Unlike *that* one."

"Evelyn is a good girl," Joseph said, defending her. "She's upset. But she's doing as she's told." Her mother started to speak, but Joseph cut her off. "That's enough excitement for one morning. It's done now."

Evelyn smiled and flopped across her bed, then reached into the nightstand drawer for the chocolates Tony had given her the night before. They would tide her over.

Like clockwork, there was a soft knock on her door after she heard the chairs scraping at the table downstairs. Miriam would have tried the doorknob first. Joseph wouldn't have entered his daughter's room without making gratuitous noise to make sure she was decent, if he ventured to her room at all.

Evelyn opened the door and yanked Vivie in, then turned the lock, took the pillow off her bed, and wedged it over the floor grate. Miriam undoubtedly knew where that grate led as well.

"I'm so sorry—" Vivie started, standing before her sister, wringing her hands miserably.

Evelyn pulled her to sit on the bed, then offered her a chocolate. "It wasn't your fault. It was mine for telling you in the first place. You know Mama can read you like a book."

"But I just ruined everything."

Evelyn's lips started to curl into a smile, but she suppressed it. Under normal circumstances, she would tell her sister; nothing was over with Tony until she decided it was. But Miriam was out for blood, and it was better for everyone if Vivie thought it was done. She'd have to find a new alibi among the girls in her class, someone whose mother Miriam didn't know. Ruthie had been a risky choice anyway—their family was Orthodox, which meant that Ruthie's parents were much more restrictive about what she could do than Evelyn's were. But that was a problem for another day.

"Boys are like buses. Another one will come along in an hour." She elbowed her baby sister. "Just don't tell Mama the next time I take the bus."

~

Evelyn planned to stay in her room until supper, but by one, her stomach was rumbling. Had she been one of her sisters, her mother would have placed a plate outside the door and knocked quietly so she would have something to eat. But Miriam wasn't going to aid and abet when it came to Evelyn. If Evelyn wanted to eat, she'd come downstairs.

She chewed her bottom lip, looking at the alarm clock on her nightstand. Papa napped on Sunday afternoons. Mama would be washing laundry in the copper tub in the kitchen. She glanced toward the window. As children, they had all climbed the pear tree that grew outside her bedroom window—it just hadn't been her bedroom then. After opening the window and leaning out, she tested the branch that she could reach. It was thick and sturdy. She looked down. It was difficult to see through the early blooms of spring, which would give way to some of the best fruit in Essex County come the end of summer, but there was a path of branches she could climb down. And more importantly, back up again.

He's Up to No Good

She grabbed a couple of dollars from her drawer and shoved them into the pocket of her skirt, then climbed over the sill and grabbed at the close branch, swinging her feet down to the limb below it. She picked her way down carefully, testing each branch before she put her weight on it, and the old tree held her, guiding her down. She touched a hand to its trunk in thanks as she reached the bottom, patting it twice. Then, making sure she circled the house to the side that would avoid the kitchen window and side yard should her mother be hanging laundry on the line, she went to the street and walked briskly down the hill toward the drugstore, where she could pick up a few sandwiches at the counter.

Armed with two for later in a bag slung over her arm and eating one sandwich as she walked, Evelyn figured she could make it through to the following morning, then slide silently into her seat at the breakfast table and not speak to them until supper that night. That should make it look believable.

But she didn't go home.

Instead, she headed toward the docks.

Evelyn spotted him working with Felipe and their father to unload cargo from one of his uncle's boats, which she only knew because she had made him point out which boats were theirs one day. She couldn't tell the difference between a fishing boat and a trawler, despite growing up in a fishing town, because her father was so adamant they stay away from the wharves. The dock boys had a reputation, after all.

Finding an empty post near the base of the dock, Evelyn sat down and continued eating her sandwich, enjoying the action unfolding in front of her. She knew her existence was sheltered, but she had no idea so many people worked on Sundays. Of course, work looked different to different people. Joseph had bought Miriam a newfangled washing machine several years earlier so she could rest on weekends. But she stubbornly still washed the laundry herself, running it through the mangle before hanging it to dry, eyeing the machine as if it meant to replace her.

When the three Delgado men finally finished, Tony and Felipe took turns drinking from a water jug. Evelyn sat another moment, waiting to see if he would notice her. But she was undeterred when he didn't, hopping down and walking toward him. "Tony!"

He whirled in surprise at her voice and frowned as he saw other workers staring. Tony said something quietly to his father, who nodded, before walking briskly to her, taking her arm firmly, and turning her around. "What are you doing here?" His grip may have been tight, but his tone couldn't mask the thrill he felt at her presence.

"I wanted to see you." She shrugged. "I thought it would be a nice surprise when you were done."

"I'm not done. We have to reload the boat, and then we have two more."

"Can't you take a break? We can go for a walk."

He glanced back at his father, who was pretending not to watch them.

Then his face changed as he realized this wasn't a normal visit. "What's wrong? What happened?"

"Nothing *happened*. I just missed you."

"Evelyn."

He looked into her eyes, and her breath caught. And she realized she had lied to her father more than she meant to. Because the boy who looked at her like that—the boy who saw through her—that *was* the boy you married. No one else realized when she was hiding something, except sometimes her mother. They all just saw what she wanted them to see. She stared back into his eyes, the rich brown of the earth beneath the pear tree she had climbed down, and felt herself shiver involuntarily.

"Vivie told my mother . . . about us—it wasn't her fault. Mama is . . ." She shook her head. "It doesn't matter. It's done now."

Tony stiffened. "*What's* done now?"

Evelyn smiled compassionately, too far gone to even be flippant for once. "Them knowing."

"Them . . . ," Tony echoed. "What did your father say?"

Evelyn waved a hand in the air. "He said I can't see you anymore. But I'm not worried about Papa." Tony looked unsure, and Evelyn gripped his forearm, noticing the hard swell of muscle beneath her hand. "He'll come around. He always does. He blusters and he hollers, but he's all bark. Honestly, he barely even barks with me. He's never going to do anything that makes me unhappy for long. And it's not like I'm saying I'm skipping college to marry you or . . . anything . . ." She trailed off, realizing what she had just said.

Tony tried, and failed, to suppress a smile.

"You jerk." She smacked his arm lightly. "It's not funny."

"No. You're definitely going to college. Even if we get married."

She threw her head back and laughed. "Papa will love you. You wait and see. It may take some time, but he will."

"I don't like the idea of sneaking around." His voice turned serious. "Promise me you'll talk to him."

"I promise." She hesitated, realizing she couldn't play her usual games with Tony. "I don't promise it'll be soon. He needs to cool down first."

He nodded, then glanced back at his own father, who had moved on to the next boat with Felipe. "I have to get back."

Evelyn grinned up at him. "Kiss me first."

"At the docks? With them"—he gestured over his shoulder—"watching?"

"Especially with them watching!"

"You'll get a reputation."

"None of them know me. You're the one who will get a reputation."

"You're going to get me in trouble, aren't you?"

She leaned in close, her lips pursed slightly. "Isn't it worth it?"

He sighed, closing the gap between them. "Absolutely." He kissed her lightly. "Now go home. I need this job if I'm going to keep taking you out."

She nodded and turned to leave.

"Wait." He plucked something from her long dark hair and held up a white blossom. "What's this?"

Her lips spread into a coquettish grin. "Oh, that? I climbed down the pear tree next to my window to get here. I'm about to go climb back up it."

He stared at her, his mouth open. "You . . . climbed down a tree? In a skirt? And are about to climb back up?"

"I told you, I wanted to see you. Unless they cut that tree down, they're not stopping me." She turned again, shooting him a last look over her shoulder. "And if they do? I'll get a ladder."

She heard him laughing as she walked away.

CHAPTER TEN

At the Woodrow Wilson Service Plaza, I checked my phone while waiting for my grandmother to finish in the bathroom. I had felt the texts come in while driving, but I couldn't read them until we stopped.

Are you ready to kill her yet? my father asked.

Is she behaving? from my mother.

Are you really on a road trip with Grandma? Did you learn nothing from my adventures in Mexico? from my cousin Lily.

And one from Brad. I looked at his name suspiciously but didn't open the message.

We had only communicated through text and email since I moved out. Except for that one phone call, when he asked me to sign the property settlement agreement and attest that our separation had been mutual so he could file for divorce quicker. It hadn't gone well. I asked if he was in such a hurry so he could marry Taylor, and he hesitated too long.

"We're not even divorced yet," I had hissed at him, careful not to yell with my parents downstairs. "You can't be serious!"

"I'm not planning to get married yet. I just—"

"YET!"

"Jenna, it's serious. I don't want to wait a full year when we both know it's over. And I don't see why you do either. I want you to be happy too."

The condescension pushed me over the edge. Was I being vindictive? Yes. I didn't want him to be happy. I wanted him to be miserable for doing this to me. I wanted him living in his childhood bedroom and single and . . . well . . . something worse than what I was doing, even if I didn't know what that was. And I wanted to move on and be happy. But the *too* of that last sentence was when I vowed to make him wait the whole year even if Zac Efron proposed to me that very night. Brad was the reason I had to tell everyone my marriage fell apart. He was the reason I hated my name every time my students called me Mrs. Shapiro. And while, yes, I could go back to being Miss Greenberg sooner if I granted the divorce, I could suffer longer if it meant he was suffering. Too.

"Why are you looking at that phone like it's going to bite you?" For an older woman with a bad hip, my grandmother was excellent at sneaking up on people. Not that a New Jersey Turnpike rest stop is quiet, so she could have been stomping like an elephant and I probably wouldn't have noticed.

"Brad texted me."

"And?"

"I don't know. I haven't opened it."

She gave me an incredulous look. "Good. Throw it in the trash."

"My phone?"

"The message. Recycle it. Wherever those things go. He can *gai kaken afen yam*."

I didn't know much Yiddish, but I was familiar with that expression, and I snorted. "Grandma!"

"What?"

I sighed. "I can't just delete it."

"Why not?"

"We're still married. It's not *done* done yet."

"From what your mother tells me, it could be." I crossed my arms. "Oh, don't make that sour face. You'll get wrinkles. That's why I don't have many. I always smile." She grinned to prove her point. "I'm with you, though, darling. Make that shmuck suffer. But you don't need to suffer along with him. Read the message if you want, but remember he can't do anything worse than he's already done. You're wearing the pants now."

She took my crossed arm and pulled me toward Starbucks. "Come on. Get me one of those frap-a-mochiatto things."

I let myself be led. "Are you going to steal all of the Sweet'N Low again?"

"Of course not. Now I'm taking the Splenda."

"Right." I rolled my eyes.

"You get the coffees."

"We should probably get lunch too."

Grandma looked distastefully at the fast-food options. "Absolutely not. I brought sandwiches."

"You did?"

"It's tradition. Didn't your mother tell you about driving to Hereford?"

"No?"

She shook her head. "Well, there are sandwiches. Get the coffee."

~

Back in the car, Grandma pulled two foil-wrapped packages from a cooler in the back seat and handed me one, along with a paper towel as a napkin. "I can drive," she offered, "so you can eat."

"Nice try. I can drive while eating a sandwich."

She shrugged. "So can I."

I unwrapped mine. It was tuna, seasoned with diced apples and a splash of lemon juice, on rye bread. The smell brought me back to my childhood at her house. The nights when I slept over, in my mother's old bed. After a bath, she would dry my hair carefully with her old hairdryer, so much gentler with the brush than my mother, who ripped through my thick hair, before tucking me into sheets that were thin with so many washings, but soft and fresh. In the morning, I would wake to the smell of French toast, made with thick-cut challah bread. Then we would do puzzles, sitting at the old oak dining table, under the chandelier that had come from her mother's house in Hereford, while my grandfather drank coffee and did the *New York Times* crossword puzzle in blue ink while sitting in his armchair in the living room. At lunchtime, I would stand on a wobbly kitchen chair at the counter and help make these exact sandwiches for the three of us to eat.

"These were your favorite when you were little," my grandmother said as she opened hers. "I hope you still like them."

I felt tears prickling at my eyes, and I tried to blink them away. The combination of the memory and the realization that not only did Grandma remember, but she made the effort to pack my childhood favorite was too much for me. I glanced in the rearview mirror, wishing I could see my grandfather back there, his newspaper folded to the crossword, the blue ballpoint pen in his hand.

Grandma reached into her purse and handed me a tissue. "If you're going to cry while you eat, I should definitely drive."

I laughed, and the moment passed. I took a bite, savoring the taste, so simple and yet so distinctive.

"What happened next?" I asked. "Did your parents stay mad at you?"

She smiled at the memory. "Papa could never stay mad at me. He didn't even make it a day. And the thought of me going to bed hungry? No. He caved by the end of supper."

CHAPTER ELEVEN

April 1950
Hereford, Massachusetts

"Supper!" Miriam bellowed upstairs. Evelyn had her nose in her battered copy of *A Tree Grows in Brooklyn*, a half-eaten sandwich on its paper wrapping next to her on the bed. Was it a kid's book? Yes. But it was comfort food nonetheless. Evelyn hadn't grown up poor, but she felt a kinship with Francie as her mother's distinctly unfavorite child.

She looked up briefly at her mother's voice. When that woman yelled, they could probably hear her all the way down at the docks. But she took a defiant bite of her sandwich and flicked the page. Miriam wouldn't call again, and that was fine. She was set until morning.

It *was* a little hard to focus on the book when she had one ear cocked toward the heating grate though. And it sounded like an awkwardly silent meal.

Maybe I should go down, she thought, not wanting Vivie to suffer. There was only one person whose feelings Evelyn put ahead of her own and that was her baby sister. The sound of cutlery clinking against plates traveled up through the grate, but no one spoke.

She tossed the book aside with a sigh and crossed her arms. This was all part of her mother's plan though. Treat Vivie like garbage until she smoked Evelyn out of her room. It frequently worked.

Not this time. She flopped onto her stomach toward the foot of the brass-posted double bed that had once been shared by her two eldest sisters. Vivie did this to herself. She could tough it out one night to help the ruse along.

It was going to be a long, dull night, though, without any company. She played idly with her hair, finding another stray pear blossom and smiling to herself as she thought of Tony and the first time she saw him. It hadn't been *quite* as sudden as she led her sister and Ruthie to believe.

She had been in Joseph's store two months earlier when she heard a commotion. Peeking around a shelf, she saw a young man dragging a boy to the counter by the ear, the boy yelling in protest.

The older one shoved the younger toward the counter, where Joseph stood, watching warily with crossed arms. "Give it to him," the young man said gruffly. "Now."

The boy looked up in defiance, saw the expression on his brother's face, and then pulled something out of his pocket and placed it on the counter. The older one prodded him sharply in the back. "I'm sorry," the boy mumbled.

"For?" Another jab.

"I took this."

"Stole."

"I stole this."

"And?"

"I won't do it again."

The older one put a bill on the counter. "I want to pay for what my brother took. You can't sell it now."

Thievery was fairly common among the children in town, and while Joseph was gruff if he caught them blatantly, he also was too kind to make a fuss if a child took a piece of candy. The Depression may have ended with the war, but it wasn't a wealthy town. And there was no softer touch with children than Evelyn's father.

She watched a small struggle play across his face. The young man was right. He couldn't sell the candy cigarettes in their current state. Taking them back meant throwing them away, which was a waste. But they *had* been returned.

Finally, he took the box of candy, leaving the dollar where it sat. "I won't take your money. He brought it back."

The young man started to protest, but Joseph silenced him. "Put it toward his education instead. The boy learned a lesson today. Let him learn another in the future."

The boy squirmed out of his brother's grip and skipped away, happy to be free of trouble, and the two men stared at each other for a moment before the younger took the bill back and placed it in his pocket. They nodded at each other, a sign of mutual understanding, before the young man turned to walk away and Evelyn saw his face.

He looked vaguely Mediterranean, tanned from the sun even in winter, with strong, even features and thick dark hair. But his eyes, the warm brown of mahogany, were full of a fire that Evelyn recognized as the match for that in her own.

As she walked home from the store that afternoon, she mused over the young man's actions. Her father didn't care about a piece of candy. But to return it *and* try to pay. Evelyn may have had a Machiavellian streak a mile wide when it came to self-preservation, but she also respected those whose moral compasses pointed due north—perhaps because her own didn't.

And it was that, as much as his eyes, that returned to her over and over as she tried to sleep. So when she saw him leaning against the side of the drugstore to light a cigarette that blustery February afternoon, she realized she wanted something sweet. And she took it.

～

Evelyn heard the chairs push back from the table and the sounds of her mother and sister clearing the dishes, then the lumbering tread of her father on the stairs. She quickly hid the remnants of her sandwich, listening as he paused outside her bedroom door. This was most unusual.

He cleared his throat to announce his presence before knocking softly. "Evelyn? It's your father."

She fought the urge to laugh. Who else could it possibly have been? But she had to play her part. She composed her face and opened the door a crack. "What is it, Papa?"

"May I come in?"

Evelyn opened the door and gestured for him to enter. He stood awkwardly as Evelyn sat on the bed, then went to the small secretary desk and sat in the straight-backed chair where she did her homework and wrote letters to her sisters. He cleared his throat again and opened his mouth but did not speak.

"Yes, Papa?"

"You need to eat," he said. Evelyn slid her foot along the floorboard, making sure no trace of sandwich wrapper was visible.

"I'm not hungry."

He wrung his hands in his lap. "What about a compromise?"

Evelyn felt her eyebrows rising. This was *quite* out of the ordinary. "What kind of compromise?"

Joseph sighed. "You can go on dates. But only with Jewish boys."

She eyed him with the look of a prizefighter circling her opponent and seeing a weak spot. "But I want to date this boy."

"No."

"Honestly, Papa, what's the difference? I'm going to college in the fall. If you're going to let me date people in town, why not *this* person?"

"You can't date someone who works the docks."

"He doesn't. He's in school."

"And when he's not?"

"He helps his family. Just like both Bernie and Sam did in the store when they were in high school. He's a good boy."

"No."

Evelyn threw her hands in the air. "Then you can keep your compromise." She lay down and closed her eyes, placing her hands deliberately over her stomach. "I'm going to sleep."

Joseph watched her for a long moment. Then relented. "You cannot marry him."

Her eyes sprung open. "I'm seventeen. I'm not marrying anyone."

"And you can't date *only* him. You have to see Jewish boys too. And nothing interferes with college."

Evelyn sat up, swinging her feet back onto the floor. "And Mama?"

He hesitated again. "Maybe—maybe you only tell her about the Jewish ones. You tell her you stopped seeing this boy."

A laugh bubbled up in her chest, threatening to escape, but she contained it. "Okay."

Looking guilty, he reached into his pocket and pulled out some brisket and a piece of bread, wrapped in a linen napkin. "Don't tell your mother about this either. I don't want you going to bed hungry."

She crossed the room and hugged him tightly. "Thank you, Papa."

"I love you, *ziskayte*," he said, pressing the napkin of food into her hand as he stood. He kissed her forehead gently, then left, closing the door softly behind him.

Evelyn set the food on her desk and twirled in a circle, thinking to herself that if she wouldn't need to climb down the pear tree anymore, she could probably fly instead.

CHAPTER TWELVE

As the driving got more complicated around New York and then through Westchester County on the Hutchinson River Parkway, my grandmother paused her story to insist I was going the wrong way. I tried to explain Google Maps to her; instead of the ten hours she was used to, we would be there in nine with stops. But she argued there was no need for a map. She could drive there blindfolded. Which was probably a step up from her actual driving, but I kept that thought to myself and told her I needed to concentrate.

By the time I realized I hadn't heard from her in a conspicuously long time, I looked over, more than a little worried she had died on me. That first glance did nothing to reassure me, as her chin sagged to her chest, the muscles slack. It took a closer inspection to see her chest rising and falling as she slept.

Steadying my own breathing, I looked longingly at the car's stereo system and wished again that we were in my car. Driving without music was a much more tedious task. But I was afraid searching the FM waves would startle her.

I drummed my fingers on the steering wheel, trying to resist the urge to click away from Google Maps and check my messages. I still hadn't read the one from Brad.

We had plenty of gas and stopping would wake her.

I won't reply, I said, justifying myself. *Reading it isn't much worse than checking the map.*

It had been so much easier to avoid thinking about it when she was awake and talking.

I lasted another three miles before I remembered my AirPods. I dug them out of my purse, slipped one into my left ear, and whispered for Siri to read Brad's message, glancing at my grandmother to make sure she stayed asleep.

I have a buyer interested in the condo, but I can't sell it until you sign the property agreement. I won't be petty and withhold the money until the divorce is final, but I am reminding you that it's been six months and you can decide to not drag this out any time you want. The ball is in your court. Hope you're well.

My chest felt tight with anger at the implication that I was being petty. I mean, okay, yes, I was being petty. I didn't want to still be married to him. But that sense of self-righteous hurt was what was getting me out of bed every day. I wasn't ready to let go of that.

I pulled the AirPod out of my ear and dropped it into my lap, wishing I hadn't listened to the message.

Maybe I should get a puppy. A puppy would love me.

Something painful rose in my chest but not about Brad. About my grandfather. I hadn't known he had been sick until the very end, when it was too late. He made everyone swear not to tell me.

I knew parents and grandparents weren't supposed to have favorites, but I also knew they did sometimes. And I was Grandpa's favorite. He loved all of us, of course. But I was the eldest, and Grandma once said she never saw that man fall in love the way he did when he first held me.

His whole countenance changed when I walked into the room. He lit up and wanted to know everything I had to say. He was the only one, in my whole life, who loved me like that. Brad should have. I thought he had. But apparently he didn't. Because a love like that doesn't evaporate into thin air.

And here I was, driving my grandma back to her hometown, probably to find this other guy, who was all she could talk about. What was I doing? Had she ever actually loved my grandfather? From what she had told me on the drive, it was obvious she thought Tony was the one for her, despite her insistence that she would never settle. Was that why my grandfather loved *me* so much? Because she wasn't in love with him? She was so blasé about her mother not loving her father. Just threw it out there. Was this some curse in my family? Our inability to be with the right person, so we wind up with someone who doesn't love us at all.

The car was too quiet. I was going to scream.

In desperation, I switched on the radio and tuned the dial. If it woke Grandma, so be it. I could ask if she loved Grandpa if she was awake. But I couldn't sit there with my thoughts.

She gave a little half snore as I settled on a classic rock station that was cruelly playing music from when I was in middle school, and I let the familiar notes drown out the disloyal thoughts.

~

She woke the moment we crossed into Essex County, as if the land shook her gently and told her she was home. "Half an hour now," she murmured, surprising me.

I glanced at my phone, which said twenty-nine minutes to our destination.

"I don't think I've ever fallen asleep on the drive before." She pulled down the visor and checked her reflection in the mirror. Then she lifted her purse onto her lap and rummaged in it for powder and lipstick.

"Are we seeing anyone?"

"You never know."

"Is this trip about Tony? Is that why we're going to Hereford?"

"Tony?" She looked at me in surprise. "Good heavens, no. Why would you think that?"

"He's all you've talked about, the whole drive."

"Is that all you heard?" I looked at her from the corner of my eye. She didn't sound like she was being facetious, although it was hard to tell with her. "He's part of the story, yes. But I haven't seen Tony in . . . twenty years? Thirty? How old are you now?"

"Me? Thirty-four."

"Thirty, then. He was at Helen's funeral."

"Helen?"

"My sister. We said hello to each other then."

"Why did my age tell you when that was?"

"Because we brought you with us, your mother and me. That's when you went to Hereford."

I looked at her, confused. "But Mom said—"

"It was a long time ago. There were a lot of people there with unfinished business. I had this grand idea that we'd go, and it would be like it was when your mother and aunt were kids. And it wasn't."

"What—?"

"What time is it?"

I wanted to know what she was talking about. I foggily remembered her in someone's face, the two of them not quite shouting, but arguing loudly. I didn't know why I could suddenly see that from the words *Helen's funeral*, but I could, and I knew the two were connected.

But no one had ever successfully pulled a story out of her that she wasn't ready to tell. And it was obvious I would get nowhere, so I sighed and told her. "A little before four."

"Good. We have time to go through town first."

"We're not staying in town?"

"No."

CHAPTER THIRTEEN

June 1950
Hereford, Massachusetts

Joseph came out of the war years a wealthy man. After growing up with little in Russia, he found it to be no hardship to live frugally during his early years in America. He had no investments, other than the store, so the stock market crash affected him only in the sense that people spent less money. But he ran the only dry goods store in town, kept his prices low, and helped people where he could, meaning when they had money, they spent it with him.

And because he was one of the few people in town in a position to invest, people came to him with opportunities. Which meant by the time the war came and the stock market rebounded with the costs of industry, Joseph found himself exceptionally comfortable, even with two children in college, and five more in the wings.

In 1946, he splurged on three things: a Ford Super DeLuxe to replace his seventeen-year-old Ford Model A, a washing machine, and two cottages on the northern edge of the peninsula that Hereford rested on. While the town of Hereford perched above a harbor that was known as one of the oldest fishing ports in the country, the coastline was rocky and the air stagnant and thick in summer, some five miles from the cool breezes of the beach. The Bergman house sat on a hill on Main Street, but it caught little fresh air off the port, and the unmistakable smell of fish began filling the town in late June, lasting through September most years. Miriam, uncomfortably hot in her girdle and starched dresses, seldom complained, though the children did frequently. But Joseph watched her wipe a bead of sweat off her forehead during a June heat wave as she placed his breakfast on the table, the day barely begun. After he finished eating, he climbed into his new car and drove the five winding miles past the swampy marshlands, which flooded in high tides and hurricanes, to the coast.

Hereford Beach was unincorporated but had a small seasonal community. There was an inn, which had a few rooms to rent, along with a restaurant, at one end of the beach, and a small general store. At the other end of the beach, on the bluffs overlooking the ocean, sat a group of imposing mansions. These were summer homes, owned by Boston's elite, who avoided the crowds of Cape Cod, choosing instead to summer in seclusion. They drove their fancy cars into town occasionally to take in a movie or buy some staples, but more often they sent their household staffs for necessities instead.

Joseph looked disdainfully at the gaudy estates, going instead toward the Inn, following the small dirt road that wound its way inland behind it. Up the hill stood a manor house that had been old when Joseph was born fifty-one years earlier. Closer to the beach were two matching clapboard structures, each with a wraparound porch. They had once been a guesthouse and an overseer's dwelling, now repurposed into beach cottages.

He parked the car and stood in front of the first cottage, inspecting it, then climbed the six steps of the front porch and turned around. A refreshing breeze caught his hair, and, peering through the trees, which provided a thick, cool shade, he could just make out the sun glittering on the ocean.

Rapping on the doors of the cottages produced no answer, so Joseph made his way to the manor house, where a much older woman answered the door.

An hour later, Joseph returned home and announced to Miriam that her days of sweltering in town were done. He had bought her a beach cottage to summer in.

She looked at him as if he had grown a second head, but Joseph was undeterred. He had bought two, he explained, so all their children and grandchildren could come for the summers as well.

"It's good for the children," Miriam said finally. "But what about you? You have to be here for the store. I will stay here with you."

Joseph went to his wife and cupped her face in his hands. "I can drive back and forth. And if I stay here, I can take care of myself."

"You don't even know how to make your tea. How would you eat?"

Chuckling, he kissed her forehead. "I can manage. You deserve time to be comfortable with the children." He released her and turned to go, his mind already on furnishing the two houses.

"Joseph," Miriam called after him, and he turned around. "Thank you."

~

By the summer of 1950, Bernie and his wife had a house in town with their three children, so they were the first to move in for the summer, claiming the smaller of the two cottages. Sam had just completed his degree after returning from service in Europe and stayed the summer in Bernie's cottage before his job began in late August. Miriam, who for the first two summers spent only weekends at the cottage, and those only when Joseph was there, now spent most of her summer in the main bedroom of the larger cottage, whether Joseph joined her or not. Margaret returned from college, and Helen brought her two children for several weeks at a time, her husband driving out to stay when he could. Gertie, carrying a newborn in her left arm and a two-year-old on her right hip, came out on the train from Boston Monday mornings and left Fridays, as her husband worked long hours during the week.

Vivie and Evelyn shuffled between the two cottages, sleeping wherever there was room, usually sharing a bed with each other but sometimes with Margaret or Gertie, helping with the children during the day.

All in all, the arrangement suited everyone. And that summer, when there were so many grandchildren to keep track of, it suited no one more than Evelyn. Because with the ever-changing sleeping arrangements, there was no way to monitor how late she got back from spending time with Tony. Miriam thought she was in Bernie's cottage, as it came to be known, while Bernie thought she was with her mother. And Evelyn quietly did as she pleased.

CHAPTER FOURTEEN

When the road split, we took the turn toward Hereford and crossed over a bridge. My grandmother rolled down her window and inhaled deeply. I did the same, trying to capture whatever essence she had claimed my soul would recognize. There was the unmistakable smell of salt air, seaweed, and . . . fish. I wrinkled my nose.

She looked at me from the corner of her eye and shook her head. "This is what home smells like."

"Fish?"

"Yes, Miss Sass. And there's nothing wrong with coming from a blue-collar town where people use their hands to earn a living."

We rounded a corner, and the ocean sprawled to our right, pure and blue, sparkling in the late afternoon sunlight, the town just up ahead. The familiar green mermaid of a Starbucks greeted us from one of the first buildings. "When were you here last?" I asked her.

"Not that long ago. Six years maybe? Layla's wedding."

"Who is Layla?"

"Your cousin. My brother's great-granddaughter. That'd make her your . . ." She worked it out in her head, her lips moving silently. "Second cousin once removed." She paused. "Bernie was twelve years older than me and had his kids young."

"That's a big gap."

She shrugged. "There were seven of us. And a few losses, we think. No one really talked about it back then, but my sisters remembered Mama being sick. And Mama was never sick except when she had us. Until the end, that is."

I shook my head to myself. That had been what drove house hunting into an imperative. A late period that might have been nothing. Or might have been something. *We don't talk about it now either,* I thought. I gestured toward the Starbucks as we passed, to change the subject. "Things may have changed a bit."

Grandma scoffed at the storefront. "They made it stay at the edge of town. It's much more upscale now. The Brooklyn of the north shore."

I suppressed a laugh as a bearded man in sandals and thick, black-framed glasses walked by pushing a stroller. She might not be wrong.

We drove along Main Street, where old Victorian houses now held shops. "Where did you grow up?" I tried to picture the version of my grandmother I knew from black-and-white photos skipping along this street and walking up the steps to one of the front porches we saw.

"There." She pointed to a bank at the top of the hill. I looked at her, confused. "The house is gone. They tried to move it—it was going to be a museum—after Mama and Papa died. Not to them. A town museum. It was such a grand house. But something about the zoning. And the house didn't survive the move."

"When was that?"

"Almost forty years ago now."

"I'm sorry."

She nodded.

We passed more shops, the street eventually giving way to newer buildings, the ocean still peeking through between the buildings on the right. Quick glances down the steep side streets revealed that the town sat upon a sharp, rocky bluff, dropping away to the docks down on the harbor, which seemed to house a combination of fishing and private boats.

"Have you been fishing?" I couldn't picture her casting a line, but it seemed to be a thing here.

"Of course, darling, and for more than just compliments." She smiled at some memory, and I wondered if it was about Tony. She said his family had owned a fishing company.

"What about—?"

"You're going to miss the turn," she said. "Bear left up there."

I glanced at my phone. "Google says to stay on this."

"The road ends. Go left."

It didn't. But I figured if she got us lost, Google could bring us back on track.

I turned left, and the map rerouted, cutting two minutes off the time.

She smirked at me. "Your little apples don't know everything."

"Apps."

"Clearly they don't know that either."

I gave up as we wound our way through a newer segment of town, my grandmother scowling at the houses. "This was all empty marshland."

~

There was a break of about a half mile where the marshes still made the ground too soft to build before we entered something resembling civilization again. A miniature golf course, three beach supply stores, a Stop & Shop, two wide hotels, and eventually the ocean stretched in front of us. "Left where the road ends," my grandmother instructed. "Then the next left at the Inn." She looked around as we drove up a hill. "This used to be all woods."

The street held a mishmash of houses, some small Cape Cods, a few McMansions, a handful of houses that would have looked at home in a suburban neighborhood, one knockoff Victorian, and finally, at the end of the street, two clapboard structures with wraparound porches.

"This is it," my grandmother said, pointing to the larger of the two. It was painted red, with six steps leading up to the screened porch.

"You rented a house?"

"It's one of those Air Bed Bath and Beyond things."

I raised an eyebrow. "An Airbnb?"

"I suppose."

"You know how to rent an Airbnb?"

"I *do* have a phone," she said sharply, struggling to unbuckle her seatbelt. I leaned over and released it, then got out of the car to help her. Once she was on her feet, she shielded her eyes from the sun, which hung over the roof, and examined the property. "I hate the color that woman painted it."

"What woman?"

"The owner."

"Have you stayed here before?"

Her lips twitched into a grin. "Darling, this was our cottage. I spent every summer here."

My mouth dropped open. I started to say something, but the porch door swung open, startling me.

"That's the property manager," my grandma said, raising her hand to wave as the man walked down the steps toward us. "Hello, Joe, darling."

CHAPTER FIFTEEN

June 1950
Hereford, Massachusetts

Evelyn always walked down the unnamed road to the junction with Sand Island Lane to meet Tony. Joseph may have given his approval to date, but that didn't mean Tony could park in front of the cottages, climb the steps, and knock on the door to pick Evelyn up. Which left Tony feeling uneasy, but Evelyn said to trust her. They just needed time.

They both graduated high school at the end of May. Tony joined his father and uncle's fishing business full-time along with Felipe while Evelyn prepared for college in the fall, and the whole summer stretched before them.

Most nights she climbed into his father's 1939 Ford Standard, and they drove out to Gloucester or Rockport, where they could walk through town without everyone knowing them, sometimes venturing as far south as Beverly. When they returned, they walked along the beach in the moonlight, setting up camp at the far end on a worn flannel blanket that Tony pulled from the trunk before building a fire. Nights in town were hot, but down on the water, there was frequently a chill in the air.

Evelyn shivered, largely for show, in her poplin sundress, and ducked under Tony's arm. For warmth, of course. Not that Tony objected either way. He looked down at her in the firelight, and she smiled up at him, then nestled closer, inhaling his clean scent, not knowing that when he left the docks each day, he raced home to be the first one in the bath, where he scrubbed himself until Felipe threatened to break the door down. Felipe was recently engaged to a girl named Beatriz from another Portuguese family. But her brothers and father worked the ships as well, and Tony rationalized that she could handle the smells that came with their work easier than Evelyn could. So he scrubbed himself raw, working at his fingernails until not a trace of dirt remained, then dressing and counting the minutes until it was time to meet her at the end of the dark road.

Leaning her head back, Evelyn looked up at the stars. "Show me the constellations again."

He lay down, pulling her with him, pillowing her head on his left shoulder and pointing out the formations, starting with Ursa Major and moving through the visible zodiac.

"How do you know all of these?"

"You learn them when you go out on the ships. It's how they used to steer."

"But how do you do that?"

He laughed softly. "If it were two hundred years ago, I could tell you. I'm not exactly crossing oceans on my uncle's fishing boats."

"I want to do that," she said, sitting up.

"A fishing boat wouldn't make it."

She rolled her eyes. "I didn't mean on one of your uncle's boats. I mean I want to see the world. All of it."

"That's a pretty tall order."

"Don't you? I want to go to Rome and Paris and Greece and London and Egypt and"—she looked at him slyly, the flames of the fire reflecting on her face, making her eyes glow in the darkness—"Portugal."

Tony laughed again and pulled her back down next to him. "Name one city in Portugal."

"Lisbon."

"You do know I've never been there, right?"

"So?"

"So, do you want to go to Russia?"

She wrinkled her nose. "It's not the top of my list. But someday. Maybe."

"You're not as far removed as I am. My family has been here for a hundred years. I'm more American than you are."

"Okay, *Antonio*."

"What's in a name?"

"Ha. Would be funnier if we weren't so star crossed."

"Are we though?"

"Papa said I can go out with you, not marry you."

Tony held her tighter. "And do you always do what your papa tells you?"

A slow, sultry smile spread across Evelyn's lips, and Tony fought to keep from kissing her. Yes, their evening would wind up there, but to do it lying down on the beach like this was more dangerous. It was easier to stop in the car. "You know I don't." She leaned in, and he sat up abruptly.

"I was thinking—I might leave the business."

Evelyn sat up too. "What would you do?"

"Well, I had two ideas. There's the Army. I could do four years and then go to college."

She shivered again, involuntarily this time, but kept her face studiedly neutral. "Is that what you want?"

"No," he admitted. They both knew young men who hadn't come home from the war. And many who came home missing body parts. Or who came home but were really still on the beach in Normandy. "But I know your father cares so much about college."

"But you'd be gone four years."

"So would you."

"I may not go far," Evelyn hedged. "If I was in Boston, we'd still see each other. If you were here."

"That's true."

"Look, if you want to go to college—"

Tony turned to look at her. "Do you want me to?"

"Only if it's what you want. You can't do something that big because it *might* make my father happy. Are you going to magically become Jewish too?"

"No."

They didn't speak for a minute. "You said you had two ideas?"

"They're looking for new police officers. I picked up an application this week."

"Is *that* what you want to do?"

He nodded slightly. "I think it is. It's not like we have gangs here. And I like helping people." He looked at her again. "And it's more respectable than cod fishing."

"Tony, I don't care if you work on the docks forever. You know that doesn't matter to me one bit."

"It matters to me. I want to be something you can be proud of."

"What will your family think?"

"My father won't be happy, but he has three other sons to leave the business to."

Evelyn leaned her head on his shoulder. "Officer Delgado," she mused. "It sounds good." She thought about the first time she saw him, when he forced his brother to do the right thing. "I think you'd be a wonderful police officer."

He leaned his head on top of hers and they sat next to each other, looking into the fire as if they could see their future together in it.

CHAPTER SIXTEEN

I looked at my grandmother with distrust as the man who exited the cottage wrapped her in a warm hug.

When he released her, she held his hand with her right, then took mine with her left. "Joe, I want you to meet my granddaughter, Jenna. Jenna, this is Joe Fonseca."

He held out his hand, and I awkwardly had to disentangle mine from my grandmother's to shake it. "Hi," he said, grinning, and a wave of annoyance flared as I looked at him. Most Airbnbs had keypad entrances, so you didn't need to interact with a human being. And while, yes, she would pick human contact over avoiding people at all costs the way my generation did, I realized instantly that this was intentional. And not just because she was watching us with the same level of interest with which she devoured episodes of *The Marvelous Mrs. Maisel.*

Under other circumstances, those rich brown eyes that crinkled at the corners when his full lips parted to flash perfect, even white teeth at me from a suntanned face would have absolutely been a welcome sight. But I couldn't imagine ever wanting to think about dating again, let alone meeting someone on vacation. And a Grandma Evelyn setup was the kiss of death, as I learned in college.

"Hi," I replied guardedly, then pulled my hand from his and turned to my grandmother. "Let's get you inside. You must be exhausted from the trip."

"Not in the slightest. I'm old—I'm not infirm." Taking Joe's arm, she led him toward the cottage steps. "You'll need to show me what that old bat of an owner has had done since I was here last. I'm not over the porch yet."

I was still standing by the car. With a sigh, I opened the trunk and began lifting the bags out.

"Jenna!" Grandma called.

"I'll get those," Joe said from the steps.

Defeated, I followed them into the cottage, hoping he would leave soon but knowing my grandmother better than that.

The front door opened into a hall, with what appeared to be a living room on the right, a dining room on the left, the kitchen straight ahead, and a staircase next to the living room's entrance. I looked at the stairs warily. My grandmother still lived in the house she had spent the better part of fifty years in with my grandfather, but she got one of those motorized chairs for the steps after Grandpa died. She said she was fine, but I knew she worried about falling, especially living alone. And she wasn't going to let me help her up and down the stairs.

I followed their voices into the kitchen, which was tastefully done, with light wood cabinets and granite countertops. Grandma was shaking her head. "Where's the charm? It was rustic when we spent summers here, but that was the appeal of it." She looked over her shoulder at me. "That and the cool air of course. We had no air conditioning back then."

"There are window units upstairs. But the house still doesn't have central air."

"What would be the point? If you don't have the windows open, why are you even here? Joe, be a dear and open the windows for us." He left her side and began doing as she said.

I came closer to her, talking low. "I know this place has sentimental value, but we might be better off somewhere without all the stairs."

She looked at me like I had suggested we take up cannibalism. "You are as bad as your mother." She raised her voice in a falsetto. "'You can't drive to Hereford because you don't have a license. You can't make it up a few stairs.'" She went back to her normal tone. "Next thing I know you're going to be telling me I can't have a drink."

"You *can't*. Mom said—"

Grandma put a finger in my face. "You would do well to cut that out. I'm not a child. And I won't let you talk to me like I'm one."

I fell silent, realizing I was in over my head. Yes, this trip had gotten my mom off my case for a week or two, but what was I actually doing? Had I come along to be helpful or to hide? It was looking like I wouldn't be able to do either.

Joe returned, and I crossed my arms defensively, trying to make it crystal clear that whatever my grandmother intended, I was the opposite of interested.

"I'll bring the bags in," he said, noting my posture and turning to her. "Just let me know which ones go upstairs and which ones stay down."

"Down?" I asked my grandma.

"The main bedroom is through there." Joe gestured to another hallway off the kitchen. "Evelyn, I assume that's where you'll be?"

"Yes, darling, thank you. Jenna can have her pick of the upstairs rooms."

When he excused himself, Grandma settled into one of the kitchen chairs. "Will you find me a glass of water?"

"What? Not gin?"

She smiled. "Well, if you're pouring. Though I prefer vodka."

I shook my head and began opening cabinets. After locating the glasses, I went to the refrigerator to see if there was a filter. "Tap is fine," she called. "The water tastes better here. Always has."

I crossed back to the sink and began to fill the glass, then realized something. "You and Joe seem to know each other well."

"So?"

"He calls you by your first name."

"What else would he call me?"

"If he just met you? Mrs. Gold."

"I tell everyone to call me Evelyn."

I stopped talking as I heard the front door open again and the sound of bags being set down. Going into the hall, I showed him which ones were my grandmother's, and he carried them down the hall to put in her room. I started to lift mine when I heard Grandma's voice. "You let Joe do that," she said. She couldn't see me, so I didn't know how she knew I was bringing mine upstairs. "Men like to feel useful."

The blood rose to my cheeks. There was no way he hadn't heard her say that. Embarrassed, I picked up the bags and took them upstairs before Joe could return from the back of the house. I placed them at the top of the stairs, then went back down. I could pick a room later.

His lips twitched like he was trying not to smile when I came back into the kitchen. "Mom said to tell you that you have to come to the restaurant," he told my grandmother.

"I doubt we'll go into town tonight, but we will this week, of course." She looked up at him warmly. "It's good to see you, Joe."

Reaching down to squeeze her arm, he said, "You too." He looked back at me. "I'll let you two get settled in. My number is on the counter if you need anything at all."

"Thanks."

"Give your mother my love," Grandma said.

"I will. It was nice to meet you, Jenna."

"You too," I said through a mouth that felt full of cotton.

Once the door closed, I turned back to my grandmother. "You know his family?"

She gave me that same look, as if I had just said something too bizarre to fathom. "Of course I know his family. He's Tony's great-nephew."

CHAPTER SEVENTEEN

July 1950
Hereford, Massachusetts

Evelyn tiptoed up the porch stairs, avoiding the third step to Bernie's cottage, which creaked. Shutting the door silently behind her, she breathed a sigh of relief in the darkness, only to gasp at the sound of a match striking, the small flame illuminating her brother lighting a cigarette in the sitting room that opened off the front hallway.

Bernie took a drag and exhaled slowly. "You're up late."

"I was helping Gertie with the baby."

"No, you weren't."

Exasperated, Evelyn flounced into the dark room and flopped onto the sofa across from her brother. "What do you want, Bernie?"

"So defensive," he murmured, flipping on the lamp next to him. "It *is* a boy, then?"

"Look, Papa knows. It's fine."

"Does he know you're out until all hours of the night with him and lying about where you're sleeping?"

"I'm not lying about where I'm sleeping. I come home every night. I'm just lying about where I am before bed."

"You're only sixteen—"

"Seventeen. Almost eighteen. Vivie is sixteen."

"Do you know how embarrassing it would be for the family if you got pregnant?" Evelyn glowered at him. "I'd hope with three older sisters, you'd know enough to stay out of trouble, but it is *you* we're talking about."

"I'm not getting into trouble!"

"If Papa knew, and you weren't doing anything wrong, you wouldn't be sneaking around, would you?"

"Papa *does* know. Mama doesn't."

Bernie looked at her contemplatively, processing this piece of information. He admittedly did not always see eye to eye with their father. But he had assumed it was Joseph, not Miriam, who was so adamant that the girls not date before college. Then again, everyone knew Evelyn had their father wrapped around her little finger.

Evelyn stayed completely still under her brother's gaze, refusing to give up anything after letting that slip about their mother.

"Who is he, then? I assume Papa knows that much."

"Why?"

"Because I want to know who this boy is who takes my sister out and doesn't come meet her family." A realization crossed his face, and Evelyn's stomach dropped. He had figured it out. There was no one in town Bernie didn't know. And had Tony been Jewish, there would have been conversations between the two families. "Evelyn," he said quietly. "What have you done?"

"I haven't *done* anything! Good grief, you're acting like I'm the Whore of Babylon out here. He's a good boy. He's just not Jewish."

"Papa doesn't know that part, clearly."

"Yes, he does, Bernie. You can ask him yourself if you don't believe me."

"And how will Mama feel about it?"

"Don't you dare."

Bernie stroked his chin as he thought, saying nothing for long enough that Evelyn realized her life was about to become more difficult.

"Tell me who it is."

"Why?"

"I'm going to pay him a visit."

"You'll do no such thing."

"It's that or I'll tell Mama. Your choice."

Evelyn glared at her eldest brother again. "What are you going to say?"

Bernie grinned. "Don't you trust your big brother?"

"Clearly not. I might do better with Mama."

He laughed loudly enough that Evelyn shushed him, afraid he'd wake the house. The battles between Evelyn and her mother were legendary. "Evie, you're a child still. I'm going to make sure he *is* the good boy that you say he is and find out what his intentions are. Maybe scare a little sense into him."

"He doesn't need any sense scared into him."

"If he thinks he can handle you, he does. And you're impossible to scare. One of you has to be the smart one."

She swore quietly, mostly because she knew he didn't approve of her doing so. Saying she was impossible to scare was a compliment, after all. Then she sighed and capitulated. "Tony Delgado." His face softened slightly in recognition. "But if you do anything to him, I swear before God and all the prophets—"

"I'm a thirty-year-old man with a family and he's a teenager who works on the docks. You think I'd hurt him?"

She looked at her brother, who wasn't large or physically intimidating, but he was smart. In another life, he would have been the lawyer or banker their mother had hoped for instead of owning a clothing store in town. And she was under no illusions about the fact that he could scare Tony if he chose to.

"He's not going to work on the docks forever."

Bernie examined his sister's face, seeing something new there. "You're serious about this boy." It wasn't a question, but Evelyn nodded. "Does Papa know that part?"

She exhaled heavily. "Like I said, I'm seventeen. I'm going to college in a couple months. The rest . . . Well, it'll work out. Or it won't. I know how I feel now."

"Papa will never let you marry him. You have to know that."

"Papa will get over it."

"Go to bed." Bernie shook his head, stubbing out his cigarette in the ashtray on the wicker coffee table. "I'll pay him a visit tomorrow." She opened her mouth to speak, but Bernie held up a hand. "I'll play nice. Now go to sleep."

Wearily, Evelyn rose and went to the stairs, her brother shutting off the lamp and following her to the hall before turning toward the back of the house, where his bedroom was.

She tiptoed up, not wanting to wake anyone else, washing her face and brushing her teeth before creeping into the room she shared with Vivie, where she pulled off her dress and changed silently into a nightgown, then inched into the bed to avoid waking her sister.

Vivie's breath caught, and she rolled over to Evelyn. "Where've you been?" she mumbled drowsily.

"Just talking to Bernie," Evelyn whispered.

"'S everything okay?"

Evelyn stroked her sister's hair, then kissed her forehead. "Yes, darling. Go back to sleep."

Vivie rolled back over and nestled into her sister, who hugged her gently and wished, as she fell asleep, that her beloved sister would never have to deal with such complications in love.

CHAPTER EIGHTEEN

My first thought the following morning was that the sheets felt wrong. So did the pillow. And the mattress. I opened my eyes, and it took me a minute to realize where I was. Light peeked around the edges of curtains, which fluttered gently where I had left the window cracked the night before. *Hereford,* I thought sleepily.

I sat up, rubbing my eyes, got out of bed, and pulled back the curtains to see what was outside. Through the trees, the ocean sparkled in the morning sunlight. I opened the window as wide as it would go and inhaled. There was no trace of the underlying fishy smell that had permeated the town. Out here there was just the salt of the ocean and the sharp, clean scent of the pitch pines that grew along the craggy coast.

For a moment, the first in half a year, there was no divorce. No loss. No sense of failure. I closed my eyes and breathed deeply. Grandma was right about it being in my blood. This was the smell of home.

Grandma.

The claustrophobia of the past months crashed over me. I wasn't here to be home. I was here to run away. Because I had no home. And no one to miss me.

I sank back onto the unmade bed, my head in my hands, focusing on my breathing to steady myself. When I finally felt under control, I checked my phone. There were no messages except emails from companies, most of whose products I could no longer afford. A metaphor for what was left of my perfect life. It was early still, only seven. My room faced due east, so the sun had woken me.

But working myself into a panic attack wasn't going to help. After a trip to the bathroom, I pulled on a sports bra, top, and leggings before going downstairs. If Grandma was up, I'd see what she wanted to do about breakfast. If not, I'd go for a run to clear away the anxiety. It usually came right back, but if I pushed hard enough, I could buy myself a little time when I could just be, not think.

~

There was no sign of her, so I made a cup of coffee, grateful that the owner had supplied a Keurig and a stock of K-Cups, and wrote my grandmother a note while I drank it.

I didn't need to consult a map. The road dead-ended at the empty lot just past the other cottage, which, according to my grandmother, had been her brother Bernie's. She said they lost this one when Sam's "wretched wife" sold it. When I asked about Bernie's, she changed the subject.

I jogged down the road to where it ended. It was less than half a mile from the cottage to the Hereford Inn, which bordered the beach. I went through the Inn's parking lot and over a dune path to enter the beach, which, except for a couple of other joggers in the distance, was empty. Away from the threat of cars, I slipped my headphones in, turned my music on, and made my way to the firmer sand by the water's edge. A small island jutted out of the ocean just offshore.

The beach spanned about a mile and a half, just a cove really, ending in a rock jetty that I stopped to stare at. These were the rocks I remembered from my childhood visit. I was sure of it. I looked for a way to climb up, but the tide was in, and there was water all around them. There were tiny snails, though, and I smiled, remembering Grandma taking my shovel and gently placing snails in my blue bucket with the yellow handle. *Helen's funeral,* I thought, trying to remember if she had been sad. She must have been. But all I remembered was the feeling of being with her on the beach because she was the sun. And when she shone her full force on you, nothing could be wrong.

Or at least that's how it felt when I was four. Thirty years later? Not so much. There was plenty wrong. And the only thing she was shining on me lately was a whole lot of crazy. *She would have been fifty-eight then. Younger than my mom is now.* Would my mother ever get a chance to play on the beach with my children? Now that I was almost thirty-five and suddenly single, it was looking less and less likely.

Ugh. The run wasn't working.

I turned around, wishing I was back in my childhood bedroom, where, yes, I was in a horrible rut, but it was my familiar rut. Not these new feelings of inadequacy.

Halfway back down the beach, another jogger approached, running with a black dog. I dodged closer to the surf to avoid them, but the dog came right at me, forcing me to stop to avoid the water.

I looked to the owner, annoyed, and my heart sank.

"Hey!" Joe said.

"Oh. Hi."

The dog jumped up, getting sandy paws all over me, and Joe yanked on the leash. "Jax, get down! I'm sorry. She's friendly, I swear."

Jax beamed up at me, her tongue lolling out of her mouth, and I couldn't help but grin back and pet her head. "It's okay. I need a shower anyway."

He smiled. "How was your night? Everything all right at the cottage?"

"Yup. All good."

Joe ran the hand not holding the leash along the back of his neck, showing off the well-formed biceps I did not want to notice. My body wasn't letting me ignore how good-looking this guy was, even if my brain wanted nothing to do with him. "So, um, your grandmother asked me to come by later."

"Okay." He looked up at me, and I tried not to flinch. I was going for neutral but came across as a little hostile.

"She . . . Well, she wanted me to show you around a bit."

My shoulders slumped. Of course she did. She was as subtle as a tsunami. "You really don't have to do that."

"I don't mind."

"No, I mean—she doesn't want you to show me around. She's trying to set us up."

"She said—"

"She lies. That's what she does. And I'm sure you're great and all. Actually, I'm not—she set me up with a couple of jerks when I was younger, but you seem nice." I was babbling and told myself to shut up. "Anyway, I'm in the middle of a divorce right now, and I'm not looking to date anyone. Or—whatever it would be—for a week."

"Uh . . . I think she actually just wanted me to show you around so you wouldn't be alone while she sees some old friends."

I felt myself blushing and tried to discreetly look at his left hand. It'd be just my luck if he was married and I misread the whole thing. No, there was no ring, which didn't mean anything. But now he thought I was a total loser who couldn't entertain herself.

"You still don't need to do that. I don't mind just hanging out on the beach."

He shrugged, looking amused. "Have you tried saying no to your grandmother? Maybe you'll have better luck than I do. If not, I'll see you in a couple of hours."

"I . . . uh, okay." He had a point there.

Chuckling lightly, he scratched behind Jax's ears, then pulled her out of my way. "Enjoy the rest of your run. The Inn has good coffee if you want to grab some."

"I didn't bring my wallet. But I had some at the cottage. I'm fine."

"Just tell them you're Evelyn's granddaughter. They won't let you pay." I started to ask what that meant, but he said he would see me later and jogged off toward the jetty.

I rubbed at my tense shoulders, brushed the sandy paw prints off my leggings, and started back. Apparently I *did* need to shower. And have a talk with my grandmother.

CHAPTER NINETEEN

July 1950
Hereford, Massachusetts

"Your brother came to see me," Tony said by way of a greeting as Evelyn came down the dirt road. He was leaning on the car, arms crossed.

"I know. He caught me sneaking in last night." She moved to kiss him, but he turned his head, and she caught his cheek instead. Taking his face in her hand, she turned his chin, so he had to look at her. "That bad?"

"We can't sneak around like this."

Evelyn leaned on the car next to him, copying his body language with an exaggeratedly gruff facial expression. He looked over at her, and she furrowed her brow further until he finally cracked a small smile. "We're not sneaking around. We're just . . . not telling people yet. And then when I leave for school, we won't have to." Her looming departure both excited and terrified Evelyn, though she would never admit to the latter. While it would be easier to slip out of a women's dormitory than her parents' house when there wasn't the chaos of summer, she knew Tony wouldn't be able to make the two-hour drive to see her often.

And once again, she wondered if she wouldn't be better off transferring closer.

"I don't want to feel like I'm a criminal for being with you."

"Is that what Bernie said? He's so dramatic. I'm turning eighteen this month!"

"Your father—"

"My father loves me. And he's going to come around. We just need to give him time."

Tony nodded. "Time is fine." He took her by the arms, his grip firm, and she felt the skin on the back of her neck tingle in anticipation of the kiss that was sure to follow. "Evelyn, I can wait forever if I have to. But if he doesn't know we're together, he's not coming around."

Disappointment flooded her as he dropped her arms and turned away. He was right, but she wasn't used to being called on her bluffs. And worse, she wasn't so sure Joseph would actually come around on Tony—at least not unless she forced his hand. While getting into the trouble Bernie worried about would do the trick, that wasn't the right way. Joseph might yell; he might threaten. But he would never actually sit shiva for her, even if she eloped. And that was what they would have to do. And he would forgive her eventually because he'd have no other choice.

Not that Tony had proposed. There had been hints, but no outright declaration of intentions. Yet that part didn't worry Evelyn. She knew how she felt and didn't worry for a moment that he felt anything but the same.

College was another obstacle though. If she eloped and then didn't get her education, Joseph really might not forgive her and certainly wouldn't forgive Tony. But if she attended college as a married woman . . . Pembroke College, where she planned to go, would definitely be too far away; she would have to go someplace closer. But that would work.

"What's going on in that head of yours?" he asked warily. She quickly wiped her face free of machinations. "I don't want to know, do I?"

Evelyn stuck out her tongue. "So serious. Does your family even know about me? Other than Lipe?"

"Yes," Tony said, opening the car door for Evelyn. She climbed inside, and he shut the door behind her. "That's where we're going tonight. My mother wants to meet you."

"Your mother?" He nodded, putting the car in drive. "You let me out of this car right now." She reached for the door handle.

He turned to look at her, amused. "Why, Evelyn Bergman. Are you afraid of my *mãe*?"

She squared her shoulders. "I'm not afraid of anything, but I'm also not walking into your"—she hesitated—"*mãe*'s house empty handed." She butchered the pronunciation—it sounded like the month instead of the Portuguese word for *mother*—but he smiled at the attempt.

"No, that wouldn't do, would it?" He reached into the back seat and pulled out a bouquet of flowers. "You'll give her these. And if you *really* want to impress her, you'll say, '*Prazer em conhecê-lo.*'"

"Won't 'nice to meet you' suffice?"

He chuckled. "That *is* 'nice to meet you.' Say it with me now. *Prazer.*"

"Praz-eh."

"No Massachusetts accents now. You're going to have to say an 'r.'"

"Not like you talk any better!"

"I do in Portuguese. Come on. *Prazer.*"

"Praz-ER," she said exaggeratedly, rolling her eyes.

"Good. *Em conhecê-lo.*"

"Em cone-ye-se-lo."

"All together now. *Prazer em conhecê-lo.*" She repeated it. "She'll love you."

"And if I accidentally say something that means 'I neck with your son in his car down by the jetty most nights'?"

"She probably won't love you as much, although she has her suspicions. You did leave a mark last week."

Evelyn grinned. "Might have gotten a little carried away. *Someone* always says we have to be good."

He looked over at her again. "Be good tonight, huh? I want my family to like you."

She leaned back against the car door and put her legs, bare in the summer heat, up on the dash near the steering wheel, her dress riding up to show sun-bronzed thighs. "They'll love me, darling."

"I hope so," he said, not daring to look at her. "Because I do."

"Pull over." She sat up suddenly, removing her legs from the dash. "What?"

"Pull over right now!"

He pulled the car to the side of the road, still two miles from town, glancing at her nervously. But as the car rolled to a stop, she climbed on top of him, straddling his lap, the steering wheel digging into her back.

"Say that again."

"What?"

"What you just said. Say it properly."

He looked into her eyes, lost forever and never wanting to be found. "I love you."

Her lips spread into a slow, sultry grin, and she wrapped her arms around his neck, leaning in to kiss him deeply. His hands came up around her waist as he forgot that he and Evelyn had plans.

But Evelyn pulled away, kissed him once more lightly on the lips, then climbed back into the passenger seat, where she pulled a compact out of her bag to check her reflection. "I'd *really* better be on my good behavior now."

He swallowed. She hadn't said it back. "Why's that?"

She looked at him, then reached over and wiped at the lipstick on his mouth. "Isn't it obvious? I love you too." She handed him a hand-kerchief. "Wipe that off well. You just raised the stakes. Let's go. I don't want to be late."

Tony scrubbed at his mouth with the square of cloth while Evelyn reapplied lipstick, looking in her compact mirror. Then he pulled the car into gear and continued toward town.

CHAPTER TWENTY

"Grandma?" I called, entering the cottage. I heard clattering in the kitchen and headed in that direction.

"Good morning, sweetheart. How was your run?"

"I ran into Joe," I said, pulling out a kitchen chair.

"Well, of course you did."

"What's that supposed to mean?"

"I texted him when I saw your note."

"What do you mean you texted him? Since when do you know how to text?"

"I know how to do a lot of things." She was at the stove, French toast simmering in a frying pan, the smell of my childhood wafting toward the table.

"When I text you, you send back gibberish."

"Oh, darling." She turned around to face me, one hand on her hip, the other gesturing with a spatula. "Have you not figured out how much fun I have teasing you and your mother?" She smiled, turning back to the pan. "Never underestimate me."

"I don't," I said through clenched teeth. "That's what I want to talk to you about. I know your game. And I'm *not* interested in a setup."

"A setup?" She slid thick-cut pieces of French toast onto a waiting plate. "What kind of setup?"

"This Joe guy. I know you think it'd be cute because he's Tony's great-nephew and all, but I'm not interested."

"Of course, you're not interested."

I narrowed my eyes. Agreeing too readily was always a sign she was about to play an ace. "I'm serious."

"I know, dear. You don't even know him yet. How could you be interested?"

"That's not what I mean!" She put a plate in front of me. There was syrup on the table and two glasses of orange juice.

"Eat," she said, setting down the other plate and sitting. "We have a busy day today."

"Oh, do we? You literally haven't told me anything about this trip."

"I certainly have. I have business to take care of."

"And you won't tell me what that business is?"

"No. It's mine. That's all you need to know for now. But that's later in the week."

"Joe said you want him to show me around the town?"

"This afternoon, yes. This morning, we need to run errands."

"Why can't *you* show me around town? I want to hear your stories about it, not some random guy's."

"He's hardly random."

"Look, historically, your fixups have been disasters."

"One time—"

"Two. And that second one was enough for a lifetime."

"You can't tell me you haven't seen that before. You've been married, after all."

I rubbed at my forehead, not wanting to relive the worst date in the history of dates. And referring to my marriage in the past tense took some of the fight out of me. "Grandma, I'm not ready. And he lives almost five hundred miles away from me."

"From your parents' house, you mean."

I looked up sharply, but she smiled innocently. So it *was* a setup, no matter what she said to the contrary. "I'm not moving to Massachusetts. Especially not for a guy."

"Sounds like you've thought things out awfully far for someone who isn't interested." I threw my hands up, exasperated. "Now eat your French toast. You'll need a shower too. I can't take you anywhere like that."

Defeated, I took a bite. "Where did the groceries come from?"

"Oh, I texted Joe a list before we left."

"You text him a lot apparently. Are you sure *you're* not interested?"

My grandmother winked at me. "Maybe. A little competition is good for you."

I shook my head.

~

I had picked the largest of the three upstairs bedrooms, which my grandmother said had held a double bed and two twins at the peak of the cottage, when everyone used to descend on the shore for the summers. Now, it was outfitted with a queen bed, an antique dresser, and a small matching desk. I turned on the water in the recently remodeled bathroom (no sign of the clanking pipes my mother described from her childhood trips) and stripped out of my sweaty clothes.

Stepping over the edge of the tub, I stood under the shower's stream, then pressed my forehead against the cool tile wall.

I *should* be interested in Joe. I knew that. A fling on vacation would be perfect. Not only could I snap some cute social media posts to make it look like I was moving on but it might actually help me do just that.

But the idea of sleeping with someone new—I shuddered.

What's wrong with me? I wondered. My mother had suggested antidepressants a month ago. But I wasn't depressed. I was . . . stuck. I knew she was right, and I should sign the settlement agreement. I wouldn't move on until I was legally free. But I wasn't ready yet. I had never truly failed before. And I wasn't quite ready to concede defeat, even though I didn't want to be with Brad anymore either.

With a sigh, I pulled my face off the wall and began shampooing my hair. If I took too long, my grandmother was likely to take the car on her own. *I should hide the keys,* I thought as I washed the lather out. Not that it would matter—she would have no qualms about going through my bag to find them. I needed to hurry up and get back downstairs.

CHAPTER
TWENTY-ONE

July 1950
Hereford, Massachusetts

The houses were smaller than the grand Victorian Evelyn grew up in, on a side street she had walked past many times but never ventured down, clustered together with a small alley behind them. Children ran wild through the neighborhood, yelling to one another in a mishmash of English and Portuguese and dashing across the road, half-clothed in the summer evening. On front porches, men sat in undershirts while women in mended dresses brought them their next bottle of beer. It was less than half a mile from her parents' house yet a world apart from the starched collars and saddle shoes of her childhood. Joseph and Miriam would sit on the porch on a hot summer night, rocking quietly in wicker chairs, but they dressed for the town to see them. Which, in their location, they did.

No one was sitting on the porch at the house that Tony stopped his car in front of, and the children who ran across the lawn did so on their way to other houses. But it looked tidy, with freshly painted shutters, a porch free of the debris of kids, and well-cared-for flowers lining the small beds bordering the porch. A pear tree grew next to the house, showing the beginnings of the young fruit it would eventually bear, and Evelyn smiled, remembering her climb through the blossoms of her family's own to find Tony.

"Ready?" he asked, offering her his hand.

"Are you?"

He shook his head, handing her the flowers for his mother. "Come on, then."

A young girl pulled the door open excitedly before they were even up the steps. "They're here," she called over her shoulder, then looked up, gawking at Evelyn. "You're so pretty!" She turned to her older brother. "Tonio, she's a movie star!"

Tony made a gesture that Evelyn caught out of the corner of her eye, and the little girl's face fell. Evelyn knelt to her level. "It's just the lipstick," she whispered, winking. She cupped a hand under the little girl's chin. "And you're one to talk! That Natalie Wood better watch her back." The girl turned pink and squirmed happily. "Now, are you Carolina, or Francisca?"

"Carolina."

"It's nice to meet you, Carolina. I'm Evelyn."

"Miss Bergman," Tony said.

"Evelyn," she corrected. "Don't you start all that formal stuff now." She stood back up and looked at him playfully. "*Tonio*."

"Lina, go tell Mãe that we're here."

"I already know," a voice from the hall said. "Lina, let them in, *filha*."

Carolina moved aside, and Tony pressed a hand to the small of Evelyn's back to guide her inside.

Before Evelyn could even offer a handshake, or the flowers, she found herself being kissed on both cheeks by Tony's mother, who then pulled back and grasped her by her elbows to look at her. Evelyn, unused to such effusive greetings, hid her surprise. "Prazer em conhecê-lo," she said, mimicking Tony's earlier inflection perfectly. He raised an eyebrow. She had been messing with him at the mispronunciation.

"*Bonita*." His mother kissed her one more time, then released her arms to clasp her hand. "It's so nice to meet you too."

Evelyn offered the flowers. "Thank you for having me, Mrs. Delgado."

"Maria." Her brown eyes, a perfect match for Tony's, twinkled warmly. "I don't care for 'that formal stuff' either." She was a petite woman, perhaps five feet tall. And while she was slender, she looked sturdy—she'd have to be. She had borne eight children, though only six survived infancy.

"Where is everyone?" Tony asked, looking around.

Maria smiled. "I said I wanted to meet your Evelyn first." She turned to Carolina. "Go tell everyone they can come downstairs now."

Carolina went only as far as the foot of the narrow staircase. "Mãe says you can come down," she yelled.

Shaking her head, Maria handed the flowers to Tony and then took Evelyn's arm. "Come. We have so much to talk about."

~

Dinner was the ever-present cod of the north shore, fried with eggs and potatoes and seasoned with garlic and a spice Evelyn couldn't identify. "I made sure this was something you could eat," Maria said to her quietly as she served the meal. "Tony said fish was fine."

Evelyn smiled. Miriam kept a kosher home, but Evelyn decided in the car that she would eat pork if that was what was served. "Thank you." Maria squeezed her shoulder.

"What happens in the fall?" Felipe asked.

"What do you mean?"

He turned to Evelyn. "Aren't you going to college?"

Carolina and Francisca gaped at her. Apparently that wasn't an option for the women in the Delgado family, let alone a requirement. Everyone stopped eating, looking at Evelyn with great interest. Rafael, Tony's father, studied her through narrowed eyes. Evelyn glanced at Felipe, whose smirk told her that he knew his father wouldn't approve.

"I am," Evelyn said measuredly. "I'll be the sixth member of my family. My father insists."

Rafael made a chuffing noise, but a murderous look from Maria kept it at that. "And what will you do after?" Maria asked, trying to pretend this was a normal conversation.

"*That* question sounds like my family." Evelyn smiled with false sheepishness and the mood lightened. "I have no idea. One of my sisters is a nurse. Another a teacher. I haven't figured that part out yet." She turned to the four younger children, who ranged in age from seven to sixteen. "Is Lipe this tough on all of Tony's girlfriends? I know you'll tell me the truth."

"What girlfriends?" Francisca asked.

"You're his first," Emilio said.

"Unless you count Clara."

Evelyn looked at Tony in mock outrage. "And who's this Clara? Should I worry?" Tony started to sputter an answer, but Evelyn turned conspiratorially back to Carolina. "I want all the details later."

A deep rumbling laugh from the top of the table made Evelyn turn her head. Rafael slapped a hand on the table. "Clara was the dog," he choked out.

Evelyn burst into a merry peal of laughter. "I don't know whether to be relieved or insulted. Mr. Delgado, apparently *you're* going to have to tell me everything."

"Rafael," he said, still laughing. "And oh, he loved that dog."

~

"That went well, I think," Evelyn said as they drove along the dark road that wound its way through the marshes toward the beach. She was pressed against Tony on the bench seat, his arm around her as he drove. "Considering you gave me about ten minutes of warning."

"Would you have come if I gave you more?"

She pursed her lips in the darkness. He had a point. No, she would have made a flip excuse instead. Meeting his family was a stark reminder that most of hers didn't know he existed. Not that she would admit to that.

"Your father didn't seem too keen on college. Would he feel that way if it were you? If you went into the Army first?"

Tony was quiet for a moment. "I don't think it was about that specifically."

"Then it's because I'm a girl?"

"No—maybe a little. I think . . ." He trailed off.

"You think what?"

They had reached the turnoff for the beach, but instead of going left to take Evelyn home, he veered right toward the jetty end, where they could park and talk. He left the car on, Peggy Lee singing softly on the AM radio. "It's why Lipe asked what's going to happen. They don't think you're serious."

"About college?"

He bit his bottom lip, looking out toward the dark ocean. "About me."

"What's that supposed to mean?"

He turned to face her. "I can't offer you anything. Even if I get a different job, it'll be years before I save up enough for a house. And I'll never learn the things you'll learn at Pembroke. You'll be two hours away—"

"I was thinking about that, actually."

"Which part?"

"The two-hours-away part. Simmons accepted me. I could cut the commute in half."

His shoulders dropped. "But you wanted Pembroke."

"I wanted to go farther away from home. I don't anymore."

"I don't know that it makes much of a difference. You—"

"I could come home more often. You could come see me more."

Tony looked at her plaintively. "It's not the distance. You'll be in a whole different world. And I want that for you. But you can't pretend you'll still want to be with me when you're there. You'll meet someone else, someone in school. Someone who will be able to give you everything you want." He looked back toward the shore, where the moon reflected silver far out over the waves.

Evelyn took his face in her hands and turned it back to her. "What I want is *you*."

"Evelyn."

"Stop. Just stop. I don't care where we live, and I don't care what you do. I care that you're honest and good and kind, and you do the right thing even when you don't have to. I care that you see me. The real me. And you make me better." He opened his mouth to speak, but she shook her head. "No, you listen. I didn't tell you to take me on a date because I liked how you looked. Sure, you're handsome, but that wasn't it. Do you remember the day Julio stole the candy from my father's store?"

He looked at her in surprise. "Your father—?"

"No, I was there. I saw you. What you did. And I thought to myself, *That's what I need*. Someone to keep me honest. To make me want to do the right thing. Maybe you haven't noticed, but I get away with a lot when people let me."

Tony smiled despite himself. "Just a bit."

"You don't let me when it matters. Maybe that's why I like the idea of you in a uniform."

He finally laughed. "How do you do that?"

"Do what?"

"Make everything okay all the time."

She leaned against him. "It's a gift."

He pulled her back to face him again. "You *are* good, you know."

"I know that. No one else really does, which is how I like it. But I like knowing that you do." She saw a cloud of worry still sitting on his brow and climbed up onto her knees to kiss the lines from his forehead. "Listen. I may go to college, but I'm not going anywhere. You hear me? You won't get rid of me that easily."

His hands went around her waist, and she felt a tingle of excitement at the touch, moving her lips down to brush his, an urgent heat moving down through her chest to her belly and continuing south. "I do love you," she whispered as he held her tighter, kissing her more intensely. He pulled her onto his lap, and she wrapped her legs on either side of him, his hands roaming from her waist to her back, around to the sides of her breasts until he suddenly wrenched her off him and back onto the bench seat.

"What's the matter?"

"We—I—we can't."

Evelyn looked at him in confusion. They hadn't gone far, of course, but they had gone farther than this.

"I want you," he said plainly. "But I want to talk to your father. I want to do this right."

"Are you—?" She held her breath. Was he saying what she thought?

"No. No. Not in a car at night with you on my lap. No." He went silent. "But if your father agreed . . . ? Is that something you would . . . want?"

Her heart was beating so hard she thought her chest would swell until it burst out. She had never felt such an ache before. "Yes," she whispered. "But he'll never agree."

"Then we start wearing him down."

"How?"

He smiled and kissed her forehead. "You're not the only one who can be charming. Let me try first."

"We'd be better off eloping."

"Never."

She shook her head. "If I *promise* to be a good girl, will you keep kissing me?" He took her face in his hands and kissed her lightly again.

"You still always get your way with me, you know."

"Yes, but you make me work for it," she said, climbing back onto his lap as he groaned exaggeratedly and pulled her in close.

CHAPTER TWENTY-TWO

Errands with my grandmother meant a trip to the "beauty parlor." She offered to pay for me to get my hair done as well, because apparently the messy bun that I pulled my hair into after the shower didn't meet her standards. I considered it, briefly, but when we walked into a pink-fronted salon literally called "the Beauty Parlor," which looked straight out of the sixties, complete with stylists who had spent the last sixty years working there, I decided to pass. Gray hair might be in, but I wasn't feeling the granny look.

Instead, I got an iced coffee from the shop a few doors down and sat outside. Instinctively, I pulled out my phone and began scrolling through Instagram. A picture of my cousin's engagement ring got a double tap, liking it despite the pang of jealousy I felt. The beginning of a relationship is so much more social media–worthy than the end.

Then I did what I told myself weekly I wouldn't do anymore, and I typed Brad's handle into the search bar. I had unfollowed him, of course, because I didn't want pictures of Taylor popping up on my feed. But a morbid sense of curiosity still sent me there. He hadn't posted anything since the last time I looked, so I went to her feed instead, where the most recent picture was of their feet on a beach, angled together to make a heart.

I swiped up to close the app and let my phone fall in my lap before leaning my elbows on my knees and dropping my face into my hands. Why did he get to be happy when I didn't?

My grandmother's words, telling me I didn't need to suffer along with him, echoed in my head. Well, he clearly wasn't suffering, even with me not signing the settlement agreement, so what was I torturing myself for?

"Enough," I whispered. Six months was long enough for wallowing. It was time to start rebuilding. And stalking Brad's Instagram was *not* going to help me do that.

"Ready to go?" my grandmother asked from behind me. I turned and saw her hair, fluffed up and sprayed heavily enough to withstand a nor'easter.

"What's next today?"

"I'm going to see a friend. Joe is going to pick you up here in a few minutes."

"I really don't need the guided tour."

"Well, I have plans, and I don't want you sitting at the cottage all mopey."

"I'm not mopey!"

She cocked her head. "Darling, I told your mother I'd get you out of the house, but not so you can do the same thing you were doing at home."

"What do you mean you told her you'd get me out of the house?"

She grinned. "You think I would have told your mother I was coming here if I didn't want company?"

"I—" I stopped. I had been played. "How did you know I'd offer to come?"

Her expression softened. "You have a good heart. You always have. What else would you do?"

110

"You would have actually just driven here yourself?"

"Of course. I've done it a thousand times."

"Recently?"

She winked at me.

"All that stuff about not having a license?"

"Oh, that was true. But I don't need one of those."

The woman was impossible. "How are you getting to your friend?"

"Driving, of course. It's just a mile from here."

I shook my head. "I'll go with Joe, on one condition—you don't drive. We'll drop you off and pick you up."

Her expression was too bland, which always meant she was up to something. *Oh no,* I thought. *This was her plan all along.*

Joe pulled up to the curb in a black SUV. "Don't bother parking," Grandma called through his open window. "Jenna volunteered you to drive me to Ruthie Feldman's house." I grimaced, but he agreed, and I helped my grandmother into the car.

～

I climbed into the front seat after walking my grandmother up the steps to Ruthie's house. She panted slightly, leaning on me. "She ought to put in a ramp," she huffed. "Even I knew when to give in and get that chair thing." But Ruthie was thrilled to see her, and the two of them disappeared into the house, arm in arm.

"It's really okay," I said as I buckled my seatbelt. "You can just take me back to the car."

Joe glanced over at me as he pulled away from the curb. "Evelyn said you'd say that."

"Well, I feel bad. You don't want to show some random girl around town."

"How do you know what I want to do?"

"I mean, do you?"

He smiled, showing straight white teeth. "She didn't strong-arm me into it. I volunteered."

"That doesn't mean she didn't orchestrate it. I volunteered to come on this trip, and today she tells me she planned for me to come all along."

"Sounds about right. She must have been something when she was young."

"Oh, she's still something."

"That she is." He grinned again, and I felt my defenses lowering.

"Okay, then," I said, enjoying the feel of the salt breeze from the open window on my skin. "Where are we going first?"

"That depends. Are you hungry?"

I hadn't thought about it, but now that I did . . . "I could eat."

"Good. You're in for a treat, then."

We drove out past the edge of town to what could only be described as a large shack on a hill overlooking the water, with picnic tables covered in red-and-white checkered tablecloths—the kind with the plastic coating for easier cleaning—held down on each table by rocks and pieces of driftwood.

"This is the treat?" The smell of grease was heavy in the air, and it looked like the birthplace of food poisoning.

"Just wait. Any shellfish allergies?"

"No?"

"Go sit. I'll get the food."

"You don't know what I like."

He was already walking to the run-down counter and called back over his shoulder, "They only serve one thing." He stopped. "Oh, wait. Diet Coke or regular?"

I hadn't had soda in probably three years, but I also wasn't sure I trusted water from this particular establishment. "Diet."

He shot me a thumbs-up, and I selected a table closer to the bluff—about two-thirds of them were taken. *I could get used to these ocean views,*

I thought, staring out at the minuscule sailboats. *Although it's probably miserable in winter.*

Joe was back quickly, carrying a tray with two cups and two red plastic baskets lined in grease-stained paper. He set the tray on the table triumphantly.

"What is it?"

"What is it? It's your new favorite food. Your grandmother never told you about Brewster's clams?"

The name rang a bell. "I think my mom might have."

"Just try it."

I pulled one of the baskets toward me, and Joe handed me a soda. I selected one of the strips and gingerly took a bite. "Wow," I said as I chewed, not caring that my mouth was full.

"Right?" he asked, taking one from his basket. "This place is famous."

I finished the strip and took another one. "This is amazing."

He smiled. "And you didn't want a tour."

"I was wrong." I passed Joe my phone. "Take a picture for my mom?" He obliged while I held the battered clam to my mouth, then handed back the phone. I sent the photo to my mother. Then, because I actually looked happy for the first time in months, I uploaded it to Instagram too. #vacation #food #BrewstersClams #HappyAsAClam.

My phone vibrated with a text immediately. My mother sent three shocked-face emojis, then wrote, Brewster's! I should have come too. That's it. I'm getting in the car. I chuckled.

"What's funny?"

"My mom is so jealous she wants to drive nine hours just to eat here."

"Can you blame her?"

"No." I took another one. "And okay, if it's all like this, show me around as much as you want."

"Now I know how to get you to agree to things. I guess food isn't just the way to a man's heart."

"It's the way to everyone's heart. No need to be sexist about it." I found myself smiling.

He laughed. "Point taken."

I willed myself not to notice how his eyes sparkled when he laughed.

CHAPTER
TWENTY-THREE

August 1950
Hereford, Massachusetts

As the days grew shorter and her departure for college loomed closer, Evelyn decided to go into Boston, ostensibly to buy clothes for school.

"Alone?" Miriam asked suspiciously. She had taken her three eldest daughters to buy their wardrobes. And Evelyn had been a little too happy, a little too eager to comply with her all summer.

"I'll take Vivie with me."

Vivie looked giddy at the prospect of an afternoon in the city with her favorite sister, and Miriam's face contorted. As the youngest, Vivie was often given the least pleasant tasks, which now meant watching her nieces and nephews so her elder siblings got a break. Evelyn offered to help, but more often than not she fell asleep on the beach. Vivie never shirked her duties, but a vague melancholy had settled over her that summer, worrying Miriam. Evelyn saw the indecision on her mother's face and seized on it.

"Look, Mama, I'll be on my own in another month anyway. You can trust me. I promise not to corrupt her. We'll just go to Filene's for a few staples, get some lunch, and be home in time for supper."

"Maybe one of your brothers—"

Evelyn smiled. "I'll bring my hat pin. I need some practice using it anyway. We'll be fine. Really."

Miriam relented. She was fifty-six by then and tired. And life in the cottage with her grandchildren was so much more pleasant than sweltering on the train and the city streets.

Evelyn kissed her cheek and promised again to behave. And the next morning, the two girls set off for the station, Evelyn driving Sam's car.

"What are we going to do first?" Vivie asked, more excited than she had been in months. "I know it's not just Filene's."

Evelyn glanced at her. "What? You don't think I told Mama the truth?"

"Evelyn! What are we doing today?"

"Well, I suppose it's safe to tell you now. I'll tell Mama and Papa when we get home anyway. I'm not going to Pembroke."

Vivie's eyes widened. "You're—oh my goodness, Evelyn, you're not going to college? Papa is going to disown you!"

"I'm going to college, you goose. Just not Pembroke. We're going to go sign the papers at Simmons instead."

"Simmons . . . but why?"

Evelyn threw another look at her sister. *No,* she thought. *I can't tell her about Tony. Mama would worm that out of her in an instant.* "I don't want to go that far away," she hedged. Vivie looked skeptical. "Besides, I'll be so much closer to Harvard and MIT. *Much* better husband-hunting grounds." She thought quickly. "And you'll be seventeen before too long. You can take the train to visit me too."

"Do you think Mama and Papa would let me?"

"We'll work on them."

Vivie was quiet as they pulled into the train station's parking lot, where Evelyn purchased their tickets. As they sat on a bench on the platform waiting for the train to arrive, Vivie looked at Evelyn. "It's a good plan."

"What is?"

"Switching schools." She leaned against her sister. "You'll be closer to Tony."

Evelyn's mouth dropped open, and she elbowed Vivie sharply. "What?"

Vivie dissolved into giggles. "I don't tell Mama *everything* I know. And I'm not blind."

"How long have you known?"

"Since you agreed to date Jewish boys. I know you better than that. And you're never where you say you are now that we're at the cottages."

Evelyn looked at her sister in wonder. Vivie wasn't such a baby anymore. "And you're not going to tell Mama?"

"I haven't yet. And she's asked. But I told her what you told me: that you'd broken things off and that I hadn't heard anything else about him since." She tilted her head. "Are you going to marry him?"

"Vivie!"

"What? It's a good question, isn't it? And who would do it? A rabbi wouldn't."

Evelyn *had* realized it would have to be a judge. Even if Tony agreed to convert, which they hadn't discussed, it would be tricky. But Jewish law dictated that their children would be Jewish, following the religion of their mother, and beyond that, Evelyn didn't care.

"We're not engaged."

"But do you love him?"

Evelyn nodded, smiling.

Vivie dropped her voice to a whisper. "Have you . . . ? You know."

"Vivie!" Evelyn clapped a hand over her sister's mouth playfully. "What do you even know about that?"

"Oh my goodness, you *have*!"

"I have *not*! Lower your voice, please. People are starting to stare." Vivie looked around. There were three other people on the platform, none of whom were paying attention to them. People came to the shore this time of year, and few left for the city if they could avoid it.

The sound of the train approaching prevented further conversation. They boarded and settled into seats. But as they pulled away from the station, Vivie returned to her line of questioning. "Do you want to? Are you going to?"

Evelyn raised her eyebrows. "And here I was thinking you would go running to Mama if you even knew he existed."

Vivie lowered her voice again. "I read *Lady Chatterley's Lover*."

"The banned book? How did you get it?"

"I found a copy in Margaret's bag."

"And you didn't share it with me?"

Vivie pursed her lips in a fair imitation of Evelyn's face. "I've had a lot of time to read before bed. You sneak in awfully late."

"Okay, well, you're giving that to me as soon as we get home."

"I put it back in Margaret's bag. I didn't want her to notice it was missing."

"What's she going to do? Admit to having it? We'll swipe it."

Vivie laughed. "I've missed you this summer. You've been here, but it hasn't been the same." Then she turned more serious. "You haven't answered yet though. Are you going to?"

It was a question preying frequently on Evelyn's mind. There was the obvious concern about pregnancy, particularly with college looming. Papa's shop did have prophylactics, but he kept them in a locked box under the counter, and he sold them only to married men and the sailors. Never to a woman. And Tony certainly couldn't buy one anywhere in Hereford. Not if he was ever going to try to appeal to Papa.

There was also the question of where. The house on Main Street sat empty most of the time with everyone at the cottage and Joseph at work. But the neighbors were nosy and posed too big a risk. And a car for her first time was simply not an option. Tony would never agree to those choices either.

Tony himself was the final obstacle. Would he agree before marriage? Evelyn liked the idea of doing the deed before leaving for school. It was a way of promising herself to him. And moreover, she *wanted* to. A year earlier she couldn't have pictured herself straddling a boy in a car and so desperately wanting his hands on every inch of her skin. And she knew, from what she could feel when she moved on his lap, that he wanted to go further too. No matter how much he argued that they shouldn't.

Evelyn licked her bottom lip. "I don't know yet."

Vivie nodded sagely. "I'll get you the book. You might need it."

Laughing, Evelyn elbowed her little sister again. "There are things you can't learn in books, you know."

"I know. But I'm not brave enough until I go to college."

"Good." Evelyn leaned her head on her sister's shoulder. "I'm glad you know about Tony though. I haven't been able to tell a soul."

CHAPTER TWENTY-FOUR

The Instagram notifications trickled in as we drove toward town. I scrolled through my feed briefly, not realizing it had been so long since I had posted anything. Life had, well, stagnated since Brad left. My social media feed had always been heavily curated to show what I wanted the world to see, and I definitely did *not* want anyone seeing that I was living in my childhood bedroom, convalescing from a failed marriage.

"Where are we going next?"

He inclined his head slightly, keeping his eyes on the road and squinting in the bright sunlight. "I was thinking we'd go to Main Street and walk around there today."

"Today?"

He glanced over. "Yeah. Your grandmother—"

"Hired you to babysit me?"

"Are you always this suspicious?"

"When it comes to my grandmother? Yes. Did you know she doesn't have a driver's license?"

Joe let out a deep laugh. "I didn't. But it doesn't surprise me at all."

"And she was going to drive herself here." I shook my head. "She's always up to *something*. And I've been on enough bad fixups from her to last a lifetime . . ." I trailed off. "No offense."

"None taken." He paused. "How many is enough?"

"Honestly not that many. But the last one—that was bad enough for several lifetimes."

"What happened?"

I felt my cheeks turn red and didn't answer. He looked over again at my silence. "Okay, now you have to tell me."

"No way."

"Why not?"

"I don't know you well enough for *that* story."

He chuckled softly, looking back to the road. "I've got a goal for this week, then. I'm going to get that story out of you."

"I wouldn't count on it."

"We'll see." He glanced at me again, and I felt a strange flutter of excitement in my lower abdomen. Or the clams hadn't been so good, after all. It was more likely that. Obviously.

Thankfully, he changed the subject. "Anyway, it's not babysitting. She said she had some business."

"Did she tell you what that was? She keeps telling me it's her business, not mine, and then telling me stories about how in love she was with your great-uncle."

"I have no idea why she's here. Do you think it's about Tony?"

I shrugged. "She said it's not. But that's most of what she's told me about." I paused. "Then again, with her it could all be a red herring."

Joe parked near the bank that used to be my great-grandparents' house and gestured down the hill. "I thought we'd go see the park," he said.

The shops we passed were mostly nautical themed, about two-thirds of them in repurposed Victorian houses. I read the names as we walked.

There were a handful of art galleries and artisan shops boasting hand-made soaps. One advertised spells and charms.

"How far are we from Salem?"

"Little over half an hour. Why?" I gestured toward the shop. "Tourist trap. I went to high school with the owner. If she's a witch, I'm Tom Brady."

About halfway down, the hill leveled out, and we reached a small park with a playground, pear trees, flower beds, benches, and large rocks lining the edge that overlooked the hill leading to the water below.

This is what he wanted to show me? I thought, unimpressed. Yes, it was cool that it overlooked the water, and it was immaculate, but I didn't see anything special about it. "It's nice," I said politely.

"Do you want to read the plaque?" He gestured toward a copper plaque on a pedestal, long oxidized to green from the salt air.

"Uh, okay." I approached it. "Oh."

Joseph Bergman Memorial Park, it read. *Hereford had no truer friend.*

I looked up at Joe, who was standing close enough to my shoulder that I could feel the electricity of his presence. I took a reflexive step away. "I feel like your great-uncle doesn't agree with that sentiment."

"Actually, he put up part of the money for the park."

"What?"

"I don't know the whole story. But there isn't any bad blood there."

I thought for a moment, trying to figure out how that could be. "Did Tony ever get married?"

"No."

"And he forgave my great-grandfather for not letting him marry my grandma? How?"

Joe shook his head. "I don't think anyone really knows what happened except Tony and your grandmother."

I sighed. She made it clear she was only going to tell me what she wanted to and in the order she wanted to. If I asked her how Tony and my great-grandfather made amends, I'd get a story about Sam or Bernie or something unrelated. She said it was all the same story, but I didn't see the connection.

Giving up, I snapped a picture of the plaque.

"Do you want me to take a picture of you next to it?" Joe asked.

I looked out at the horizon. "How about one of me by the rocks with the water in the background instead? I want to look like I'm having an amazing time."

He looked mildly amused. "You're one of those people on social media?"

I shrugged self-consciously and tried to play it off. "Mid-divorce and all."

"Got it. Go sit on the rocks."

I obliged, and he took my picture. When he returned the phone, he had taken multiple shots.

"You're good," I said, swiping through them.

"I should be."

"Why's that?"

"I'm a photographer."

"You—wait, I thought you were the cottage's property manager?"

He shook his head. "The owner is a family friend. I help out sometimes. That's all."

"Oh. So like, you shoot weddings and stuff?"

"That's part of it. I've got an art gallery in town."

I had pegged him as a townie who rented properties, not a legitimate artist, and I cringed at how judgmental that was. "Can I see it?"

"Sure." He checked his watch. "Probably not today if we're going to see the harbor though."

I wanted to ask if he did a lot of business. I couldn't imagine art being enough to make a living in a town like this. And I wanted to ask about his family—I knew he came from fishermen. Was that still a family business? But it felt like prying and like I was too interested. So I didn't.

Instead, I posted the pictures to Instagram. No, I wasn't going to spend my time going through Brad's pictures anymore, but if he was still looking at my feed, he'd wonder who took the picture. I looked so carefree, my face turned toward the sun, hair blowing in the breeze, sunglasses on top of my head. If he did, I hoped he felt a pang of regret at throwing me away.

CHAPTER
TWENTY-FIVE

August 1950
Hereford, Massachusetts

Tony proudly thrust a letter into Evelyn's hands as she reached his car.

"What's this?"

"Open it."

She pulled the flap of the envelope and removed the paper. It was Tony's acceptance to the police training program. He would begin the following week.

Evelyn would be gone by then.

So soon, she thought, as she did whenever she realized her departure date was charging at them. But she pushed that dread aside and kissed him, then rummaged in her bag.

"It's like I knew we needed to celebrate tonight." She grinned wickedly, pulling a half-full bottle of Canadian Club from her handbag.

He shook his head. "I can't celebrate my acceptance into the police by doing something illegal."

Evelyn wrapped her arms around his neck. "You're going to be absolutely insufferable now, aren't you? It's a good thing you'll look so handsome in a uniform."

Tony kissed her lightly. "I had an idea, actually. Now that I have this."

"What's that?"

He hesitated slightly. "What if . . . What if I talked to your father? Before you leave."

She felt the excitement of the moment fall like a stone into her chest. She wanted him to ask *her*, not her father. Joseph would say no. But *she* would say yes. "I think you'd do better talking to me."

"I already know what you'd say."

"Oh, do you now?"

He pulled her in close and kissed her deeply, his body pressed to hers, but she didn't kiss back. "Don't I?" he asked quietly, his face close to hers.

"Yes," she whispered. "But he won't say the same thing."

Tony released her. "Evelyn, I won't run off with you."

"Then where does that leave us?" She turned away. "You're never going to be Jewish. You're still going to come from a fishing family. He won't say yes unless we force his hand."

"I could convert."

She tilted her head. This was a new development. And it could be enough after the fact. Maybe. But the mere promise of conversion wouldn't be enough to get Joseph's blessing.

"You would do that?"

He nodded slowly. It wasn't something he had given much thought to. But he believed in Evelyn more than religion, though it would kill his heavily Catholic mother.

She grabbed him tightly. "Then let's do it now. We'll go to Maryland. We can be married tonight."

He shook her off. "I said no. Look, I would give you the moon if you asked for it, but this is the one thing I can't do."

"Why?"

Tony sighed, crossing his arms as he leaned against the car. "Because even if your father forgave you, he would never forgive me. And that would be a problem for the rest of our lives. And how happy could you be with your father and husband always at odds?"

Evelyn leaned next to him, and they looked down toward the beach together, neither speaking for a long time.

Finally, she broke the silence. "You can't ask him yet."

"Why not?"

"It's too close to me leaving for school. He'll see it as a threat."

Tony looked disappointed but nodded. "When, then?" He looked to Evelyn and could practically see the wheels turning in her head.

"I'll write to Vivie that I'm seeing someone—she knows about you—but I'll get her to plant the seed without saying who it is." She paused, thinking the next step through. "Then, when I come home at the end of the term, I'll . . . I'll tell Papa that my boyfriend is coming to meet him. Mama will insist on making a dinner. Papa won't turn you out when you show up. And you'll have the meal to warm him up."

"And if he says no?"

"He will. At first." She stuck out her chin. "But then you let me work on him." Something in her demeanor changed, and a spark glinted in her eye as she suddenly shot past him to the driver's side of the car before pulling open the door, climbing in, and leaning toward the open passenger window. "But now, get in. I have a surprise for you!"

"Only if you scoot over," Tony said, going to the driver's side, but Evelyn started the car and put it into drive. Tony hopped back, his toes in jeopardy. "Hey now!"

"What? I can drive!"

"Terribly."

"I haven't died yet, have I?"

"I'm not letting you drive."

She pulled the car forward five feet, then jerked to a stop and leaned out the window to look back at him. "Doesn't look like you have much of a choice, does it?"

Sighing, he went to the passenger side, only for Evelyn to jerk the car forward another five feet. "Oops. That one was an accident."

"The surprise better not be you killing us," he grumbled, climbing in but sitting close enough to grab the wheel if he needed to. "Where are we going, anyway?"

"You'll see," she said, turning on the radio.

They always avoided town on their evenings together, as any gossiping neighbors who spotted them would surely tell Miriam. But Evelyn parked the car crookedly in front of the house on Main Street. The sun had just set.

"No," Tony said, seeing where they were. "Evelyn, what are you doing?"

"Ease up. No one is home. Papa is sleeping at the cottage."

"And the neighbors?"

"The Kleins are in Maine, and the Fultons went to a wedding on Cape Cod."

She didn't show it, but Evelyn felt nerves prickling through her stomach and along the back of her neck. She hadn't expected this chance, but when it came, right before she was due to leave, she took it.

"Come on," she said, and they climbed the steps to the wide front porch. Evelyn unlocked the heavy door and shut it quickly behind them without turning on the light, then took Tony's hand, leading him through the darkness up the staircase and to her bedroom, where the moonlight shone through the window. Tony reached for a light switch, but Evelyn pulled his hand away, placing it on her hip instead before kissing him.

"This is dangerous," he whispered.

"We're practically engaged." She pressed herself closer. "And I want this." He didn't respond. "Don't you?" She brushed a light hand across his pants.

He groaned. "You know I do. But we can't."

"Yes, we can." She pulled him toward the bed.

"And if you get pregnant?"

The moonlight illuminated her grin, sheepish this time, an emotion Tony had never seen on her. "Well . . . there are ways around that."

"I don't—"

Evelyn reached into her bag, then dropped it on the floor, the bottle clinking as it hit the wood and then rolled away. "I do."

Tony recoiled slightly, knowing what she was holding. "Where did you get that?"

"I swiped it from Papa's store." She sat and began unbuttoning her dress as Tony stood frozen next to the bed. When she was down to her brassiere and panties, she reached for him and he let himself be pulled onto the bed, falling into her kiss, the feel of her bare skin under his hands, his mouth. He pulled the strap of her bra down over her shoulder and reached into the cup, hearing her gasp, her back arching into his touch as he moved his mouth to her. He barely felt her hands unbuttoning his pants, so intent was he on what he was doing, but when he felt her touch under his shorts, he stiffened and pulled away sharply, propelling himself off the bed.

"What's wrong?" she asked, her voice husky. "Tony—?"

"No," he said. "Not like this."

She sat up, pulling her bra back up to cover herself. "Not like *what*? We're not in a car. We're planning how to get married."

"We should be married first. Or at least actually engaged."

"Then propose. And you can have me. Right now."

He looked away. If he looked at her, like that, on the bed, he would say yes. And he couldn't.

"No."

She turned on the lamp next to the bed and went to him, forcing him to look at her. "I'm leaving in three days. If we do this, it's proof we love each other. That the distance and the time won't matter."

"I don't need proof."

"And if I do?"

He looked into her eyes, memorizing the sight of her. She was the most beautiful thing he had ever seen. Maybe more than ever now, when she was laid bare of all the pretense. Then he reached for her hands and turned them up, kissing each palm. "Let this be your proof, that I won't until you're really mine."

"I *am* yours."

"And I'm yours. But that's why we'll do it right."

She sank onto the bed and put her head in her hands. "This is *not* how I imagined tonight going."

He handed her the dress. "Put this on before I lose my willpower."

She looked up, the veneer of flirtation back in place, and reached threateningly to the back of her bra. "And if I take more off?"

He shook his head. "It'll be a long walk back to the cottage."

"You wouldn't!"

He leaned down to kiss her forehead. "No. I wouldn't. But get dressed. Please. We only have a couple of nights left before you leave."

She stepped into her dress and buttoned it swiftly. Tony stooped to retrieve the bottle of whiskey, which had rolled to a stop next to her desk. He looked at it for a moment, then untwisted the cap and took a long swig before offering it to Evelyn.

"I thought you weren't drinking."

"That was before." He gestured at her and the bed.

She smiled grimly and took a sip. "Goodness, that's terrible."

"Let's go back to the beach."

Evelyn took his proffered hand, disappointed, but not embarrassed, and returned to his car, where she let him drive as she nestled beside him in silence, feeling the breeze from the open windows as they wound through the five twisty miles of dark marshland.

CHAPTER TWENTY-SIX

We walked the full mile of Main Street to the harbor at the bottom of the hill, where a restored factory, still bearing the faded logo of the old fishery on the brick, now held several chain stores and a couple of boutiques. Wide walking avenues lined the street, leading to a pier that people fished off at the far end. Hotels and restaurants, built to look like grander models of the Victorian houses on Main, lined Harbor Avenue, looking out over the water, where sailboats dotted the horizon.

I turned to Joe. "I get the feeling it didn't look like this when my grandmother was a kid."

"Not so much."

"Does Hereford still have a fishing industry?"

"Not really. Gloucester is close and still does because Gorton's is there. But it started to die out in the 1970s here."

"What happened to your family's business?"

"Long gone. Lack of interest mostly."

"I know Tony became a police officer."

"Chief of police eventually."

"The chief? Really?"

Joe looked at me curiously. "Do you want to meet him?"

"What? No. Why?"

"You seem very invested."

"I—I didn't know he existed before yesterday." *Was it really only yesterday?* "But like—he could have been my grandfather." Joe tilted his head, studying me, and I felt my cheeks burning. "He isn't—I mean— Grandma said—oh no, you can't trust anything she says, can you?" I tried to turn off the babbling, but it was like plugging a hole in a dam. "I just meant they could have gotten married. If my great-grandfather hadn't stopped them. And like—I didn't know there was anyone before my grandfather and it—"

Mercifully, he cut me off. "If that's how you say no, what do you do when you *do* want something?"

I huffed slightly. "Anyway. Tony became the chief of police—what about his brothers? Whose grandkid are you?"

His lips twitched, and I realized he was trying not to laugh at me. "What?"

"Nothing," he said. "Tony's older brother, Felipe, was my grandfather."

"Was?"

Joe nodded. "He died a long time ago. I never knew him."

"I'm sorry."

He nodded again. "That was part of why the business went. My great-grandfather's heart wasn't in it after my grandfather died. Emilio went to Korea and then college on the GI Bill and he didn't want any part of fishing, and once Emilio did it, Julio wanted to go to college too." He paused, looking out at the water. "Things started to change for a lot of the Portuguese families here after World War II. We were second-class citizens before. It's better now."

I had a million questions. But his suggestion that I was too invested meant I kept them to myself.

We walked along the promenade next to the water in silence, and I felt a sense of dread rising the longer we went without speaking. I cursed my grandmother for making me spend time with this stranger instead of letting me have the beach trip I had assumed I was getting. Yes, I should have known better with her because nothing she did was ever straightforward. But still.

A boat cut through the water near us, and I looked over at it. The logo on the side boasted "Whale Tales and Tours."

"That's a thing here?" I asked, gesturing to the boat, grateful for a topic other than Tony.

He shrugged slightly. "Tourists love it."

"Have you ever seen a whale?"

"A few times."

"Why are you not more excited about that?"

The corners of his eyes crinkled when he smiled. "You obviously didn't grow up on the water."

"Like forty-five minutes from the Chesapeake Bay. If that counts."

"It doesn't." He looked over. "Do you want to go whale watching?"

I sensed condescension at the idea of a tourist activity and said no. "But do they know a 'whale tail' is a girl's thong sticking out of her pants?"

Joe laughed, and I felt tension drop from my shoulders. "I didn't know *that* had a name."

I nodded sagely. "You learn things like that when you grow up forty-five minutes from the Chesapeake Bay." I was rewarded with another laugh.

～

The ship was fading into a dot on the horizon, so I let my eyes wander over the shop windows as we passed instead, not paying much attention until—

"Wait," I said, retreating a few steps, back to the picture that had taken a moment to process. Joe followed, and I stopped in front of a store called Hereford Heirlooms, looking at a framed black-and-white photo that had caught my eye. I was sure I must have been wrong, but I wasn't. "That's my grandmother."

She stood on the front of a parade float; the name of my great-grandfather's store just decipherable on the side. She couldn't have been more than sixteen or seventeen, and two other Bergman-looking girls flanked her—the younger one had to be Vivie, but I always got confused about which of the older sisters was which. Margaret maybe? Not that anyone watching that parade could have been focused on anyone but my grandmother. Vivie looked uncomfortable in that gawky, early teenager stage, and the older sister looked bored and like she had been strong-armed into being there. But my grandmother? She had a hand on one hip and the other in the air, waving exuberantly to the crowd as if she were royalty and they, her subjects, were all there to catch a glimpse of her.

I felt Joe's eyes on me and looked up.

"You look like her," he said.

I shrugged noncommittally, glancing at my reflection in the shop window, then looked back down at the picture. Features-wise, maybe. But that confidence, the absolute sureness of who she was, that was all I saw when I looked at the picture. I didn't have that.

"Come on," Joe said, opening the door, a blast of air conditioning hitting us. "Let's find out the story on it."

He held the door open for me, then reached into the window display to grab the frame, which he carried to the counter at the back of the store, where an older woman sat. She looked up, and her face split into a smile as she looked at Joe.

"Aunt Lina," he said as she came around to embrace him, standing on her tiptoes to kiss his cheek.

Lina, I thought. Would that make her Tony's sister? She looked about the right age.

She asked him something in Portuguese, but he shook his head. "Aunt Lina, this is Evelyn's granddaughter, Jenna. Jenna, this is my great-aunt Lina."

I found myself smushed into a tight hug, then held out at arm's length. "I should have known. You look just like her."

"I—uh—thank you."

"I thought she was the most beautiful girl I had ever seen when Tony brought her home." She smiled sadly. "Such a long time ago now." She noticed the frame in Joe's hand and took it to look, smiling broadly again in recognition. "This one's a funny story."

"It is?"

There was an old dining table with matching chairs to the left of the register, and she gestured for us all to sit. "Your grandfather took this picture," she said to Joe.

Joe tilted his head. "You mean Tony did?"

"No. Lipe took it. He had a secondhand Brownie box camera."

Joe looked to his great-aunt in surprise. "I have that camera."

Lina patted his cheek. "You're a better photographer than he ever was. But he took this during the Memorial Day parade in"—she thought for a moment—"must have been forty-nine. It was before Tony met her."

A bell chimed at the door as a customer walked in. Lina rose. "Take the picture. But tell your grandmother to come see me. It's been too long."

"How much is it?"

Lina shook her head. "I won't take your money," she said over her shoulder as she went to greet the woman who had walked in.

I looked at Joe, who sat studying the photograph. "You should have it," I said.

"Nah. This was your find."

"But I still have my grandmother. You should have this."

"My grandfather's camera is more meaningful." He ran a thumb over the glass, then picked up the frame and handed it to me. "That camera was why I wanted to take pictures. I always wanted to play with it, and my mom wouldn't let me. She gave it to me when I graduated from college."

"Does it still work?"

"It does actually. But the film is expensive, and the quality isn't great." He pushed his chair back and stood, and I followed, holding the frame. I thanked Lina as we left, she patted my arm, and then we were back outside in the blinding sunlight.

We had walked about a block when Joe pulled his phone out, an incoming call on the screen. "Sorry, it's a work thing. Is it okay if I take this?"

"Of course," I said, studying a shop window to avoid eavesdropping as he walked a few feet away and began discussing the price of something. But I wasn't really looking at the dress in the window. Instead I was looking at my own reflection.

I glanced back down at the picture in my hand. That self-assuredness that made her so special wasn't something that came with age. I had assumed that she just lost her filter as she got older, like so many people do when they grow out of caring about what others think. But one look at this picture told me that my grandmother had burst out of the womb much as she was now.

Looking up at the window again, I put my shoulders back and fought the urge to emulate her posture in the picture. I smiled, and my reflection did look like the photograph in my hand, giving me a little boost of confidence.

Joe's reflection appeared next to mine, and, for a split second, it wasn't the two of us, but my grandmother and Tony in the shop window.

"I'm really sorry," he said, shattering the illusion. "I need to stop by the gallery to deal with a customer. You could come with me if you wanted?" He checked his watch. "But it's almost time to pick up your grandmother. If I walk you back to your car, are you okay to pick her up on your own?"

"Definitely. You don't have to walk me though. I can find it."

"I don't mind. I need to go that direction anyway."

I agreed and followed him up a side street.

"So today was fried clams, Main Street, and the harbor. What's the plan when you babysit me tomorrow?"

He turned his head, his eyes traveling over my legs, and I felt a flutter in my stomach. "Wear sneakers. And probably long pants."

Ugh. He was looking at my shoes, not my legs. "Why?"

"I'll show you tomorrow."

Was I imagining the flirtatious tone? Maybe. But it was the first time I had really looked forward to something in months. Not that I was interested. But I had maybe, kind of, a very little bit, almost thought about it. And that excitement felt like a tiny piece of myself clicking back into place.

"Do I get fried clams again?"

He grinned. "You don't have to convince me."

"Then it's a date." I looked at him defiantly to see if he challenged that, not regretting it until he didn't.

Not a date, I reminded myself as I approached my grandmother's car, willing myself not to turn around as he walked away. *Just a vacation adventure.*

CHAPTER TWENTY-SEVEN

October 1950
Boston, Massachusetts

Evelyn sat on the grass by the water just off the Emerald Necklace path, scribbling furiously. It was unseasonably warm, but she barely noticed the sunshine as she leaned on a textbook, trying to cram in as much reassurance to Tony as possible. In her last letter, she recounted the double date she went on at her roommate's insistence, thinking her complete lack of interest would amuse Tony. It did not. Their phone call after that ended badly, and Evelyn was determined to fix things—she would take the train home that weekend if she had to, but the letter would have to suffice until then.

"Darling," she wrote, "I would no more be upset were you to—" But how to finish that sentence? Because now that she thought about it, she probably *would* be upset if he had gone on a date. Not that she would admit that. But she also wasn't going to write that she wouldn't be upset because that gave him a free pass to see other girls. She crumpled the paper and sighed. She pulled another sheet from her bag and scrawled her salutation across the top, then stared down at the blank page, willing the letter to write itself.

"Homework or a letter?"

Evelyn started and looked up at the young man standing before her. "I beg your pardon?"

He grinned. She was unimpressed, but he sat down next to her. "Looks like you're struggling with it," he said mildly, nodding to the three balled-up pages around her. "I'm Fred."

Under other circumstances, Evelyn wouldn't have seen the harm in playing along. But she had to finish this letter, and he was breaking her concentration. "Look, *Fred*, I'm quite busy right now, so if you don't mind—?"

"Not at all," he said, making no effort to leave. Instead, he lay on the grass, pillowing his head on his arms, and stretched out, closing his eyes to the sun.

She glared down at him. "Do I need to move?"

"Why? You're not bothering me. And I'm perfectly content to stay quiet until you're done."

"And if I don't want to sit with a strange man while I write a personal letter?"

He opened a blue eye and squinted at her. "Ah, so it is a letter, then. Let me guess: Stole a friend's fella?"

"Excuse me!"

He chuckled, closing the eye. "Okay, not that, then. Breaking up with your boyfriend back home?"

"Quite the opposite."

"Why so hard to write, then?"

"I—why . . . That's none of your business!"

Fred sat up. "Ouch, what did you do?"

"Good grief, are you always this impertinent?"

"Possibly. My mother always said I asked too many questions." He shrugged. "Here's another: What's your name?"

"Evelyn," she grumbled.

"Well, Evelyn, you can tell me. I'm perfectly safe. I'm engaged, after all."

She looked at him sideways. "You are?" He nodded. "Then what are you doing talking to strange girls in the park?"

"Are you strange?"

"To you I am."

"Fair enough. I normally wouldn't, but you seemed to be having such a difficult time, and as a gentleman, I decided to offer a friendly hand."

"By sitting here until you annoyed me into talking to you?"

"It worked, didn't it?"

She rolled her eyes and put the textbook on the grass, another book on top of the paper to keep it from blowing away. Her hat pin was stuck through the top of her bag, easily accessible if he turned out not to consider his engagement an obstacle. "I'm engaged too." She saw him glance at her hand, and she looked at him defiantly. "We haven't gotten a ring yet, but we don't need one for it to be real."

"Parents don't approve?"

This was too much. She started to stand, but he waved her back down. "Stay. I'm just being nosy."

With a sigh, she resettled herself. "No. He's not Jewish."

"I got lucky there. Betty is."

Good for you and Betty, Evelyn though unkindly. Then she rearranged her face. It wasn't this man's fault Tony was who he was. It also wasn't his fault she was in a sour mood. She had made her own bed there.

"That's not why the letter is hard." He nodded at her encouragingly. "I went on a date as a favor to my roommate, and I didn't think it was a big deal."

"And he did?"

"Apparently."

"Do you think it was now?"

"It wasn't. But I guess I see why he's upset."

"So tell him that. He'll get over it. And if he doesn't, is that really who you want to be engaged to?"

Evelyn looked at him carefully to see if he was being flippant or making a pass, but he seemed genuine. "I suppose you're right."

Fred lay back down in the grass. "So which school are you at?"

"Simmons. You?"

"Harvard."

"And it took this long to bring that up in conversation?"

Fred let out a hearty laugh. "I could tell I liked you. I admire a girl who speaks her mind."

"Well, don't like me too much. Betty definitely wouldn't approve."

"No, she probably wouldn't. But we're both engaged and away from home, and as I see it, there's no harm in having a—strictly platonic, of course—friend."

"Oh, we're friends now?"

He opened the one eye again. "I'd warrant I now know more about that fella of yours than your parents do. So yes. I think we are."

Evelyn smiled, despite herself. "Touché."

He sat up and then stood and dusted off his pants. "Well, friend, I'll let you finish your letter. What do you say to grabbing a cup of coffee one day?"

"I say I'm already in enough trouble and don't need more."

"Hah. I don't need any either. Suppose I'll see you around, then."

"I suppose so. Goodbye, Fred."

He tipped an imaginary hat at her. "Evelyn." And he walked away. She wasn't watching when he turned to glance back at her.

CHAPTER
TWENTY-EIGHT

My grandmother's face lit up when I showed her the photograph. "Wherever did you get this?" I told her the story of finding it in Lina's shop. "Well, that explains a lot. Lipe must have been in love with me first."

I rolled my eyes. "How did you get that from a picture?"

"You don't take—or keep—a picture like that of someone you don't like. It explains why he didn't seem to want me and Tony to be together."

Or he figured out you weren't going to be able to stay together, I thought. "What happened to him?"

"It was a terrible tragedy. There was a fire on a cargo ship, and twenty or so men went out to try to rescue the crew. Lipe and three others didn't come back. Joe's mother was only two." She shook her head. "What else did you do with Joe today?"

I told her about the fried clams, and my grandmother closed her eyes, savoring the taste of the memory. "Brewster's alone is worth the trip."

"Mom said it made her want to get in the car and come up."

"She's not invited." She reached across the kitchen table and put a gnarled hand on top of mine. "This is our trip."

I found myself smiling. It felt good to be wanted instead of being the prodigal daughter, returned home after her failure of a marriage to live off her parents while trying to build up the courage to return to the world.

I also realized I desperately wanted to know more about this place. When I was little, she'd told me stories about growing up in Hereford, but they were all anecdotes about her ridiculous family, and I often confused them with my mother's battered copies of *A Tree Grows in Brooklyn* and the All-of-a-Kind Family books, as well as the movie *Avalon*. Now, her tales were so blurry with age that I couldn't remember which were real and which I had seen elsewhere.

"What happened to the cottage?" I asked.

"I told you. That woman sold it."

"But why didn't the rest of you buy it?"

She sighed. "She sold it without telling me. And Bernie and Margaret . . ." She trailed off.

"Bernie and Margaret?"

She clapped her hands once. "They're gone now. Leave them be." After rising with an effort, she made her way to the kitchen cabinets, which she began opening and closing, one by one.

I came to help her. "What are you looking for?"

"This." She pulled a vodka bottle from a cabinet and waved it triumphantly.

I tried to take it from her, but she had an impressively strong grip on the bottle. "Mom said you're not allowed to drink."

Her eyebrows rose almost to her hairline. "Your *mother*," she said icily, "isn't here and doesn't get to tell me what to do."

"But your medications—your heart—"

"My heart is fine, and I haven't died yet, have I?" She took two glasses down and poured a healthy splash of vodka into each one, then went to the refrigerator, where she pulled out the orange juice. "And if you're going to be all nosy, you'd best have a drink with me while you do it."

I tried to stay firm, but she thrust one of the glasses into my hand, then made her way to the front porch, leaving me little choice but to follow.

She was unusually quiet as she sipped her cocktail.

"Grandma?"

"Yes, darling?"

"Are you okay?"

"Whatever do you mean?"

"I—we didn't come up here for you to die or something, did we?"

She laughed. "Where did you get such a morbid streak?" She took another drink. "No, darling, I'm not going anywhere anytime soon. And even when I do, don't you think I'm ever leaving you. I'm going to be that little devil sitting on your shoulder telling you to get into more trouble. You always worried too much about what other people thought to have any fun. That's one of your problems."

"One of them?"

"Yes. Would you like me to tell you what they all are?"

I shook my head. I already knew my flaws much better than she did. And I didn't feel like having them listed by someone who pulled no punches.

"What were you being all quiet about, then?"

"The screens." She gestured around us. "They're the one good change. The mosquitos are something fierce otherwise. If you sat outside when we were young, you'd be up all night scratching." She smiled at some memory. "Of course, we did it anyway."

"Did Grandpa come here with you?"

Her expression changed. She was thinking about the before time, when it was her parents and siblings, not her own children and family.

"He used to come up for his two weeks of vacation. And every other weekend or so. But I drove up myself with Anna, Joan, and Richie in June, and we stayed through August every summer."

It never occurred to me that the summers they spent in Hereford meant being away from my grandfather for the better part of three months. And I wondered again if there had been something fishy going on.

Wasn't he suspicious of you and Tony? was on the tip of my tongue, but I bit it back with a sip of the screwdriver. Even before I knew about Taylor, I would have been suspicious at that much time apart had it been Brad—especially if it was in his hometown with his first love. But despite knowing she was an inveterate liar, I believed that she didn't cheat on my grandfather. Maybe I just wanted to believe it and not tarnish my memory of them as happy. But moreover, there was something playful when she lied, and she had been serious about that.

She met my grandfather in college. I knew that much. But I didn't know how she went from planning to marry Tony to marrying Grandpa. She was telling me stories in a painfully linear fashion. I was never one to skip ahead in a book, but had this been one, I would have.

"You and Joe," she said, changing the subject as if she could hear my thoughts. "You sound like you two clicked this afternoon."

"He seems nice." I hesitated. "Why isn't he married?"

She grinned over her drink. "Who says he's not? Besides, you're not interested."

I threw my hands up and quit, letting her lead the conversation back to the stories she was willing to tell, getting up to fix us a second drink at her behest, though I made them significantly weaker than the first ones on purpose. I didn't want hers to clash with her medications, and I wanted a clear head the following day.

CHAPTER TWENTY-NINE

November 1950
Hereford, Massachusetts

Evelyn's entire body hummed with excitement as the train rumbled along the track toward Hereford Station. In the nearly three months since she had left for school, she had seen Tony only four times, when he could both take the car and have enough time to see her, factoring in a two-and-a-half-hour round trip. And while it was heavenly to go out in public with him, to a restaurant and a movie, and then walk through town arm in arm after a summer of sneaking around, time was always far too short. Especially because he was working nights at the docks while he trained with the police department, and he was tired.

But now, at Thanksgiving, which was one of the only holidays they celebrated in common, his training was finally finished. And as of two weeks earlier, he was officially on the payroll of the Hereford Police Department—which, having been founded in the late 1600s, had a long and storied history. Or so he said in his letters. Evelyn's interest in town history prior to her own arrival was scant at best.

Which meant that Saturday night, once the sun set, he was hers.

The intervening days of knowing they were only a mile apart yet she couldn't see him were torturous, but Evelyn still savored being home with her family. The house was crowded, and she was forced out of her room and into a bed shared with Margaret (poor Vivie consigned to a pallet on the floor of her own room) because Gertie and her husband slept in her room, their baby in a dresser drawer. But there was a sense of normalcy in the chaos. Sam was back in his room that he shared through childhood with Bernie, who now lived in town with his wife and children, where he put up Helen, her husband, and her rowdy brood of children for the holiday, as the Main Street house had finally reached its limit and could not contain another fully formed family.

Sam picked Evelyn up at the station, lifting her in a large bear hug and swinging her around as she squealed to be put down. He had returned the day before and was charged with ferrying people from the train station as they arrived.

"How's college treating my favorite sister?"

She smiled. He told all of them they were his favorite. "I'm enjoying it."

He glanced sideways at her. "Oh yeah? How much?"

Evelyn laughed. "Not *that* much. I'm a good girl, after all."

"Yeah. And I hear I might be named the next pope." He was rewarded with a jab to the ribs.

"How sad—I suppose that means you won't be getting married, then. Unless you plan to have a lot of 'nephews' like the old popes did."

"Which one of our sisters has the big mouth?"

"Margaret. Tell me who she is."

Sam sighed. "Louise. You'll meet her Wednesday. I've already met her parents."

"Is it official, then?"

He shook his head. "I spoke with her father, and I have a ring. I haven't asked her yet."

"What are you waiting for?"

"The right time, you heathen. You can't just do it in a car like you're asking where to go to eat."

Evelyn scowled, then rearranged her face. It wouldn't do for Sam to know. He might be her favorite brother, but he couldn't keep a secret to save his life—as evidenced by having already told Margaret—and probably the rest of their siblings—about Louise.

Thankfully, he was too focused on the drive to notice her expression. "And what about you? You got a fella yet?"

"Maybe."

"Is he Jewish? Or you gonna get yourself in trouble again?"

This time she let him see the scowl. "Did it ever occur to you that we're living in the twentieth century and the whole idea of only marrying people like us is ridiculous and old-fashioned?"

He shook his head. "No, I can't say that it did. Especially not after what I saw in Europe at the end. There are about six million fewer of us than there used to be."

There was no way to argue once that point came out. But she could always fudge the truth a little. Besides, she *had* met a Jewish man, even if she wasn't interested in Fred. "Don't you worry." She patted Sam's arm. "Papa will approve."

He glanced at her again, and she wondered briefly if Bernie had told Sam about his talk with Tony. But then he changed the subject back to Louise, and Evelyn exhaled. Sam had the biggest mouth in the world. Bernie wouldn't tell him. And as long as Miriam didn't pry it out of Vivie, her secret was safe.

Of course, by bedtime, Margaret and Gertie were peppering her with questions about who the new boy was. *Sam,* Evelyn thought, shaking her head.

"Where does he go to school?" Margaret asked.

"How did you meet him?"

"Is he Jewish?"

Evelyn looked at her sisters appraisingly. This was new territory; Evelyn had never been treated as one of the big girls before. She glanced down at Vivie, who sat cross-legged on her floor pallet, a pillow hugged to her chest. At not-quite seventeen, Vivie was now the last of the little girls. Evelyn wondered if that would change when she went off to college or whether it would always be the case; Margaret was graduating this year, and Vivie would always be a full step behind everyone except Evelyn.

With the new terrain, however, also came the question of whether she could trust them. Historically, that hadn't been wise. But a broken plate or a trip to the movies on Shabbat were in a whole different league from the secret she was carrying now.

She looked at Vivie again. *Two can keep a secret if one of them is dead,* she thought. Evelyn held a conspiratorial finger to her lips. "It's still early—I don't want to jinx anything."

Margaret elbowed her playfully. "Come on."

"Nope. You'll find out eventually—assuming it goes the way I want it to."

"She must be serious," Gertie said to Margaret, swaying gently when the baby stirred. "Imagine Evelyn not bragging."

"Hey!"

"Am I wrong?"

Evelyn grinned. "Not in the slightest."

But when the rest of the house had gone to sleep, Evelyn climbed out of the bed and snuggled in behind Vivie on the floor.

"Missed you," Vivie murmured sleepily.

Evelyn hugged her tightly. "Missed you too."

~

The girls all helped prepare the Thanksgiving meal, taking turns rocking, feeding, and cooing over Gertie's baby, who finally slept in a basket on the table, on top of a soft blanket that Miriam had crocheted. When dinner was ready, the family would crowd around Miriam's elegant dining table, extended to its fullest with extra leaves but still not big enough for the addition of so many spouses and children. It would be Evelyn's first year at the adult table.

Vivie was to be at the children's table with Bernie's three children, Helen's three, and Gertie's eldest. Vivie sighed as she counted the seats at the tables, and Evelyn saw the disappointment on her face.

"Mama," Evelyn whispered to Miriam. "Move Vivie to the adult table." Her mother looked at her. "Please?"

"She's not an adult."

"She's not a little kid either."

"She'll help them behave."

"Let her have this early. She's only a year younger than me. Please, Mama."

Miriam looked at Evelyn, watching to see if there was some ulterior motive. But she saw only love for the youngest child Miriam herself doted on and nodded her acquiescence. "It'll be your job to arrange it."

Evelyn kissed her mother's cheek, surprising her. "You won't even know we squeezed in a spot," she promised. "Thank you."

Miriam returned to the kitchen, smiling at the idea that a little heartbreak and some distance had helped her second-youngest daughter mature.

And the look on Vivie's face when Miriam instructed her to sit between Evelyn and Sam made Evelyn's heart swell.

Until Sam, tired of being the subject of ribbing over the impending family meeting with Louise the following day, changed the subject.

"How's the new fella, Evelyn?" he asked. "You gonna bring him home soon?"

If looks could kill, Sam would have been six feet under. But Bernie, a couple of drinks in, turned to his sister. "New fella, huh? Another Portuguese, or is this one Irish?"

Joseph slammed a hand on the table, his fork clanging loudly enough to silence all conversation. "What do you mean, Bernard?"

Bernie glared at his father, suddenly sober. He had just been teasing, but clearly he had struck a nerve.

Evelyn held her breath.

Bernie didn't answer, and an interminable moment ticked by with no one speaking.

"My Evelyn is a good girl," Joseph said through clenched teeth. He looked at her as if daring her to say differently.

"Yes, Papa," she said quietly as he and Bernie exchanged murderous glances.

"Enough," Miriam said calmly but firmly, holding Joseph's gaze until he looked away. He and Bernie did not speak to each other for the rest of the meal. Evelyn stayed focused on her food.

~

Louise came with her parents Saturday afternoon, leaving Miriam too distracted to be suspicious when Evelyn left to "see some friends in Gloucester." Joseph handed Evelyn his keys, kissed her forehead, and told her to have a good time. She looked back at the scene of her family gathered in the crowded sitting room, laughing and joking and cooing at children, and felt a twinge of guilt. But who knew when she would find time alone with Tony again?

She drove the winding road toward the beach, making the three turns to the cottage. There was a light on in the big house at the end of their street—Mrs. Gardner lived there year round. She was a widow who had lost her only son in the same fishing accident as her husband, years earlier. If she had other family, no one ever saw them. The Bergman children did small errands and chores for her during the summer; she rewarded them with coins when they did well, with sharp words when they did not. But her hearing was terrible, and Evelyn didn't think she would notice the two cars outside the cottage. Tony's was already there when she arrived.

The air was cold, but Tony's embrace was warm as she leapt into his arms, wrapped her legs around his waist, and kissed him in the darkness.

"Hello to you too," he said, coming up for air.

She grinned and he released her, sliding her to the ground. "Let's go inside. There's no heat, but there's also no wind."

She had warned him about the lack of electricity in the off-season, and he pulled a kerosene Coleman from the trunk, along with a heavy down comforter and several crocheted afghans, then followed Evelyn up to the porch, where she used the key from Joseph's ring to unlock the door that was never locked in summer.

Inside, the furniture was covered with sheets, the wicker porch furniture stacked in the corner. Tony lit the lantern, and she pulled the sheet from the living room sofa, which had been recycled from the Main Street house when Joseph purchased a new one. She shrugged off her heavy coat and sat; Tony set the lantern on the table, pulled off his thick peacoat, then spread the heavy blanket over her and climbed under it as well, putting an arm around her. She nestled in against him, holding his hand in hers, her head on his chest, soaking in the feeling of his presence.

He sighed, and she looked up at him, seeing his furrowed brow in the flickering lantern light.

"What is it?" She took his face in her hands. "Tell me."

"It's nothing." He took one of her hands and kissed her palm, but she shook her head.

"Tell me."

Leaning back, he rubbed his knuckles across his jaw. "This is harder than I thought it would be."

"What is?"

"All of it. You being gone. The new job. Keeping everything a secret. Not knowing what your father will say. Everything."

A small stab of guilt ran through Evelyn. She missed him desperately when she was at school. But she was also gone and experiencing an entirely new world. It hadn't occurred to her that he was living in the same place with a huge, gaping hole shaped like her, while she was out with new friends, going new places and even sometimes agreeing to double dates.

Not to mention she knew exactly what her father would say.

That was going to be another difficult conversation soon, though she hoped they would get some time together before it came up. But maybe if she steered him away from the most sensitive parts—

"What's wrong with the job? Do you not like it?"

"It's an adjustment."

"What does that mean?"

"I—I know the town looks down on us. But I mostly stayed with my own people before. I'm the only Portuguese in the department. The only one ever. And it's constant." He saw the look on her face. She was ready to jump in the car, drive to the police headquarters in town, and give them all a piece of her mind. "It's fine. I can take it. They'll stop eventually. They're like this with anyone new. It's just harder than I expected. Especially when I don't have you."

Evelyn felt her heart breaking. She had always been selfish—oh, she had a good heart, but she had always done exactly as she wanted without a thought to consequences because things just worked out. But she had been off enjoying herself, telling him nonchalantly that she was going to this party and that, while he never complained about what he was suffering for her sake.

She climbed onto his lap and kissed the tip of his nose playfully. "You always have me."

"Do I?"

"Always." She brushed her lips lightly against his. "I'm yours." Then a deeper kiss. "Forever."

"Even when you're not here?"

"I'm always here," she whispered, touching his heart. She took his hand and pressed it to her chest. "And you're always here." She kissed him again, greedily this time, moving his hand lower until it cupped her breast and she felt him stirring beneath her.

He reached up, untucking her blouse from her skirt and running his hands up her abdomen to her chest, the feel of his fingers electric along her skin. She reached down and felt him stiffen. He pulled back and looked at her.

"Don't stop this time," she said, holding his gaze. "And you'll know, no matter what, that I'm yours and you're mine."

He stared into her eyes another moment, losing both himself and his desire to do what was honorable in their depths. Then he kissed her again, leaning her back onto the sofa, himself on top of her, and did as she asked.

~

When they were finished, they lay pressed against each other on the sofa, huddled under the blanket against the cold of the cottage. Evelyn traced her fingers along his chest silently.

"Are you all right?" Tony asked quietly.

She looked up at him. "Never better." He squeezed her even closer to him.

"I do have to speak to your father now."

"That might be a little awkward *right* now."

"You know what I mean. When you come home after the term. Like we planned." He felt her tense against him. "What?"

She hesitated. "I don't think that's wise."

"Why not?"

"He—Bernie made a comment the other night . . . and he—well—he didn't react well."

"What does that mean?"

"What does it matter? He's going to say no. I don't care what he thinks. I know what I want and it's you."

He leaned forward, surprising her as she fell back against the sofa. "Was this a setup? To trick me into running off with you?"

"What?"

"I know you, Evelyn Bergman. Don't think for a second that you can put one over on me. I love you, but I'm not going to let you do what you do to everyone else."

She sat up, genuinely stung. "You claim you know me, but that's what you think this was?"

He swallowed dryly, his Adam's apple bobbing. "You tell me."

"Well, if it was, I did a terrible job of it. I wouldn't run off with you right now even if you were Frank Sinatra!" She turned away, arms crossed over her chest.

This elicited a smile that she didn't see, but he pulled her elbow until she was facing him again, which she did reluctantly, still miffed. "You swear?"

She looked up finally. "Fine. If you were Frank Sinatra, I'd *think* about it."

He laughed, wrapping his arms around her. "How long do you want me to wait?"

"Until summer maybe. Can you bribe someone to rob his store so you can save the day? Find a way to ingratiate yourself?"

"I'll do my best."

"It'd be a start."

"What time do you have to be home tonight?"

"Midnight."

He checked the watch on her wrist, a high school graduation present from her father. "Then we still have time."

CHAPTER THIRTY

"Where are you going today?" I asked my grandmother, sniffing the orange juice she gave me to make sure it was just juice. Then, after checking that she was still at the stove, I smelled the juice in her glass as well. I wasn't taking chances.

She put a plate of French toast in front of me. "Your cousin Donna is picking me up for lunch."

I took a bite. "I have a cousin Donna?"

My grandmother made an exasperated noise. "Yes."

"Is she my age?"

"Is she—no, she's—" She stopped to think for a moment. "She's seventy-six—no, seventy-seven. She'll be seventy-eight in . . . Now, when is her birthday, again?"

I could vaguely picture an older woman named Donna at my wedding, hugging me repeatedly. I thought she was one of my grandmother's friends.

"How are we related?"

"She's my niece, so she'd be your . . . first cousin once removed."

I still didn't understand the removed thing, so I nodded politely. "Whose kid is she?"

"Bernie's. She made me an aunt."

"So you used to watch her here?"

"Next door. That was Bernie's cottage. Bernie and Papa—well, it was better they not spend too much time under the same roof."

"Why not?"

"Too similar, I suppose. Or too different. Or both."

I knew better than to question how that could all be true at the same time. "And you're telling the truth? She's driving?"

"You sound more and more like your mother every day."

"I get the feeling that isn't a compliment."

"Oh no. It isn't at all."

"You didn't answer the question."

She sighed dramatically. "I offered to drive because she just had a hysterectomy last month, but she says she's fine."

I ate another piece of French toast, shaking my head.

"Where's Joe taking you today?"

"I have no idea. He just told me to wear long pants and sneakers."

She nodded. "Hope he brings bug spray. You're going to need it."

"You know where we're going from that?"

"I believe I do. He's taking you to see Dr. Foster."

"Who?"

"I don't know if he'll get that joke. It depends on whether your mother told his mother and whether she told him."

"Mom knows his mom?"

"Of course. They played together every summer as children."

I felt my brow furrow. "Grandma, *what* are we doing here? You're telling me bits and pieces, and I get the feeling you have some big plan."

"Me?" she asked innocently.

"Yes, you."

"I told you. I have business to attend to."

"And is that business just visiting your friends and family?"

"No."

"Then what is it?"

"If it were your business, I'd happily tell you. But it's not."

159

I sighed dramatically, irritated. "Will you tell me when it's done?"

She shrugged. "I don't know the answer to that yet."

"You're impossible."

"Maybe. But that's why I'm interesting, darling. What are you?"

My jaw dropped open.

"Close your mouth, dear. You'll catch flies. Speaking of which, maybe I'll text Joe about the bug spray. You'll get eaten alive out there."

I pushed my chair back and took my plate to the sink. "I have some."

"Make sure it's the beat kind."

"The beat kind?"

"Yes. To beat the ticks away."

I looked at her for a moment, trying to figure out what she was saying. Then it clicked. "DEET?"

"What? No, your feet should be fine if they're covered."

Shaking my head, I went upstairs to get ready.

~

When Joe arrived, he had a backpack, water bottles, and a can of OFF!, which he offered to me. "I put stuff on already."

"Is it the deep woods kind?"

"Are we going into deep woods?"

He nodded, and I took the can and sprayed myself liberally with trepidation. Hiking wasn't exactly my scene. Going for a jog along the beach? Yes. A walk through a seaside town? Lovely. *Outdoorsy* wasn't an adjective one would use to describe me though. But my grandmother's comment—*What are you?*—echoed in my head. I was never going to be as difficult as she was, but I refused to be boring. So I pulled my hair up into a ponytail, knelt to double-knot my shoes, and said, "Let's go."

I expected we would drive somewhere, but Joe led us past the cottage to the end of the street, where there was an empty, overgrown lot before the forest started in earnest. The remains of a rock wall led along the edge of the property, and we walked beside them. I pointed to a pile of rocks in the middle of the tall grass. "What's that?"

"It was the Gardner house."

"I don't—"

"The family lived there for a hundred and fifty years or so. They gradually lost their money, and the last one died in the fifties. There was some legal issue with the property being entailed, and that's the only reason there aren't McMansions or some horrible townhouse complex there."

"This many years later?"

He shrugged. "I don't know who owns it. But the house was torn down before I was born."

"When *were* you born?" He looked approximately my age, but I was curious.

"A year before you."

I rolled my eyes. "Is there anything my grandmother hasn't told you? The song I danced to in the sixth grade talent show? How I like my steak? My bra size?"

He glanced at my chest, and I blushed. That had just popped out of my mouth. But I stood my ground and didn't cross my arms even though I wanted to. My grandmother wouldn't have. She would have owned it.

He grinned. "None of the above. I know you're a teacher, we're about the same age, and you're divorced."

"Going through a divorce. Not divorced yet."

"Are you getting back together?"

"No."

"Then is there that big a difference?"

I didn't respond, and we walked past the tall grass to a narrow path that led into the woods.

But a few hundred feet in, all signs of the path disappeared.

"How do you know where we're going?" I asked.

"There's a trail."

"Where?"

"It's a little overgrown. Not many people come out this way anymore, I guess."

"You're not bringing me out here to murder me, are you?"

"No."

"Okay, but see, you didn't laugh at that one." He finally did. "I'd hate to find out this mysterious business of my grandmother's was to have me killed."

"Why would she do that?"

"Maybe she's working for my hus—soon-to-be-ex-husband."

"And divorcing you isn't good enough?" I didn't reply, and he looked back at me. "Ouch. What did you do?"

"Nothing! He's the one who wanted the divorce. I was blindsided."

"Then why would he have you killed?"

"He wouldn't. I just . . . DC law lets you divorce after six months if both parties agree that it was mutual . . ." I trailed off.

"And you didn't agree?"

"Not yet." I shook my head. "Don't get me wrong, I don't want him back or anything. I just . . ."

"Want him to suffer."

"Is that *really* so wrong? He's living with his new girlfriend."

He looked back over his shoulder at me, a wry smile on his face. "Then you're right. Let him suffer."

I grinned slightly, not sure why I liked his approval, but I did.

We walked in silence for another minute or two. "Where are we going, anyway? My grandma said something about a doctor?" He looked puzzled. "She said you wouldn't get the joke unless my mother told your mother?"

"Ohhhh," he said. "Yeah, it was a rhyme my mom used to say. 'Dr. Foster went to Gloucester.' It was their explanation for why the town was deserted. That the people left for Gloucester. Which was partially true. But it's an old rhyme about the Gloucester in England, not here."

"What town that's deserted?"

"We're almost there."

I was thoroughly confused, but he didn't say more about the town, so I changed the subject. "Did you know our mothers were friends?"

"My mom told me. When I said I was taking Evelyn's granddaughter around town."

It hadn't occurred to me to ask my mom about anything. I reflexively pulled my phone out of my pocket. No service. I held it over my head, looking at it to see if it picked anything up, and promptly tripped over a tree root. The next thing I knew, I was on the ground—except it wasn't the ground. I had fallen into Joe, knocking him down in the process.

My phone was faceup in the dirt, about a foot from his head.

"Sorry. I'm so sorry, I wasn't—" I pulled myself off him and stood up. He pushed up on his hands before rising, then stooped to pick up my phone and handed it to me.

"Do you text while driving too?"

I started to protest and explain myself. But it was almost like I felt my grandmother's presence, whispering in my ear that I was being boring. And I wasn't boring! Instead, I shrugged. "Only if there's a cute cop nearby to stop me." *Jenna, what are you doing?* I didn't back down, and he eventually shook his head and continued walking. But I saw the hint of a grin as he turned away, and I felt my nerves crackling with electricity.

Flirt a little, that's fine, I reminded myself. *But you're going home next week. And you're still married.*

We walked in silence for the next quarter mile until Joe stopped. "We're here," he announced.

I looked around. The trees were less dense, and there were a lot of rocks, but I didn't see anything that resembled a town. He was looking at me expectantly. I looked around again. "Uh . . . what am I looking at?"

He spread his arms expansively. "Welcome to Rockland."

"You're putting me on, right?"

"Huh?"

"Rock Land?" I gestured to the rocks littering the ground.

"They weren't real creative with place-names in the 1600s, I'll give you that. Most towns in Essex are named for places in England and the rest are about the terrain. But this was a real settlement up until around 1800."

"Did they live in the trees like Robin Hood?"

"A lot of the trees came later. You can see them growing in the ruins of houses. Come on, I'll show you." He began picking his way through the flora until we came to something that was square enough to let me see that it was man-made.

"So why did the people leave?"

"Most left because it was safe to live on the coast again after the Revolutionary War. And the fishing industry started to really be a thing . . ." He trailed off.

"And the rest?"

He looked up at me, a spark of excitement in his eyes. "Well, you asked about Salem."

"Witches?"

"That's what they say. When everyone else left, this was a safe space for them."

I felt a slight shiver of excitement. "You don't believe in that stuff, do you?"

He shrugged. "Not really. But they did back then. And some of them were pretty well known."

"So what happened to *them*?"

"Maybe they're still here. People say it's haunted."

I tried not to look apprehensive. I didn't believe in magic. But in the middle of nowhere with a strange guy and no cell service . . . I laughed nervously. "You . . . uh . . . you meant it when you said you didn't bring me out here to kill me, right?"

"They do like their sacrifices."

There was a zero percent chance I could find my way back through the woods. *What did you do, Grandma?*

He laughed. "I'm messing with you." Then he turned more serious. "It's actually a sad story. People came from Hereford and burned what was left of the town. You can still see charring on some of the foundations."

"Why?"

"Bad harvest one year. Someone decided it was the witches."

"And they killed them?"

"Depends who you ask. I don't doubt people died, but they say that the women knew the men were coming and hid. They just lost their houses."

"Just," I said, thinking about the fact that I was now living with my parents.

"On the plus side, if they really were witches, I bet they hexed them good after that."

"And if they weren't, they starved."

"I told you it was a sad story. But you seemed interested in witches, so here are Hereford's. And they do say these woods are haunted."

"And what do *you* say?"

He grinned. "We used to come out here to drink in high school. On Halloween, even. And I never saw anything out of the ordinary."

"Maybe the witches just like you."

"Maybe. I don't bother them, they don't bother me."

"Probably smart. You don't want two-hundred-year-old witch ghosts mad at you."

"No." He looked at his watch. "Do you want to walk back or Uber?"

I pursed my lips. "Funny."

"I'm serious."

"Oh, okay, let me just use my nonexistent cell service to get an Uber to pick us up in the middle of the woods. Do the witches get a discount?"

Joe pointed through the trees. "There's a road about a quarter mile that way. And cell service another tenth of a mile up the hill once you're out of the trees."

"And we just walked—how far did we walk?"

"About three miles."

"When we could have driven?"

"Where's the adventure in that? Besides, it's good for you. Builds character."

I shook my head but passed him my phone. "If I had to hike all this way to an abandoned witch town, I need a picture. And now that I know you're a photographer, I want something artsy for my Instagram feed."

He handed my phone back, set his backpack on the ground, and pulled out a camera. "I work better with my own equipment. Come on, there's a more complete foundation on the way to the road, and the light is better."

Joe led the way, stopping to pick a few wildflowers. When we reached the foundation that had the recognizable remains of a real wall, he told me to sit, then posed me with the flowers, instructing me to put one leg up on the wall, then guided it to the exact angle he wanted with a gentle hand under my knee, before positioning my arms and turning my face to the side to shoot me in profile.

"Take your hair down," he said, looking at me critically. I reached up and pulled it free from the ponytail holder. He ran his fingers through it, adjusting pieces. It felt oddly intimate, and I was suddenly shy. He stepped back and looked at me through the viewfinder but didn't take the picture. "Relax your shoulders and tilt your head up toward the sun." I did what he asked, and he looked again. I saw him shake his head from the corner of my eye, and he came over and sat on the wall by my foot. "Don't be nervous." I started to protest, but something in his demeanor stopped me. He was a professional, after all. "Tilt your head up and close your eyes." I closed my eyes, leaning my head back. "Imagine the sun is washing away everything that's bothering you. Anything you're afraid of, it can't touch you when the sun is on your face out here."

I heard a dry leaf crunch under his foot as he stood, and I wondered for just a moment, with my eyes closed, my head tilted back, if he was going to kiss me.

Instead, I heard the snap of a shutter. "Perfect," Joe breathed as he looked at the image on the camera's screen. "Do you want to see it?"

I climbed down and went to him, where he offered me the camera. I was bathed in a beam of sunlight that created a circle around me where it came through the trees, and I looked ethereal, like a wood nymph in a serene yet sensual pose.

"How did you do that?"

"Do what?"

"Get *that*"—I gestured toward the camera screen, then toward myself—"out of *me*."

He smiled again. "That *is* you. I just capture what I see."

I didn't know what to say. *That* was what he saw when he looked at me? He put the lens cap on his camera and the strap around his neck. "Come on. The road isn't far, and it's lunchtime. I'll transfer the shot to my phone after I call an Uber, and then you can put it on Instagram. Just tag me as the photographer."

CHAPTER
THIRTY-ONE

December 1950
Boston, Massachusetts

"Let's go see the lights on the Common," Fred said. "My parents used to bring me into town to see them when I was a kid."

"How gauchely gentile of them," Evelyn said dryly, but she punctuated it with a wink. "Mine didn't, even though we used to beg them to when our non-Jewish friends would talk about them." Evelyn had met him at the South Street Diner for coffee, which led to hamburgers as a cup of coffee stretched into two, then three, and was then close enough to supper that they might as well stay. As long as they split the check, it wasn't a date, and besides, he was engaged, and she was the next-best thing to it. She hadn't intended to see him again, but after running into him three more times, always near the Simmons campus, she asked if he was following her.

"I have a feeling I'd meet the business end of that hat pin if I were."

Evelyn shrugged. "Depends on my mood. I've got a mean right hook too."

"I would expect no less."

"What *are* you doing this far from home? Harvard is an awfully long walk and across the river."

"I like long walks."

Evelyn shot him a suspicious look. "In Boston. In December?"

"I don't see you curled up by a fire."

He had a point. She had established a loop that took her about three miles daily, four if the wind wasn't too harsh or she felt like more. It was a way to keep her figure with the starchy campus food, but moreover she needed to move. She always had. And growing up by the water, she could stand the cold.

"Where are you from, anyway?"

"Plymouth."

She shook her head. "Plymouth *and* Harvard. You're insufferable, aren't you?"

"You're the one who keeps bringing up Harvard. I'm extremely modest. And my parents are absolutely frowned upon by the original families. My father was born here, but in Fall River, and my mother came as a baby from Russia."

"How tragic."

"I know. I can't tell anyone at Harvard for the shame of it all."

Evelyn peered at him to see if he was serious. He wasn't.

"Where are you from?"

"Hereford."

"Yet you don't smell like fish. Look at us breaking stereotypes."

"Are you this impertinent with everyone you meet?"

"Only the people I like."

"And how do you know you like me? We've bumped into each other three times."

"Four counting today. We're practically an item."

Rolling her eyes, Evelyn stopped walking and turned to face him. "Really now, this is too much. I told you I'm engaged and—"

He held up his hands in a gesture of surrender and interrupted her. "Don't get your feathers all ruffled—I'm only teasing you."

"It would take more than you to ruffle my feathers," she said, gloved hands on her hips.

"Well, either way, settle down. It was a joke, and I don't need to meet that famed right hook." She took her hands off her hips, and she and Fred continued walking along the path. "That's better. And see? This is how I know I like you."

"Because you might get clocked at any second?"

He grinned, showing off a dimple in his left cheek, the corners of his eyes crinkling into what would become smile lines as he aged. "Absolutely. I like to live dangerously. And I like someone who can keep up with me."

"Fred, darling, I can run circles around you."

"I don't doubt it," he said, chuckling. "I enjoy being kept on my toes. Do you know how uptight those Radcliffe girls are?"

Evelyn did. "I take it Betty isn't one of them, then?"

Cocking a finger at her, he smiled again. "And that right there is how I know you like me, too, no matter what you say. You wouldn't remember her name otherwise."

"Maybe I just have a fantastic memory."

He closed his eyes and turned toward her. "What color are my eyes?"

"Excuse me?"

"Let's test that memory. Come on. What color are they?"

She glanced at his dark hair. "Brown."

"Are you sure?"

"Yes, you fool."

"Well, they're blue. Now who's the fool?"

"You really are the most irritating man."

"I will take being the 'most' anything."

She sighed. "I'm going to have to find a new walking route, aren't I?"

"Nah. I can take a hint if you spell it out explicitly enough. You want me to leave you alone if I see you again?"

She should say yes. She knew that. But there was something charming in his endless energy and nonstop chatter. Something witty and confident and sassy that matched the same qualities in herself. And he *was* engaged. Was there any harm in having a male friend as long as there really was no interest?

She knew the answer—Tony wouldn't like it. He trusted her—she knew he did. He just didn't trust anyone else.

But Evelyn was a big girl, and she could take care of herself just fine. And bantering with Fred felt more like being with Sam than flirtation. It was like he knew her already—how to push her buttons, how to calm her back down after riling her up. And whether she would admit it to Fred or not, she *was* enjoying his company.

"I didn't say that," she said. "Besides, you keep the criminals and perverts away."

"Little do they know you're the one to fear, between the fists and the hat pin. Can I see it, by the way?"

"The right hook?"

"Preferably the hat pin." She pulled it from her wool cloche hat and held it up for him to see. "Yes, that could do some damage. I'll make sure I behave."

"See that you do."

He offered a sweeping bow. "I shall be a perfect gentleman." When he straightened, he offered his arm, which she took delicately after replacing the pin. "There now. So tell me more about this fella of yours and why he hasn't put a ring on your finger yet to make sure everyone knows he claimed you."

"How do you know I'm not wearing a ring? I have gloves on."

"Did he cough one up over Thanksgiving, then?"

She removed her hand from his arm and scowled in reply.

"I suppose that's a no. So what's the problem there?"

"There's no problem."

"You haven't said his name yet. That's how I know there's a problem."

"Maybe I just don't tell everyone everything that's ever happened to me like you do."

"First of all, I haven't told you the half of what's happened to me. You don't know I had my tonsils out when I was eight or that I'm extremely allergic to paprika."

"I do now."

"That's true. Do you want to know about my cousin Herbie? He ate a grasshopper once."

Evelyn finally laughed. "I hope you don't have a roommate. The poor fellow must want to murder you in your sleep if you do."

"Charlie? Nah. Well, maybe. Let's not give him a hat pin." He offered his arm back, and she took it again. "So what's his name?"

"Tony."

He shook his head. "No, can't play that one off as Jewish when your parents find out." She didn't reply again. "Come on, you can tell your dear old uncle Fred the whole sad tale."

"Another time." They were nearing the turnoff toward her dormitory.

"I'll walk you home."

"You'll do no such thing. I don't need the gossip."

"Coffee, then? Tomorrow night?"

And against her better judgment, Evelyn found herself agreeing, which led to the dinner they had just finished eating and the discussion of the Boston Common Christmas lights.

"Then let's go see the lights."

"And what would Betty say if she knew you were walking around Boston Common with a beautiful girl doing something as romantic as looking at all the Christmas lights?"

"Who says I'm going with a beautiful girl? I'd be going with you!"

Evelyn threw her head back and laughed. "I should be mad at you for that one."

"Look, there's no denying you're attractive, but if I start telling you that, where will we be? You're my friend. Why can't two friends look at some lights outside in a public place?" She didn't reply, and he sensed her wavering. "Besides, it's not romantic unless you're a gentile. Jews don't kiss under mistletoe. We'll talk the whole time about how tacky the *goyish* couples are for thinking it means anything."

She felt a twinge of guilt. Tony had been reassured by what happened between them over Thanksgiving, and she didn't want to break that trust. But it wasn't like she was interested in Fred—sure, she might have been had Tony not been in the picture, but poor Fred never stood a chance. Not that he seemed to want to—as far as she could tell, he didn't have any interest in her beyond friendship, which did make Evelyn wonder more than once if Betty was destined for an unpleasant surprise with this particular husband.

"What are you afraid of?" Fred asked.

Evelyn looked up at him. "Absolutely nothing." She pulled a couple of bills from her wallet and slapped them on the table to cover her share. "Let's go."

CHAPTER
THIRTY-TWO

We sat on a boulder by the side of the road, waiting for the Uber to arrive. There was just room enough for both of us, with an inch or two preventing our shoulders and hips from touching. An inch or two that I was very aware of for reasons I didn't want to think about.

"Where does this road go?" I asked, trying to get my bearings. And maybe to distract myself. Not that Joe was paying much attention to me. He had his camera in his lap and his phone in his hand, and he was downloading the picture.

"Into town that way." He nodded to the left. "And up toward Ipswich the other." He switched the camera off, set it gently in the backpack at his feet, and then turned to me. "What's your number?" he asked, gesturing with his phone.

"You can just AirDrop it."

The hint of a smile played across his lips. "Or you can give me your number."

I wanted to kick myself as I recited the ten digits.

My phone vibrated as the message came in, and I opened the picture, using two fingers to zoom in and see it more clearly. I hadn't looked that spectacular in a photo—or in person for that matter—since my wedding. I shook my head slightly.

"You don't like it?"

I glanced up, unaware that he had been watching my reaction. "No, I do—I love it. I don't think you're a photographer though. You're some kind of wizard." I remembered where we had just been. "Or a witch, maybe. When in Rome and all." I returned to my phone, saving the image, then opening Instagram. I had a dozen new notifications. I had posted the previous two pictures partially to seem happy if Brad was looking. I didn't know if he was—but my friends, whom I had effectively shut out except for sporadic texts to reassure my three nearest and dearest that I was alive, were. And I had forgotten, when I was hiding so no one could see what a mess I was, that there still were people who wanted to see me. Who missed me. And who, until that moment, I hadn't realized I missed as well.

I scrolled quickly through the comments. I would respond to every one of them later, I told myself, then clicked the plus to upload the new picture. I thought for a moment about the caption, smiling as inspiration hit, then typed out Glinda's line from *The Wizard of Oz* about only bad witches being ugly.

"What's your handle?" I asked Joe. He told me, and I tagged him as the photographer, then hit the share button, resisting the urge to look through his feed then and there.

He unlocked his phone and touched the notification, grinning slowly as he read the caption. "Perfect."

A car approached—the first we had seen in the fifteen minutes we had sat there—and Joe rose, saying it was the Uber.

"Where to now?" I asked when we were in the car.

"I'm hungry. Lunch?"

"Solid plan. Brewster's again?"

"Liked it that much?"

"Um, that was the whole reason I went on this hike."

He shook his head. "There's more to Hereford than fried clams on a picnic table."

I looked down at my yoga pants—I was sweaty and not dressed for a real restaurant. I would have liked to shower and change into nicer clothes first. But he was just as grungy as I was. And it wasn't like I would run into people I knew. So I told the voice in my head that questioned every decision to get over it and watched out the window as the woods gave way to the marshes that led to town in one direction and the beach in the other.

The Uber driver eventually pulled to a stop in front of an unpretentious bistro with a green awning by the harbor, with outdoor seating overlooking the water. "Gimme Shell-ter," the sign read. We seated ourselves outside, and a waiter soon brought waters and menus.

I picked mine up, then looked at Joe. "What's your recommendation?"

"Everything is good."

I made a face. "Okay, but I want Brewster's-level good."

He smiled and gestured to the waiter. "Two lobster rolls," he said, pronouncing it "LAWBstah."

"Lobster?" I asked when the waiter left. "Really?" It sounded so fancy.

"You asked for the best thing on the menu."

I looked out over the water, suddenly aware, as we fell silent, that our situation was awkward. It was one thing when we were actively doing something, because we could talk about the woods or the town or my grandmother, but I had just spent six months frozen in time and the previous six years in a committed and all-consuming relationship. What did I have to talk about?

The melancholy began to rise, but I battled it down, casting around anxiously for a subject to wedge into the conversational lull. Another whale-watching boat went past, close to the shore, having just left a nearby dock, a painting on the side: a rotund cartoon whale standing on a scale, holding up a sign that read "Whale Watchers."

I pointed to the boat. "That's a terrible pun."

"Aren't all puns terrible?"

"Says the guy who brought me to a restaurant whose name is a pun from a Rolling Stones song."

"I never said the name was good. I said the food was."

"I guess you would know—doesn't your mom own a restaurant?"

"She does."

"Please tell me it has a pun for a name."

He shook his head. "As straightforward as they come. La Tasca Sofia."

"What does it mean?"

"Sofia's restaurant."

"And your mom . . . ?"

"Sofia."

"Is it Portuguese food?"

"No, Thai," he deadpanned.

I scrunched up my nose. "Stupid question, huh?"

He softened. "No, I'm just teasing. It's actually a lot of my grandmother's recipes."

"Does that mean that you cook too?"

He nodded.

"Are you married?" I blurted out, then clapped a hand over my mouth. "I'm sorry. I don't know where that came from."

"I—um—wow—okay . . ." He rubbed at his suddenly ashen face, and I felt my stomach drop. What had my grandmother said? *Who says he's not?*

Of course. He's married. Grandma, what did you do?

That reaction does mean he was *flirting with you though.* I pushed that thought aside. I wanted nothing to do with a cheater.

"Sorry. I—"

"It's not what you're thinking."

I waited.

"I'm not, but I was."

My shoulders dropped—I hadn't realized I had tensed them. "Why didn't you tell me you were divorced too?"

He rubbed the side of his hand across his forehead again. "Because I'm not. She died."

Half of me wanted to wrap my arms around him. The look on his face was heartbreaking. The other half wanted to dive off the retaining wall into the ocean to escape my embarrassment.

"I—I'm so sorry."

"It was almost four years ago now. I'm okay. You just caught me off guard."

"What happened? I mean—you don't have to talk about it—you don't even know me—I—" *THAT was what Grandma meant? She couldn't have warned me?*

"Drunk driver. She was coming home from a shift—she was a nurse."

I exhaled loudly. "That's—"

"I know."

"I'm sorry."

His glanced down. "Thanks."

We sat in silence, and I desperately flailed for the right thing to say. My go-to was always to break tense or awkward moments with humor, which I definitely couldn't do about his dead wife.

But if one of us didn't say something soon, I wasn't going to be able to stop myself.

"Do—do you want to talk about it?" I stammered to avoid saying something regrettable.

"Not really, no."

And back to silence.

He closed his eyes momentarily, took a deep breath, and when he opened his eyes, I could see he was going to save me with a safe subject. "Listen, it's—"

"Jenna!"

I turned my head, horrified, toward the sound of my grandmother's voice. She was waving excitedly and entering the restaurant's terrace with another older woman.

"We were walking by, and suddenly there you two were. How did you get here so quickly from the woods?" She started to pull a chair over, but Joe jumped up to do it for her, getting a second chair as well.

"We walked to the Ipswich Road and Ubered back to town."

"Well, that explains it." She sat, gesturing for the other woman to sit too. "Jenna, darling, you remember your cousin Donna. Donna, do you know Joe Fonseca?"

Donna peered at him over her glasses. "Sofia's boy?" Joe nodded. "But you were a baby just yesterday!"

"Not quite yesterday," he said amicably.

Donna shook her head at my grandmother. "They grow up so quickly."

"You're telling me. They're already as old as I was when I was spending summers here with three kids."

The waiter reappeared with menus and asked if they would be joining us for lunch.

"Why yes, I think we will," my grandmother said. "But we don't need menus. The lobster rolls, of course." She said it the same way that Joe did, with a long, accented "lawb" and an "ah" instead of "er" at the end.

"Oh, I don't think I could eat a whole one," Donna said. "You know how big they are here."

"You'll take it home. Martin will be thrilled with the leftovers."

"That's true."

The waiter said he would rush the order.

Grandma dug through her purse and pulled out a baggie of assorted pills, which she dumped into her hand, then picked out several small, ruddy pentagons. "Xanax, anyone?"

Joe and I shared an alarmed look, while Donna helped herself to a pill.

"Grandma, you can't just give out Xanax!"

"What are you talking about?"

"It's prescription only."

"No it isn't. I got a big bottle at Costco."

"Yes it . . ." I trailed off, realizing that it wasn't Xanax. She was the queen of malapropisms. Like the time she got pulled over for driving alone in the high occupancy vehicle lane and insisted to the police officer that she took the "HIV lane" all the time with no issues.

He let her go without so much as a warning.

I changed tactics. "What do you take it for?"

"What do you think I take it for?"

"I have no idea. That's why I'm asking."

"Heartburn, you silly girl. I can't even look at a French fry without it."

"Zantac," Joe and I said at the same time.

"That's what I said."

I looked back at Joe. "Didn't they pull that off the market a couple years ago? Caused cancer or something?"

"I think so."

"Well, I'm still here, aren't I?"

Joe was trying not to laugh and excused himself to go to the bathroom. I watched him crack up once he was out of my grandmother's line of sight, then I turned to her.

"What are you *doing*?"

"What?" she asked innocently.

"I—" I stopped myself. She was playing dumb to get me to admit that I liked Joe and that she was intruding. "Nothing," I muttered.

A second later, she was holding my arm in a surprisingly firm grasp, her bony hand wrapped around my wrist. "You were mucking it all up."

"I—what?"

"Donna and I were walking by and saw you, and I said, 'Let's see how she does.' And you weren't doing well. I'm here to help."

"What's that supposed to mean?"

"A man doesn't make a face like that when you're entertaining him. What were you talking about, anyway?"

"His dead wife," I said through gritted teeth. "Maybe if you'd told me about that, it wouldn't have come up over lunch."

She shrugged. "It wasn't my business to tell."

"You literally told me that Donna just had a hysterectomy!"

"Well, I did," Donna said mildly.

I closed my eyes and shook my head. "You're not helping."

My grandmother was smiling broadly when I looked back at her. "And you aren't interested, so what do you care?"

The waiter came out with all four sandwiches, and Joe returned just as he finished setting them on the table.

"Everyone watch Jenna take her first bite," my grandmother directed, to my mortification. "I honestly wish I could go back in time and experience this for the first time." She turned back to Donna. "A day after Brewster's too."

"The best," Donna agreed.

"You all can eat," I said. "Please don't watch me."

Joe picked up his sandwich. "Don't have to tell me twice." He shot me a quick smile before taking a bite and averting his eyes.

My grandmother elbowed me sharply in the ribs, raising her eyebrows.

Steeling myself for a long afternoon, I lifted the sandwich and took a bite. My shoulders dropped. "Why is this so good?" I asked after swallowing.

"It's the sea air," my grandmother said. "Everything tastes better here."

"Not everything," Donna said. "Remember how horrible Louise's cooking was?"

"Darling, everything that woman did was horrible."

"You're not going to see her, then?"

I looked up sharply. "Sam's wife? She's still alive?"

"If you can call it that," Donna said. "She's ninety-five and in a home. Alzheimer's. Terrible."

My grandmother shook her head. "No. The last time I went, she got extremely agitated. Apparently she still remembers the funeral."

The last time she went? I thought. Everything she said on this trip was more bizarre than the last. I had never heard her spew such venom as she did about Sam's wife, but she still went to visit her?

"It's because the lobster is so fresh," Joe said, bringing me back to the food. Donna and my grandmother were still discussing the sins of Louise. "They probably caught it this morning."

"Makes sense." I took another bite. "And I'm guessing you're only taking me to the good spots."

"That too."

"When do we go to your mom's restaurant?"

"Whenever you want."

"I don't think I've ever had Portuguese food."

"Then we'll go."

My grandmother and Donna had gone quiet. I looked over to see them watching us like a tennis match.

I rolled my eyes at Joe and mouthed, "I'm sorry."

"What did you say?" Grandma asked.

I pursed my lips. "I said, 'I'm sorry.'"

"What are you sorry for?"

"You."

Her eyebrows rose again. "Joe, darling, my granddaughter seems to think I'm imposing. Am I?"

"No, ma'am."

"Well, darn. I hoped I was." I could feel the color rising in my cheeks. "Jenna, I told you that you needed to be more interesting." She turned back to Donna. "Speaking of interesting, did I tell you my Lily is engaged?"

"No! To that groomsman?"

"The one from the bog, yes."

I puffed out my cheeks, then exhaled. "Does Massachusetts have the death penalty?" I asked Joe quietly.

"No," he said, grinning.

"Excellent. A jury would totally believe that she fell into the ocean on her own. Especially with all that Xanax in her system."

He laughed.

CHAPTER
THIRTY-THREE

December 1950
Hereford, Massachusetts

Evelyn pulled the cigarette out of Tony's mouth and took a long drag. He looked at her with a raised eyebrow. "What happened to the girl who didn't smoke?"

"She went to college." Evelyn took one more pull before putting it back between his lips as they lay together in an upstairs room in the cottage. If they piled enough blankets on and stayed close to each other, they barely noticed the cold anymore.

"And whose cigarettes are you smoking?"

"My own."

He shook his head. "Liar."

"Excuse me?" She sat up, feeling slightly guilty. She wasn't lying exactly—just not telling the whole truth either. Her first—and many of the subsequent smokes until she bought a couple of packs of her own—had been Fred's.

"I know you, Evelyn Bergman. You're bumming them off people just to see what you can get away with." She laughed and settled back into the crook of his arm.

"So what if I am?"

"So nothing. I trust you."

She plucked the cigarette from his lips and stubbed it out in the coffee can they used as an ashtray to take the evidence with them, then climbed on top of him and kissed him fiercely. She had a month at home before the second semester began and she intended to make the most of every moment. Even if those moments were stolen, sneaking away from her family to meet him at the cottage.

When the sky began to darken, they dressed to leave. Evelyn couldn't miss Shabbat dinner without a solid excuse, and Tony worked the night shift all week.

"Wait," he said, his voice catching as she walked toward her father's car after kissing him goodbye.

Evelyn turned, her head tilted curiously.

"I—I have something for you." He reached into his pocket. "It isn't much. And it's not—I'm not *asking* yet. But—" He opened the box in his hand, where a small diamond shone against a gold band. Evelyn's eyes widened. "I'll get you a bigger one. I promise you that. I'll save every penny. But I wanted you to have . . . something."

She wrapped her arms around his neck in a crushing hug. When she finally released him, she held out her left hand. "Put it on me."

He did as she asked, pulling it gingerly from the box and placing it slowly on her ring finger, both of them feeling the solemnity of the moment, the vow it represented for the future. Evelyn admired it, her eyes shining, before a look of disappointment crossed them.

"You don't like it?"

"Don't be ridiculous." She shook her head. "I love it. But I can't wear it around my family."

"I thought of that." He pulled a packet of tissue paper from his pocket and unwrapped it to reveal a thin, gold chain. "You can wear it on this for now."

"I don't want to take it off," she admitted.

"Someday, hopefully in just a few more months, you won't have to."

She wanted to repeat her plea, that they drive south that very night. But she knew it would only sour this moment, which she wanted to keep sweet. And he would cave eventually when he realized her father wouldn't. It was the thought that kept her going when the doubts crept in—she had yet to meet an obstacle she couldn't get around; it was impossible to imagine one so obstinate that it could defeat her. So she put her shoulders back and agreed, pulling the ring from her finger and placing it on the chain, then holding her hair up to allow Tony to fasten the clasp around her neck.

"I love you," she said, hugging him tight again. "I don't have a ring to give you to remind you, but know that it's just as real."

He nodded, looking as if he didn't trust himself to speak.

"Sunday? Same time?"

"Sunday," he agreed.

~

Lying in bed that night, Evelyn held the ring on its chain tightly in her hand, savoring the memory of the afternoon.

Not that her family suspected anything. True to her word, Vivie channeled her older sister's bravado and revealed nothing when Miriam questioned her. And Sam's declaration at Thanksgiving that she had a Jewish "fella," as incorrect as it was, took them all off the scent. Her ebullience was attributed to Fred's fictional suitor status.

Of course, it helped that Fred had called the day before. He was bored in Plymouth and wanted to know if she felt like going for a drive.

"You're two hours away, you fool," she laughed, checking to make sure no one was close enough to hear her, and then lowering her voice. "And it doesn't bode well for poor Betty that you're bored enough to call me."

"Maybe not. But I miss my friend. What do you say?"

"I say I'll see you in a few weeks."

"Whatever happened to the girl who's up for anything?"

Evelyn laughed. "She's quite content where she is, thank you very much."

"You're really going to make me stay here with my family for the whole month?"

"Absence makes the heart grow fonder and all that jazz."

He sighed dramatically. "Well, I suppose if the Pilgrims could survive Plymouth, I can make it another month. But if you change your mind—"

"You'll be the first to know."

Miriam, in the kitchen, had paused her work and tiptoed to the door frame, where she could hear better. She didn't make out what her daughter said when she spoke quietly, but the laughter and the general tone of merriment reassured her enough to trust that her instincts in crushing the dalliance with the Portuguese boy had been correct. Her vivacious penultimate daughter had done exactly as she had hoped. And she therefore didn't worry when Evelyn borrowed the car and went out on errands and to meet friends.

But when Evelyn heard a footstep outside her bedroom, she quickly thrust the ring and chain back inside her nightgown as the door creaked open.

"Are you awake?" Vivie asked, slipping quietly inside.

"Why do you ask that?" Evelyn scooted over to make room for her sister, who crept across the cold floor to climb into the bed. "If I wasn't, you'd have woken me."

"Seems polite," Vivie said, pulling the covers up and facing Evelyn. "Tell me everything."

"About what?"

"Everything!"

Evelyn laughed. "We'll be up all night, then."

"So?"

"So I'm tired."

"Fine. Tell me about the boy who called."

Evelyn rolled her eyes. She didn't want to talk about Fred. Not tonight, not with Tony's ring resting between her breasts, still warm from her hand. "He's a friend."

"How good of a friend?"

She sighed. "That's not the exciting news."

"It's not?"

Evelyn shook her head and pulled the chain from her nightgown. "I saw Tony today."

Vivie grabbed for the ring and reached behind her to switch on the bedside lamp.

"Evelyn," she breathed. "Does that mean—?"

Evelyn nodded. "Not officially. But unofficially . . ."

"What about Papa? You'll have to elope."

"I know. But he's going to ask him this summer anyway."

Vivie switched the light back off and settled back on the pillow next to Evelyn. "I want that."

"What? Someone Papa won't approve of?"

"No. Someone I love enough to risk everything for. Someone who loves me that much too."

Evelyn smiled gently and brushed her baby sister's hair from her face. "You're only sixteen."

"I'll be seventeen in a month. And that's how you old were when you and Tony met."

She had a point there.

"But you still have so much time. And so many more options when you go to college. And in New York!"

"If Barnard accepts me."

"They will. You'll see."

Vivie nestled deeper into the pillow and yawned. "Will you bring me? When you elope?"

Evelyn would have liked nothing better than to say yes. "You know I can't. Mama and Papa would know if you went missing with me."

"Wait till I'm off at school, then. You'll drive past New York anyway if you go south."

"Okay," Evelyn said. Vivie made no move to go back to her own bed, and Evelyn let her fall asleep beside her, the soft, even rhythm of her breathing eventually lulling Evelyn to sleep as well.

CHAPTER THIRTY-FOUR

"Donna couldn't get over how much you look like me."

"Do I?" I asked, picking at my leftover lobster roll distractedly.

My grandmother set her utensils down with a loud clatter. "Spill it."

I looked up at her. "Spill what?"

"Whatever happened that made you get so quiet."

"Nothing happened."

Leaning forward enough that I worried her pendulous chest would land in her food, she peered at me through the glasses that she seldom wore—they made her look old, after all. "Is *that* the problem, then?"

My shoulders sank as I rolled my head back in exasperation. "You really have to stop."

"Stop what?"

"Trying to play matchmaker."

"Who's playing matchmaker? He's not even Jewish." She hummed a couple of bars of a song that took me a minute to place. Then it clicked as "Matchmaker, Matchmaker" from *Fiddler on the Roof*.

"You'll stop when you're dead, won't you?"

"Oh, I don't plan on doing that."

"Stopping or dying?"

"Either, frankly. Neither seems like much fun."

"Let's talk about you, then," I said.

"What about me?"

"When are you going to see Tony?"

"Tony?" she asked in either genuine surprise or the best imitation of it. "Why on earth would I see Tony?"

I had done the math. "Because the last time you were here, Grandpa was still alive. What are you waiting for?"

She blotted her lips with her napkin. "Darling, we broke up nearly seventy years ago."

"But he's practically all you've talked about."

Her head shook as she waggled a finger at me. "You haven't been paying enough attention."

"I asked you why we were coming here, and you've spent the last three days telling me about your love affair with Tony. Grandpa seems like an afterthought."

"Neither of them is why we're here."

"Then why?"

She sighed. "I have business to take care of. I've told you that."

"And Tony is no part of it?"

A flicker of something I couldn't recognize crossed her face, then was gone. "He was . . . then. Not now."

"What does that mean?"

"It means you ask too many questions," she said brusquely. "Isn't that what got you into trouble this afternoon? Asking about Joe's wife?"

"I wasn't in trouble. It was an awkward moment, but we got past it."

"Yes. You're welcome for that."

I rolled my eyes. "You know, if you *did* want something to happen, crashing our lunch wasn't the way to do it."

"You two looked just fine once I got things moving again." I started to argue, but she held up a hand. "Besides, you told me you don't want anything to happen. Has that changed in the last"—she looked at her watch—"three minutes?"

"You're impossible, you know that?"

"So I've been told. By you, in fact. But nothing is impossible, my dear, not even me."

~

After dinner, Grandma changed into a nightgown, then insisted that I watch a movie with her, which turned out to be some hideous made-for-TV thing that was too poorly acted to watch. Instead, I opened Instagram, intending to look through Joe's feed. But first I clicked on my notifications.

There were a lot. I never posted anything artsy, and it was an amazing shot. As I scrolled through the comments, I reminded myself to ask to see his gallery again. Then—

Oh.

Joe liked eight of my pictures.

Not the ones he took—older ones.

Meaning he had gone through my feed.

My friends were all old and married like me—well, like I had been. But I did know one person who was an expert, if a somewhat infamous one, in social media and dating.

I texted my cousin Lily.

What does it mean if a guy you just met likes old Instagram pictures of you? I asked.

The three dots appeared immediately. Her phone was always in her hand.

Is it the guy who took that picture of you? she wrote back. **I stalked his profile. He's H-O-T.**

I rolled my eyes, completely unsurprised that she had already looked him up. **Maybe. But what does it mean?**

You know what it means, Jen. Three dots again. Is this a Grandma fixup?

She's trying.

Oh no. Trust nothing. He's probably our cousin.

If Tony was actually my grandfather, Lily was right on the money. But that was too far, even for my grandmother. I hoped.

So he's interested?

Yup.

I bit my lip as I replied. That complicates things.

Why? You're single . . . or about to be. And you're totally allowed to bring a date to my wedding.

I laughed, and Grandma looked over sharply. "What are you laughing at?" she asked over the television, which was at a decibel level that would probably relegate my hearing to the quality of hers soon.

"Lily."

"Billy who?"

"LILY."

"Oh." She lost interest and returned to her movie.

Thanks.

Let me know if Grandma does anything crazy. I'll blog about it. My readers love her.

I summarized the Xanax/Zantac debacle. Lily could have that one.

Then I switched back to Instagram and went to Joe's feed. He had posted the picture of me as well, without tagging me, but using my *Wizard of Oz* caption. The rest of his pictures were mostly artistic shots mixed with pictures of Jax, a couple of him with friends, and a few with an older couple, identified as his parents in the caption.

If I liked a picture, did it tell him I was interested?

And moreover, did I want that?

Another notification popped up.

He had liked a picture of me in Greece from six years earlier—Brad had taken it on our first trip together. I was lying on a wall in Mykonos, my chin resting on my hand, making a kissy face at a stray cat. My hair was wild in the breeze, my skin tanned, and I looked younger and happier than I could ever remember being.

I had deleted the photos with Brad in them, which was a significant portion of my feed, but kept the ones Brad had taken of me because otherwise there would be almost nothing left. But there were still enough that finding a picture from six years ago was significant.

And he was looking at my feed right now.

I glanced over at my grandmother. She wouldn't hesitate.

So I didn't think. Instead, I went back to the picture of me in the woods, double-tapped it, and commented, "Copycat. Come up with your own caption," with a winking face.

Then I closed the app and dropped my phone facedown on my lap.

It vibrated a few seconds later with a text.

Imitation is the sincerest form of flattery . . . Besides, it was the perfect caption.

I looked back at Grandma. She was still immersed in the TV.

It was the perfect shot.

The three dots appeared, then disappeared, then reappeared. **It's easy with a good subject.**

Lily was right. He was flirting. But why would he be interested in *me*? I knew I needed to reply, but I froze.

The three dots appeared again. **Do you want to grab a drink?**

I could feel my heart pounding. Yes. I wanted to. Very much. So much that I didn't want to at all. No good would come of this.

Now? I asked, hedging.

Yeah. We could just go down to the Inn.

Grandma's eyes were closed, her jaw slack. I hated when she fell asleep; she always looked dead at her age. I would need to tell her I was going so she wouldn't worry when she woke up. And—I looked down at my sweats—I would have to change.

No. It wasn't smart to go.

She gave a half snore, and her eyes popped open. "Why are you looking at me like that?"

"Like what?"

"Like you're figuring out what to bury me in. I told you I'm not dying."

"Maybe I was just figuring out which jewelry to take."

"Clever. But not clever enough. Your mother and aunt have a list of who gets what."

"Because you don't trust them or because you don't trust your granddaughters?"

"I don't trust any of you vultures." I smiled. My phone buzzed in my hand, and I looked at it. "And who is that?" she asked, leaning over to try to see.

"Lily," I lied.

"You don't look that quickly when it's your cousin. Tell Joe I say hi." I stared at her, wondering if growing up that close to the ghosts of colonial witches had rubbed off on her.

She would go, I told myself. *And not care about the consequences.* I stood up. "I think I'm going to go out for a little bit."

Her eyebrows rose. "I didn't think you had it in you."

"What is *that* supposed to mean?"

She winked. "I'm going to bed. And I'm a heavy sleeper."

"Ew, Grandma!"

She stood with effort. "Make sure you use a prophylactic. Or maybe don't. You don't have that much time to waste at your age."

I watched in horror as she made her way toward her bedroom.

CHAPTER

THIRTY-FIVE

January 1951
Hereford, Massachusetts

Felipe's wedding was set for the first weekend of the New Year. Both Maria and Beatriz's mother tried to convince them to wait until spring, when Beatriz could do the traditional walk to the church without everyone freezing in the Massachusetts winter, but the young couple was adamant that they didn't want to wait any longer. And the mothers, eyeing Beatriz's waistline suspiciously, reluctantly agreed.

Tony sighed when Evelyn said she was coming to the wedding. "Why are you still arguing this? If it gets back to your father, we're sunk before I've even had a chance. And the old man is finally warming up to me." Okay, *maybe* Tony had given Emilio a whole precious dollar to "accidentally" break one of Joseph's store windows with a baseball while Tony was walking by so Tony could haul the culprit in by the ear and let Joseph decide his fate. Joseph remembered the young man who forced his brother to return the candy he stole (and Tony had been wise enough to choose a different brother to commit this second crime).

Joseph, of course, said that no, the window was an accident and to let the boy go, which Tony did after a vicious scolding. He tipped his hat to Joseph and turned to leave, but the older man stopped him and offered him a Coca Cola from his newly purchased machine.

Tony offered to pay but was told he had earned it. He would take that praise as a start. Even if the soda in question really cost him twenty times its retail value in payment to Emilio.

"I want to be there."

"And I want you there." He put his arm around her. They were in his car, parked by the beach, the sky gray and cold. "But it's not worth the risk. Everyone in town knows who you are. And people talk. It would get back to your father."

He was right, but *defeat* wasn't in Evelyn's vocabulary. She leaned into him, breathing in his smell. She had another week and a half until she returned to Boston and would miss these stolen moments.

Tony dropped her off on a deserted side street a few blocks from her house, the cold biting through her coat and wool stockings as she walked up the hill.

But as she climbed the steps, the front door opened, and Minnie Goldblatt, Ruthie's mother, hurried out. She was bundled so heavily for the two-block walk home that Evelyn could only positively identify her from her exposed eyes and the fringe of her *sheitel*—the wig that peeked out from under the brim of her hat. An Orthodox Jew, Minnie kept her real hair covered when she was with anyone who wasn't in her immediate family. And because the Goldblatts had money, instead of the kerchief that most women wore, Minnie indulged her vanity with a pair of wigs—a synthetic one that she wore for everyday and the expensive one from New York that she wore for special occasions.

"Hello, Evelyn." She looked up nervously at the sky. "Do you suppose it'll snow?"

"Smells like it," Evelyn said, the wheels in her head turning as she looked at her friend's mother.

"I'd better hurry," she said, going down the stairs. "Goodbye!"

"Wait." Evelyn turned and followed her down the steps. "I'll go with you, if that's all right. I wanted to talk to Ruthie."

"Of course."

Evelyn took Minnie's bag to help her, and they walked as quickly as Minnie could manage.

Safely ensconced in Ruthie's bedroom, Evelyn locked the door and pulled Ruthie to sit with her on the bed. "What are you doing?" Ruthie asked, confused.

"Shhhh. I need you to help me."

"Oh, Evelyn," Ruthie whispered. "What have you done?"

"Nothing! What do you think I've done?"

"I never know with you."

"Good grief. I just need to borrow something."

Ruthie looked at her suspiciously. "What?"

"Don't look at me like that. I'll have it back before she even knows it's missing."

"No."

"You don't even know what I'm asking for yet!"

"Look, if you want something of mine, you can have it. But if it's not mine, I can't give it."

"Ruthie," Evelyn said quietly. "You're the only one who can help me."

Ruthie sighed. "What do you want? I'm probably not giving it to you, but what is it?"

"Tony's brother is getting married this weekend. And I want to go."

"You're still seeing Tony?"

"Yes, and you can't tell anyone. But I need to go to the wedding."

"In a church?"

Evelyn nodded, and Ruthie exhaled loudly. "Evelyn, why are you doing this? There are a million Jewish boys out there."

"There are," Evelyn said. "But there's only one Tony. And he's the boy for me."

"And how am I supposed to help with that?"

Evelyn told her. Ruthie protested, but by the time Evelyn left a half hour later, she had secured a promise that Ruthie would try. As Evelyn walked home through swirling snowflakes, she smiled, her plan taking shape.

~

Evelyn paced her bedroom floor, checking her watch every few minutes. Ruthie was late. And if she was much later, it would be a problem.

Finally, she heard footsteps in the hall and flung open her bedroom door to see Ruthie with Vivie. She grabbed Ruthie's arm and yanked her into the bedroom. "Did you get it?" she hissed.

Ruthie nodded. Vivie's eyes were wide with excitement as Ruthie pulled her mother's blonde wig gingerly out of her bag. She didn't hand it over though.

"You *have* to be careful with it. She doesn't wear it often, but she takes good care of it. It's the expensive one."

"I'll treat it like it's a baby," Evelyn promised. "You're an angel, Ruthie. A true angel."

"I'm going to be a dead angel if you mess this up."

"I won't. I swear on . . ." She pulled Vivie to her. "On my sister."

"Hey!"

Ruthie smiled grimly. "I don't know why I'm doing this."

"Because you love me." Evelyn took the wig gently and placed it on her head in front of her vanity mirror. "And I love you." She tucked her hair under it, turning her head this way and that. "How do I look?"

"Different," Vivie said. "You might just be able to pull this off."

"I've got Mama's good hat too. If I keep my head down, no one will get a real look at my face."

Ruthie shook her head again. "Just make sure I get it back tonight."

"Tomorrow," Evelyn said, admiring her reflection. "I may be late tonight. I don't want to wake your whole house and give us away." She saw Ruthie's nervous expression in the mirror. "I'll have it back to you first thing in the morning."

"What are you telling your parents?"

Evelyn grinned. "Mama and Papa both nap on Saturday afternoons. The timing is perfect to sneak out."

"And when they realize you're not home?"

"She went down to Beverly to have dinner and see a movie with Alice from school. Papa, she told you she was going, don't you remember? She'll be back late tonight," Vivie recited. Evelyn reached up and patted her cheek lovingly. She had grown up a lot in the last year.

"Perfect, darling."

"This whole thing is mad. You know that, don't you?"

"We're all mad here," Evelyn said, eliciting a small smile at the reference to one of their childhood favorites. She stood and kissed Ruthie's cheek, thanking her, then removed the wig to dress.

~

Sneaking out of the house in Minnie Goldblatt's wig, her mother's favorite hat, and her own best dress didn't faze Evelyn. But she did hesitate briefly at the steps of the church. She had never been inside one before. Attending mass in a Catholic church felt blasphemous. Would she be conspicuous for not taking Communion—a step too far even for her? The town was fairly tolerant of the Jewish population, though there had been a few swastikas drawn on doors during the war—done by children, but done nonetheless. Would anyone recognize her and be offended by her presence?

But self-doubt never had a firm grip on Evelyn's psyche. So she squared her shoulders, angled her head down, and walked through the large doorway, selecting an inconspicuous pew in the back of St.

Peter's, named for the patron saint of the town's Portuguese fishermen population.

The ceremony itself was conducted in a combination of Portuguese and English. Evelyn watched Tony, beaming from under her hat at how handsome he looked in his suit. And she was relieved to see many of the congregants refusing Communion as they had not yet been to confession for the week.

It lasted longer than her brothers' and sisters' weddings, though when she was ten and wearing uncomfortable shoes, she thought Bernie's wedding was the longest thing she had ever experienced. And when it was over, she flowed out with the rest of the crowd, waiting until the photographer had snapped some family photos and Felipe and Beatriz were safely ensconced in a car on their way to the reception before grabbing Tony's arm. "*Parabéns*," she said, having practiced the pronunciation after learning it from Beatriz. He turned at the sound of her voice, then stared at the familiar face framed by blonde hair before laughing.

"You're too much." He shook his head, reaching up to touch a blonde lock. "Where did you get this? Don't tell me it's your real hair?"

"Might have swiped Ruthie's mother's good wig. But if you like it, we can talk about a dye job."

He covered his face with his hands briefly, then put an arm around her waist. "Is there anything you can't do?"

"I'm not sure I can fly."

"If you set your mind to it, you probably could. Will you come to dinner in your disguise?"

She smiled. "Try and stop me."

~

The dinner was unlike any wedding reception Evelyn had attended, with a buffet and open seating, in the town's social hall. No one danced the hora or lifted the new couple in chairs, a napkin held between them, but the air was festive, and the small band played traditional Portuguese music while the liquor flowed freely.

Tony's younger siblings eyed her warily, clearly an intruder whom their brother should not be talking to so closely until they got a better look at her. Carolina recognized her first, elbowing Francisca sharply and gesturing wildly before running over. Evelyn turned just as Carolina was about to cry out her name and put a finger to her lips. The little girl hugged her fiercely around the waist all the same, followed quickly by Francisca.

"What are you doing here?" Francisca asked while Carolina questioned what she did to her hair.

"It's a loaner," Evelyn said, fluffing the ends slightly. "My family doesn't know I'm here." She looked at the two girls conspiratorially. "What should my name be as your brother's new girlfriend for the night? I need something Portuguese-sounding."

"Maria something," Francisca said immediately.

"But that's your mother's name!" The girls and Tony all laughed. "What?"

"That's all of our names," Carolina said. "I'm Maria Carolina and she's Maria Francisca."

Evelyn turned to Tony. "Don't tell me you're Maria Antonio."

"It's got a nice ring to it," he said.

She shook her head and turned back to the girls. "Okay then, Maria what?"

They studied her. "Teresa," Carolina offered after a moment, and Francisca agreed.

"Maria Teresa it is," Evelyn said, turning back to Tony. "Your girlfriend would be furious."

He put an arm around her waist and pulled her toward the dance floor. "Let her be." Carolina and Francisca watched them, wondering when they would be old enough for someone to be as in love with them as their brother was with Evelyn.

He twirled her and she laughed. They had danced on the beach before, but this was their first time together in public as a couple. And with her wig, on the crowded floor, the freedom was intoxicating.

A slower song played, and Evelyn leaned her head against Tony's chest, their hands held together just below her chin.

"What are you thinking?" he asked in her ear.

She turned her head up to look at him, her round brown eyes sparkling, wild and beautiful even with the ridiculous wig. "How happy I am."

"Even if we can't ever have this for ourselves?"

"What do you mean?"

"If your father says no—"

Evelyn pressed a finger to his lips. "You're ruining the mood, darling. Let's be happy now. And if he says no, as long as I have you, I don't need any of this."

He pulled her in close again, and they stayed like that even after the tempo of the song changed.

CHAPTER THIRTY-SIX

I should have worn the sundress, I thought, looking down at my jeans and tank top. But then would I look like I was trying too hard? A dress was definitely trying too hard. And I wasn't trying at all.

Or did a dress say, *Hi, I'm confident enough to wear what I want?*

The Inn was such a short distance from the cottage. I could go back and change. Especially because I had driven—it was an easy walk, but if I walked, I had no excuse to nurse one drink and stay utterly inhibited, which was obviously the smart decision.

I took three steps back toward the car, then heard my name and froze, cursing silently.

"Hey," I said, turning.

"Everything okay?"

"Huh? Oh—yeah. I thought I forgot my phone." I pulled it from my back pocket. "But here it is." I was a terrible liar, but if he noticed, he didn't call me out.

He inclined his head toward the door. "Let's go in."

We found a table on the patio, which overlooked the water. There were a handful of people, but it seemed to be a quiet night.

I glanced down at my watch—I had lost track of the days. It was Sunday.

"I'm guessing this place is packed on Fridays and Saturdays."

"It is."

A waitress came and took our drink order. Joe asked if I wanted food too, but I shook my head as it was nearly ten.

"Do you live near here or in town?" I asked, curious.

He turned, pointing across the beach to the far side where the handful of large houses sat on the bluffs, looming over the beach. "On that side."

"In the big houses?"

He smiled. "No. But it was a guesthouse of one of them."

"Ah, still East Egg though." I bit the inside of my cheek. He wasn't going to get that.

"Is that the old money side or the new money side? I always forget which is which."

"Old."

"Then no, that's your side—the old estate that the cottage was part of. The big houses on my side are the new money summer people."

"Summer people?"

"The ones who come in for the summer from Boston—the old joke goes that 'Some're people, some're not.'"

"That's terrible."

He shrugged. "I didn't say it was a *good* joke."

The waitress brought our drinks, and we each took a sip, then sat in silence for a moment.

"Listen," he said. "I . . . wanted to apologize. For earlier." I looked at him, confused, thinking he meant for making me hike when we could have driven. "I didn't expect Emily to come up."

"Emily? Oh! I—no—I'm sorry. I didn't know." *Great. That's why he asked me for a drink,* I berated myself. But that did make the most sense.

"Why would you?"

"Well, my grandma could have told me, considering how much she's told you."

"She hasn't told me that much."

I took another sip of my drink. "She tells me too much. She told me to use a"—I made air quotes—"'prophylactic' when I said I was meeting you."

Joe choked on his drink, coughing loudly enough for people to look over, and I turned pink, wishing I hadn't said that.

"That's both hilarious and so, so gross," he said when he caught his breath.

"It's hilarious when it doesn't happen to you."

"Like that bad date you wouldn't tell me about." He gestured to my drink. "Have some more. I want that story."

"Not sure this place has enough alcohol for that one. Besides, I drove tonight."

Something painful crossed his face, and I kicked myself. He had lost his wife to a drunk driver. My grandma was right. I was *not* good at this on my own. I glanced over my shoulder to see if she was coming to bail me out.

"Guess that saves you tonight, then," he said lightly. "But I'll get it out of you."

"Unlikely." But I was smiling. I tilted my head. "What do you do for fun when you're not showing around sad almost-divorcees?"

"Are you sad?"

"Not really," I said, realizing for the first time that it was true. "Okay, so when you're not showing around merry almost-divorcees?"

"*Merry* might be a stretch."

I shook my head. "Fine, totally boring, middle-of-the-road almost-divorcees. You're a real buzzkill, you know that?"

"Just honest. You're not boring either though."

"You know how I was just trying to ask about you? Let's go back to that."

He shrugged. "I'm the boring one, I guess. I work. I go running. I read a lot."

"No one that artistic is boring." He looked at me like he was trying to figure out what I meant. "I couldn't have gotten a picture like you did today. Or even the iPhone ones you took of me. I wish I could see the world the way you do."

"It's easier through a lens sometimes."

Maybe I was feeling the drink—it was almost gone, and other than my grandmother's concoctions the night before, I couldn't remember the last time I'd had more than a small glass of wine. But that statement sounded so incredibly profound. And wasn't that how I was living before everything fell apart? Posting everything through a filter on Instagram to make my life look perfect when it wasn't?

"That's . . . deep."

"I didn't mean it to be, but I guess it is." The waitress passed by, and he gestured for two more drinks.

"I shouldn't."

"I can walk you home. You can pick up your car in the morning."

"It's my grandmother's car."

"Explains the dents."

I laughed. "You don't know the half of it."

He leaned in conspiratorially. "Should we check the glove compartment for prophylactics?"

I cracked up and he did too. "Oh man—if she had them, I'd die."

We were still laughing when the waitress brought the drinks. I sipped mine, then returned to what he had said earlier. "Wait, did you walk here? Isn't that far?"

"A little over a mile and a half along the beach. Not a bad walk."

"After that hike today?"

"If we hadn't Ubered back, maybe I would have driven."

I looked toward the beach, the idea of walking back across it with him in the cool evening air dancing through my mind intoxicatingly.

207

The moonlight reflected on the waves, except where a sandbar had appeared, leading toward the island offshore.

"Can you walk out there?" I asked, gesturing to the protruding land mass, trying to take my mind off what lay at the end of that imagined journey across the beach.

Joe turned and studied the sandbar briefly. "You can. You have to watch the tides carefully though. If you time it right, you can get about three hours out there. If you don't . . . Well, you're out there for twelve."

"Does that happen?"

"Your mother never told you that story?" I shook my head. "She and my mother got stuck there once. Your grandmother and Tony rescued them."

I wanted to know more. But I also didn't. If Tony helped rescue my mom . . . Well, he and my grandmother were clearly still on extremely friendly terms when my grandfather was home working. And after the amount of detail my grandmother had used in describing their relationship, right down to the prophylactics—I didn't see how you could go from that madly in love with someone to strictly platonic friends.

"What's out there?"

He grinned, then checked his watch. "Do you want to see? If we left at about ten thirty tomorrow morning, we'd have time to explore."

"Is it worth it?"

I wanted to go before he answered. The slow smile he gave me made me want to down the rest of my drink and tell him to take me home—and not to the cottage where my grandmother waited. "Yeah. It's worth it."

"Okay, then." I smiled back flirtatiously. It was surreal. Who was I? Not the Jenna who had spent six months in her childhood bedroom, too afraid to resume her life. I thought about the picture of me in Greece that he had liked on Instagram—I felt like that girl again. Carefree and desirable and . . . well . . . not the kind of person you'd leave for someone else, that was for sure.

I remembered the feel of his hands positioning me on the wall that morning. The breathless wonder of what would happen with my eyes closed. And, feeling brave, I pulled my phone out of my pocket, unlocked it, and slid it across the table to him. "Take my picture again."

He studied me for a moment, then picked up the phone, rose, and walked around the table. "Put your arm on the railing," he directed. I did as he said. "No, like your elbow. I want you to lean the side of your forehead slightly on just your index finger." When I didn't get it right— admittedly, a little deliberately—he took my hand and positioned it for me, then touched my cheek to angle it just right. "There. Now cross your legs toward the railing." I debated letting him do that too, but the direction was unmistakable. He took a few steps back and looked at me again, this time through the camera's screen, adjusting the image with two fingers. "Good," he said, more to himself than me. "Now smile." I smiled. "No. The way you smiled at me before. When I said seeing the island was worth it."

"I was smiling back at you then." The same sultry grin spread across his face, and I reflexively returned the look. He snapped it and then handed the phone back to me, our hands touching as he did.

I looked down to see what he'd gotten, and I felt goose bumps rising along my arms. There was something so intimate in the picture. It was posed, but it looked like he had captured a spontaneous moment of flirtation.

"Good?" he asked.

"I—how do you get a picture like that with a phone? I mean— here," I said, taking a quick shot of him and turning the phone for him to see it. "My pictures don't look like that."

He laughed. "You also didn't look for lighting or try to create a mood; you just snapped." He handed the phone back. "Close your eyes." It was the second time that he'd asked me to do that today, and there was something exciting in the request. I closed them. "Picture me. Not the picture you just took. How do you actually see me?"

I thought about the smile he'd given me. He had smiled like that at the caption on the earlier picture too. Like there was a secret we shared. And the promise of more to come. He was vibrant and alive, and he made me feel like I was too.

I opened my eyes.

"Now tell me where to go and what to do."

Looking around, I gestured back to the railing. "Angle your body toward the island," I said slowly, thinking. I stood along the railing as well, farther down, parallel to him, then came back and turned his head so he was looking at me, my hand lingering a second too long, and I thought his face moved a fraction closer to mine.

But I wasn't sure.

So I pulled away and went back to the spot I had staked out, five feet from him, and took a deep breath.

"Am I going to like whatever is out on the island?" I asked. When his lips curled into that same smile, I took the picture, then looked at it.

"So?"

I held the phone out for him to see. It was the best picture I had ever taken. Not on par with his, of course, but better than anything I had done before.

"I like how you see me," he said, taking the phone and sitting back at the table, zooming in to examine the photo. "You're good."

"I've got a good teacher." I sat as well and took another sip of my drink. He reached out to hand me my phone, and I leaned in to take it, and for a moment, we both held on, our hands touching. I looked at them, his right and my left, which still looked so naked without its wedding ring.

I took the phone and leaned back in my seat. It was too inebriating. The whole situation. Being away from home, the sound of the waves crashing on the beach, the drinks, the way he looked at me, the moonlight. And while I knew full well what my friends, my cousin, and, hell, even my grandma would tell me to do tonight, I couldn't. I didn't have a vacation fling in me. It wouldn't make me feel better. I wasn't Stella getting her groove back. If I tried to get over my failed marriage by sleeping with someone new, I'd only wind up even lower than I had been. And that was all this could be. I needed to remember that.

"I—I should head back," I said, rummaging for my wallet.

He looked at me quizzically. "What just happened?"

I shook my head, not trusting myself to speak. If I let my mouth open, I had no idea what kind of disastrous truth about how I felt would come spilling out. And while I wasn't ready to act on anything, I also didn't want to scare him off, which I knew I would if I answered his question.

"Okay." He gestured toward the waitress for a check. "Are you good to drive, or should I walk you back?"

Under other circumstances I would have driven. I'd only had two drinks. But his wife . . . "You don't have to walk me home. I know the way."

He lowered his head and leveled a gaze at me. "I won't try anything. But it's pitch black up the hill. I'm not letting you walk back alone."

"I didn't mean—I wasn't saying—" I was somewhat saved by the arrival of the check. Joe started to put a credit card down, but I had clearly just insulted him. "Let me," I said, putting a hand over his. "As a thank you. For today. And yesterday." He started to protest, but I cut him off. "Fine, as payment for services rendered—that picture from tonight is going to be my new social media profile picture."

He finally smiled again and let me put my card down instead. "How do I pay for the picture of me, then?"

I heard my cousin Lily's voice in my head as clearly as if we had spoken on the phone instead of texting. *You know what it means.* I grinned back. "You've got tomorrow at the island to figure that out."

∼

I lay in the brass bed of my room that night, having changed into pajamas, washed off my makeup, and brushed my teeth, looking at the picture I took of him. *I like how you see me,* he'd said.

Sitting up suddenly, I swiped back to the picture of me and zoomed in. I looked glamorous and flirtatious and confident and so, so beautiful. That—was how he saw me?

I was still smiling when I finally put the phone down to go to sleep.

CHAPTER
THIRTY-SEVEN

June 1951
Hereford, Massachusetts

When Evelyn returned home for the summer, the cottages hadn't yet been opened for the season. Which suited her just fine. It wasn't nearly as cold as it had been for their previous assignations, and she and Tony could take their time without needing to dive under a blanket for warmth.

But always, the impending conversation with Joseph loomed in the background.

"When, then?" Tony asked when Evelyn again said to wait. "I'll wait until you finish college to marry you, if that's what he wants, but I don't want to sneak around for three more years."

Evelyn felt something tighten in her chest every time he brought the subject up. There had never been a situation where she couldn't manage her father. But this—this was different. She was confident she could gain forgiveness. But a blessing would never come. It was somehow the one subject she couldn't make Tony budge on either—and she had tried every trick in her arsenal, including attempting to extract a promise to elope during an exceptionally compromising moment. Even that failed.

Her only hope was that when Joseph rejected him, he would change his mind rather than lose her. But if he didn't . . . The thought was too much to bear. Evelyn feared nothing except that the two men she loved most would be incapable of meeting in the middle for the sake of her—the woman they both loved most. No, it was better to keep to the status quo for as long as she could get away with it.

Finally the weather turned hot, and Miriam brought Evelyn and Vivie to the cottages to clean and outfit the beds with linens, the bathrooms with towels, and the kitchens with food.

Vivie slipped something into Evelyn's hand when Miriam climbed the stairs with an armful of towels. "Yours, I presume?" she asked archly. Evelyn looked down at her palm. It was a cigarette butt.

"I should have done a sweep before Mama got here."

"We'll blame Sam if there's anything else."

Evelyn smiled. "Like that wet mop he's marrying would ever do anything as interesting as meeting him here alone. Honestly, what *does* he see in her?" Their wedding was set for the end of the summer. Evelyn fantasized about bringing Tony as her fiancé to the wedding. It was just a dream, and she knew it. But if she could get him to elope—

Vivie was shaking her head. "She's not that bad."

"I had lunch with her in Boston. She doesn't have a single opinion of her own."

"Sam likes to be the exciting one, I guess."

"He'd still be the exciting one even if he married someone with a *little* gumption."

"She's a good girl," Miriam said from behind them. Both girls jumped. "You could take a lesson from that," she said to Evelyn, whose toes curled in her shoes but her face stayed steady. Miriam didn't know anything, Evelyn decided, studying her mother. She was just fishing to see if she got a reaction that she could learn something from.

"I'm as good as gold," Evelyn said. "Honestly, Mama, you always suspect me of being so much worse than I am."

"I've known you since before you were born," Miriam said tiredly. "I know exactly who you are."

Even though Miriam couldn't know about Tony, a chill went through Evelyn as she looked into her mother's eyes, which somehow missed nothing. And she realized that even if by some miracle Joseph was won over, the more formidable obstacle might be standing in front of her now.

~

Bernie's family moved into his cottage, Helen and her brood into the other along with Miriam and Margaret. Gertie came every weekend with her children in tow. Sam took up residence in Bernie's house, and Evelyn and Vivie once again crowded in wherever there was a bed for them at night.

But unlike the previous summer, finding time to see Tony was difficult. As one of the newest officers, he frequently worked night shifts. But with everyone together during the day, Evelyn's absence was noticeable the one time she snuck off—she blamed it on cramps and needing to lie down, but there were only so many days a month she could use that excuse.

Each day, the entire clan gathered for the beach together—an ordeal with seven children under nine years old. Mornings were an assembly line of first breakfast, then preparing stacks of peanut-butter-and-jelly sandwiches, which were stuffed back into the bags that the loaves of bread came in for lunches, filling canteens of water, packing the towels and blankets that had spent the night airing on the railings of the cottage porches, dressing the children in their bathing suits, and waddling down to the beach, loaded up with chairs and blankets and toys, like a line of baby ducklings.

Joseph spent more and more time at the cottage as well, leaving the store in the care of his two clerks to enjoy the hard-earned fruits of his labor with his ever-expanding family.

Evelyn's time with Tony was then limited to the mercy of his nights off—and even then, the beach was no longer safe. Sam had taken to bringing Louise out for bonfires, which her older siblings frequently joined them around once the children were in bed. Now, when she snuck down the road to his waiting car, they had to find other places to go.

"Evelyn," Tony said. They had driven out to the woods off the Ipswich Road and were sitting on a boulder together with a lantern. If the woods were haunted, the spirits didn't bother them.

She sighed heavily at the tone of his voice. He didn't need to say it. "I know."

"This week?"

For a long moment she said nothing. Then, quietly, "If he says no, they won't let me see you. What then?"

He wrapped his arms around her. "We wait. And he'll see how unhappy you are. And then we try again. He likes me."

"He likes you. But that doesn't mean he wants you as his son-in-law. He's still got one foot in the old country."

"And one foot here. Remember that."

She nodded, then leaned against him.

～

They settled on Monday, in two nights' time, when Joseph would return to the cottage for supper after a day at the store. Gertie, Helen's husband, and Margaret would all be gone, making the scene less chaotic.

Supper ended and Joseph retired to the porch to smoke a cigar in the twilight. Evelyn dropped two dishes, and Miriam finally banished her from the kitchen. She went to the living room and paced instead.

"What is the matter with you?" Miriam asked, coming to the doorway, a dishtowel in her hand. "Evelyn." She turned to look at her mother, whose face went pale when she saw her daughter's wild eyes. "What did you do?" she asked in a whisper. "*Chas vehalilah.*"

The sound of a car approaching and then pulling to a stop came in through the open windows, followed by a door closing. Evelyn and Miriam both ran to the window.

"Officer Delgado," Joseph said pleasantly. "Is everything all right?"

"Delgado?" Miriam asked.

"Mama, hush!"

Under normal circumstances, Evelyn wouldn't have gotten away with that, but Miriam wanted to hear what was happening outside as badly as her daughter did. They had missed Tony's reply, but whatever it was, Joseph invited him to sit and offered him a drink and a cigar.

Evelyn's heart was racing. The hospitality was beyond what she could have hoped for—whatever Tony had done to lay the groundwork, he did it well.

"No, thank you, sir. But I'm here on an important matter." Evelyn could just make out the tense set of his shoulders through the screen, her mother next to her. She felt him take in a breath. "I don't know if you know this, but your daughter Evelyn—"

Joseph's free hand gripped the armrest of his rocking chair tightly. "What did she do now?" he asked. "I'll pay for whatever the damage is. Thank you for coming to me instead. I thought she had grown out of that mischievous streak—"

"Sir, no, she didn't do anything wrong."

"She didn't?"

"No. I—I'm here tonight because I'm in love with her. I want to ask your blessing to marry her."

Miriam and Joseph drew in a sharp intake of breath simultaneously, Miriam grabbing her daughter's arm with a viselike claw.

Joseph rose to his feet and Tony followed suit. "No," he said stonily, then turned toward the open window and bellowed Evelyn's name.

Evelyn struggled out of Miriam's grip and ran out to the porch, stopping short at her father's face.

"Did you know he was coming here to ask this?" Joseph asked her. She nodded, afraid to speak.

"This—this was the boy—all that time ago—?"

"There's—" Her voice cracked hoarsely, and she took a deep breath before trying again. "There's never been anyone else, Papa. I love him."

"I forbid this!"

Evelyn looked up at him, drawing from a reserve of courage that surprised even her. "You can't."

"What?"

"You can say no, but you can't stop me from loving him. And you can't stop us from getting married."

"Evelyn," Tony warned.

Joseph's eyes narrowed. "Do you know what you're saying?"

Tony came to stand between Joseph and his daughter. "Sir, no. I won't do that without your permission." He turned back to Evelyn. "Go back in the house." Then quieter. "Please."

"Don't you tell her what to do!" Joseph grabbed his daughter's wrist, but she flung his hand off.

"Don't *either* of you tell me what to do! I won't sit here and let the two of you negotiate over me like I'm some prized goat. Papa, I love him. And you should know that the only reason we haven't run off is because *he* wanted to get your blessing. So you might as well give it unless you want to lose me."

Her breathing was ragged, and she could feel not just her mother's presence at the window but Helen's, Vivie's, and the children's too. She didn't care. She was gambling everything on her father being unwilling to sit shiva for her—or that he would later forgive her even if he did.

"Mr. Bergman, I—this—isn't how I wanted this to go. You have my word that unless I have your blessing, nothing will happen. I'm sorry." He looked at Evelyn, pleading silently with her. "Family is everything," he said finally, then lifted her hand to his lips, kissed it, and went back down the porch steps to his car. No one spoke as he drove away.

"Papa," Evelyn said finally. "Look at me, Papa."

But Joseph walked past her into the house without a word.

CHAPTER
THIRTY-EIGHT

There were three places set at the table when I came down for breakfast. I shook my head.

"Are you expecting company?" I asked my grandmother. She was at the stove, cooking a monstrously huge breakfast.

She turned around. "I suppose it's too much to hope that Joe is in the shower."

I pressed two fingers to the bridge of my nose and shook my head. "Is this how you were with Mom and Aunt Joan?"

"If they'd been your age and single, I would have been." She turned back to the stove and slid the contents from the pan onto a plate.

I sat heavily at the table. "I don't need to be with someone to be happy, Grandma."

"Who said you did?" she asked, bringing a plate to me. "But you're not happy now. And if you don't try something different, you never will be."

I opened my mouth to reply that I was happy, but nothing came out. If I was happy, I wouldn't have pulled away the night before, because I wouldn't have cared about the consequences. I would have acted on what I wanted.

Instead, I changed the subject.

"We're going out to the island today. Do I wear a bathing suit or regular clothes?"

She squinted at me in concern. "Joe has the tides timed right?"

"He said he does."

"I'm too old to steal a boat to come save you."

"You—what?"

She waved her hand. "Another time."

"So what do I wear?"

"Depends how brave you're feeling." I asked what she meant, but she was finished on that subject. "I mean it though: don't get stuck. We have plans at four."

"What plans?"

"You're not very spontaneous," she said, studying me. "You shouldn't worry so much. It causes wrinkles. Just be home and dressed by then."

Back upstairs, I looked at my wardrobe choices spread across the bed. My weather app said it would be hot in town, though it was always cooler by the beach. And if we did wind up walking back through any water, I didn't want to be in pants.

Depends how brave you're feeling.

I'm braver than she thinks, I thought, yanking off my clothes to put on a bathing suit. I studied my reflection in the mirror over the dresser. No. I wasn't brave enough to wear JUST a bathing suit. Instead, I covered it with denim shorts and a T-shirt. Then, looking in the mirror again, I pulled off the shirt and switched it to a tank top. What was the point in wearing the brave outfit if it didn't show?

Picking up my phone, I saw a text from Joe. Bring sneakers.

I recalled seeing a lot of green at the top of the island, and I frowned. More hiking. I had been excited for the beach day. Okay, I replied. Leaving now.

Perfect. See you soon. He included a smiley face with sunglasses.

"I'm heading down to the beach," I called to my grandmother.

"I meant it," she hollered back. "Don't get stuck."

~

Joe was waiting for me by the entrance to the beach across from the Inn. "Morning."

"Hey." I felt the littlest bit shy. There had been another moment at the driveway to the cottage the night before when we *could* have maybe kissed but didn't. He seemed normal at least, though, which helped. "Does the Inn have coffee?" I asked, looking at a couple walking out with plastic cups.

He glanced at his watch. "Yeah. We have a few minutes. We'll have to bring the trash back with us, but there should be room in the bag." He had a strange-looking backpack over his shoulders—almost like it was made from wetsuit material.

"Waterproof?" I asked, gesturing toward it.

"Comes in handy, just in case."

"My grandma thinks we're going to get stuck."

A smile played across his lips. "Apparently it was very dramatic when our moms got stranded."

"Dramatic or traumatic? She actually looked worried."

"Both maybe. It was before cell phones. Come on. Let's grab coffee and get out there. The sandbar is going to show up any minute."

Armed with iced coffees, we made our way to the almost-visible sandbar, and Joe told me to give him my shoes to cross the wet sand. He brushed them off and put them in a Ziploc bag, which he then placed into the backpack. I saw water bottles and sunscreen in there as well.

"No camera today?"

He shook his head. "The phone will have to do."

"Are we swimming back or something?"

"No. Not if we go now." He glanced at me. "You *can* swim, right?"

"Yeah."

"Come on, then." He took a few steps into the shallow water and gestured for me to follow. A couple of minutes later, the water receded off a thin strip of sand, which soon widened into an area where we could walk side by side. I looked down, seeing at first a shallow, then increasingly deep drop-off next to the sandbar.

"This will hold us, right?" I asked, suddenly a little nervous.

He looked up at the tone of my voice. "It definitely will."

We walked on. It was farther from the beach than it looked when the tide was in, maybe half a mile, and the island loomed much larger than it had seemed as we approached it.

"What's the story with this island, anyway?"

"No real story. The coastline is dotted with them up here. Just kinda cool."

"Then what was that secret smile last night?" It appeared again. "That one. If it's just a natural formation, why are we out here?"

"Be patient." He looked down. "And watch your step. It gets rocky as we get closer." I narrowly avoided stepping on a sharp rock. He pointed toward an outcropping at the end of the sandbar. "We'll sit there and put our shoes back on. Then we climb."

"Climb?"

"There's a path."

"When do you just let me lie on the beach?"

"Whenever you want. But you don't need me for that."

Maybe I want you for that, I thought. But it was too flirtatious to say. "Maybe after the island. I apparently have to be back at the cottage and dressed by four."

"As long as we don't miss the tide, you'll have plenty of time." My eyes widened. "I'm kidding. We'll be back. What's at four?"

"I have no idea. That crazy woman won't tell me anything. I still don't know why we're here. I'm half convinced she's dying and tying up

223

loose ends, but she swears she's never going to die and is going to haunt me when she does."

"So it's her funeral, while she's still alive to see it, at four?"

"That or we're robbing a bank. Or performing open heart surgery. Or summoning those dead witches in a séance. Who knows with her?"

"Let me know if you need a getaway driver. I'm not much help as a medium."

"Thanks." We reached the rock he had pointed to and brushed off our feet before putting our shoes and socks back on. Joe rinsed the coffee cups and flattened them to put in the backpack. Watching him do that, I realized the coffee had been a mistake. I had to pee. And I wasn't going to make it three hours. And there were no full trees, just low, scrubby bushes. I looked toward the shore, where people gathered on the beach. I could ask Joe to turn around, but I was still in the sight line of the shore. *Ugh.*

"What's wrong?" I hadn't realized he was looking at me as I studied my choices. "I promise, I know the timing. I was just teasing before. I've never gotten stuck out here."

"No, it's not that."

"Then what?"

I scrunched up my face. This was the exact opposite of the sensual goddess I looked like in the pictures he had taken of me. "I have to pee."

He looked toward the shore. "I don't think anyone could tell what you were doing if you did." I remained unconvinced, so he placed the backpack on the ground and pulled a thin towel from the bottom of the bag and held it out in front of him, turning to face the shore. "Better?"

I went a few yards away behind a bush, making sure I was still blocked by the towel, and squatted. When I was done, I walked back to the water's edge and rinsed my hands, thoroughly embarrassed. "Thank you."

"I don't need the towel, but uh . . . I'll take a turn, too, if you want to stay over here." My shoulders relaxed. I didn't know if he actually had to go, but either way I felt better. He returned a minute later. "Ready to climb?"

I craned my neck up to see how steep it really was—the answer was steeper than I would have liked. But something about Joe gave me confidence. "Let's do this."

Even Joe was breathing heavily on parts of the climb, and he was in better shape than I was. But he stopped frequently to check on me.

"What's up there, anyway?" I panted.

"You'll see in a minute."

I expected a stunning view. Or maybe a colony of wild goats.

I was not expecting what I saw.

As we crested the top, the ruins of a small castle sat below us, nestled into the hillside. One turret remained largely intact, along with several walls, the rest caved into piles of rocks. "What on earth—?"

"Come on." Joe led the way down the hill to a stone staircase that delivered us onto the parapet, where an oxidized cannon sat, green from the sea air.

"What *is* this?"

"Do you want the real story or the one the kids all told each other?"

"Both."

"The first governor of Massachusetts, before the Revolutionary War, decided he was going to be the king of America and built his castle here. When the British heard what he was doing, they shelled him out, and this is all that's left."

"That's not real. Is it?"

The corners of his eyes crinkled. "Not in the slightest. They filmed a movie here in 1920 and built the castle for it. They just left it because it was going to cost money to take it apart, and no one really cared. Then the hurricane hit in 1938 and ruined a good chunk of it."

I stepped gingerly back toward the edge built into the island. "Is it safe?"

"What's here has been pretty much the same since I've been coming. And the old folks say not much has changed since the hurricane. So probably."

"It's kind of crazy, isn't it? What was the movie?"

"It was called *The Kingdom by the Sea*. No surviving copies that anyone knows of. And it was apparently terrible." He looked over at me. "Do you want to go up into the tower? The view is spectacular."

I grinned, and he led the way, ducking to get through the doorway as I followed. There was a corroded set of scaffolding stairs leading the way up past graffiti-covered walls, which spoiled the illusion. But a stone bench, just wide enough for the two of us to sit with our hips touching, provided a place to look out the tower's window. The ocean sparkled below us, a perfect deep blue all the way to the horizon.

"Wow," I breathed.

"Worth it?" Joe asked quietly.

I nodded, feeling the sudden heat of his thigh against mine, afraid to turn my head toward his. There was something about this place, this person, that was crushing my self-control.

Instead, I kept my eyes fixed on the horizon. "Do you think we could see a whale from up here?"

"You really want to see a whale, don't you? You keep mentioning it."

I started to say no, then I stopped myself. "You know what?" I looked at him. "I want to see a whale."

"Then that's what we'll do tomorrow."

"That's not too touristy for you?"

He shrugged. "I'll live."

"When do we need to head back to not get stuck?"

His eyes flicked down to his watch. "Pretty soon."

"I feel like the way back down is going to be harder than the way up."

"Depends. How brave are you feeling?"

I looked at him sideways, the repetition of my grandmother's words making me nervous. "Why?"

"Well, we can go back the way we came, but you're right, it's kind of treacherous. Or we take the stairs from the castle to that ledge down there." He pointed to a rock that jutted out over the ocean like a natural diving board. "And then . . . jump."

"What do you mean 'jump'?" We were literally at the top of a small mountain in the ocean. He wasn't serious. Was he?

"It's about a fifty-foot drop into open ocean. Then you swim onto the beach around the side and walk back to the sandbar from there."

"And people survive that?"

He laughed again. "Yes. No one has died doing it. At least not that I've ever heard of."

"Has anyone ever actually tried it?"

Joe grinned. "Why do you think I brought the waterproof backpack?"

Apparently my grandmother's comment about my bravery determining my outfit had *nothing* to do with my comfort level surrounding Joe seeing me in a bathing suit. Why was she like that?

He was still talking. "I won't judge if you're not up to it."

I wasn't remotely sure I would survive it, but I trusted him. "Let's go."

"You're sure."

"You've done it before?"

"Dozens of times."

"And you'll jump with me?"

He smiled again. "Unless you want to go first and I'll get a picture?"

I shook my head. "Definitely not brave enough to do it alone."

"Then we go together."

We left the tower, then went down the stone stairs outside the castle, which stopped at a shelf about seven feet above the flat rock Joe had pointed out from the tower's window. "Once we jump down this part, there's no turning back," he warned. "Decide now."

"I can do it." He sat, then hopped down and held his arms up to help me as I went down. "What now? We just jump?"

"You *probably* want to give me your phone and shoes first. And your sunglasses."

I pulled off my sunglasses, then my sneakers and socks, and handed them to him one at a time, then my phone. He put the shoes back in plastic bags, packing them into the backpack, then pulled off his shirt and wrapped our phones and sunglasses carefully in it before putting them into another plastic bag. I tried not to stare. He had a hint of a farmer's tan and muscles that told me he didn't just go running with his dog on the beach to stay in shape.

"Wait," I said, then stripped off my tank top and shorts and handed them to him as well. I didn't want to walk back in wet jean shorts. And I felt a hint of satisfaction at the look on his face.

He secured everything in the bag and put it on. "Ready?"

"You promise I'm not going to die here?"

"I promise." He held out his hand and I took it. "Running jump on the count of three?"

I felt like if he looked, he could have seen my heart pounding in my chest. Grandma's pool had a high dive when I was little. My sisters and cousins all loved it. I never worked up the courage. I had never been skydiving. Never jumped off the rocks into a quarry like in the movies. I had never even leapt into the ocean from a boat.

I took a deep breath and grabbed his outstretched hand. "Okay."

"One. Two." I took another deep breath. "Three." We ran the six steps, and suddenly we were flying, my legs still running in the air. I heard a noise that I didn't recognize as my own scream until we plunged into the ice-cold darkness of the water. I don't remember swimming, but my body knew what to do and propelled me upward until my head burst out, and I sputtered as I treaded water in the relative still of the cove we had jumped into.

"Joe?" I looked around in a panic. "Joe!"

He surfaced—I had only been alone for a second or two at most, but that was the most terrifying part. He smiled and let out a victorious, wordless yell.

I was shivering but smiling. "Did I just do that?"

"You did!"

"That was—I think I want to do it again."

He laughed. "If we do it again today, you're going to be late for your grandma." I swam closer to him, and he suddenly looked embarrassed. "Um. You might want to . . . adjust."

I glanced down. My bikini top had ridden up when I hit the water, and nothing was covered. The thrill evaporating, I quickly pulled it down as well as I could while trying to stay afloat, also now aware that the bottom of my suit had wedged itself into a position where not much was covered there either.

"Think I'll wear a one-piece if we try again."

"I won't object either way." I laughed. I should have still been embarrassed, but I couldn't be after that jump. "Come on. The beach is over there." He started swimming toward the shore. I followed, pausing to look up at the impossibly high ledge I had just conquered.

I learned to fly today, I thought giddily, swimming after Joe. My teeth were chattering from the chill of the New England water, and I couldn't have cared less. I had been in suspended animation for six months. No—longer than that. Much, much longer. But now? I was alive now. And I wondered if reviving me was the mysterious business my grandmother had in Hereford all along.

CHAPTER
THIRTY-NINE

June 1951
Hereford, Massachusetts

If Evelyn thought she'd find sympathy in her brothers and sisters beyond Vivie, there was none. Not once Joseph and Miriam put their collective foot down to forbid Evelyn to see Tony. Joseph hadn't spoken to her in the week since the proposal, and Miriam had only to scold her. But her siblings and their children were suddenly attached to her like glue. If she picked up the phone, her nieces and nephews appeared, making such a racket that she couldn't hear a word, and they were completely unfazed by her cajoling, offers of bribes, and eventual threats.

Joseph's car keys sat in a basket at the front door when he was in residence. But now they, along with Sam's and Bernie's, lived in the men's pockets and were hidden in their bedrooms at night. Her pleas to her brothers fell on entirely deaf ears.

If she left for a walk, Helen, Margaret, or Sam accompanied her—usually after a furiously whispered conversation with Miriam, but they did it nonetheless. And when they wouldn't leave her alone about her "mistake," Evelyn turned on her heel and went back to the cottage, locking herself in a bedroom, where she paced the floor until long after the rest of the house had gone to bed, locking even Vivie out.

There was no word from Tony.

Not that he ever contacted her when she was home with her family. Whenever she called him before, it was always under the guise of talking to a friend from school, while she spoke in coded conversation. They arranged their next meeting at the previous one.

The only evening she successfully evaded everyone and made it to the end of the street, praying his car would be parked there waiting for her, it wasn't. And just as she was debating begging the Inn to let her make a call, she heard Bernie say her name.

"Be a good girl, and come back now, Evie." His tone was sympathetic as he put an arm around her shoulder.

Evelyn shook out of his grip. "I thought you were on my side!"

Bernie looked at her levelly. "I'm on your side. Which is why I told you last year that Papa would never let you marry him. And I told Tony the same thing. Why you two couldn't have been smart about this and tried to meet more suitable people, I will never understand."

"And that's why you married Doris? Because she was 'suitable'?"

"It's why I went out with her in the first place. Because I wasn't looking to just have some fun. I wanted to get married and have kids."

Evelyn had never slapped anyone, but she considered it then. "Fun?" she spat. "You think it's been *fun* having to hide the person I love from my family? Especially when I'm in school and can't even see him without lying when I come home?"

"You know what I mean."

"And if you can't tell that that isn't what this is, then you don't know me."

"Are you pregnant?"

"No, you fathead!"

"I had to ask." Bernie softened. "Ev—you're a good kid. And I suppose I love you best out of all the girls. Which is why I'm going to tell you the truth right now. You can't marry him. You were never going to be able to marry him."

Evelyn scowled. "You just watch me." She stormed back into the cottage and went straight to the phone. Six-year-old Connie raised the alarm, calling for her siblings to make "the phone noise" with her, but Evelyn ignored them and dialed Tony's number.

The children screamed, making it impossible for her to hear if anyone had even answered the phone.

"It's Evelyn," she yelled into the receiver. "You tell Tony they won't let me out, but I'll find a way yet." And with no chance of hearing a reply, she replaced the receiver, swatting at the child nearest her before climbing the stairs.

She tried to sneak out in the night, determined to hitch a ride or, failing that, walk the five miles to town in the dark. She leaned out the window, looking for any purchase that would prevent her from hitting the gravel below too hard, but found none. Had she been in a room at the front of the house, she could have climbed down onto the porch, but she wasn't. And a broken ankle would rob her of any chance of getting to Tony for months.

She'd have to go out the front door.

Walking along the side of the hallway, avoiding the creaky middle floorboards, she tiptoed to the stairs. As long as she went slowly, she could be silent. She took a step down. Then another. Skipped over the fifth step entirely because it groaned at any weight. Another step. One more. Almost there now. Just three more.

"Go back to bed, Evelyn," Miriam said from the darkness of the living room.

Evelyn froze.

"Now."

Instead, Evelyn walked down the remaining steps. In the moonlight that came through the living room window, she saw her mother on the sofa, which she had made up into a makeshift bed, knowing what Evelyn was going to do before she did.

And Evelyn understood that the battle she needed to win was in front of her, not snoring loudly in the downstairs bedroom.

Steeling herself, she went in and knelt on the floor at her mother's side. "Mama, you have to listen to me."

Miriam said nothing, so Evelyn continued.

"I didn't fall in love with him on purpose. But it's done now. And he's good, Mama. He's a good man. So much better than me. The first time I saw him, he was dragging his brother, who had stolen something, into Papa's store to make him return it and to pay. That's who he is. He does the right thing every time. You can't hate someone who does the right thing. And he makes *me* do the right thing. He makes me want to be good like him. Isn't that what you always want me to be?"

Miriam still didn't reply.

"Mama, I know it's not what you wanted, and I know it's not how you were raised, but it's different now. The old ways—they don't matter as much anymore." Her eyes had adjusted to the dark, and, seeing Miriam's posture stiffen, she changed tactics. "Besides, our children would be Jewish because I am. Isn't that the most important thing, anyway? Who cares if he doesn't come to temple a couple of times a year?"

Evelyn took her mother's hand. "Mama, please."

Something in Miriam's face changed. For a moment, she wasn't Evelyn's fifty-seven-year-old mother. Her eyes were fixed on a spot behind her daughter as her face softened at a memory before contorting in an unspoken grief. Miriam rose and walked to the window; Evelyn felt her hopes rise. She was considering it!

But when she turned back to face her daughter, she was shaking her head. "No. And if you leave this house to go to him, you'd better be sure he'll have you. Because you will be dead to this family." She took her pillow and blanket from the sofa and went to the bedroom at the back of the house.

Evelyn slumped to the floor and wept.

CHAPTER FORTY

Joe and I got pizza from the café next to the Inn and ate it at a table outside, shaded by a red-and-white-striped umbrella. I put a hand giddily to my cheek. "I still can't believe I did that."

"Next time, if you're brave enough to jump alone, I'll get pictures."

Something tingled along my spine at the idea that he treated the fact that there would be a next time as a certainty. "I may need a little more hand-holding first." He held out his hand across the table, and I started to laugh. "Not to eat pizza!"

He withdrew his hand but was smiling. "The offer stands."

My phone vibrated on the table, and Joe's did a moment later. I looked down. A text from my grandmother. WAU. "She does *not* know how to text," I muttered.

Joe held his phone up to me, displaying the same message. "Does this mean anything to you?"

I said it didn't, pressing the button to call her and holding the phone to my ear. "You should be back by now," was her greeting. "If you're stuck on that island, I swear to God—"

"Grandma, we're having lunch. At the café. By the Inn."

"Good. You need to be ready by four."

"I know." I hesitated. "What did your text mean?"

"What text?"

"The one you sent to me and Joe. *WAU?*"

"Where are you?"

"I told you. We're at the pizza place." Her memory really wasn't what it once was.

"Yes, you said that."

"But what did the text mean?"

"It meant 'Where are you?'"

I put a hand on top of my head. "You can't just make up random acronyms and expect people to understand them."

"You do it."

"I use the ones everyone knows."

"Everyone knows that one. You ask Joe. He knows it."

"I—okay. I'll be home soon to shower."

"Tell Joe he's a good boy for not getting stuck, unlike your mothers."

I hung up and turned to Joe. "You're a good boy for not getting us stuck like our mothers. And the text meant 'Where are you?'"

He nodded. "Everyone knows that one." I smacked his arm with the back of my hand.

"I swear, if you act like you knew that to her . . ."

"You two should have a TV show. You could make millions."

"I'd tear my hair out in the process."

"You could afford a wig."

"I'd lose it diving off the island."

"True. I like your real hair better anyway." He reached out and touched the end of my ponytail, still damp from the ocean.

"I should get back." I stood up too quickly, bumping my thighs against the table. He rose too, and I hated myself for being so awkward. He clearly liked me. I definitely liked him. Why couldn't I do this? "We're still going whale hunting tomorrow?"

He looked at me strangely, then laughed. "Whale *watching*. We're not hunting an endangered species, you weirdo."

"Potato, potahto," I said, but even a faux pas with him felt comfortable, like he was laughing with me instead of at me. "You'll let me know what time?"

"I'll text you. Just don't show up with a harpoon."

I grinned. "I make no promises."

It took every ounce of self-control I had not to look back as I walked away.

~

I was showered and dressed nicely, with blow-dried hair and makeup applied per my grandmother's insistence by four sharp.

At which time I went to check on her, only to find she was still in a robe and putting on makeup at a small vanity table.

"I thought you said four?"

"I didn't. I said four thirty."

I took a deep breath. There was no point in arguing with her. I sat on the bed and watched as she applied eyeliner, sighed heavily, then wiped it off with cold cream and tried again. "Can I help?"

I expected to be rebuffed, but she held the pencil out to me without a word. She closed her eyes, and I bent, pulling gently at the corner of her wrinkled lid to get a straight line, then did the other eye. She turned to the mirror and moved her face from side to side, examining my work. There would be no punches pulled if it didn't meet her standards.

"How do you make your eyebrows look like that?" she asked eventually, examining me in the mirror. "I have almost none left."

I looked at her face. She wasn't wrong. "Let me get my brow kit."

She held up her pencil. "I have this."

I looked at it and shook my head. "We'll use my kit." I went and grabbed it from the upstairs bathroom, then drew on brows for her as naturally as I could. They were too dark for her hair, which had been my color when she was young, then had been gradually dyed a sandy blonde rather than allowed to go gray. But she preened in front of the mirror, admiring them.

"I look so glamourous. Like a movie star." I didn't say what I was thinking, which was that the movie star was Faye Dunaway playing Joan Crawford in *Mommie Dearest*.

"Where are we going tonight, anyway?" The last time I saw her this done up was for my cousin Amy's wedding.

"You'll see," she said, applying the bright fuchsia lipstick that all women seem to be issued at eighty.

"Why do you never tell me anything?"

"I tell you plenty. You're impatient, that's your problem."

"I thought I was boring."

"It's all the same problem. The excitement comes from not knowing." She stood and removed her robe, revealing only a pair of literal granny panties.

"I'll let you get dressed," I said, exiting quickly. Not that modesty had been a trait of hers when she was younger, but no shreds of any that once existed remained now.

It was nearly five before my grandmother emerged, and I had dozed off on the sofa. "Are you sleeping? We'll be late." She shook her head at me.

"Aren't we already?" I checked the time on my phone.

"No. We need to be there at five."

"Then why did you tell me four thirty?"

"I never said four thirty."

I sighed, picking up my purse.

～

"How do I look?" she asked as we approached the restaurant that she directed me to.

"You look fabulous, Grandma." I found myself wondering if Tony was inside. But would she drag me along for that?

We stepped into the cool blast of air conditioning, only to be assailed by dozens of voices as a crowd swelled forward, swallowing my grandmother.

I took an instinctive step backward, bumping into the door. There were people everywhere, and she was hugging them all. I stayed put until I nearly fell when an older couple opened the door behind me, then pushed past me to embrace my grandmother.

"Darlings," she said, her voice silencing the group as she gestured to me. "This is my Jenna."

Suddenly the crowd was on me, hugging, kissing my cheeks, holding me out at arm's length to admire me and pronounce me the very image of "Aunt Evelyn."

"You're . . . cousins?" I asked.

The woman who was patting my cheek laughed. "Of course we are," she said. "I'm your cousin Laney."

Grandma appeared at my side, her grip firm on my arm as she led me from person to person, introducing me to the whole room. They all looked vaguely similar, the Bergman genetics dominant, but there were too many of them for me to retain names. I recognized Donna, but the rest overwhelmed me.

We were eventually seated around banquet tables in a private room. I tried to count how many people there were, but they kept getting up to talk to each other, and they looked so much alike I couldn't be sure I wasn't counting anyone twice.

"These are your brothers' and sisters' kids and grandkids?" I asked my grandmother. She nodded, content in her role as reigning queen of the room. "There are so many of them."

She laughed. "Well, darling, there were seven of us. Granted, only six had children." She paused for a moment, clearly remembering Vivie, who died at twenty-one. But she shook her head, and the mood passed. "This isn't even everyone. Just the people in the general Boston area."

"There are more?"

"I'll make you a list."

"A list?"

"It's important to know where you come from," she said. "Who you come from."

I agreed, looking around the room but thinking that what I had learned from her and from being here, in the place that my family was from, had taught me so much more than a list could.

The eldest of them had been eight when my great-grandparents forbade her to marry Tony, which I doubted they really remembered. The stories they told over dinner revolved around their time at the cottages, most of them referencing later years, when my grandmother would come for the entire summer with my mother, aunt, and uncle.

I cringed guiltily. My mother had called while I was getting ready, and I had forgotten to call her back. I had texted her that I went to the island, and she had replied, OMG does your grandmother know you went out there? Then she called, but I was in the shower by then. Mom, Aunt Joan, and Uncle Richie should be here for this, not me. I didn't know these people.

A cousin named either Diana or Diane (there was one of each, and I couldn't tell which was which) was in the middle of a story about a goat that Joseph had purchased for the grandchildren when I felt my phone vibrate. I checked it discreetly from my lap, assuming it was my mom.

But it was Joe. Whatcha up to?

Impromptu family reunion at a restaurant. Apparently my family is huge.

Yeah. I've got one of those families too. I'll let you go. Pick you up at 10 tomorrow for whale watching?

My heart sank a little. I didn't want him to let me go. They're telling a story about a goat that ate through all the beach towels. I think I can talk. What are you up to?

I watched the three dots greedily, waiting on his reply. Over at the gallery. Do you want to come by when you finish?

It was after nine, and the waitstaff had already cleared the tables. Good girl Jenna would stay until her grandmother was ready to leave. But I looked over at her as she was chiming in regularly to correct details in her niece's story. *She* would go.

Touching her arm to get her attention, I leaned toward her ear. "Are you okay if I bail a little early? You can text me when it's time to go back, and I'll come get you."

She turned and eyed me sharply, the corners of her mouth twitching into a grin. "One of them will take me home. Give Joe my love."

"I—"

"Go."

I stood and kissed her cheek. "Okay."

"You're leaving?" Donna asked.

"She's meeting Joe."

I sighed as a group discussion of my social life began. "Nice to meet you all," I said loudly, then left and texted Joe for the gallery's address.

CHAPTER
FORTY-ONE

June 1951
Hereford, Massachusetts

Word of Miriam's ultimatum spread rapidly through the two houses. Everyone watched Evelyn warily, especially as she picked at her food listlessly instead of eating it, but she regained a semblance of freedom. If she went for a walk, no one followed her. Instead, when she came back to the house, everyone looked up anxiously, then pretended they hadn't been waiting on *shpilkes*, counting the seconds to see if she would return or if they would have to pretend she was dead if they encountered her in town.

Once, when the phone rang, she heard Joseph say, "She can't come to the phone," then hang up.

She couldn't breathe.

She pulled open the screen door, slipped on a pair of beach shoes from the front porch, not caring that they weren't hers, and padded rapidly down the steps. But instead of going toward the end of the road, she crossed through the line of trees to the bluffs overlooking the water.

She reached the edge and laid down on one of the rocks, her hands over her eyes, struggling to pull enough air into her lungs.

When her breath eventually calmed, she sat up, legs dangling off the rock over the cliff edge, and leaned her head in her hands, her elbows on her knees.

"Does that fella of yours know you're this upset?"

Evelyn whipped her head around so fast at the strange voice that she almost lost her balance. An older woman peered out from the trees, wearing a brightly colored muumuu and a straw sun hat. "Hello, Mrs. Gardner," Evelyn said, wiping at her eyes.

"What'd he do?"

"What'd who do?"

"Your fella. That one you came up here with all winter."

Evelyn looked at her in alarm. "I don't know what—"

Mrs. Gardner came closer, leaning on a walking stick. "Don't bother lying. I don't go telling other people's business." She looked Evelyn up and down. "Doesn't look like you've gotten yourself into any trouble."

Evelyn felt her cheeks reddening. It was one thing when Bernie said it, but she didn't know this woman. "N-no," she stammered.

"Your pa doesn't approve? Or he doesn't want to marry you?" She spoke in the thick accent of someone who spent her lifetime on the north shore, her family probably among the earliest settlers.

Blinking heavily, Evelyn sighed. "The former. Although I think it's more my mother."

"No, I s'pose they wouldn't approve. Looks Portuguese."

"He is."

Mrs. Gardner shook her head. "Never understood the fuss myself. But don't you fret too much. Things have a way of working themselves out the way they're supposed to. Give him some time to make something of himself, and your folks'll come around yet."

"I thought so too. But I'm not so sure now."

"Then make them. Haven't you ever heard that old expression? Easier to ask forgiveness than permission. You don't strike me as the permission type anyway."

Evelyn looked at this weathered woman, who knew more of her secrets than her family did without having ever exchanged more than a passing greeting. "You were married, weren't you?"

"Near on forty years, before he died."

"Is it worth it? If you have to give up your whole family?"

For the rest of her life, Evelyn would remember the kindness in Mrs. Gardner's eyes as she replied. "That question doesn't depend on the marriage—it depends on you, child. And I think you already know the answer. If you were going to run off, you wouldn't be here." She looked out toward the sea. "Give your pa time. He's a good man. Proud, but they all are, men. If your young man is worthy, your daddy will see that. And your ma'll fall in line." She gestured with her walking stick. "Now come away from those rocks and walk an old woman home."

CHAPTER
FORTY-TWO

The lights were on, though a Closed sign hung in the door, the words *Fonseca Photography* stenciled on it. I tried the door, but it was locked, so I rapped lightly.

Joe came from the back, Jax bounding behind him, and unlocked it for me.

"Hey," he said.

"Hey." Jax nudged my hand with her head, and I scratched her ears, her tongue lolling happily. I inclined my head toward the Closed sign. "You've got to lock the door too?"

"People just wander in if the lights are on."

"I kind of forgot you actually had like . . . a job."

He grinned sheepishly and ran a hand through his hair. "To be fair, I don't work a nine-to-five or anything. I have an assistant who runs the shop."

"Give me the tour?"

"It's not much of a tour." He gestured around him. It was one large room with white walls and framed photos in a mix of black and white and color. Toward the back there was a rather austere table with several portfolios on it, and a couple of doors in the back corner.

"Is it all your work?"

"Right now it is. I do guest shows sometimes though."

I began at the wall closest to us and moved around the room. There were a lot of local scenes that I recognized, including some of the castle. "I'm guessing you didn't jump if you had your camera with you."

"Nah. I went out with a boat that day. I didn't want to worry about the tides or timing."

"You have a boat?"

"A small one. Mostly for things like that."

I shook my head slightly, examining the next picture, which was of the Gloucester fisherman statue, and pondering what a different world he lived in. I was sure there were schools and teachers and people here who lived similarly to how I did—or how I had before I moved back home. But I had never lived near the water or thought about a job where you could just hop in a boat and find something that looked appealing.

It wasn't all scenery though. He had shots from weddings, including one of a flower girl pouting in her poufy dress that I couldn't help but smile at, and several of Jax that emanated happiness. Then an older man, silhouetted against the water, and I knew before I looked at the title card that it was Tony. I studied him for a moment. "You look a little like him."

"A little." He shrugged. "We have the same nose. But so does everyone in our family."

"At least it's a nice nose." I bit the inside of my cheek, but he didn't say anything.

When we got closer to one of the two doors, he turned to me. "I wanted to ask you something. But it's okay to say no. I won't be weird about it."

A nervous anticipation tingled in my stomach. This was where it was going to get weird. Saying that meant it would. Oh no. What was he about to ask?

"Okay."

He led me through one of the doors into a workroom, with a large table covered in framing supplies in the center, a computer desk with two oversized monitors along one wall, and another table along the back wall with a massive printer and paper cutter.

The center of the worktable held a framed, poster-sized print, and as I walked closer, I recognized it as the picture of me in the woods. Everything in it was black and white, except for me. I looked up at him, confused.

"I wanted to display it—if you're okay with that." I stared at the image. The color contrast against the black and white made me look like a time traveler in my hiking clothes. But there was a sense that I belonged there too. When I didn't reply, he kept talking. "If not, you can just have this one. If you want it. I mean, I can print another one for you, too, if you're okay with me showing it."

I was suddenly very aware of him standing just behind me, at my shoulder. We weren't touching, but I could feel him there all the same, just like I could feel my chest rising and falling with the effort to keep breathing. I heard my grandmother's words in my head, about a man not keeping a picture like that of someone unless he felt something for her.

"It's okay to say no," he said again, quietly, and I turned toward him.

It took a moment. Or maybe it didn't, and time just felt like it slowed down. Maybe I leaned in first or maybe he did or maybe whatever cosmic force that propelled my grandmother away from Tony and toward my grandfather was pushing us together. But then it happened. His lips on mine, so gently, as if he were still asking permission. He pulled back slightly, brushed a piece of hair from my forehead, then ran his fingertips down the side of my face to my bottom lip. I leaned forward and he kissed me again, firmer this time, a hand wrapping itself in my hair.

And for once, I didn't overthink or panic about the consequences—I couldn't have if I tried.

"Sorry." He pulled away again. "That's probably not a fair way to ask about the picture, is it?"

I laughed and pressed a hand to my eyes. "Is that how you get all of your work?"

"Just you. And Jax." She was lying by our feet and picked up her head at her name.

It should have been awkward. It was my first kiss since Brad, and, well, Brad hadn't kissed me like that in years. Maybe not ever like *that*. Which should have been a clue that we weren't going to last.

But it wasn't awkward.

"Who's the better kisser?"

"Definitely you. Jax licks her own butt sometimes."

I burst into giggles. "I'm not sure that's a high bar."

We looked at each other, and I realized I needed to leave. If I stayed, things were going to happen. Probably right there. On the table where the picture was. I glanced down at it, biting my bottom lip. Definitely had to head back.

"I should go," I said. His face dropped, and something in my chest jumped at his disappointment.

"Are you sure?"

My eyes darted to the table again. "Yeah," I said lightly. "But I'll see you tomorrow when we go whale hunting."

He shook his head, chuckling. "Watching."

"I've never seen one. It's a hunt for me."

"Do you want to think about the picture?"

"I don't need to. It's yours."

"Are you sure?"

"Yeah." I paused. "Do I get a cut if you sell it?"

"I'll take you to a really nice dinner."

"How nice?"

"Lobster and champagne."

"Ooh la la." We stood there smiling like idiots, and I desperately wanted him to kiss me again before I left.

"I'll walk you to your car." He went to the desk and picked up a leash for Jax.

"It's only a couple of blocks. I'll be fine."

"I know you'll be fine." He clipped the leash on to her collar. "But maybe I want the extra ten minutes with you."

My heart beat faster.

He turned off the lights and locked up the shop as we left, then took my hand, his other holding the leash, as Jax frolicked around us.

White holiday lights decorated the trees, giving Main Street a festive feel in the warm summer air, and we walked the long way, going six blocks instead of two.

When we reached my grandmother's car, we stood awkwardly for a moment saying goodbye, then kissed again, deeper, more urgently this time, my back pressing into the door of the car as I felt him against me. If he asked me to go home with him . . . But he didn't.

"I'll see you tomorrow morning," he said, kissing my cheek, then my lips once more, softly.

I nodded, not trusting myself to speak.

"Good night, Jenna."

"Good night." He opened the car door for me, and I sank into the seat.

~

I climbed the steps to the cottage, the light of the television flickering through the front window and reflecting onto the porch. I didn't call out as I swung the door quietly open in case she had fallen asleep in front of the TV again.

"Jenna?" she called. "Who's there?"

"It's me, Grandma." I went to the doorway of the living room.

"What are you doing here?"

I looked at her, concerned. She had probably just woken up, and being disoriented was normal at her age, but still concerning. Especially because she had been drinking at the dinner.

"I drove you to Hereford. Remember?"

"I know that. I'm not an idiot. Why are you here instead of at Joe's?"

I exhaled loudly. "Seriously? I just met the guy."

"Prude. When it's right, it's right. What are you waiting for? It's not like you're a virgin."

"Oh my—no. I'm going to bed. Good night."

"It's not too late to call Joe if you don't want to do that alone."

"Good night, Grandma."

"I don't know where I went wrong with that girl," she muttered as I went up the stairs.

CHAPTER FORTY-THREE

July 1951
Hereford, Massachusetts

Three more days crept by while Evelyn tried to decide what to do. Mrs. Gardner's voice would come back to her and she would resolve to leave, going so far as to pack a bag. But Vivie slipped into the room when Evelyn went to get her toothbrush.

She looked at the bag on the bed and back at her sister, eyes welling up.

"Vivie, please don't."

Vivie brushed at her eyes with the back of her hand and took a deep breath, trying to blink the tears away. "Mama said—"

"I know what Mama said." She took a deep breath. "But you know Papa will cave eventually."

"Not if she doesn't."

And there it was. The wild card Evelyn hadn't counted on when she planned to run off with Tony if Joseph said no. Joseph would forgive her. But would he go against Miriam?

Evelyn sank onto the bed. "What am I supposed to do?" she asked. "I love him. I can't live like this."

Vivie wrapped Evelyn in her arms. "I don't know." She kissed her sister's hair. "But I don't know what I'd do without you."

Guilt ridden, Evelyn unpacked the bag before crying herself to sleep.

~

As the family prepared for the daily trek to the beach the next morning, a car pulled to a stop outside the cottage, and the children ran to the front porch at the sound.

"Well, hello there." A male voice drifted through the screened windows. "Is your auntie Evelyn at home?"

Evelyn was in her room. She hadn't been to the beach since she last saw Tony and wasn't about to help anyone prepare for the day's adventures. But her ears pricked up at the sound of the car, and a ray of hope traveled through the screen with the familiar voice.

She ran to the mirror over her dresser—she looked frightful. Pale and thin with huge circles under her eyes. She couldn't even remember the last time she brushed her hair.

Straining to hear the conversation as Joseph went outside to talk to the man, she hurriedly put on some makeup and a dress and tugged a hairbrush through her matted hair.

When she came downstairs, Fred was seated in the living room, a glass of lemonade in front of him, and both Miriam and Joseph fawned over him as if he were the Messiah himself, having realized from his last name that he was the Jewish suitor who could end their worries.

"Hello, Fred."

He rose, smiling. "Evelyn."

"What are you doing here?"

"I've been calling—when I couldn't reach you, I figured I'd take a drive."

"Two hours?"

He grinned. "I missed you." Miriam grabbed Joseph's hand with her left and pressed her right to her heart, which Evelyn saw as her window of opportunity opening.

"We were going to the beach," Miriam said. "We could find you a suit, if you'd like to join us."

"Mama," Evelyn said. "With everyone? All the kids?" Fred started to protest that it was fine, but a look from Evelyn silenced him. "Is it all right if I go into town with him?"

"Of course," Miriam said. She rose, touching Fred's arm. "It's so nice to meet you." She shooed Joseph out of the room, stopping to brush Evelyn's hair from her face as she went.

Evelyn waited until they were gone, looked behind the sofa for spare children, then grabbed Fred's arm. "Come on," she said, pulling him toward the door.

"What's the hurry?"

"I'll explain in the car. Let's go. Now."

He let himself be led down the porch steps and opened the door of his Studebaker for her. Once in the driver's seat, he turned to her. "Are you okay?"

"No. Drive down to the end of the road and turn left, then the first right."

"Are we robbing a bank?"

Evelyn sighed, exasperated. "No. What are you really doing here?"

"I was worried. I called the house a few times and kept being told you couldn't talk. Then they hung up without taking a message. Are you a hostage?"

"Yes, actually."

"Now I'm really confused."

She sighed again. "Tony asked my father for his blessing. And everything went south."

"Oh no," Fred said. "I'm sorry."

"Mama said if I went to see him, I wasn't coming back."

"It'll be okay, you know. I know you really wanted it to work out, but it's a big world out there and—"

"No, you don't understand."

"I don't?"

"We're going to find him now. I have to talk to him."

Fred was quiet for a moment. "I see."

There was a tense pause.

"You're the only one who can help me," Evelyn said, ignoring his obvious disapproval. "You have to."

He kept his eyes on the road but nodded.

"Thank you."

When they pulled up to Tony's house, Evelyn got out.

"I'll just wait here, then," Fred said.

Evelyn leaned down to look at him through the open car window and thanked him again. "You don't understand how much this means to me."

"Good luck." He smiled grimly.

Evelyn walked up to the house, took a deep breath, and knocked on the door. Maria opened it a moment later, her eyes widening as she saw who was on her step.

"I need to see Tony."

"We don't want any trouble," she whispered.

"Trouble?" Evelyn asked, confused.

"Your father—he's powerful in this town. He said no. And—"

"No, Maria, no. He'll take it out on me. Not you. He's not like that. Please."

She looked unconvinced but called for her son, who came down the stairs, bleary and unshaven, freezing momentarily at the sight of her.

254

The moment passed, and he rushed to fold her in his arms, where she sank against him in relief, not realizing until it didn't happen that she was worried he would turn her away.

Maria wrung her hands, looking at them. "Do you . . . want to sit out here? To talk?" she asked.

Tony nodded and his mother went into the house, shutting the door carefully behind her to avoid hearing anything.

"I'm so sorry," Evelyn said, the words pouring out of her. "They wouldn't let me use the phone. They wouldn't let me out of the house. I didn't know how—"

"It's okay." He took her hands in his. "I understand."

"It's not him. I thought it would be Papa, but it's my mother. She isn't going to let him give in but . . ." Now that she was here, she knew what she wanted. "We'll elope. You have to see. It's the only way."

She raised her eyes to his, and what she saw terrified her.

"Tell me you didn't do anything irreversible to get here today." His voice was quiet, and he dropped her hands.

"I—no—Fred showed up and they thought—but I made him bring me here."

"Fred?" he asked dully.

Evelyn pointed to the car at the curb. "He's my friend. From school. He's engaged. I've mentioned him." She paused, suddenly not sure that she had. "That doesn't matter. Look. We can go tonight." She grabbed for his hands, which felt limp and cold in hers.

"He's Jewish, if they let you go with him." It wasn't a question. "Maybe he should matter."

Evelyn's mouth fell open.

"Go home, Evelyn. Be with your family."

"No."

"I told you all along I wouldn't do it this way."

"I'm not leaving."

"Yes. You are."

"I'll sleep out here. You won't have a choice."

"Is that what you want? To force me to do something I know is wrong?"

"I—" She stopped, desperate. "Why are you doing this?"

He stood and walked to the edge of the porch, looking toward Fred's car. "Your father came to see me. He offered me money to stay away."

A look of horror crossed Evelyn's face. "You didn't—?"

"Of course not. But he made it clear that you'll have no family at all if we run off. And I can't take that from you."

He turned back to her, leaning against the railing of the porch, arms crossed. "I love you. And I can't be the reason your heart breaks when your family isn't at your wedding. And when you have a baby who doesn't meet his grandparents. And when you can't be at your sisters' weddings. And every other time you'll want your family and not be able to have them."

A tear trickled down her cheek. "But I want *you*."

"I love you enough to let you go. And if you love me, you'll go. Don't make me be the one who steals those moments from you." He paused, finally meeting her eye. "You have to go home, Evelyn."

"What am I supposed to do without you?"

"Be happy," he said lightly. "Please."

"I can't."

He closed his eyes for a moment, then crossed to her and kissed her forehead. "You have to."

He pressed his lips to her forehead one more time and then went into the house, leaving her on the porch, tears rolling down her cheeks.

CHAPTER FORTY-FOUR

I woke up before my alarm, scrunching my face at the memory of the previous night, pressing my fingertips to my cheeks. Did that really happen? I was dreaming, right? I removed my hands and looked around the room. I was definitely in Hereford. In the cottage. Was it something in the air? In the water? Whatever it was that spawned the ridiculous force of nature that was my grandmother was healing me here. It wasn't just Joe—she could have dangled him in front of me at home a week earlier, and I wouldn't have cared at all.

I grinned. I was going to see a whale today.

Joe had warned me that we might not find one. But I knew better. If I wanted it enough right now, I could manifest that whale myself.

I sat up, swung my feet onto the wood floor, and went to the window to open the curtains. Another beautiful day.

Humming softly to myself, I went to take a shower.

~

I didn't wait for Joe to come to the door when he arrived. Grandma had already figured out that something had happened, and despite her insistence that she was helpful, the last thing any budding flirtation needed was my grandmother giving sex advice. Instead, when I heard his car pull up, I kissed her cheek and ran out the door and down the steps.

"Hi," he said when I jumped into his car.

"Hey."

"You're really excited to see a whale, huh?"

"That, and I didn't want my grandma giving you the third degree about last night."

He smiled sheepishly. "Appreciate that one. And glad you didn't bring a harpoon."

"Didn't really go with my outfit." I glanced in the back seat and saw a backpack. "Did you bring your camera?"

"I did. Please don't tell me you want a picture of you riding a whale."

I laughed. "You don't think that'd work?"

"It'd be a great shot. But I think it's illegal to ride an endangered species."

"What a dumb law."

"I know. Such a bummer."

"What's the point of even going, then?" He looked at me for probably longer than he should have while driving. "What?" I brushed my hair behind my ears self-consciously.

He shook his head. "I didn't expect to have this much fun this week. When your grandmother asked me to keep you busy for a couple days."

"I *knew* she hired you to babysit me."

"No, just—I said yes as a favor. She didn't ask me to take you out yesterday or today."

I bit my bottom lip, embarrassed. "Oh." I had just assumed my grandmother had arranged for him to show me around all week.

He looked over again at my tone. "I wanted to." I didn't know what to say. But he took my hand, holding it until we parked by the docks.

Instead of going to one of the whale-watching ships, though, Joe led us to a sailboat.

"We're not doing one of those cruises?"

"Definitely not."

"Is this your boat?"

"Nah. It's Tony's."

"I should have known." I looked it over. "Tell me it's not named for my grandmother."

He gave me a strange look. "He hasn't spent the last seventy years pining over her. You know that, right?"

I didn't know that at all. Everything I'd heard so far made it sound like the two of them were so in love that they'd never get over each other. She also hadn't seen him since we'd been in town, so I didn't know what to think. "To hear her talk, no one she's met has ever gotten over her."

"You may have a point there." He climbed onto the deck and held out a hand to help me up. "Let's go find you a whale."

I took a seat at the back of the boat while he prepared to leave and watched him setting everything up, his muscles rippling as he pulled the various ropes and moved the tiller.

"How did you learn all of this?"

"My family were fishermen for a hundred years here. I don't even remember learning." It seemed fantastical to know something so complicated so intrinsically, but I thought about the hamantaschen my grandmother made every Purim, rolling out the dough, cutting the circles with a drinking glass, adding a dollop of fruit or poppyseed filling, and pinching the corners. I'd have to follow a recipe for the dough and the baking times, but it was still something ingrained in me, something that she had learned from her mother, that I learned from her so young I didn't remember learning it.

We motored through the harbor, and then Joe opened the sail, positioning it to catch the wind just right, and soon the town grew smaller behind us.

"How do you know where to find a whale?"

"I asked around. And we'll see how we do."

"So we just sail around until we do?"

"Basically. We have to go out a ways."

Once we were in open water, Joe came to join me. "You don't need to steer?" I asked.

"It has an autopilot. I'll check it in a bit, but I set a heading, and the wind is steady. We're good for now. Do you want a drink?"

I glanced at my watch. "Like a *drink* drink?"

"I meant water or a soda or something, but I'm sure Tony is stocked."

"Water is great."

Joe went to the small cabin and returned with two bottles, handed me one, then sat beside me, pulling down the brim of his baseball cap and leaning back. "Good night."

I elbowed him. "Don't you dare. I know nothing about boats."

"Do you want me to teach you?"

"Nah." I shook my head. "Are you really going to put up that picture of me?"

"It's already up. I went back last night and hung it."

I held my hands under my chin, creating a frame. "Hashtag 'famous.' Or something."

He laughed. "You kind of are—my mother wants to meet you." I recoiled. "Calm down. She said that before I even met you—remember, she knows your mother."

My shoulders relaxed. "I forgot that part."

"Will you come to the restaurant tonight? With your grandma, of course."

"Do we have to bring her? She's going to make meeting your mom much more awkward."

"Depends—do you prefer awkward or guilt when you tell her she's not invited?"

I scrunched up my face. "Neither. We live on the ocean now. We're voyagers."

"We'd run out of food pretty quickly. I only brought snacks."

"What happened to the century of fishermen running through your veins?"

He rolled his eyes with a wry smile. "They didn't live on their boats."

I sighed exaggeratedly. "Neither option is good. She's either going to make inappropriate comments or guilt-trip me for the rest of my life."

He tilted his head slightly. "Is that why you came to Hereford? Guilt?"

The question caught me off guard and I looked down at my ringless hands.

In the pregnant pause that followed, I realized two things: the truth was complicated, and I didn't want to lie to Joe.

"Not guilt exactly." He didn't respond, and I looked up to see him watching me, his eyes warm, waiting for me to be ready to continue. "I was . . . stuck, I guess. You remember when a CD would start skipping, and you had to kind of bang on the Discman?" He smiled at the reference from our middle school days. "I moved home—to my parents' house—when my . . . well, when everything fell apart. And I got stuck."

"And your grandma banged on you?"

"No—well—sort of. She announced she was coming here, and I realized I needed to shake myself out of it, and that this was something new. Different. Even if it was really something old. If that makes sense."

He leaned back, settling in. "What happened? When things . . . fell apart? You know my sob story. What's yours?"

I froze, panicked.

"Or not." He rose to adjust the sail that probably didn't need adjusting. "Sorry." He glanced back at me over his shoulder, then went to the helm and checked the autopilot before coming back. "New subject: we have officially entered the area where we could start seeing whales."

How to explain that I had stopped mattering in the marriage? I didn't think it had always been like that, and I couldn't pinpoint when it happened, but a shift occurred at some point. When it stopped being about us and became all Brad, all the time. His job, his preferences, his timing. And fighting changed nothing, so I just went along because what was the alternative? Not that it had mattered in the end. All that silence and swallowing my feelings and sacrificing what I wanted, to keep things on an even keel, ended in the same result I had been trying to avoid.

My thoughts were spinning on a hamster wheel, going nowhere, and I knew I had to say something. "I wasn't happy either," I blurted out.

He nodded, as if I hadn't started two-thirds of the way through a story he didn't know.

"I just—it looked so perfect. On the outside. And I thought that mattered more. It—it was okay that we didn't talk that much or that we—well, he said we were fighting a lot, but we kind of weren't by then. We'd stopped bothering. It was—" I looked down at my lap and then held up my phone. "It was like Instagram. You post all the good stuff and don't let anyone see that it's held together with tape and safety pins and not really anything special at all."

When I finally looked back at Joe, I was sure I'd said too much. But his face was sympathetic. "Sounds like you'd been stuck for a while." I nodded. One side of his mouth curled into a small grin. "I can't picture you not talking much."

I let out an embarrassed laugh that almost turned into a cry, but didn't. "Tells you how bad it got, when I was okay with that."

"You stopped looking happy in your Instagram pictures a couple years ago."

"What do you mean?"

"You were still smiling, but it wasn't the same as earlier pictures."

Suddenly vulnerable, I resisted the urge to open the app and go through my feed. If he could see through me when we'd just met, could everyone else see it too?

He took his phone from his back pocket and pulled up a picture of me from the previous summer at the beach. At the time, I had thought it was the perfect shot. But I remembered how annoyed Brad was that I made him take so many to get it. "Look at that versus this one." He scrolled down until he came to a different picture of me in Greece, the blue of the Mediterranean behind me, my smile radiant. Then he went back up to the picture of me at the Inn. "Or this one."

My eyebrows went up. "Are you saying you make me happy?"

"I didn't mean ——" he stammered slightly, and I put a hand on his arm.

"I'm teasing. Let me see again." He handed me his phone, and I studied the pictures, swiping between them. He wasn't wrong. I was smiling in the one from last summer, but not like I used to. "Does that mean everyone knew my marriage sucked? And no one told me?"

Joe shook his head. "Photographer's eye. I capture emotions for a living."

"You're also admitting you went through my whole Instagram feed."

"Purely photographic research." He grinned. "What's your excuse?"

"I'm ridiculously nosy."

The silence that followed made me realize that if we just sat there smiling at each other alone out on the water, we were going to quickly find ourselves in territory I wasn't ready to be in. I broke the moment by turning toward the vast expanse of ocean leading to the horizon. "How will we know when there's a whale?"

"Either we'll see a tail or spray from a blowhole. Sometimes they jump."

"We came all this way, and we *might* see some water spray up?"

"If we see that, we'll see tails, too, probably."

"And we just watch the water?"

"We just watch the water."

I scrunched up my nose. "Okay, I get why you didn't want to do this."

"Who says I didn't want to do it?"

"You said it was touristy."

"It is—if you go out on one of those cruises. This is two people enjoying a nice morning on a sailboat."

"You're not bored?"

He looked at me, and I almost changed my mind about what I was willing to do this soon. "I'm not bored."

I was in over my head. I looked back at the water because if I kept looking at him, things were going to happen. And I saw a fin. I grabbed Joe's arm. "Is—is that a shark?"

He followed my gaze and laughed. "No. Dolphin."

"How do you know?"

"Dolphins swim up and down so their fins bob. The fins are also curved. And they travel in pods." He followed the line behind the dolphin's fin and pointed toward a dozen or more tiny fins bobbing farther away but heading in our direction. "They like boats. They might stick around for a while."

I looked down in wonder as it swam alongside us, clearly visible in the water next to the boat. It surfaced, looking at me as it swam along, Joe at my side. "Did you see that?" I asked, whacking his arm repeatedly. "The dolphin looked at me!"

"They're very smart." He grabbed his backpack and pulled out his camera.

"Yes! Get a picture of this!" I glanced at him, but the camera was pointed at me, not the water. "Not me! Get the dolphin!"

The rest of the pod joined us, splashing around the boat, one of them even jumping as Joe lowered the sail so we could watch them longer. I had seen dolphins at the National Aquarium when they still did shows, but never anything like this. They stayed with us for about half an hour, then, as if on some command we couldn't understand, they turned and left us.

"That was incredible." I collapsed into my seat next to Joe. "How do you not just want to take a boat out every day and see that?" He was looking at me. "What?"

"I'm used to it." He paused. "It's better seeing it through your eyes."

"Going to put another picture up in the gallery?"

"I might."

"Of me or a dolphin?"

"You'll have to wait and see."

I elbowed him, and he pulled me in and kissed me. Slowly, like he had all the time in the world.

When we surfaced, he brushed a windblown piece of hair from my face. "Let's go find you a whale."

I smiled broadly at his back as he went to raise the sail and resume our course.

When a whale eventually flipped its tail at us from a distance and spouted some water an hour later, it was almost anticlimactic after what we'd already seen. But even if it lacked the sheer joy of the dolphins, I felt a deep sense of satisfaction at that huge tail. Because it was my choice to come out on the ocean and see it. And I had spoken up, said what I wanted, and made it happen. It had been a long time since I was whole enough to do that.

On the way back to town, I let Joe teach me how to steer, him standing behind me as he showed me how to maneuver. When he finished instructing and told me to do it myself, I remembered nothing but the feel of his arms around me and joked that I just wanted to go do the *Titanic* pose at the front of the boat.

"We could."

"But who would take our picture?"

"No one. You'd have to live with the knowledge that it happened without anyone seeing it on Instagram."

"What's the point of bringing a professional photographer everywhere with me, then?"

He kissed the side of my neck, and I felt a shiver run down my back. "Do you want to be king of the world or not?" he asked close to my ear.

I turned around in his arms. "I'm good right here." And that time I kissed him, my arms around his neck, his at my waist, our bodies pressed together against the motion of the boat.

"Have dinner with me tonight," he said, pulling out of the kiss.

"With your mother and my grandmother? So much for romance."

"I think it's extremely romantic. I want you to meet my mom. And have Portuguese food. And spend time with me."

Even though I had no desire to spend time with my grandmother and Joe together now that we were—well—whatever it was that we were and was somewhat terrified to meet his mother, I found myself agreeing.

CHAPTER FORTY-FIVE

August 1951
Hereford, Massachusetts

Evelyn sent four letters to Tony in the weeks after seeing him. The first angry and tearstained. The second pleading with him. The third reasoning. And the fourth calling him a coward. She walked defiantly past her family to hand them directly to the mailman, then waited on the porch each day for the mailman to return, not trusting her family to give her Tony's reply.

No reply came.

For one more week after the final letter, she wallowed. Refusing meals, dropping weight she didn't have to spare, replacing food with cigarettes that Miriam protested only once before falling silent when she saw the haunted look in her daughter's eyes.

And then, on the eighth day, Evelyn rose before the sun and went to the beach, where she sat on a rock and watched the sun rise. When she returned to the cottage, no one in her family could place the difference in her, but it was there all the same. On that rock she accepted that Tony was right—she could force his hand, but if she did, they wouldn't be happy. Which meant letting him go was all she could do.

There were just two weeks until she went back to school, and that evening she called Fred.

"If I don't get out of this house, I'm going to lose my mind," she said, quietly, aware that there were ears around every corner. "Any chance you feel like taking another drive?"

"Tomorrow?"

"Perfect." She hung up without saying goodbye.

His car had hardly stopped when Evelyn ran down the front steps and threw herself into the passenger seat. "You don't want me to come in? Throw your parents off the scent?"

She looked at him dully. "There is no scent."

"Oh—I—when I didn't hear from you, I thought—" He stopped, flummoxed, and looked at her. "You always find a way."

"I didn't this time."

Fred studied her for a moment, realizing her phone call had been a genuine plea. "Do you want to talk about it?"

"No."

"Okay, then." Fred put the car into drive. "Tell me where to."

Evelyn didn't want to go to town, where the possibility of running into Tony existed, so instead they drove to Rockport to walk around the artists' colony.

Fred followed her directions and parked on Bearskin Neck, looking around and spotting an ice cream shop as they stepped out of the car. "Perfect," he said.

"What is?"

"Ice cream."

"I don't want ice cream."

"You look like you need some."

"I'd rather have a drink."

Fred offered her his arm, and she slipped a hand into the crook of his elbow. "It's too early for that," he said lightly.

"Well, it's too early for ice cream too, then."

"Nonsense. Besides, you're too thin. Did they stop feeding you when they locked you in the tower?"

"Hah."

"Now let me guess. Butter pecan?" Evelyn made a face. "No, you're right. Too simple. You wouldn't go for a plain flavor." He stared at her for a moment. "Rocky road?"

She smiled wanly. "Lucky guess."

"No. I know you, Evelyn Bergman. Like it or not. And I know something else—there's not a broken heart on this earth that ice cream won't help." Evelyn let herself be led into the ice cream parlor, where Fred ordered two rocky road cones.

Evelyn touched her tongue to the ice cream initially to satisfy Fred, but it was hot out, and she found herself eating to keep it from dripping everywhere.

"It's melting too quickly," she said, trying to keep up.

"You're telling me." Fred circled his with his tongue.

"We're going to be a sticky mess."

"We can clean off in the ocean."

"And you'll drive two hours home in wet clothes?"

"If it put a smile on your face, I would." Evelyn shook her head but did smile briefly before licking her cone again to keep it from dripping all over her hand. "Don't you feel better now?"

"You may have been right about the ice cream," she conceded.

"Ice cream? I'm mortally wounded that you didn't see through that one. There's no magic in ice cream. It was my charming company that made you feel better."

Evelyn rolled her eyes. "Honestly, Fred, you are impossible."

He stuck out the hand that wasn't holding his ice cream. "Hello, pot. I'm the kettle. It's nice to meet you." She laughed, and he gave up, throwing the rest of his cone in a trashcan. "Come on. Show a stodgy old Plymouth guy around this bohemian town." She switched hands for her ice cream, suddenly hungry enough to finish the whole thing, and put a sticky hand in Fred's proffered arm.

~

They ate a late lunch after their walk through town, then wandered down to the small beach dotted with rocks. "Not the most creative with names up here, are they?"

Evelyn bent to undo her shoes, and Fred followed suit. "Says the man whose hometown was named for a rock."

"Yes, but a very famous rock. This is just a port filled with undistinguished rocks."

She shrugged, picking up her shoes and gesturing for him to follow her down to the water. "Yes, but it's one of the only towns *not* named for someplace in England. We can give the Pilgrims who settled here *some* credit." Evelyn waited as Fred bent to roll the hem of his pants into cuffs, and then they walked along the water's edge, the waves licking their bare legs. "Besides, what would you have called it?"

"Evelynport."

"Cute. I wasn't born yet when they founded this place."

"That's no excuse for a lack of foresight."

"Witches and seers historically didn't fare well here."

"Fair enough."

Evelyn stepped on a rock and stumbled. Fred caught her, holding her a second too long, then took her hand. She looked down at her hand clasped in his. "Probably not the best idea," she said lightly. "What would Betty think?"

"I doubt she'd care much anymore."

Evelyn's head tilted away so she could look at Fred more carefully, a tingle of alarm running down her spine. "Why's that?"

"I ended things with her months ago."

She was too startled to even pull her hand away. "Months ago?" she repeated. "But—I thought—you—why? What happened?"

"Isn't it obvious?"

"No, clearly not if I'm asking."

"Because once I met you, there was no way I was going to marry her. Didn't seem fair to string her along."

Evelyn's eyes were wide, her mouth open. "But—I—you—"

Emboldened by the fact that her hand was still in his, he pulled her in close to him, and, wrapping his other arm around her waist, he leaned down and kissed her softly. Evelyn was too surprised to respond, but Fred didn't seem to mind. He broke the kiss, still holding her hand but dropping the one around her waist.

"Just wanted to plant the seed. I know you're not ready. And that's okay. I've waited this long. But I'm here. And I'm not going anywhere until you tell me to."

And with that, he started walking again, pulling her gently along.

She followed, her mind reeling. She had never been kissed by anyone except Tony, and it felt strange and different. Not bad, just . . . different. And Tony didn't want her—no, that wasn't right. He did. He just wouldn't be with her. It was all so confusing. *Maybe he should matter,* Tony had said. She stole a glance at Fred, who wasn't looking at her. He was handsome. Taller than Tony. A good, straight nose. Cornflower-blue eyes. So different. And they did get on so well. She realized with a start that he was her closest friend after Vivie and Ruthie. And deep down, she knew there was a reason she hadn't told Tony about him. Her heart was racing, her breathing ragged.

"Stop." She yanked her hand free from his. Fred turned to look at her, his chest rising and falling as rapidly as hers—he was scared, she realized. Scared he'd made a mistake in admitting how he felt and was about to lose her. And that made up her mind. "Try that again."

"Which part?"

"The kiss, you fool."

Fred smiled and closed the gap between them, wrapping her in his arms, and kissing her for real this time, with all the passion he had felt since the day he first sat in the grass beside her. And Evelyn kissed him back, resolutely pushing thoughts of Tony out of her head as soon as they entered. What was past was past. And this was her future.

CHAPTER FORTY-SIX

Ruthie was over when I got back to the cottage, her car parked at a forty-five-degree angle in the driveway, leading me to wonder about the validity of her driver's license as well.

I called to my grandmother when I walked in, but neither of them heard me, so I went through to the kitchen, where they sat huddled together around a photo album.

"Hi," I said, going to the cabinet for a water glass.

"How was whale hunting, darling?"

"She went hunting? At this time of year?"

"Whale watching," I clarified. "We didn't hunt anything."

"I should hope not. Messy business, that." My grandmother turned to Ruthie. "She went with Joe."

"Spending a lot of time with him, it sounds like," Ruthie said. "I had hoped you'd want to meet my David, but I suppose it's too late for that."

"She's not married to him yet."

I held up my hands. "Stop. Both of you."

"Isn't it funny how life works out sometimes?" Ruthie said, ignoring me completely. "If you'd run off with Tony, they'd be cousins."

"I wound up right where I was supposed to be," my grandmother said. "Just like Jenna is now."

"Not divorced yet," I reminded them. "And I'm standing right here."

"Might be time to take care of that," my grandmother shot back. "You'll be committing adultery soon if you haven't already."

I opened my mouth to remind her that she had told me not only to sleep with Joe but also to not use a condom to hurry things along, but she wanted me to argue with her. It was impossible to win an argument against her because she changed the rules as soon as you learned them. Instead, I announced that I was going upstairs to shower and maybe take a nap. "We're having dinner at Joe's mother's restaurant tonight. Be ready at six."

She raised an eyebrow but said nothing as I took my water glass and went upstairs.

"How much of this did you plan?" I heard Ruthie ask in the kitchen. My grandmother laughed in reply.

~

I had one sundress left that Joe hadn't seen, and I slipped it over my head, then inspected myself in the mirror. Crazy tan lines crisscrossed everywhere from our time outside in bathing suits, tank tops, and T-shirts after a summer spent primarily indoors. But I didn't think he'd mind.

I should have been nervous. I was a wreck when I met Brad's parents the first time. But this felt different. I didn't know if it was because Joe's mother already knew my mother and grandmother, or if it was because I was different now. Then again, we had been dating seriously for a couple of months when I met Brad's family. This was—well, I didn't know what it was, but it wasn't that.

I dug in my bag for the lipstick I had thrown in at the last minute before leaving home. It was an older one—I hadn't worn lipstick in months. I applied it carefully in the mirror, then stopped and looked at myself. *No.* I grabbed a tissue and rubbed it away, leaving only the hint of a stain, and dropped the tube in the trash as I left to check on my grandmother. I was tired of trying so hard. I just wanted to be me and have that be enough.

Grandma was sitting in the living room, fully dressed and ready to go. I looked at her, tilting my head. "What's that face for?" she asked.

"Your eyebrows look good."

"Of course they do."

I didn't bite. "Ready?"

"Are you?"

"Yeah. I am."

"Then let's go." She struggled to rise, and I offered her my hand, which she took then shook off in favor of the railing, to go down the stairs to Joe's waiting car.

~

La Tasca Sofia was in town, not on the harbor, but it sat on the water side of Main Street in what had once been a house, with a back patio overlooking the marina, twinkling lights threaded above it to mimic stars. "This was the Abbotts' house," my grandmother said, looking up at it. She shook her head. "A million years ago."

"Wait until you see what she's done with the patio," Joe said. "I think it was still the old deck when you were here last."

I looked at my grandmother curiously, marveling at the fact that she knew Joe before I even met Brad. She had this whole secret life that I knew nothing about. I wondered how much my mother knew.

A woman came bounding down the stairs toward us before we even reached them. She wrapped my grandmother in a tight hug, kissing both of her cheeks before turning to me. "Jenna?" she asked. I nodded, and she hugged me as well.

"I—it's nice to meet you, Mrs. Fonseca."

"Sofia." She held me at arm's length to look at me but showed no sign of letting go anytime soon. "You look more like your grandmother than your mother." She released my right elbow to pinch her son's cheek warmly, then took my arm. "Joe, help Evelyn in—we're getting a ramp installed. It should have been done already, but it's my cousin, and he works slowly."

"I don't need a ramp. You think the cottage doesn't have stairs?" She did, however, take Joe's offered arm.

"You should have a ramp there too," she said. "I'll send my cousin over. If he ever finishes ours." She held the door open and gestured for us to walk inside. "I saved the best table outside for us."

The interior of the house had been gutted to become a large dining room, with a kitchen in the back right, a handful of pillars where there had once been load-bearing walls. The floors were finished in hardwood, and there was a nautical theme, tastefully done, with antique anchors, driftwood sculptures, and large, framed black-and-white seascape photographs that had to be Joe's. Sofia led us through to the patio and a table at the far edge with a Reserved sign. She told us where to sit, putting me and Joe next to each other, seating herself across from me.

"I'm sorry my husband isn't here," she said as a waiter appeared with wine. "He's in Sonoma this week."

"Jenna doesn't need to meet the whole family," Joe said, smiling.

"Who said the whole family? I didn't invite your sister."

I felt uneasy suddenly. We had talked about my family, of course, and Emily. And he had talked about his mom, but mostly in the context of my family again. I didn't know he had a sister. I didn't know if he knew I had two sisters. He hadn't talked about his dad, so I hadn't asked. What else didn't I know?

Another waiter brought menus and laid them in front of us, telling us to take our time. Sofia told him he could bring the appetizers now, then turned to me. "How is your mother? I see her on Facebook, of course, but . . ." She shrugged. "You know how that goes."

"She's good. I think she'll retire in another couple years."

"And then what?"

"Travel probably."

"I hope she'll come here. It's been too long. You were so young the last time she was here."

I tilted my head. "We met then?"

She smiled warmly, Joe's smile. "You and Joe played on the beach together. You were what? Five?"

"Almost," my grandmother said.

I tried to remember, but there was nothing beyond my grandmother and the rocks. I turned to Joe, and he shrugged.

Puff pastries filled with fish appeared on the table, as well as bread, shrimp, and an egg dish. I put my napkin in my lap, letting Sofia explain what everything was.

"I used old family recipes as a base for most things."

"I still remember the first time I ate at your grandmother's house," my grandma said, helping herself.

"Her *bacalhau a bras* is on the menu," Sofia said. "That one I couldn't bring myself to change."

I took a bite of one of the pastries, then looked over at Joe. "Saving the best food for last?" I asked quietly after I finished chewing.

"Better than Brewster's?"

"Might have to go back there for a second taste test. But yeah. I think so." He touched his leg to mine under the table. No, we hadn't discussed *everything* yet. But maybe that was because conversation with him was just so easy. It felt like we already knew each other. Which, apparently, we kind of did.

I asked what he recommended when we turned to the menus, and he deferred to his mother, who recommended her grandmother's dish for my first experience trying Portuguese food.

"Have you ever been to Portugal?" I asked Joe.

"No." He shook his head. "I'd like to go someday. Mom has been a few times now."

"Your great-grandfather insisted I go before I opened the restaurant. He bought my plane ticket."

I put down the shrimp that had been on its way to my mouth and stared at her. "My great-grandfather?"

She nodded.

"But—" I turned to my grandmother, extremely confused. "Your father?"

"Of course."

"I don't get it."

"What's not to get?" my grandmother asked. I looked at her more carefully—she was enjoying herself, which meant she had deliberately left important information out.

"The last thing you told me was that your parents wouldn't let you marry Tony."

"They wouldn't."

"Then . . . ?"

Sofia smiled kindly. "My father died when I was just a little girl. Your great-grandfather approached Tony—he wanted to help. I guess he felt bad about . . . all that. Tony said no, of course. Then Joseph caught me stealing from his store one day when I was seven or eight. I was terrified, but he was so kind. He told me I didn't need to steal; I could just ask. Then he went to my mother, and she accepted his help. I used to go help him in the store—he didn't need me, of course, but I was curious about him." She took a sip of her wine, remembering fondly. "He paid for me to go to culinary school—he wanted me to go to college, but that wasn't the path for me. He was a wonderful man."

I remembered Joe saying Tony and my great-grandfather forgave each other eventually—this was how apparently, though I knew there had to be more to the story.

But Sofia was still talking.

"I wouldn't have all of this without him. It's why I named Joe for him."

I looked from Sofia to Joe, shaken. "You're named for my great-grandfather?"

He was amused at my confusion. "I thought you knew. It's not exactly a Portuguese name."

I looked to my grandmother, who winked at me and then laughed.

~

My grandmother was, miraculously, on her best behavior. There were no overt sexual comments or even innuendos. In fact, most of the conversation she dominated with Sofia, reminiscing about the summers she spent here and people I didn't know. Joe explained what he could, and Sofia was good about filling in holes. My grandmother just enjoyed having an audience.

"Of course, he didn't give you the ticket," Sofia said, laughing as my grandmother finished a tale of an escapade from years past. "Tony wouldn't have allowed it."

"Your uncle's moral compass always pointed due north. Even when I was around. He'd have let him."

Sofia shook her head. "I still believe he joined the force just to make sure you stayed out of trouble."

Something twitched in my grandmother's face, but it was gone so quickly I could have imagined it. "What trouble? I swear, the whole town built my reputation around that movie theater eighty years ago."

"And the boat. You can't forget the boat."

Grandma pointed a finger at Sofia. "That one was your fault. You and Anna scared me half to death."

Sofia turned to me. "Did you know your grandmother was a boat thief?"

I looked at my grandmother. "Honestly, I don't think anything would surprise me. Did you ride with Butch Cassidy's gang too?"

She crossed her arms. "Don't be impudent. They were dead before I was even born." Then she cocked her head and smiled. "I did meet Paul Newman in the sixties though. Had I not been married, Joanne Woodward might have had some competition."

I turned to Joe, speaking low. "I've heard *way* too much about her sex life this trip." He tried to hide his laugh by taking a sip of water. My grandmother may not have been able to hear what I said, but she was watching us shrewdly. She missed nothing. And I wasn't so sure she needed those hearing aids as much as she pretended to.

After dessert, which Sofia insisted on, Joe excused himself to use the restroom, and my grandmother stood to follow suit. "I'll take you," I said, starting to stand.

She fixed me with a withering look. "If you don't stop hovering over me, you're going to find the walk home from Massachusetts to be a long one." And, unsteadily after the wine she shouldn't have drunk, she tottered into the restaurant.

"She'll be fine," Sofia said, leaning across the table toward me. I turned away from my grandma's progress, suddenly aware that we were alone and equally aware that my grandmother likely did not actually need to pee.

"This was lovely," I said, but Sofia reached out and took my hand.

"He really likes you."

I didn't know how to respond. I really liked him too. But this was his mom. And she seemed to want a reply. I swallowed dryly and nodded, afraid to speak.

"Sometimes family makes things complicated. Sometimes the complicated part is in our own heads." She patted my hand. "It's good to see him smiling so much."

"Mom, stop scaring Jenna."

I looked up at Joe and pulled my hand reflexively out of Sofia's.

"Who's scaring anyone?"

He looked at me. *He really likes me,* I thought, and I smiled.

～

Sofia hugged me goodbye while Joe got the car, telling me not to be a stranger, her perfume smelling of honeysuckle, before embracing my grandmother. "You bring her back soon," she said. The two women exchanged a look, and Sofia turned back to me. "Or you come back yourself." I was hit again with a sense of foreboding, like this trip was the closing of some chapter for my grandmother.

"I'll work on Anna," my grandmother said. "The two of you have so much to discuss now."

Sofia laughed merrily, and I shook my head as Joe pulled to the curb.

When we got back to the cottage, Joe walked my grandmother up the steps, and she turned to us at the door. "I'm going to watch TV in my room. With the volume up. Then go to bed. You two make yourselves at home. I won't hear a thing." Then she stumped past us into the house. We lasted about six seconds before we started laughing.

"We can't go in there."

"No," he agreed. The porch lights provided two halos of light, enough to see that his eyes were fixed on my lips, his body close to mine. "Do you want to come back to my house? For a drink?"

I nodded, and he opened the porch door, leading the way back down to his car, where he held my hand, his fingers intertwined with mine, his thumb tracing electric circles in my palm.

The drive was short along the road parallel to the beach, then a left at the end to the small peninsula that jutted out at the end of the cove. He turned into a long driveway, stopping at an old Cape Cod, the moonlight twinkling on the water behind it.

"You really live right on the water?"

"You should see the view at sunrise. It's spectacular." He led me to the front door, and I realized as he put the key in the lock that I was probably going to be there for sunrise. I shivered slightly with anticipation. There wouldn't be a drink. We would be kissing each other as soon as we were in the door. Then there would be a trail of clothes to the bedroom, and then—

Jax came bounding out of the darkness and would have knocked me down the front steps if Joe hadn't caught me. Joe's arms were around me, but it was Jax's large tongue all over my face, and it took me a second to get my bearings.

"Jax! Down! Down!" He pushed her off me. "I swear, she doesn't usually jump. She really likes you."

I brushed myself off and tried to discreetly wipe the slobber off my face. "I have to admit, I didn't think she was who I'd be making out with."

He laughed and covered his eyes with a hand. "I'm not good at this, am I?"

"We'll blame Jax."

"How about that drink? And we try again?"

I agreed and followed him to the kitchen, where he poured us each a glass of wine and suggested we sit in the living room. He let Jax out into the backyard, then sat next to me on the sofa.

I took a sip. "This is really good."

He shrugged. "I don't really know much about wine. I should, with my dad and all. But I just have what he gives me to try usually."

"You haven't mentioned him much."

Joe took a sip. "He travels a lot. Wanted me to be a lawyer, not a photographer. But we do well otherwise."

"And your sister?"

Jax scratched at the back door to come in, and he went to open the door for her. She jumped right into his spot on the sofa and put her head in my lap for me to pet her.

"Jax! For the love of—you're not helping!" He tried to pull her off the sofa, but she had dug in.

"Is she like this with every girl you bring home?"

He laughed nervously. "She's *never* like this. Jax! Treat! Come on, girl!" She jumped down at the word *treat* and ran toward the kitchen, while Joe quickly claimed the cushion she had vacated next to me. He took a big swig of his wine, then looked at me. "Hi."

I set my glass down. "Hey." We were facing each other, and he inched closer, putting one arm behind me, brushing my hair back with the other hand. I had forgotten this sense of anticipation, the delicious moments before a kiss happened, when it felt like gravity was pulling you into someone in slow motion.

His lips touched mine, and then everything moved quickly again. His hand was in my hair, and I was on his lap, kissing him with an overwhelming urgency as he pulled a strap of my sundress down my shoulder. I pulled my arm out and reached down to start unbuttoning his shirt when I felt his tongue along my neck.

Wait. I pulled away. That wasn't his tongue. His had been quite busy with mine. We both looked at Jax, then at each other and started to laugh.

"Bedroom?" I asked. He nodded. I stood and he followed, his shirt untucked and half-buttoned.

Jax ran down the hall ahead of us and jumped onto the bed. "Oh, come on, Jax. Out!" She wagged her tail happily from the middle of the bed, but Joe repeated his command and she slunk sadly into the hall. He shut the door and turned to me. "I have a confession. I haven't actually brought anyone here since—well—I got Jax three years ago. So . . . this is new to her."

It was sweet. And special. And desperately romantic.

He really likes you, Sofia's voice said in my head.

He moved closer to kiss me again. I looked at the king-sized bed that he had shared with Emily and no one else since.

And I panicked.

"I can't do this." I pulled the dress strap back onto my shoulder self-consciously and turned around, looking for my purse, not remembering that it was on the kitchen counter. "I—I need to go back. I'm sorry—I—"

"What just happened?"

I couldn't look at him. I didn't know how to answer that question. The honest answer was that it got too real, and I was scared. But I couldn't say that. I couldn't admit that. Instead, I opened my mouth and something else came out. "I don't want a one-night stand."

He touched my elbow. I hadn't realized I'd crossed my arms. "I don't either. That's not what this is."

I stepped back. "It is though. I'm going home in a few days. And I'm still married. I don't want to get over one guy by getting under another."

Joe recoiled and was quiet for a long moment. "I'll take you home." He began rebuttoning his shirt.

"I can walk."

He blinked hard, clearly refraining from saying what he wanted to. "You're not walking two miles in the dark by yourself."

My shoes were in the living room, but they were heeled sandals. I could take them off on the beach, but the walk up the road to the cottage would probably result in a broken ankle. I nodded and opened the bedroom door, Jax bounding through to jump back onto the bed.

We drove in silence, my head spinning as I argued with myself over whether I had done the right thing or whether I should try to fix this. Joe didn't look at me.

He pulled to a stop in front of the cottage. I unbuckled my seatbelt but didn't open the door. I turned, looking at him in the dim light from the porch. "I'm sorry."

He was staring straight ahead, his thumbs playing on the steering wheel. "Yeah. Me too."

I got out and ran up the cottage steps without looking back, the tears starting to fall before I was even on the porch. I opened the front door, shut it behind me, and then slid to the floor against it, sobs shaking my body as I heard his car pull away into the darkness.

CHAPTER FORTY-SEVEN

June 1952
Hereford, Massachusetts

Evelyn's bare feet hung out the car window as they crossed the bridge, her head pillowed contentedly on Fred's lap. Her left hand rested against her thigh, where she could see the diamond, shimmering whenever the sun hit it, sending sparks of fiery light bouncing around the car.

"Do you smell that?" she asked, sitting up suddenly.

Fred inhaled. "Fish?"

She smacked his arm lightly. "Salt. Seaweed." She paused, taking another deep breath. "Home."

He looked at her, making sure she wasn't changing her mind. He had just graduated and accepted a position at an engineering firm in Boston, but there was a bigger job in New York that he had his eye on. Their plan was to stay in Boston the next two years while she finished school, hopefully marrying and getting an apartment together before she finished, and then . . . Well, they'd see how his job situation played out.

She sat up and leaned on her crossed arms at the open window to better breathe in the sea air, and Fred smiled, watching her.

When they pulled up to the house on Main Street, he held out his hand.

Evelyn pouted and held her left hand to her chest, covering it with her right.

"Come on. You promised."

"I changed my mind."

"About me or the plan?"

She smiled coyly. "I think it's stuck. We'll just have to leave it and tell them together."

"Evelyn."

"I don't see why this matters so much."

"Because we want your father's blessing. Now give me the ring. If all goes well, you'll have it back tonight."

She would have kept it going, but there was a flicker at the drawing room curtain, which meant Miriam was watching. "Fine." She pulled the ring off, low enough to avoid prying eyes, and passed it to Fred, who put it in a velvet box that he then slid into his pocket. "But if he says no, I'm taking it back anyway."

"I don't doubt it." Fred opened his car door and went to her side before retrieving their bags. He had been to the Main Street house during each of Evelyn's breaks from school this year, but this time was much more important.

She climbed the steps holding her handbag and a hatbox, while Fred carried a suitcase. Her trunk would require two people to lift if she didn't empty it first. Throwing open the front door, she announced loudly, "The prodigal daughter has returned for the summer!"

When no one replied, she looked left into the drawing room, where Miriam sat sedately knitting in an armchair.

"Oh, hello," Miriam said.

Evelyn rolled her eyes as Fred walked in behind her. "You can quit the charade. I saw you at the window."

Miriam put her knitting down, prepared to argue, when Vivie came bounding down the stairs, throwing herself at her older sister. "You're home, you're home, you're finally home!"

"Did you think I wouldn't be for your last summer before college?"

Vivie tilted her head toward Fred. "I didn't know *what* you two had planned." Evelyn held her at arm's length to look at her sister, a baby no longer. She had lost the last of the chubbiness that lingered around her cheeks and had bobbed her hair, framing her face elegantly.

"You look so grown up!"

"Well, I *am* eighteen."

"That's true." Evelyn pursed her lips, then turned to Fred. "Who do we know to set her up with? We'll have to go on a double date."

"No dates," Miriam said, coming to the hall where her daughters stood. "We don't break that rule anymore." The air hung heavy with the unspoken remainder of her sentence, all four of them knowing what Miriam meant.

Fred dissolved the tension as Evelyn glowered at her mother. "Mrs. Bergman, thank you so much for having me this weekend."

Miriam's countenance changed. Evelyn always brought out the worst in her. "Of course." She patted his arm fondly. "You'll stay in the boys' room. And Evelyn, you'll stay with Vivie."

Evelyn laughed finally. "Mama, you can trust me to sleep in my own room." Fred blushed.

"Vivie's room," she repeated. "Vivie, call down to the store and see if one of the stock boys can help carry Evelyn's trunk in."

"Yes, Mama," Vivie said as Miriam retreated to the kitchen.

"I wonder if she'll still make me sleep with you after we're married," Evelyn said once Miriam was gone.

Vivie's eyes lit up. "Are you—?"

"Fred is asking Papa tonight. Darling, let her see the ring."

288

"*You* aren't supposed to have seen it yet."

Both girls looked at him from a shared pair of eyes, practically blinking in unison until he sighed and pulled the box from his pocket. "Heaven help the man who ever tries to stand up to a Bergman woman," he said. "It certainly won't be me."

After Vivie admired it, Fred concealed the ring again, and Evelyn asked where their father was. "At the store. He'll be home for supper though."

"Good." Evelyn looked at her watch. They still had several hours to go. She turned to Fred. "Go get settled in Sam and Bernie's room. I'll freshen up, and then we can go to the drugstore for an ice cream. Vivie, you'll come too." She brushed her lips lightly against Fred's, then picked up her hatbox and climbed the staircase, bypassing Vivie's room for her own.

~

After supper, Fred asked Joseph quietly for a private word. The women watched them walk toward Joseph's study as they cleared the table.

"I'll be right back," Miriam said, putting down the plates she was holding and going into the kitchen.

The second she was out of the room, Evelyn bolted from the dining room and tiptoed down the hall, only to find her mother had gone the other way through the kitchen and was already listening at the study door. Miriam made a shooing motion with her hand.

"Absolutely not," Evelyn whispered, leaning against the door next to her mother. "This concerns me more than you."

Miriam was too busy trying to make out the conversation to argue. The heavy wood door muffled the voices, so neither was able to decipher much until there was a loud clink, and Joseph's voice raised in the traditional toast of *L'chaim*.

Evelyn and Miriam looked at each other, their eyes wide, then both turned and fled back to the dining room, colliding with Vivie at the doorway, which knocked all three of them to the ground, where Joseph and Fred found them.

"What happened here?" Joseph asked, taking his wife under the arms and helping her to her feet. Evelyn started to laugh, followed by Vivie and eventually even Miriam, who answered her husband in Yiddish, calling the three of them a *grupe fun yentas*, or bunch of meddlers.

Joseph looked confused, but he kissed Evelyn's cheek and told her that it was a nice night to go sit on the porch with Fred. She opened her mouth, ready to tell her parents that she had already accepted, when Fred took her arm and propelled her out the door.

"What's the big idea?"

"We're going to pretend I'm asking you for the first time now."

"Why?"

"Out of respect to your father."

"Why does everyone care so much about respecting my father? Worry about respecting me."

Fred chuckled and, taking her hand, got down on one knee. "Evelyn Bergman. I've loved—and respected—you from the day I met you. Will you marry me?"

"Aren't you going to hold the ring out?"

"No. I'm afraid you'd snatch it and run. You have to say yes first."

She smiled, then knelt in front of him. "Yes. Just like I said the first time you asked."

He reached into his pocket and pulled out the box, then opened it and put the ring on her extended finger. "Then you get this. For real this time."

Evelyn leaned in and kissed him, wrapping her arms tightly around his neck. "I do love you, Fred Gold."

~

Half-drunk on the champagne that Joseph had produced—he'd purchased it just in case, he claimed, though Vivie said it had been in the icebox since Christmas break—Evelyn went back to her own bedroom.

She sat at the vanity and smiled at her reflection before looking down at her hand again. Sighing happily, she picked up her hairbrush. But when it was halfway to her head, she set it down and went to the bookshelf in the corner. She pulled out the copy of Shakespeare's works and turned to *Romeo and Juliet*, where she had used a razor to cut a small hole in the pages. And there, right where she had left it, was the ring from Tony.

I should return it, she thought, touching the thin gold band. She pulled it from its hiding spot and held it next to the ring that now rested on her left hand. The two rings couldn't be more different and yet—

She put Tony's ring back in the book, shut it firmly, and replaced it on the shelf.

~

Negotiations began in earnest the next day.

When Evelyn came down to breakfast, Joseph was already deep in conversation with his future son-in-law, solemnly expressing how important it was that Evelyn finish college.

"—toward a house later, as long as she has a degree." Evelyn stood at the doorway a moment, trying to figure out what she was walking in on.

"Sir, she'll complete school no matter what. You don't need—"

"What are we talking about?" she asked loudly, causing both men to jump. "If it's me, shouldn't I be present?" They looked mildly shamed, but Fred stood and pulled out a chair for her. She crossed her arms, not moving.

"Don't look like that," he said. "I was just explaining to your father that you and I already planned for you to finish school. Whether we get married first or not."

Her brows went up. "Do I get a say in when that is?"

"After you finish college," Joseph said.

Evelyn cocked her head at him, and he lowered his eyes, refusing to meet her gaze. She stayed where she was for a full minute before taking her place at the table, trying to hide the smile that threatened to give her away. In marrying Fred, she would win her freedom as well.

~

Between Miriam's friends, who received telephone calls, and the party lines that meant everyone knew everyone else's business better than their own, news traveled quickly. Evelyn and Fred were congratulated by everyone they walked past on the street, causing Fred to jokingly call Evelyn the mayor.

"Hardly," she said. "Considering the town was ready to tie me to a mast and set me out toward Norman's Woe when I crashed Papa's car into that movie theater."

"Toward what?"

Evelyn felt the slightest twinge of discontent. Anyone from the north shore would have gotten the reference to the Longfellow poem "The Wreck of the Hesperus," as the rock that the fictional ship crashed into was in Gloucester. But it wasn't Fred's fault that the only famous rock he knew was Plymouth. She shook her head. "Nothing."

Fred left a few days later after making plans to bring his parents to meet hers in two weeks. He would then move into his new temporary apartment in Boston—he'd find them a bigger place when they got married. If they stayed in Boston, that was. And then come out to the cottages to be with her as many weekends as he could. Sleeping arrangements would be tight to accommodate another guest who couldn't bunk with any of the unmarried girls, but Helen and her husband had just moved to Buffalo and would only be back for a week all summer, to Miriam and Joseph's disappointment.

And Evelyn and Vivie accompanied their mother to open the cottages, as they did every year in June.

It was Miriam who found the mouse—she screamed so loudly from the other cottage that they thought she was being attacked. They both dropped what they were doing and ran out the door, down the cottage steps, across the small yard, and up the steps of the other cottage, panting by the time they found their mother standing in the kitchen, a frying pan raised above her head.

The two girls exchanged a look.

"Mama?"

"A mouse," she explained. "It ran right in front of me."

"Are you planning to cook it?" Miriam looked at Evelyn blankly, and Evelyn gestured to the frying pan.

"Don't be rude. We'll need traps. Where there's one, there are more."

"I'll go," Evelyn said. She had driven the three of them, and the keys were still in her skirt pocket.

Miriam nodded, letting Vivie lead her to the sofa and pull the sheet off for her to sit.

Evelyn went down the stairs to the car. Truth be told, she didn't want to be there until it was filled with people. The memories of the previous summer still stung like the salt of the ocean in a wound. She could have gone to the small grocery store across from the beach, but driving back to town and getting traps at her father's store would buy her more time, even if it meant more work for her sister and mother.

She hummed along with the radio, tapping her nails on the wheel as she drove, frequently admiring the gemstone on her left hand.

The spots in front of Joseph's store were all taken, so she parked a block and a half away and walked down the street.

Ten minutes later, she left the store armed with a bag full of traps and had just started up the hill when a police officer stepped out of a car in front of her.

They made eye contact and froze.

Then Tony turned down the side street and walked away.

Evelyn followed him. "Hey!" Tony turned to look at her. "You're not even going to say hello to me?"

For a moment he said nothing. "Hello."

Evelyn shook her head, emotions reaching a boiling point. "That's it?"

"What do you want me to say, Evelyn?"

She didn't know the answer. But she knew she wanted to feel that it was all right. That there was no bad blood between them. In the end, all she could say was his name.

"You can't do this to me. Not now." He reached for her left hand and held it up to her eye level. "Go back to your fiancé. The real one." He released her hand and turned to walk away, but she dropped the bag of traps and grabbed him by the shoulder.

"You have some nerve! *You* were the one who ended things! *You* were the one who left me crying on your front porch! *You* were the one who said that Fred should matter! And now—"

"I didn't mean marry him out of spite!"

"Spite? Not everything is about you."

"No, that much is obvious. There isn't room for anything to be about me when you're around."

Evelyn's breathing was shallow, her chest rising and falling rapidly. "I was willing to give up everything for you," she hissed. "Everything. And you turned me away."

"Because I loved you. Not because I didn't. Which was the right choice if you could marry someone else so quickly."

"You don't want me to marry him? Fine. Leave with me. Now."

"You don't mean that."

Her eyes were blazing. "Try me."

They stared at each other, both suddenly aware that the distance between them had shrunk. And for a moment, they each almost lost their internal struggle.

And then the moment passed.

Evelyn shook her head. "Goodbye, Tony." She picked up the traps, turned, and walked as measuredly as she could up the street, rounding the corner to return to the car, where she sat in the driver's seat, gripping the steering wheel so tightly that her knuckles turned white. *What did I almost just do?* She asked herself. *What would I have done if he had said yes?*

She didn't know the answer.

She peeled shaking hands off the wheel and fumbled in her purse for a cigarette, which took several attempts to light, before pulling away from the curb and trying to compose herself to return to her mother and sister at the cottages.

CHAPTER FORTY-EIGHT

I pretended to sleep late the following morning, hoping to avoid my grandmother's questions. It was going to be obvious that things hadn't gone the way she expected, and I knew what she would say about my reasoning; I was saying the same things to myself already.

But when I finally crept downstairs to make a cup of coffee, she barely noticed I was there.

"Everything okay?" I asked her eventually, cringing at the onslaught that was sure to follow.

She looked up distractedly from the photo album a cousin had brought her, which lay open on the kitchen table. The people in the images were in black and white, and I couldn't tell who they were from where I was standing.

"Of course, darling." She put a finger on one of the pictures. "Can you believe I was ever this young?"

I came behind her to see, mug in hand. The picture she was pointing to was taken on the beach, her sisters with her. "How old were you there?"

"Fifteen. Almost sixteen." She pointed to the rest of the women in the picture. "Vivie would have been fourteen. Margaret eighteen. Gertie twenty-two, Helen twenty-five." She touched the image of Vivie. "It was before everything. Before I met Tony. Before Vivie—" She didn't finish the sentence. Instead, she turned the page and showed me her parents, her brothers, the house on Main Street.

I wanted to look. To put faces to the names she had spent the week talking about. But not right then. I needed time alone to clear my head.

I took another sip of my coffee, then set the mug down. "I think I'm going to go for a walk."

She continued turning pages. "Enjoy."

"What are you going to do today?"

"I have lunch plans. Then we'll see."

I kissed her cheek and went out to the porch to put on my flip-flops, then began the half-mile walk to the beach.

Part of me said to go literally anywhere else. The beach ended practically at his door. But there was nowhere else to go. I wasn't confident enough to go into the woods myself with the vanishing trail, and the road into town didn't have much of a shoulder. I just had to hope he wouldn't be doing the same thing as me.

Or maybe hope he would. I didn't know.

There was a fog on the beach, which should have burned off by then but lingered, mirroring the haze of my mood. Ducking into the Inn, I grabbed a to-go iced coffee and took it with me onto the deserted beach. I walked about halfway down the beach, carrying my shoes in one hand, the coffee in the other, until I was just past the island, then I sat in the sand. I put the coffee down and wrapped my arms around my raised knees, staring out at the fog-covered waves, the island barely visible, and wondered what was wrong with me.

I knew the answer better than anyone else did. I was terrified. If I didn't let Joe in, he couldn't hurt me. If I never got comfortable, no one could pull the rug out from under me again.

But had it really been Brad who set me adrift? Or had I done that to myself?

I put my head on my knees and sat like that for a long time, trying to pinpoint the exact moment when everything had gone wrong. Was it when Brad ended things? Was it when I let my friendships with people who weren't "our" friends deteriorate? Was it even before that?

How did I go from that picture of me that Joe liked, happy and carefree, to this girl who was too scared to take a chance on someone incredible?

It was stupid. I was stupid. Sofia even told me he liked me. But what chance was there? I lived 475 miles away from him. I was still married. And there was the ghost, real or imagined, of his dead wife to contend with, even if we worked our way through unpacking my baggage. How could we possibly overcome all of that?

I didn't come up with any answers.

But when I eventually rose, my legs stiff, and pulled my phone from my pocket, more than two hours had passed. Just like the previous six months. And the six years before that. My shoulders drooped as I picked up my shoes and the barely touched coffee, the ice melted and sand stuck to the condensation on the cup, to walk back toward the cottage.

I had just turned onto the cottage's street when my phone vibrated. For a split second I let myself hope. Then I saw my grandmother's picture on the screen.

"Hey. I'm almost back."

"Jenna," she panted. My eyes widened. "I—" She was breathing heavily, and I started to run up the hill.

"I'll be there in a second. What happened? Are you okay?"

"Not—at the cottage—took the car."

I stopped short as I reached the cottage. The car was nowhere to be seen. *Oh no.*

"Where are you?"

"Salem."

298

"Salem! Okay. I—I'll get there somehow." I took a deep breath. "Are you okay?"

"I'm okay," she said finally. "I just had a little spell and don't think I should drive back."

You shouldn't have driven at all, I thought. And *a little spell* could mean anything from dizziness to a stroke or a heart attack with her. And admitting she couldn't drive back—she had to be in rough shape. I asked for exactly where she was, and she named the shops she could see around her.

Then I took another deep breath and called Joe.

He didn't answer.

I tried again. Still no answer.

Then I texted him. My grandma drove to Salem, and something happened. She took the car. Need your help. Please.

The phone rang a moment later.

"Where are you?"

"At the cottage."

"I'll be right there."

I ran inside to grab my purse, stopping to take her bottle of heart medication just in case, then jogged down the hill to meet him.

He stopped the car when he saw me, and I climbed into the passenger seat. He made a three-point turn and peeled out to get us to the main road. "Where in Salem?" I told him, and he nodded, knowing where he was going. "Is she okay?"

"She said yes. But she said she couldn't drive back, so probably not. I don't know."

He drove a little faster.

"Joe, I—"

His head shook. "Please don't."

I stopped talking, and we rode in silence the rest of the way, me chewing on my cuticles out of fear of what condition we'd find her in.

~

When we arrived, she was sitting on a bench under a store awning, clutching her handbag and looking pale. I jumped out of the car practically before it had stopped, and Joe parked illegally at the curb, then came around as well.

"What happened?" She shook her head. "Grandma, please."

"I'd like to go home now."

"Were you in an accident? Are you okay?"

"An accident? No. I'm a wonderful driver. I just—" She stopped talking, shaking her head again, then she reached into her bag and handed me the car keys. "It's down there." She pointed down the hill.

"Can you stay with her a minute?" I asked Joe. He said he would, and I went to get the car, pulling up at the curb behind Joe's. He helped her up, escorted her to the passenger side, and handed her gently inside, where I hooked her seatbelt for her.

"Can you find your way back? Or do you want to follow me?" he asked through her open door.

"I can do it."

"Okay." He patted my grandmother's shoulder. "Take care of yourself, Evelyn. Rest and fluids."

She didn't argue or make a flippant comment, which scared me further. I plugged our destination into Google Maps and pulled away, not speaking until we were on our way out of town.

"What happened?" I finally asked once we were on the road back to Hereford.

Another shake of the head. "I'm tired." She closed her eyes. I didn't think she was sleeping, but she didn't talk again until we reached the cottage. Her eyes opened when the car came to a stop, and I went to her side to help her out. She let me lead her up the stairs, where I settled her in her bedroom, then got her a glass of water.

"Do you need any of your pills?"

"No. I'm just going to lie down for a little while."

"Are—are you okay? I'm going to call Mom."

This elicited the ghost of a reaction. "What's your mother going to do? Let me lie down. I'll be . . . fine."

"You promise? You seem—"

"Jenna."

I brushed her hair back and kissed her forehead. "I'm not going anywhere. If you need anything, just call for me."

She was already asleep, snoring softly, as I tiptoed out of the room.

~

I cleaned the kitchen and used Uber Eats to order from a restaurant in town for when she woke up. Then I sat at the kitchen table, looking through the photo album she had left there. My grandfather was in the album, young and handsome, carrying my grandmother through the surf while she laughed. A picture from her wedding, Vivie standing next to her as her maid of honor. And then the album ended, blank pages left in it. I rested my head in my hands when I reached the end, saying a silent prayer that my grandmother was okay.

She reemerged around five, looking older and tired. I jumped up to guide her to a chair, then went to get her more water. "I ordered food. Are you hungry?"

"No." She took a sip of the water, then held the glass out to me. "I'm going to need something stronger than this."

"Absolutely not."

She cocked her head. "And why not?"

"Because you had a . . . spell today. And Mom said you're not supposed to drink with your medication and—"

"Oh, darling. That wasn't a physical thing."

"It—what?"

"Pour us a drink and sit. It's time you knew about Vivie."

The hairs on the back of my neck rose as I gripped the kitchen counter. Then I poured orange juice into two glasses, added vodka from the cabinet, and joined her at the table, my eyes wide as she took a sip and then began to speak.

CHAPTER FORTY-NINE

June 1955
Hereford, Massachusetts

Fred couldn't get away from his new job, so Evelyn took the car, picked Vivie up at the station, and drove the four hours from their rented house in New Rochelle to Hereford. He could take the train into the city for work, and Evelyn missed the salt smell of the air, the feel of the sand between her toes, her parents, and most of all, her youngest sister.

Vivie attended Barnard, and they should have seen each other more frequently once Fred and Evelyn moved to New Rochelle—that was one of the selling points for Evelyn to leave Boston. But it was over an hour of travel in each direction between the train and then the subway or cab from the 125th Street station. And Vivie was always so busy, not just with school, but with friends and the boyfriend who consumed more and more of her time.

George Eller was three years older than Vivie, and they met when she was a freshman and he a senior at Columbia. Vivie knew immediately he was the one for her and began a campaign that bordered on obsession to make him realize the same. For two years, they were friends. He called her "kid."

And then, one night, everything changed.

Vivie lobbied hard to stay in the city for the summer, citing Evelyn's proximity as a reason she could be trusted, offering even to live with Evelyn and Fred (without her sister's permission, though it would have been granted), but to no avail. Both Miriam and Joseph stood firm; the children all came home for the summer while in college, and Vivie would be no exception.

Evelyn was at the cottage for a week, staying up late into the night talking with her sister, the topic of George dominating the conversation. Evelyn had met him twice, both times in the city. She and Fred tried to get Vivie to bring him to dinner at the house, but it never happened. Evelyn found him handsome, arrogant, and dull in his sense of self-importance. But with his inflated ego, he treated Vivie as, if not his equal, then very close to it. And Vivie, never quite as radiant in her own sphere as Evelyn, shone fiercely in his presence. Which was all that mattered to Evelyn.

She returned to New York at the end of the week, promising to come back at the end of the month when Fred would take his vacation time. Evelyn would stay another week or two when he left, soaking in as much of Hereford as she could. If she stayed mostly at the cottage, she ran almost no risk of running into Tony—not that she had anything to say to him if she did. The book with his ring had stayed in her childhood bedroom when she married, and she sometimes went weeks without thinking of him in her new life.

But when Evelyn and Fred joined the family at the cottage, they found a house in turmoil.

"No," Miriam was saying. No one even noticed Evelyn and Fred standing in the front hall. And while Evelyn typically announced her entrance in great style with the loud flourishes reserved for royalty, the raised voices that they heard through the living room windows precluded that.

"But, Mama—"

"No. If it's what you think, he'll come to the house."

Vivie stomped her foot like a child, one hand on her hip, the other gripping the yellow paper of a Western Union telegram. "He's not *like* you with your old-country ways. Don't you see how backward you're being?"

Joseph shook his head from his armchair, a newspaper discarded next to him. "It's not backward. It's respect."

"It's *respectful* to ask *me* what *I* want, not *you* what *I* want."

"We've never met this man. How can you expect your father to give his blessing?"

"I don't care about a blessing! I'm going and that's all there is to it."

Miriam's hands went to her hips as well. "You are not."

Vivie turned to leave and saw her sister and brother-in-law standing in the doorway. "Evelyn," she sighed. "You'll talk sense into them."

Evelyn looked at her sister's wild eyes, then at the telegram clutched in her hand. Prying it gently from her fingers, Evelyn took the paper and read the message.

MEET ME TOMORROW. MADE MOST IMPORTANT DECISION OF MY LIFE. YOU HAVE TO COME. GEORGE.

There was as little doubt in Evelyn's mind as in her sister's that a proposal was imminent. And from what she had seen of George, no, he wouldn't think he needed some immigrant's blessing to marry the woman he had selected to be his wife.

"I'll try," she whispered, kissing her sister's forehead, then went into the living room to her parents, leaving Fred, who was disinclined to enter any Bergman family spat, still holding his hat in the hall.

Vivie flew up the stairs in a fit of angry tears, and Evelyn kissed her father's cheek, then flopped onto the sofa. "Oh, hello there," she said, pretending to just notice her parents. "Lovely weather we're having."

"Stop it," Miriam said.

"Hello to you too, Mama. Why yes, we *did* have a nice drive."

"You won't change my mind."

Evelyn reached up and took her mother's hand, pulling her down onto the sofa next to her. "Mama. When have I ever been able to change your mind? Papa, pssh, he's a pushover." Joseph harrumphed but didn't object. "But not you."

Miriam eyed her daughter suspiciously. "She's not going."

"What's your objection? That you haven't met him? Because I have." Fred crept gingerly into the room and perched on the arm of the chair opposite Joseph.

"You aren't her parents."

"No. But New Yorkers are a different breed, Mama. This George, he . . . Well, he thinks a lot of himself. But he treats Vivie well. He makes her happy. And he's Jewish. Vivie's not wrong—his family has been here much longer than ours. His parents don't even speak Yiddish. But, Mama, let her go. It's not like she didn't have plenty of opportunities to be alone with him all year. And he'll come here once he's asked her. Fred asked me first, after all."

Miriam and Joseph both turned to look at Fred, who grinned shamefacedly before making an excuse about needing to bring their bags in.

"It's how things are done these days. He'll come and ask Papa once they have things settled between them."

For a moment, Evelyn thought Miriam would relent. She always had a soft spot for Vivie.

And then her expression changed.

"If he wants to marry her, he'll come meet her parents. She can't marry someone we've never laid eyes on. She doesn't leave Hereford."

Evelyn took a deep breath, knowing full well she was about to anger her parents but hoping everything would work out for the best in the end. She agreed, then went upstairs to help Vivie concoct a plan.

~

Evelyn knew from experience that Miriam would be sleeping on the living room sofa to prevent Vivie from leaving. But Evelyn and Fred were in the room just over the porch this time. And if the two girls climbed onto the roof of the porch and down the side and left the car in neutral, starting it only once they were down the hill, they could get Vivie to the station for the six a.m. commuter train to Boston, where she could transfer to the New York line.

"I don't like this," Fred said. Evelyn stood at the mirror over the dresser, applying cold cream to remove her makeup.

"Well, I don't love it either, but it'll work. And they'll be fine once it's done."

"This is really how we're going to start our vacation week?"

Evelyn wiped the cream away and went to sit beside him on the bed. "Wouldn't you have climbed out a window for me?"

"Of course, but George is such a pill."

Evelyn whooped with laughter, then pushed Fred over. "I'll be back before anyone wakes up. They won't even know I took her."

He raised an eyebrow. "And how are you getting back upstairs?"

She grinned. "You think this is the first time I've climbed out and back in a window?"

He rolled on top of her. "You don't need me to make a rope out of tied-together sheets, then?"

"If it'll make you feel useful, darling, you can."

Shaking his head, he leaned in to kiss her.

~

Evelyn woke and dressed before the sun was up, then opened her bedroom door a crack for Vivie, who slipped silently inside, a small valise in her hand. "Be careful," Fred murmured sleepily. Evelyn kissed his forehead, saying she would be back before he knew it. And the two girls went out the window to the ground below, Evelyn climbing down onto the porch's roof, then the railing, then taking the bag that Vivie handed her before Vivie climbed down as well. They both froze momentarily, listening for any noise in the house, but there was none.

Evelyn put the valise in the back before slipping the car into neutral, and together they pushed it gently, then hopped in, clutching the doors closed but unlatched to avoid making any sound. Once they were far enough away, they shut their doors, and Evelyn started the car, putting it into gear and turning at the end of the street.

Vivie could barely sit still. "D'you think he'll want to elope right away? Or want a big wedding? His family has money—they'd want a wedding. But he doesn't always do what his family wants. Evelyn, I could be married *tonight*."

"Is that what you want?"

"Goodness. I hadn't even thought about it." She sat in contemplation for approximately five seconds. "Honestly, I wouldn't mind. Mama and Papa would, of course. But they've had six other weddings. Let this one be just mine."

"No matron of honor?"

"I'll send a telegram either way. You'll be the first to know the news."

"I'm teasing, darling." Evelyn reached out and took her sister's hand, bringing it to her lips. "Be happy."

"I am."

Evelyn nodded and suppressed a yawn as she pulled into the station. "I'll wait for the train with you," she said, parking the car.

"I'm fine. Go back before everyone wakes up."

Evelyn glanced at her watch. It was five forty. She'd be cutting it close, as the earliest risers among the cottage residents began stirring between six and six thirty. But this was Vivie. "Nonsense."

They walked toward the entrance of the same station their father had arrived at after falling asleep on the train so many years earlier. They were nearly there when two male figures rose from a bench in the darkness and moved to block their path.

Vivie gripped Evelyn's arm, and Evelyn instinctively reached for her hat pin, which she did not have.

Then one of them spoke. "Awfully early for you two to be out and about."

"Bernie," Evelyn breathed. "You scared us." She looked to his left at Sam. "What are you doing here?"

"Bringing Vivie home," Bernie said.

Evelyn felt a chill. Her mother had seen right through her agreement the night before. She wasn't sleeping in the living room at all. They could have walked out the front door.

"I'm not a child," Vivie said shrilly.

"Mama said not to let you on that train." There was a mildly apologetic note in Sam's voice.

"You two can't be serious," Evelyn said. "This is ridiculous. She's twenty-one, for heaven's sake!"

"Come with us," Bernie said. "I'm tired and want to get some sleep. Be a good girl now."

Vivie glanced at Evelyn, then tried to run past her brothers, but Bernie was quicker and caught her arm.

She fought back, hitting him in the stomach, but it was no use. Sam picked her up and carried her over his shoulder, as she kicked and yelled that she would never forgive any of them. He reached Bernie's car, which he forced her into like a cat into a bath, while Bernie held off Evelyn, who fought to try to get to her sister.

"You get on home too," Bernie called to Evelyn as he started the car. Evelyn stood on the sidewalk breathing heavily, her shoulders drooping.

Everyone was awake when Evelyn returned to the cottage, the residents of both houses crammed into the one. The murmured conversations ceased when she walked in, and everyone turned to stare. Fred took two steps toward her, but Evelyn could hear Vivie sobbing from upstairs, so she bypassed her family and went to her sister, knocking at the locked door and asking to be let in.

When the door didn't open, Evelyn went to her own room, found a hairpin, and proceeded to pick the lock. Vivie didn't even look up as Evelyn lay down on the bed beside her, where she stroked her sister's hair.

Eventually Vivie's weeping calmed enough for speech. "I'll never forgive them for this," she said hoarsely between hiccups.

"Of course you will." Evelyn wiped her sister's tears with her thumbs. "He'll come here because he'll have to see you, and once you have this whole thing tied up in a pretty little knot, you'll be able to laugh about it."

"No. I won't forgive Mama."

"I said the same thing," Evelyn reminded her. "But, darling, look at how things worked out." She touched her stomach instinctively. No one knew yet. Not even Fred. And she wasn't *really* sure. But she'd never been this late before either.

"You think he'll come?" Vivie's voice was barely a whisper.

"I know he will." She paused. "Okay, he might be annoyed you didn't come and make you wait a week or two because he thinks if he beckons, even the Messiah himself should show. But then he'll come."

Vivie started to cry again.

"Oh, darling, I was joking. He'll come. I promise. Just give him a little time. Men get so wounded when they don't get their way. But you tell me what to say, and I'll send a telegram so he knows you weren't standing him up."

Having this project settled her, and Vivie went through four drafts before handing Evelyn a paper with a message.

"Come down to breakfast?"

"No. I couldn't eat. And I want nothing to do with them."

Famished, Evelyn left her sister and went to face her mother's wrath in exchange for some eggs, toast, and coffee.

～

Evelyn dutifully went to the Western Union office and sent George the telegram after breakfast, then returned to the cottage, where Vivie was still locked in her room. Remembering her own similar behavior, she whispered a quiet prayer that George would respond soon. While she had no doubt that her sister would wind up with as happy a resolution as she herself had, she wanted Vivie's suffering to be brief.

When there was no reply, Vivie wrote a letter, filling pages and pages with her looping script.

Another week passed. Fred returned to New York, and Vivie moved into Evelyn's room, her sister rubbing her back as she sobbed each night.

When they reached the day Evelyn was due to leave, she called Fred to explain she couldn't come home yet. He agreed, albeit with a sigh, that she should stay another week to comfort Vivie. When she did return to New Rochelle, it would have to be via train, as Miriam insisted Fred take his car with him or Evelyn could not stay. She knew her daughters, and, with a car at their disposal, the two would have made a nighttime escape to New York.

Finally, a letter arrived that Vivie clutched to her chest before running upstairs to read. She held it out wordlessly when Evelyn came to their room a few minutes later, sitting dry-eyed on the bed.

It was a single sheet, in block letters.

Viviest,

There'll be more opportunities. Enjoy your summer.

—George

"Viviest?" Evelyn asked.

"His nickname for me. As in Vivie dearest."

"The *more opportunities* part sounds promising."

"The *Enjoy your summer* does not."

Evelyn read the letter again. "No. But I did warn you he would need to nurse that bruised ego a bit."

"But now I need to wait almost two more months? 'Enjoy your summer'? Evelyn, this is torture."

Vivie buried her face in her hands, and, free from her sister's sight, Evelyn shook her head. George was clearly punishing her for ruining his plans. But what was the best course of action to advise? Play it cool or try to make him jealous? Either could backfire with a temperament like George's. It was so much simpler with someone like Fred, who didn't make you play games to find out where you stood.

Well, maybe that straightforward approach was what was best here.

"Grab some paper," she told her sister. "We're writing him another letter."

"Dear George," she dictated. "Wait, do you have a pet name for him too?" Vivie colored. "I don't want to know. Just use it." Vivie wrote out a salutation. "I do wish I could see you sooner than the end of August, but my mother is adamant that I not venture into the big, bad city to meet strange men. And while I know you're not so strange, she, unfortunately, has not had the pleasure of your acquaintance, which is why she hired my brothers to kidnap me from the train station. If you wanted to come to Hereford for a day or two on the beach, we could rectify that situation. But if not, I suppose I'll see you when the fall term begins."

"Evelyn, no one talks like that."

She leveled a gaze at her sister. "You see, that right there is your problem. Go find yourself a man who would laugh at that letter, or it's your own fault when you wind up married to the fuddiest duddy there is."

Vivie shook her head. "I've got the gist of it."

Evelyn peeked over her sister's shoulder, curiosity winning out. "Georgeous?" She made a retching noise.

And for the first time since receiving George's telegram, Vivie smiled.

~

Evelyn went back home a few days later, promising to return in a month's time.

She came back a week early, however, driving at breakneck speed to deliver the news she had read in the *Times* that morning before anyone else could tell her sister what had happened. For the first time in her life, she didn't inhale deeply to take in the smell of home as she crossed the bridge into Hereford. She just pressed her foot further toward the floor, dreading the news she had to tell.

Five hours after she had let the newspaper fall to the kitchen table, her mouth open, Evelyn pulled to a stop in front of the cottage, her waist perhaps a fraction thicker than it had been when she left, but not noticeable to anyone else. She left her bag in the car and ran up the stairs.

"Vivie?" she called out.

"Evelyn?" Miriam's voice came from the kitchen. "What are you doing here?"

"Where's Vivie?"

"At the beach with the children."

Evelyn turned and left the house, her mother calling after her. "What's wrong? What's happened?"

She stopped and took a deep breath. This was her mother's news as well; Vivie would hold her responsible. She pulled the page of newsprint from her pocket and handed it to her mother, who read it, then put a hand to her heart.

"But—"

"I know."

"*Kinehora*," her mother said, warding off the evil eye, then sinking into one of the wicker porch chairs.

"I have to go to her."

Miriam grabbed her daughter's arm. "Don't. She's been happy. Let it wait."

The phone rang from inside the house. "That'll be one of her friends from the city. There's no waiting, Mama. Either I tell her or someone one else does. This wasn't in some Yiddish rag. It's the *New York Times* wedding announcements."

Miriam nodded weakly, and Evelyn drove down to the beach, where she double-parked outside the Inn and crossed the dune path to find her sister, who was playing catch with the various nieces and nephews in the surf.

"Evelyn!" Donna screamed in delight. "It's Evelyn."

A swarm of wet children came running to embrace her, her older siblings turning their heads at the migration but remaining in the chairs where they sat together with their spouses, smoking and enjoying their break from parenting.

Vivie pushed through the children and threw her arms around Evelyn's neck. "Why didn't you tell us you were coming?" Then she pulled back and looked at her sister's face.

"Let's go back to the cottage."

"Whatever for?"

"Vivie." Evelyn was pale, her fingers clenching and unclenching nervously.

Vivie turned and grabbed her towel, wrapping it around her waist before taking her sister's arm and shooing the children back toward their parents.

"Is it Fred? What did he do?"

Evelyn waited until they were back at the car and made her sister get inside. "It's not Fred. It's George."

"George?"

"Vivie—he—" She took a deep breath. "George married someone else. Yesterday."

"That's impossible." Vivie's tone was quiet, but confident.

Evelyn pulled the clipping from her pocket and handed it to her sister, who read it. "I came right away. I read it this morning, and I was in the car ten minutes later. I—oh, Vivie, I don't know what to say."

"Take me back to the cottage, please," Vivie said quietly.

CHAPTER FIFTY

My grandmother stopped talking. She took a sip of her screwdriver, then shook her head. "I wish I still smoked."

"He just . . . married someone else?"

She nodded. "We didn't know if he'd known her before or if he met her after Vivie didn't go to the city. The newspaper clipping had a quote about not wanting to wait when you knew it was right."

"And Vivie?"

"That night, she couldn't sleep and went out for a walk. It started to rain, and she slipped on the wet rocks. They found her the next morning. It was horrible, but an accident." She tilted her head. "At least, that's the story Papa and I told everyone."

"What?"

She took another sip and began again.

CHAPTER
FIFTY-ONE

July 1955
Hereford, Massachusetts

Vivie went straight to her room, admitting no one until bedtime, when Evelyn threatened to pick the lock again. Evelyn was tired and nauseous and wanted nothing more than to lie in bed and let her family spoil her. But Vivie mattered more.

Evelyn sat on the bed, and Vivie resumed the frantic pacing that everyone had heard, glancing uneasily at the ceiling of the living room as they sat after dinner. "You should sleep."

Vivie looked at her, eyes wild. "Is that what you did? When she ruined your life?"

She opened her mouth to make a flippant comment about how she did, actually, but something in her chest tightened. Evelyn took a deep breath, then another, before she spoke. "Vivie." Her voice was quiet. "Mama—" She stopped again, unable to say that their mother had been right or wrong in what she had done. Because, at least in Evelyn's case, she had been both. "Mama doesn't live in the world we live in.

She—it's like . . . She's a fish. And you're blaming her for not knowing how to breathe air."

"And in the meantime, she's drowning me trying to force me into her world."

"You're drowning yourself. She may have pushed you under, but, Vivie, do you really *want* a man who would marry someone else this quickly? You deserve someone who will worship you. And that was never George."

"You don't know what George was! You and Fred sat there judging him for not being like you, but we were happy being like us. And you couldn't understand that. Not everyone is like you and can just turn off their feelings for one person, snap their fingers, and have someone better appear."

Evelyn sat up straighter, stung, but said nothing. Vivie turned, poised to say more, but when she saw her sister's face, her shoulders slumped, and she sat beside her on the bed. "I didn't—I'm—"

"I understand."

Vivie nodded and stood, resuming her path across the room and back.

Evelyn's eyelids threatened to close at any moment. She remembered her older sisters complaining about how drained they were in early pregnancy, but she had never imagined this feeling of absolute exhaustion that weighed her limbs down. "I need to go to sleep. I drove up here today and all." Vivie continued walking. Had she been crying, Evelyn would have made more of an effort, but the pacing seemed a good sign. She was angry. And anger would give way to acceptance. "Will you get in bed? Or should I go sleep in Margaret's room?"

Vivie shook her head. "I can't."

Evelyn rose from the bed and went toward the door. Just as she was about to open it, Vivie hugged her, then kissed her fiercely on the cheek. "I love you."

Evelyn held her sister close. "I love you too. Please go to sleep soon."

Vivie said she would try, and Evelyn went to Margaret's room, falling asleep as soon as her head hit the pillow.

~

Evelyn woke to the sound of rain. She rolled over to go back to sleep, but Margaret was snoring. She could tolerate it in Fred, but not in her sister. And so, with a sigh, Evelyn sat up, swung her feet over the edge of the bed, and padded barefoot down the hall to Vivie's room. The curtains were drawn and the sliver of deep gray dawn that peeked around the edges failed to illuminate the bed. Evelyn walked slowly, a hand out unnecessarily as she knew each inch of the room, until she reached the bed, where she lay down to snuggle into her sister.

Except Vivie wasn't there. Evelyn patted around the bed, her eyes snapping open when she touched a piece of paper. She reached to turn on the nightstand lamp, almost knocking it over in the process, her eyes adjusting slowly to the paper in front of her, which fluttered to the bed after she read it, her hand clasped to her mouth.

She went down the stairs swiftly in the darkness, toward her parents' room, the paper clutched tightly in her hand, but there was a light in the kitchen. *Vivie,* she thought in relief, bursting through the doorway.

But it wasn't Vivie.

Her father sat at the kitchen table, drinking a cup of coffee. "You're up early," he said.

Evelyn sank to the floor at his feet. "Oh, Papa," she sobbed.

"What's this? What's wrong?"

"Vivie—"

"Vivie will be fine. You were."

Evelyn looked up at him, tears pouring down her face. "Papa, she's gone."

He stood. "She went to New York? After—?"

319

"No. Papa, she left a note. She—" She couldn't say the words, holding the paper out to her father, who took it, his dark complexion turning ashen as he read.

"No."

"We have to call the police—"

Joseph wiped his brow, then rose and went to the kitchen sink, pulling a book of matches from his pocket. He struck one and lit a corner of the letter as Evelyn watched, horrified.

"What are you doing?"

He waited until the letter was gone before turning back to her. He had never looked old to Evelyn until that moment. "We will tell the police she is missing. But whatever happened, it was an accident."

Evelyn's mouth dropped open, her eyes narrowed in pain. "That's what you care about? People knowing?"

Joseph crossed to her and gripped her arms tightly. "Just one person. Don't you understand? This will destroy your mother."

"She deserves it," Evelyn said bitterly, her own pain too great to worry about her mother's. "She's not innocent."

Her father's shoulders fell, and Evelyn saw the tears in his eyes. "Please, Evelyn. If you won't for her, then for me. We have to make them believe it was an accident. I—I can't lose her too." He released her arms and collapsed to the kitchen table, his body wracked with silent sobs that Evelyn watched with alarmed fascination. She had never seen a grown man cry, let alone her father.

Evelyn stood, fighting her own grief as she realized what she needed to do for her father's sake. "Don't call the police yet. You need—you need to pretend you don't know. We'll find that she's missing together. When I get back."

"Where are you going?"

"To see someone who can help us." Evelyn tiptoed out of the kitchen, tossed a slicker that hung on a hook by the front door over her nightgown, and slipped silently down the cottage steps in the misty rain.

For an interminable moment, she stood at the edge of the road, peering through the trees and scanning the bluffs, hoping against hope that her sister would still be standing there.

But there was no one.

Wiping her eyes with the back of her hand, she climbed into the car and looked at her reflection in the rearview mirror. *Well,* she thought grimly, *he won't think I'm there to win him back.* She put the car in drive, her heart pounding, and went to the only person who could help her.

CHAPTER
FIFTY-TWO

"Tony," I breathed, my eyes wide.

"He was a lieutenant by then. He rose quickly."

"And he . . . ?"

She smiled wryly at me. "Am I telling this story, or are you?"

CHAPTER FIFTY-THREE

July 1955
Hereford, Massachusetts

She sat for a moment behind the wheel, working up the courage to go pound on the door until someone told her where to find him. But then Tony walked out, peering up at the sky before pulling on his uniform hat.

Evelyn moved quickly, stepping out of the car and calling his name. He whirled around in surprise at her voice.

"What do you want, Ev . . ." He trailed off when he saw her face, his tone changing immediately. "What happened?"

Evelyn swallowed bravely, but her knees buckled, and Tony raced to catch her before she hit the pavement.

She woke up on the living room sofa, a cool, damp cloth across her forehead. She studied the unfamiliar ceiling for a moment before she remembered where she must be and why she was there. Turning her head, she saw Tony, who sat on the floor next to her, and she scrambled to sit up.

"Easy," he said, and her heart broke all over again. She wished that she had found the words to explain to Vivie that it was possible to love two different people in entirely different ways without one being more or less than the other.

But what was done was done. And it was safer to stick to why she was there.

"I need your help," she said dully.

"What have you done now?" He was almost smiling. Under any other circumstances, she would have pretended to bristle at that, which he knew.

"I can't explain it all—but Vivie—" A tear slipped down her cheek, and she took a breath to compose herself. "Vivie wasn't there when I woke up. And she—she left a note. Papa is going to call the station when I get home and say she's missing. But it—Tony, it has to be an accident."

There was genuine pain in his face as he realized what Vivie had done. But the rest—"I don't understand."

"My mother can't know it wasn't an accident. Papa—Papa will be okay as long as Mama doesn't know."

Tony stared at her. "You want me to risk my career . . . for your parents? The people who took everything from me?"

Evelyn wanted to shake him and say that he took everything from himself. But it would solve nothing to rehash that argument. Instead, she took his hands. "No. I want you to do it for me."

He looked into her eyes for a long moment, then exhaled audibly. "Destroy the note."

"We already did."

"Do you know where to look?"

"The water. Below the bluffs by the cottage."

"And in a storm at night." He rubbed at a muscle in his neck, then swore before looking back at Evelyn. "Why did she do it?"

Evelyn bit her lower lip. "She fell in love. And he—he married someone else."

Tony looked back at her, the ice of his gaze ripping off another chunk of what was left inside her chest.

"Tony, I—"

But he wouldn't let her finish. "Go back to the cottage. Call the station. I'll try."

She rose, and Tony held out an arm to steady her, but she didn't need it. "Thank you."

He nodded curtly, and she returned to her car, feeling as if she had aged a hundred years since the previous morning when she'd lazily scanned the newspaper over a cup of coffee and plate of eggs.

CHAPTER
FIFTY-FOUR

"And he did?"

She nodded. "No one else ever knew. Not my brothers or sisters. Not my mother. They all died thinking Vivie slipped, which was what the police determined officially."

"Did you know . . ." I trailed off. "Were there any clues she would do something like that?"

My grandmother sighed heavily. "Looking at it now, maybe. Then, no one talked about those things. I think depression ran on my mother's side. It was that darkness my father was afraid of if she knew the truth. That's why I went to Tony."

I sat in stunned silence, wondering at this man, whom I still hadn't met, who loved my grandmother enough to do something like that and then keep the secret of it. Brad hadn't loved me enough to stay faithful. Or even take out the trash without me asking four times, for that matter.

I looked at my grandmother. She had removed her makeup after her nap, which was why she looked older, and the telling of this story had left her tired.

Which reminded me—

"What happened today?"

She held out her empty glass. "I'm going to need another first."

"I'm not pouring you another. You're not supposed to be drinking."

"Then I'm not telling you anything."

Another drink was unlikely to kill her. And I had to know. So I got her another and topped off my own.

"I had lunch with George," she said casually, taking a sip of the new drink.

I knocked my glass over, the drink spilling across the table as I scrambled for napkins. "You *what*?"

"Well, of course, darling. That's why we're in Hereford this week."

I stared at her again, my mouth moving silently as I tried, unsuccessfully, to put all of the pieces together.

"I don't understand."

"He added me on Facebook."

Her Facebook profile picture was her engagement picture with my grandfather cropped out of it, meaning she was twenty at the time. My cousin Lily had set it up for her. She said at the time it was so her old boyfriends could find her, which we thought was a joke, but apparently wasn't because Vivie's boyfriend had. "He was going to be in Boston for the week and asked if I wanted to have lunch if I ever still came up here."

"Why would you meet him? After—"

"I had questions," she said. "I wanted to know exactly why he wanted Vivie to go to New York if he could just up and marry someone else less than two months later."

"And—?" I held my breath.

She shook her head. "That *bastard* says, 'I wanted her to meet my Phyllis. They would have been such friends.'"

"Phyllis is his wife?"

My grandmother nodded and took another long drink.

"He was never going to propose."

"No."

"And if she had gone . . ."

She shrugged. "Maybe it wouldn't have changed anything. But she believed if she'd gone . . ." She sighed heavily. "She said in the note that she hoped our mother would be happy now. If she'd known going to New York wouldn't have made a difference, I think she would have spent the summer miserable and then been okay. But he never cared about anyone but himself. And he never realized her death had anything to do with him."

"Did you tell him?"

"Haven't you been listening? No one knows but you and Tony."

I was silent again, marveling at her—what was the word she would use? *Chutzpah.*

"What did you say when he said that?"

"I didn't say anything. I got up and I walked out." She held up her glass at me, the liquid level already low again. "I *should* have thrown my drink in his face. Let that be a lesson to you. You get so few opportunities in life to throw a drink. Take them."

Neither of us said anything for several minutes as we processed what we had learned. Then her hand shot out and encircled my wrist, gripping it tightly.

"You can't let it break you. Things don't work out the way you want sometimes, but you have to keep going."

I couldn't breathe. She wasn't talking about Vivie anymore.

When she released my wrist, I rubbed it, still feeling the fire of her grasp. She stood with great effort and put a hand on my shoulder. "I'm going to bed. It's been a long day." Putting her hand under my chin, she turned my head, so I was forced to look at her. "I'm okay. I promise." She tilted her head toward the door, winked at me, then shuffled slowly to her bedroom.

The door shut behind her, and I jumped at the sound, my mind reeling with this new information.

You can't let it break you.

No. I was never going to be the girl who threw herself into the sea, though I shuddered at the thought of how close those bluffs were to where I sat right now. But the last six months and then Joe—

I jumped up, my chair almost tipping from the force, grabbed my purse and keys from the table by the front door, pausing only long enough to slide on the flip-flops on the porch, and ran down the steps to the car.

In the six minutes it took to reach Joe's house, I came no closer to figuring out what I was going to say. All I could hear was my heartbeat thudding in my ears, my breath shallow and rapid. I climbed his front steps and pounded on the door, Jax barking at the sudden noise.

He opened the door and crossed his tanned arms, leaning against the frame. "What do you want, Jenna?"

I brushed a piece of hair behind my ear and tugged on the sleeve of my sweatshirt, realizing what a mess I was in yoga shorts and an old University of Maryland hoodie that had seen better days.

But—

"You," I blurted out.

He shook his head. "What was it you said? You weren't looking for a one-night stand? Well, I'm not either."

"No, that's not—" I took a deep breath and looked at him, his eyes narrow and guarded, and I almost gave up. But then what? Go home and keep hiding so I wouldn't have to face the possibility of failure again?

No.

"I got scared."

He hesitated before responding. "And you're not scared anymore?"

"I'm terrified! I'm scared you're going to say that no, I missed my chance. I'm scared you're going to realize you don't actually like me. I'm scared I'm going to leave in a few days, and that this is going to be too hard." I blinked, then brought my eyes to his. "But I'm more scared of knowing I didn't try."

We looked at each other for a long minute, neither of us moving. Then his posture relaxed, and he took my arm, pulled me inside, and shut the door, then pressed me up against it, his mouth on mine, one hand in my hair, the other on my waist, traveling upward. I shifted my weight, allowing him to move closer, wanting to touch every inch of him, when I felt—

"Jax!" We both looked down. She had pushed her way between his legs, her nose nuzzling into my crotch.

I started to laugh as Joe tried to step over her without falling, and I took her face in my hands. "Sorry, girl. I think I'm stealing your bed tonight."

Joe laughed and shook his head. "Do you want a drink?"

I said I would love one and followed him into the kitchen, where he poured two glasses of wine from the same bottle as the night before. I was leaning against the kitchen island, musing how it felt like so much longer than just a day ago. Joe was leaning against the opposite counter, watching me.

"Where are you right now?" he asked.

I set my glass down and held out a hand to him. "Right here."

He didn't need another invitation. He picked me up and sat me on the island, our faces level as he kissed me hungrily. I wrapped my legs around his waist, and he groaned softly. I felt one of his hands under my sweatshirt at my back, and it was too much material between us, so I reached down to remove it, only breaking the kiss long enough to get my head out of the hoodie, then tugged at his shirt as well until he pulled it off and reached around to unhook my bra.

Leaning over me, he pushed gently until I was lying on the island, and I ran my fingers through his hair as he kissed my neck, my body on fire at his touch. His thumbs hooked into the waistband of my shorts, and he slid them down over my thighs before discarding them on the floor. His head moved lower, and he looked up at my sharp intake of breath.

Our eyes met, and he shook his head slightly.

"What?"

His lips spread in a slow smile that absolutely melted me. "You're beautiful," he said, moving up to kiss me again, slower this time.

Then he stopped abruptly and looked to his right. I turned my head to see Jax's face and paws at the edge of the island as she stood on her hind legs, her tongue lolling out as she watched us.

"What is *wrong* with her?" he asked.

I sat up and brushed my lips against his. "Bedroom?"

He nodded and offered me a hand as I jumped down from the island.

I glanced back at him over my shoulder as I walked out of the kitchen. "Please tell me you have condoms."

"Don't you mean prophylactics?"

I let out a shriek of laughter as he grabbed me around the waist and planted a kiss on the side of my neck, and whispered that yes, he did.

"Good," I said as he shut the door, keeping Jax outside, and the two of us fell, still laughing, onto the bed together.

~

I smiled in the darkness after, pillowed in the crook of Joe's arm as he drowsily ran his fingers up and down from my belly button to my collarbone. Just that light touch felt like it was setting off a chain reaction to every nerve ending in my body.

I turned to face him, pressing my body against his side, and he looked down at me. "Do I get to hear the bad date story yet?"

I made a face. "Do you *want* to?"

"Desperately."

I shook my head. "Okay, so she tells me she's fixing me up with this guy whose grandma she knows, and I agree to go. And we meet at a restaurant, and he seems normal and all, and we wind up going back to his place to watch a movie."

"How old were you?"

"Maybe nineteen?"

"So you knew what *watch a movie* meant?"

"No, I mean, yes—normally. But we were actually just watching the movie. And then I looked down and—" I stopped talking.

"And?"

"It was just . . . out."

"What was—oh!"

"Yeah. Like this guy hadn't even kissed me. And it was just out."

"What did you do?"

"I said I had to go home, and I left! But like . . . What did my grandma tell his grandma about me if he thought *that* was appropriate on a first date fixup?"

Joe laughed. "I guess the bar was set pretty low for me, then."

I looked up at him. "It could have been set at the moon. You still would have passed it."

He held my gaze for a long moment, and I stopped breathing, wondering if I had said too much. Then he rolled on top of me, kissing me slowly, pressing his body deliciously into mine.

"Stay the night?" he whispered. I nodded as he kissed me again.

CHAPTER
FIFTY-FIVE

July 1955
Hereford, Massachusetts

Evelyn stood dry eyed at the funeral, her hand cool in Fred's despite the humidity of the summer day. The cemetery was farther inland, and the day was hot, the sun merciless against their black clothes. She hadn't cried when the police came to the door, first to get information from a panicked Miriam, who was convinced Vivie had run off to New York, and a stoic Joseph, who was a terrible actor. Nor had she when they returned a couple of hours later with the news that left her mother weeping on the floor. She had slipped quietly to the room she shared most recently with her sister and sat on the edge of the bed, willing the tears to bring some sort of release. But they didn't come.

She and her father had hardly spoken in the two days since. The funeral was arranged quickly, as Jewish custom dictated that the deceased be buried as soon as possible. Fred took the train up that day, the rest of the family arriving with their children, crowding the Main Street house, Bernie's house in town, and both cottages.

Numbly, she recited the Mourner's Kaddish from memory, murmuring the Hebrew words along with her family through a mouth that felt like it was full of cotton. The casket was lowered into the ground, and the rabbi handed a small spade to Joseph, who, crying openly, took it and shoveled a small pile of dirt into the grave, the sound making Evelyn wince.

I can't do it, she thought, taking an involuntary step backward. Fred looked over and wrapped his arm around her. She wanted to shake him off and run away. Her breathing intensified as her mother's shovelful of dirt made the same muffled thud.

"You don't have to do it," Fred whispered. "It's okay. Not everyone does."

Evelyn swallowed dryly. "It's a mitzvah," she whispered back. "It's the last thing I can do for her."

He squeezed her briefly and then released her as she took her turn to scoop a small pile of dirt to cover her sister.

She stood at the edge of the grave holding the spade of soil and looked down at the plain pine box that already had a fine layer of earth scattered over it. *Oh Vivie,* she thought. *I'll never stop missing you.* She let the dirt fall and stepped back quickly, handing the shovel to Margaret, who was bawling. But still Evelyn could not cry.

Returning to Fred, she looked around the mourners, trying to distract herself from the muffled thumps as more clods hit first the wood and then the previous dirt. Ruthie was there, of course. And Vivie's friends from school. Some had come from New York, news traveling quickly because Evelyn had called Vivie's roommate. There was no sign of George—her sisters had questioned if he would come and what they would do if he did. But Evelyn knew he wouldn't be there.

Ruthie's father sat down, fanning himself, and Evelyn's eyes widened. Tony stood behind him. Their eyes met across the grave, and they held each other's gaze for a long time, each trying to communicate so many of the things left unsaid through the air.

If Fred noticed, he said nothing.

Then the funeral was over, and the mourners moved to the Main Street house to sit shiva for the customary seven days. The mirrors were covered, the chairs low, armbands available to rend, a pitcher of water at the door to wash before entering. And platters upon platters of food brought by a seemingly endless supply of neighbors.

"I wish we didn't have to do this," Gertie said quietly as she sat with Helen, Margaret, who was still crying, and Evelyn, who still hadn't. "It should be just us. Not the whole town."

Evelyn looked around the room, a plate of food untouched on her lap. Fred was in the other room with Bernie, Sam, and her sisters' husbands, all ostensibly smoking, but actually drinking. She didn't *think* Tony would come to the house for shiva, but she hadn't expected him at the funeral either.

Instinctively she placed a hand on her stomach. She knew she should eat. But everything felt like rubber in her mouth. And there was the distinct chance she would bring back up anything she ate anyway. She speared a small piece of Mrs. Rosen's sweet noodle kugel and took a tentative bite before setting the plate aside.

But when she heard her father's raised voice from the front hall, Evelyn was up in a flash, knowing immediately what it meant. Her sisters and the visitors stared after her as she dashed out of the room and skidded to a stop in the hall.

"You cannot be here," Joseph said as Tony stood in the doorway.

Tony looked apologetically at Evelyn. "I just wanted to pay my respects," he said quietly to Joseph. "I'm sorry to have bothered you." He turned and went down the front steps.

Evelyn started to follow, but Joseph grabbed her arm. "Don't you have any honor? Your husband is inside."

She stared at her father, her chest heaving in anger. "Me? You don't even realize, do you?" She heard footsteps coming down the hall, so she pulled her father forcibly onto the porch, then shut the heavy oak door behind them. "*Tony* is the reason people think it was an accident. He risked everything because I asked him to. After what you did, he still helped." She shook her head, barely keeping her rage in check. "So don't you dare lecture me about honor."

And with that, she flung her father's hand off her arm, leaving him gaping at her, deathly pale, as she ran down the stairs following Tony, calling his name as she neared him. He turned around, and she threw herself into his arms, the tears coming at last.

"I'm sorry. I'm so, so sorry," she said, weeping, into his shirt. He held her as the sobs shook her body, rubbing her back softly until she calmed enough to look at him.

"I'm sorry too."

"We made such a mess of things, didn't we?"

He brushed a piece of hair back from her face. "We did. But it's our mess, Evelyn. Not theirs." He used his thumbs to wipe her tears away. "Do you love him?"

For a split second, she wondered what would happen if she lied and said no. Would he—but no. It didn't matter now because it couldn't. And she was too bone tired to lie.

"Yes. But I love you too."

Tony took a deep breath, then kissed her forehead, his lips lingering there for a long moment. "Then go back. Because I love you."

Another tear slipped down her cheek as she savored being in his arms for the last time before he released her. They exchanged one final look before Evelyn turned and walked back up the hill to her parents' house.

CHAPTER FIFTY-SIX

I woke to muted sunlight coming through the windows, a curtain fluttering delicately in the ocean breeze. I smiled as I remembered where I was, and I rolled over to snuggle into Joe.

Instead, I got a dog tail to the face.

"Jax," I groaned as she licked my arm, her tail wagging faster with happiness.

It took him sitting up and using both arms, but he moved her to the end of the bed as I wiped the slobber away, and he slid into her spot beside me. "Hi." He was leaning on an elbow, his hair mussed, dark stubble across his jaw and chin, smiling down at me. I wished I could freeze that moment in a photograph, capturing it the way he could, to save it and pull back out any time I wanted to feel this way.

"Hey."

"Do you want some breakfast? Or do you need to get back?"

I sat up. I had completely forgotten about the series of events that led me to Joe's house. "What time is it?"

He checked the clock on his nightstand. "A little after nine."

"I should just call and make sure she's okay."

Concern crossed his face as well. "Of course."

I went to get out of bed, then remembered my clothes were all in the kitchen. "Can I borrow a shirt?"

He tried to suppress a smile as he went to the dresser and grabbed one. "Any objection to the Red Sox?"

I wrinkled my nose. "Yes, but we'll discuss that one later."

He tossed me the shirt, and I pulled it on as he slid on a pair of boxers and shorts, then I went to get my phone from the kitchen while he took Jax outside.

There were no missed calls, which wasn't necessarily a good sign or a bad one.

I pulled up her contact and pressed the icon to call her. There was no answer. I tried again immediately but got the same result. I tried texting her, then called again, panic setting in.

When Joe came back with Jax, I was pulling on my shorts. "How's Ev . . ." He trailed off, looking at my face. "Let me grab a shirt. I'm coming with you."

I didn't argue, handing him the keys to my grandmother's car. I was too worried to drive.

I shouldn't have left, I thought as Joe sped across the road parallel to the beach. I glanced at him, grateful that he was with me to help with whatever we might find. *I shouldn't have spent the night.*

Joe parked the car at an angle, and we both jumped out as soon as the engine was off and ran up the stairs together. The door was unlocked. "Grandma?" I called loudly from the doorway as we raced through the hall to the kitchen, both of us stopping short and almost falling over each other at what we saw.

My grandmother was in a robe at the table, which was piled high with breakfast. Next to her sat an older man with white hair, wearing an undershirt. He turned to look at us, and I saw the shared nose before anyone spoke.

My mouth dropped open.

"Uncle Tony?" Joe asked, his eyes wide.

"Good morning," my grandmother said. "I wasn't expecting you, but there's enough breakfast if you're hungry."

I looked from her robe to his undershirt and back to her face, then held a hand to my mouth.

"Grandma!"

She mirrored my tone. "Jenna!" Then she turned to Tony, who didn't quite seem to know where to look, and put a hand on his arm. "Darling, I want you to meet my granddaughter, Jenna. Jenna, this is Tony."

He mumbled something that sounded like *Nice to meet you.*

I nodded, still too stunned to talk to him. He didn't have shoes on.

Joe cleared his throat. "Well, this is—"

"Not what we expected," I finished. "I called you," I told my grandmother. "We wouldn't have . . . interrupted . . . if you'd told me you were okay."

"I must not have heard it," she said, gazing at Tony.

I almost argued. The stupid thing rang right in her hearing aids through an app, and I knew it. But I also wanted to get out of there as quickly as possible, and she was clearly enjoying our discomfort. I caught Joe's eye and inclined my head toward the door. He nodded.

"Okay, then. We're gonna go."

"Have fun." She still wasn't looking at us. Joe and I exchanged a look, and we both struggled to keep our composure.

"Um. Bye, then."

We turned to leave, but she called after us. "Oh, dinner is at seven tonight."

"Dinner?"

"The four of us—at Sofia's tonight."

"I—uh—okay."

Joe grabbed my hand and pulled me out the door, where we laughed until we had to hold on to each other to keep from falling over.

"What just happened?" I asked.

"I—wow—can they even still—at their age?"

"She was in a robe, and he wasn't wearing shoes."

"Holy—"

"Do you think they—" I doubled over, unable to say it.

He held a hand to the side of his face. "Prophylactic," he gasped.

I collapsed onto the wicker love seat. "This is so gross."

He nudged me over and sat next to me. "It's sweet too though."

I shook my head again. "I just—she told me she was going to bed. And she practically told me to go to you." I looked over at him again. "Do you think she was getting rid of me so she could—?"

"Aren't you glad you listened to her? Can you imagine if you'd still been home?"

I made a retching noise, then got serious as I realized something. "Oh no. I have to go back in there."

"Why?"

"I need clothes and stuff." I glanced at the door. "Okay. They're probably still eating. If I run upstairs, grab what I need, and come back down without looking at the kitchen, it'll be okay, right?"

He glanced over his shoulder through the window screen. "Go fast."

I kissed his cheek and made a beeline up the stairs. I grabbed my toiletry bag from the bathroom and an armful of clothes from the dresser, hoping I had enough to make an outfit, and hurried back down.

"Let's go."

~

I sat at the kitchen island, sipping a mug of coffee while Joe cooked breakfast, both of us still trying to figure out the scene we had just witnessed.

"My mother always said he'd go running if she crooked her little finger." He slid a plate of eggs and pancakes in front of me and came to sit on the other barstool with his own plate.

"My grandfather said my grandmother would bring a date to his funeral. I didn't realize he meant a specific date."

"How long has he been gone?"

"A little over five years."

"Why now, I wonder?"

I shrugged and took a bite to avoid giving away that I thought I knew the answer. "Did your grandmother ever remarry?"

He shook his head. "She could have. She was young when my grandfather died."

I looked at his left hand as he picked up his coffee cup. He wasn't wearing a ring, but there was still a line of skin that was ever-so-slightly paler than the rest of his hand. Glancing at my own, I didn't see the same line. I'd stopped wearing my ring when Brad left.

"Am I really the first girl you've been with since—well—you know?"

He choked on his coffee. I hadn't meant to ask that. It just came out. "I—um—no, that wasn't—" He set the mug down and fidgeted with a napkin. "I just hadn't brought anyone . . . here."

I felt the blood rushing to my cheeks. "Sorry, I didn't mean—"

But he took my hand, tracing the outline of it with his index finger, then brought my palm to his lips. Such a simple gesture, but I wanted to sweep the dishes to the floor, hop onto the counter, and reenact the previous night, minus Jax's interruption.

Pulling my hand to his chest, he smiled slowly and placed one of his knees between mine. "What do you want to do today?"

I leaned in and kissed him, embarrassment forgotten. "You," I whispered.

He looked over his shoulder. Jax was lounging in the sunlight by the window. "Think we can beat her to the bedroom?"

Jax picked up her head. We looked at each other and laughed. She put her head back down as I began to tiptoe exaggeratedly, Joe following me.

~

After a day in bed—and the shower—and a return trip to the kitchen, Jax whining slightly from the shut bedroom, I was a little nervous about dinner. Yes, Sofia had given her seal of approval two nights earlier. But there was a big difference between telling me Joe liked me and seeing her after what we had just spent the better part of the last twenty-four hours doing. But my curiosity about Tony and my grandmother was stronger than my apprehension.

Joe's father was due back the following day, Sofia said as she greeted us, kissing me firmly on both cheeks and holding out my hands to look at me. I marveled that so much had happened in the span of a business trip to California.

Then again, I was on my grandmother's "business trip" as well. That thought was sobering. No, she hadn't set a return date, and yes, she might drag it out a little longer now that she and Tony had reconnected. But eventually we would have to go home.

We sat at the same table, clearly the spot of honor, Tony greeting his niece with a paternal hug and kiss. Sofia laughed merrily every time she saw any sign of affection between my grandmother and her uncle.

"What is it? Seventy years?" she asked. "And you're like teenagers."

My grandmother looked at Tony, a sparkle of humor in her eye. "We were much worse as teenagers."

Joe nudged my knee under the table, and I suppressed a grin. I knew way too many details.

"Please, you were worse in your thirties," Sofia argued.

I looked at my grandmother accusingly. "You said nothing happened after you married Grandpa."

"She means the boat," Grandma said, sighing dramatically.

"I saw how Uncle Tony dove in after you," Sofia said. "You two weren't fooling anyone."

"Is that when you stole a boat?" I asked.

"I didn't steal anything."

"She tried to steal a boat," Tony said. "But she didn't know how to drive it, so I had to steal it for her."

"Excuse me," my grandmother said. "First of all, I *borrowed* the boat. It was returned in perfect condition. Second of all, if you"—she pointed a finger at Sofia—"hadn't gotten stuck out there, I wouldn't have needed to steal a boat."

"I thought you didn't steal it?"

She grinned.

CHAPTER
FIFTY-SEVEN

July 1968
Hereford, Massachusetts

"Lunch!" Evelyn called, standing at the big cooler they had dragged down to the beach. Kids of all ages came running, from the teenagers down to Bernie's and Helen's young grandchildren.

The children grabbed the peanut-butter-and-jelly sandwiches that hadn't changed in the twenty years since Joseph bought the cottages, made in the morning, assembly-line-style, before everyone trekked down to the beach. Not that Joseph and Miriam stayed in the cottages anymore. The house on Main Street had air conditioning units now. And someone was always willing to drive into town to get them and bring them to the beach when they wanted to watch their grandchildren and great-grandchildren play in the surf.

Evelyn surveyed the chaotic scene. She and Margaret were the ones who came to stay for the whole summer, Evelyn running the main cottage while Margaret manned Bernie's, shuffling kids between the houses as their siblings came in for a week here, two weeks there. Fred came up every other weekend, then would be there for two weeks in August.

Doing a head count was impossible among the moving children, but she scanned faces, knowing someone was missing.

"Joanie," she called to her middle child. "Where's your sister?"

Joan's face fell, and she turned to flee, but Evelyn grabbed her nine-year-old's arm.

"Where?" she asked again.

"I told her not to go."

"Told her not to go where?"

Joan pointed with her free hand to the island. Evelyn dropped her daughter's arm and walked closer to the water, shielding her eyes with a hand as she gazed out toward the island. There was no one visible. Evelyn looked down at the water and swore. The sandbar was almost gone. They hadn't made it back in time for the tide. And the rule was if you went to the island, you told an adult first to prevent this exact situation.

"Sofia is with her?" Joan nodded, and Evelyn's lips narrowed to a line. It hadn't been much of a question. The two were inseparable each summer, sending letters through the rest of the year. But Sofia, as a local, should have known better.

With a sigh, Evelyn went to the semicircle of lawn chairs where her siblings sat, smoking and drinking sodas spiked with whiskey, and knelt at Margaret's side. "I need to go to town."

"What for?"

"Don't make a fuss."

Margaret turned to look at her sister. "What about?"

"Anna and Sofia went out to the island."

Margaret looked across the water, lowering her sunglasses. "And they aren't back?" Evelyn shook her head, and Margaret pursed her lips. "Well, if you ever wondered if she was yours, there's your proof."

"Thanks."

"What are you going to do?"

"What do you think? I'm going to go get them."

"By going to town?"

"Just keep everything under control here." Evelyn looked toward the island one more time, then left the beach, walking swiftly up the hill to the cottage to grab the car keys. She drove at breakneck speed to the marina, where she strode purposefully down a dock, climbed into a waiting motorboat, and started the engine.

It was sheer bad luck that the boat's owner was just down the dock, worse luck that he didn't believe she was a police officer commandeering the boat, and even worse luck still that she had no idea of how to helm a boat, as she would have just left when he called for her to get out of his boat if she had.

The owner, a summer person, boarded the craft as well and was threatening to throw Evelyn overboard when a loud whistle broke up their argument.

"What's going on here?" Evelyn's head snapped to her right. She would know that voice in her sleep.

"Officer," the irate man said. "This crazy woman is stealing my boat."

Tony turned to look at her, his eyes widening. They had seen each other from afar in town but hadn't done more than raise a hand in greeting in years.

"Evelyn, what—?"

"Anna is on the island. The tide is in. Sofia is with her."

There was a beat.

Then Tony stepped onto the boat. "Sir, I'm afraid I'm going to need to commandeer this boat."

"But—I—no!"

Tony gently guided him back down to the dock as he sputtered in protest. "The city of Hereford thanks you for your commitment to saving two stranded children. We'll make sure you are officially thanked for your cooperation and service." He threw the line off as he spoke, then turned to Evelyn. "Life jacket. And sit."

"I don't need a life jacket."

A muscle ticked in his jaw, and she sat. He put the boat into gear, reversing it out of its spot at the dock, then pulled expertly into the channel.

"Why couldn't you call the station like a normal person?" he growled once they rounded the small cape and he no longer needed to dodge the sailboats and fishing boats.

"Well, hello to you too, darling. You look well."

He shook his head. "I guess that's like asking a leopard to change its spots."

"Would I be me if I did things like everyone else?"

"How long have they been out there?"

"I'd guess a couple hours. They missed the tide to get back."

"Sofia knows better."

Evelyn rolled her eyes. "So does Anna."

Neither of them mentioned the possibility that they had run into trouble.

After a few minutes of silence, Tony glanced at her. "I like your hair like that. It suits you."

She touched it but said nothing as the island came into view in the distance.

"Which side?" he asked.

"Two twelve-year-old girls? You know where they are."

Tony gave her another look. "Is your girl going to be up for the jump?"

That was a more interesting question, but Evelyn set her jaw. "She'll be fine."

Tony didn't reply as they sped toward the island, veering right to reach the castle side and not get beached on the sandbar, hidden by only a foot of water.

"There." He pointed, and Evelyn shook her head, the problem apparent even from that far below. Sofia was on the ledge. Anna was perched above it.

"Get under them and cut the engine. They may be able to hear us."

"If you'd called the station, we could have come out with a megaphone," Tony grumbled.

"Coulda, woulda, shoulda. It'll be fine." Tony got as close as he could and turned off the engine as instructed. Evelyn stood and cupped her hands around her mouth. "Anyone need a ride home?"

"Mom!" Anna screamed, and Evelyn felt a pang in her chest at the fear in her daughter's voice.

"You need to jump."

Anna shook her head.

"You can do this."

"I can't."

Tony touched Evelyn's arm. "We'll pull the boat around the other side. I'll go get her."

"Sofia's on the ledge."

"Sofia can jump."

Evelyn shook her head. "I have to go up."

"No."

"Tony, she doesn't know you. She's scared. And she needs to do this."

"There's nothing wrong with climbing down the other side."

"I'm not raising a coward. Besides, you've seen me drive a car. Do you want me trying to steer a boat?"

He ducked his head to hide his smile. "Promise me you'll be careful."

She gave him the old look, and, for a moment, they were eighteen again, together and free. "You told me once you thought I could fly. We're about to see if you were right." She called up to her daughter and told her to stay put. "I'm coming up."

Tony drove the boat to the cove on the other side. Evelyn pulled off her caftan, then hopped out in the shallows and waded ashore to begin the climb to the top. "I'll see you on the other side," she called over her shoulder.

But Tony waited until she reached the top before he returned to the girls.

It wasn't an easy climb, especially in sandals. But Evelyn made it, then climbed down the castle's stairs, calling to her daughter, who wrapped herself around her waist, burying her tear-streaked face in Evelyn's swimsuit.

"Hey now." Evelyn stroked her hair. "What kind of adventure ends in tears?"

"It's my fault we missed the tide. Sofia jumped down and I got scared."

"Well, let's fix that now."

Anna looked up at her mother. "Mom, no."

"Yes."

"I can't."

"You can. And you will."

The tears started to flow again. "I'm not brave like you are."

Evelyn cupped her daughter's chin in her hand, turning her face up to look at her. "I'm scared of things every day. But you have to make a choice: Do you let fear win, or do you go out there and look it in the eye and say, 'You will not defeat me today'?"

She dropped her hand, then went to the edge, sat, and hopped down. "Come on." She held out a hand to Anna. "We do this together."

Anna looked unsure, but she followed her mother's example, sitting, then taking Evelyn's hand and jumping down onto the ledge.

Evelyn peered over the edge. Tony was in the boat, waiting.

"Whose boat is that?" Sofia asked.

"It's a long story." Anna still looked frightened. "Sofia, darling, show us how it's done."

Sofia turned to look at Anna. "You're okay?"

"She's fine. Unless you're afraid?"

Sofia scowled at Evelyn as only a twelve-year-old girl can. "I'll see you down there," she said to Anna. And then she took a running jump.

Anna dashed to the edge and watched her friend fall. She hit the water feet first and surfaced a moment later. Her head bobbed as she got her bearings, then she swam to the boat. Tony pulled her in and hugged her tightly before smacking her gently on the head. She wriggled out of his grip and gestured up to Anna, yelling something indecipherable.

"It's time to go," Evelyn said firmly, taking Anna's hand. "We take a deep breath, run, and jump. Stay vertical, hit the water feet first, then swim up."

"You won't let go?"

"Not unless you do."

Anna looked at her mother and nodded once.

"Deep breath," Evelyn said. "We go on three. One. Two. Three."

The two ran in unison, leaping off the cliff, hands together as they fell through the air.

Anna surfaced first, sputtering, looking for her mother, whose hand she lost when they hit the water.

Evelyn didn't appear.

"Mom!" Anna screamed.

Tony scanned the water for her, then, with no hesitation, dove into the ocean, swimming with a strong stroke toward Anna, who thrashed, looking around panicked.

"What are you two doing all the way over there?" Evelyn called, her foot on the rung of the boat's ladder.

"Mom!"

"Come on, darling. I haven't got all day, you know."

Tony shook his head. "You are the absolute worst thing that ever happened to me, you know that?"

"I make life more interesting."

He turned to Anna, who seemed dazed. "Are you okay to swim?" She nodded and started toward the boat. Once she was in, he pulled himself up the ladder and stripped off his soaked uniform shirt, shoes, and belt. "You may owe me a new gun," he said to Evelyn.

"Put it on my tab."

"I swear—"

"Little pitchers have big ears," she warned, inclining her head toward the two girls, who sat huddled together in the back of the boat.

He stopped talking and started the boat back toward the marina.

When they returned, the furious boat owner was still there, along with another police officer. Evelyn put a hand on Tony's arm as they neared the dock. "Take the girls home. I'll deal with this."

He looked at her, holding her gaze for a long moment. "You take them home. I can handle the owner."

"You're sure?"

Tony nodded. "I didn't mean what I said, you know."

Evelyn planted a long kiss on his cheek. "I know." She wanted to say more, but she felt Anna's eyes on her. "And thank you."

He took her hand and squeezed it, then released her to ease the boat into its slip.

"Arrest them!" the owner cried.

The poor officer on the dock was at a loss, seeing his superior officer shirtless and damp, handing a woman and two children off the boat. "Captain?" he asked, scratching his head.

"To the car," Evelyn said to Anna and Sofia. "Go. Now." She turned to the irate man. "It's all right now. The girls are safe. My dear sir, you are a hero. Thanks to your gallantly selfless performance of civic duty, Captain Delgado"—she looked back at Tony—"Captain? Impressive." Tony suppressed a laugh. "Captain Delgado was able to rescue my daughter and his niece. I'm sure the newspaper would even write a story about your heroism today in lending us your boat, you wonderful, wonderful man." She hugged him, still damp, kissed him on both cheeks, then flashed a dazzling smile at Tony. "Captain."

And without a backward glance, she walked off toward her car.

"Wha—what just happened?" the other officer asked.

"Evelyn Bergman," Tony said. "She's a force of nature."

CHAPTER
FIFTY-EIGHT

Joe held my hand as we walked along the beach in the late morning, Jax playing in the waves next to us, the water lapping against our bare feet and ankles. When we got back, he picked up sandwiches from a shop across from the beach while I showered; my grandmother had asked me to take her to the cemetery in the afternoon, and Joe needed to pop into the gallery for a couple of hours.

"I'll text you when we're done, and I can just go to the cottage if you're not back yet," I said as I was leaving.

He shrugged and kissed me. "If you want. But I'll leave the door unlocked. You can come back here whenever."

My grandma was sitting on the sofa in the living room, shoes on, purse on her lap, when I arrived. There was no sign of Tony. "Where's your boyfriend?" I asked.

"Where's yours?" she replied tartly, rising from the sofa. I offered her a hand, and she swatted it away.

"What's the cemetery called?" I asked, pulling up Google Maps.

"The cemetery."

"No, like what's the name, so I can find it?"

"It doesn't have a name."

I sighed and searched for Jewish cemeteries near me. "Is it in Gloucester?"

"I know the way."

I set the Gloucester cemetery as our destination and followed the map's first direction.

"Are you and Tony like together now?"

She peered at me over her ridiculously large sunglasses. "Are you and Joe?"

I laughed. "I think we are."

"Then you should thank your great-grandmother at the cemetery for not letting me marry his great-uncle. You'd have been cousins."

"Ew, Grandma, why?"

She grinned. "Because it's fun to make you squirm, darling."

The cemetery was small and labeled only with a sign that said "Jewish Cemetery" from the main road, the words *Mt. Jacob* almost illegibly carved on a stone at the entrance.

I parked the car in the tiny lot and helped her out. She stood for a moment, and I saw the weight of loss in her face. Her whole family was here except my grandfather. Then she took a deep breath and strode purposefully through the headstones. I followed, careful not to step on any graves, though she had no compunction about that.

Finally, she came to rest at a large, shared headstone that read *Bergman* at the top. The left said *Joseph*, giving only the year 1895 for his birth, and his death on June 8, 1980. Miriam's birthdate was present on her side, in 1894, and her death in October 1978.

"Less than two years apart," I said quietly.

"Papa was lost with her gone." She stared contemplatively at the earth in front of her. "And then he had a stroke, a heart attack, and another stroke." There was a slight tremor in her voice. "That was when Bernie sold his cottage. Between Papa's medical bills and the full-time care he needed by then—he didn't want to leave the Main Street house, you see. We had a family meeting and agreed one of the cottages had to go to pay for it all." She sighed heavily. "I probably drove back and forth fifty times those last two years. But we lived so far away, and Richie wasn't in college yet. I wasn't much help."

"When did you move to Maryland?"

"Well before that. Your grandfather took the government job in . . . Let me think. Anna was fifteen, so it would have been seventy-one."

She took my hand. "Mama, Papa, I want you to meet your great-granddaughter." She didn't speak for a moment, and I wondered if I was expected to say something. *Nice to meet you* would be a little weird under the circumstances. But she shook her head. "They would have loved you. Papa loved children more than anything. And you're the good girl Mama always wished I was."

She pulled me with her to the next grave. *Genevieve Bergman*, the stone read. Who was Genevieve? I read the dates. January 1934 until July 1955. "Genevieve?" I asked, confused. "I thought Vivie was short for Vivian?"

"Why would it be Vivian? You're named for her, after all."

"I—what?"

"Your mother thought Genevieve was too old-fashioned. The older names weren't in style when you were born. So she chose Jenna."

"Why didn't you tell me that?"

"I thought you knew."

"I didn't." I stared at the stone.

"I couldn't say Genevieve when I was little. My nickname for her stuck." She looked down at the ground, then up at me. "Go on back to the car. I have things to tell her."

"I think she knows already."

My grandmother put a hand on her hip. "And I think she needs to hear some of it from me."

I didn't like leaving her there in the sun, but I did as she asked, starting the car and putting on the air conditioner, but making sure I could still see her. I was named for Vivie. On the one hand, no wonder I had been so miserable. My mother didn't mean to curse me, but oof. What a legacy to saddle a child with. I looked over at my grandmother again. She was engaged in an animated, albeit one-sided, conversation. I wondered if she was telling her sister about George or Tony, or all of it.

Eventually she shuffled back to the car, and I scrambled out to open her door for her.

"What did Vivie have to say?"

"Not a whole lot. But I think she can rest a bit easier now."

I started the car. These people felt so real to me after this trip that it was bizarre to think all that was left of them was buried under those plots of grass. I glanced in the rearview mirror, half expecting to see their specters waving from among the tombstones.

"What about your parents?"

"What about them, darling?"

"Do you think they're resting easy after . . . everything?"

She turned her head to the window, and I wondered if she was looking for them as well.

"My father made his own peace."

"How did that happen?"

"It took time. They were both so proud. But if Tony had two great loves in his life, they were me and Sofia. Papa wanted to make things right and because of Sofia, he could."

It made sense. They hadn't been able to resolve their differences over my grandmother, but they got a new chance in Sofia. But how could my grandmother ever get past what her mother did first to her, then to her beloved baby sister? "What about your mother?"

"My mother . . ." She stopped for a moment. "I forgave my mother when I met Frank. And I have to hope that's enough."

"Frank?"

She turned to look at me, her eyes compassionate. "Life is complicated and messy for everyone. It took me a long time to learn that lesson."

CHAPTER
FIFTY-NINE

October 1978
Hereford, Massachusetts

They reopened the cottages in October because there wasn't room for everyone when Miriam died.

She was diagnosed the previous spring, but was mostly fine until the last month, when the cancer moved quickly and aggressively. Her children all agreed it was best she didn't suffer long, but they worried deeply about Joseph as they gathered in the Main Street living room after Joseph went to bed the night before the funeral.

"He can move in with me," Bernie said. He and his wife had already discussed the inevitable conclusion as the only ones who still lived in Hereford. Helen was close, in Boston, Sam even closer in Beverly. But Bernie was the eldest, and the responsibility, in his mind, was his.

"He won't," Helen said. "I talked to him last night about coming to live with us. He said he's not leaving Mama's house."

"Stubborn old fool." Bernie shook his head. Evelyn was secretly relieved. She couldn't imagine selling the Main Street house.

"How will he eat? He's never even made himself a sandwich, let alone done any housework." Gertie was chewing on her thumbnail, which Evelyn hadn't seen her do since she was a little girl.

"We'll have to get someone in to help him." Bernie looked around at his siblings. "They took a hit with Mama's treatments, but he's got the money for that." He deliberately avoided looking at Evelyn. "But he isn't so healthy himself. If anything happens—" He swallowed, looking down at his hands. "If anything happens, I'm going to sell the smaller cottage."

Evelyn looked around at her siblings, who all nodded their assent. She didn't want to agree; her summers in Hereford were what she looked forward to all year. But no one else came for as long as she did anymore. And with Anna and Joan in college and Richie in high school, they no longer wanted to spend the whole summer away from their friends. So as long as they still had the one cottage, she could agree to that.

She also knew that her father had paid Sofia's culinary school tuition and used the sale of the store to help her open her restaurant. She wasn't positive her siblings knew that, but if they did—

"I agree," she said quietly, and everyone let out a collective breath.

"Good." Bernie wiped his palms on his pants. "Next up, I think you girls need to sort through Mama's things. We don't want to make Papa do that."

"We can," Margaret said. "We have all week with shiva."

The rest of the sisters agreed, then they retired to the multiple houses for the night, knowing they needed their strength for the funeral the next day.

~

Fred left with the children two days later, dropping Anna and Joan at their colleges on the way. Evelyn kissed them all goodbye, telling Fred she would let him know when to pick her up at the train station.

"I can come back and drive you home," he said.

"It's okay. I don't want to make you do that."

"I don't mind."

Evelyn put a hand to his cheek. "I know. And I love you. But I'm okay. I promise."

He embraced his wife before herding the now-grown children into the car, Richie volunteering to drive.

"A little different from the old days, isn't it?" Fred asked from the passenger window.

Evelyn shook her head. "It goes by in a flash. I'll call you tonight." And she watched them drive away.

The following afternoon, the sisters quietly excused themselves from the living room, where Joseph sat with Bernie, Sam, and various neighbors, including Ruthie's mother, who hadn't stopped crying and didn't show any signs that she would soon.

Helen went into the closet, Margaret took the jewelry box and sat on the bed to begin divvying things up, Evelyn went to the chest of drawers, and Gertie sat on the floor, opening the trunk in the corner. They quickly established a pile for each sister and the much larger give-away pile, where most of the clothes went.

"This one is mine," Margaret said about a ring. "I don't care what else I get, but I'm taking this."

"What about Mama's good hat? Does anyone want that?"

Evelyn smiled at the memory. "I do."

"When's the last time you wore a hat?" Helen asked.

"Sentimental value."

Helen shrugged and added it, still in its box, to Evelyn's pile.

"What are these?" Gertie asked, pulling out a bundle of letters, tied in a ribbon. Everyone looked over.

"I have no idea."

"I've never seen those."

"They were in the trunk?"

"At the bottom," Gertie confirmed. "In a hatbox under an afghan she made." She untied the ribbon and lifted the top letter, looked at the front, and then turned it over. "It's addressed to her. But it's not opened." She lifted the next one. "None of them are."

They all gathered around Gertie, sitting on the floor around her, each picking up a letter.

"What do you think they are?"

"Who are they from?"

"Frank Corrigan. Who is that?"

"I've never heard of him."

Evelyn ripped open the envelope she was holding.

"Stop! What are you doing?" Helen asked, reaching for the letter, but Evelyn pulled it away from her sister's grasp.

"There's only one way to find out what they are," she said, skimming the rough cursive. Her mouth dropped open. "These are *love* letters. To Mama!"

"What?"

"Let me see!"

Evelyn handed the letter to Margaret, who eagerly read it, Gertie looking over her shoulder, then picked up the stack, flipping through postmarks.

"They came on her birthday every year—look. And they started in 1919—the year she married Papa."

"Corrigan. He wasn't Jewish."

"Irish, I'd guess."

The four of them looked at each other in awe.

Evelyn picked up the letter from 1919 and opened it.

"I don't think we should read these," Helen said.

"Well, I do."

Gertie looked at her older sister, who stood with her hand on her hip, and silently rose, going to the dresser to continue working there while Helen returned to the closet. Margaret stayed on the floor with Evelyn, reading each letter after she finished.

"I think we should call him," Evelyn said when she had read them all.

"What?"

"He should know she's gone."

"He can read it in the newspaper."

Evelyn stood and looked at Helen. "He loved her. And I know she loved Papa, but this Frank meant *something* to her if she kept his letters all these years."

"She didn't even read them!"

Evelyn lowered her eyes to the envelopes and letters now scattered across the floor. They were poorly spelled but brimming with the affection this strange man held for the woman they thought they knew so well. Evelyn understood she was doing this for herself, but that had never stopped her before. And it *would* be a kindness to return the letters.

"That's how I know she cared. She couldn't bring herself to read them or to throw them away."

"I want nothing to do with this," Helen said.

"Then have nothing to do with it." She turned to Margaret and Gertie. "Will you meet him with me?"

They both nodded.

Helen's jaw was set in a firm line. "He doesn't set foot in this house."

"Of course not," Evelyn said, though she hadn't thought that far ahead. "We wouldn't do that to Papa."

The party line was long gone, and there was a phone upstairs now too, so Evelyn, a recent letter in hand, went to the chair next to the phone in the hall, Margaret and Gertie following her. She dialed directory assistance and gave Frank's information, then agreed to be connected through.

On the third ring, a man answered, the craggy tone of a longshoreman who spent his life smoking, and with the "r"-dropping accent of someone who had never left the north shore except to go out to sea.

"Hullo?"

"Mr. Corrigan?"

"Who's there?"

"Mr. Corrigan, my name is Evelyn Gold—er—Evelyn Bergman. I'm Miriam Bergman's daughter."

There was a long pause. "She's gone, then?"

Evelyn took a deep breath. "She is. We—her daughters—we found your letters."

"She kept 'em?"

"She did. We—well—three of us—we'd like to meet you. If you would."

Another pause. "Ayuh."

Evelyn suggested the diner in town the following afternoon, when Joseph usually took his nap and their absence would be less noticeable. He agreed, and they returned to Miriam's bedroom to complete their work. Evelyn sat on the floor, attempting to match letters to envelopes before stacking them in order and retying them carefully with their ribbon.

~

The man who entered the diner the following day looked much older than their father, his skin browned and spotted from years on the water. But he was kind, shaking each of their hands.

"You look like her, all of you. Different ways though."

He waited until they sat to sit, his hat in his lap. "How'd she go?"

"Cancer. But it was quick."

He nodded. "Thought she'd have more time. But in my mind, she's seventeen still."

Evelyn pulled out the stack of letters and passed them across the table. "We thought you'd like to have these back."

He reached for them, touching the ribbon gently. "She used to wear this."

The three daughters looked at each other, trying unsuccessfully to picture their mother ever wearing a ribbon in her hair, being young enough to do such a thing.

"Can—can you tell us how you two met?"

"Ayuh." He ran a crooked finger across the top letter. "She was seventeen. Walking home from school, and she dropped her books. Later, I find out she did it on purpose."

Frank picked up the books for her and carried them home. He was two years older, already working on the ships, but he started meeting her and walking her home every day that he could.

"Her father wouldn't allow it, of course. Threw me out. He was a mean one. Not a'cause of me. I'da understood that. But her ma was sick. He said if Miriam left, her ma'd die. So I left fo' a couple years. Figured it'd be easier for her. Then her ma died, and she married your father." He took a sip of the water that the waitress had placed in front of him. "I understood. He gave her a good life. Better than I coulda." He looked down at his hands. "Much better." He wiped at his eye with a gnarled hand. "Was she happy?"

"Yes," Gertie said defensively at the same time that Evelyn said, "I don't know."

"This explains a lot, I suppose," Evelyn said quietly. Margaret reached over and patted her hand.

"Means the world to me that she read 'em though."

"She di—" Evelyn kicked Gertie under the table, and Gertie stopped talking.

He rose, wiping at an eye again and picking up the letters. "Thank you for these. An' for telling me she's gone."

"Thank you," Evelyn said softly. "And I'm sorry."

"I'm sorry," he said. "She was your ma, after all."

They nodded. He said goodbye, apologized again, choking up, and then he left, quite suddenly.

"That's why she . . ." Margaret trailed off.

"I know."

"And Vivie—"

"I know," Evelyn said again, standing. And without another word, she walked out of the restaurant, leaving her sisters staring at each other, wide eyed.

She nearly ran two blocks, then turned down a side street, realizing with a hysterical half laugh that it was the same spot where she had told Tony, years ago, that she would run off with him instead of marrying Fred. "Oh," she gasped, leaning against the wall, pressing her hands to her face. "Oh, Mama."

Miriam trying to prevent her from falling in love with Tony in the first place. She knew. She knew what she was trying to save Evelyn from. She thought she knew better by not letting her marry the fisherman. And Vivie—Miriam just wanted to be sure, before she let Joseph say yes, that her youngest daughter was making a smart choice and not falling in love with the New York equivalent of a longshoreman. She couldn't have known what that would do.

Evelyn shook her head, realizing that everything she knew about her mother was only a half truth. That she really believed she had her daughters' best interests at heart all along. And honestly, maybe she did. Could Tony have given her the life Fred had?

Wiping the tears from her face, Evelyn took a deep breath. It was time to go home. Not to the Main Street house, but to her family. But first, she would go back to the cemetery, the earth still fresh from the clods she had helped to throw, and tell her mother that she understood and forgave her.

CHAPTER SIXTY

When we pulled up to the cottage, Tony was sitting in the wicker rocking chair on the front porch, reading a newspaper and looking as if he
lived there.

"What made you call Tony?" I asked my grandmother, gazing up
at this man who played such a pivotal role in her life, yet who hadn't
existed to me a week earlier.

"Who says I called him?"

"Pretty amazing timing if he just showed up here with a boombox
held over his head the other night."

She pulled a compact out of her purse and lifted her sunglasses to
apply powder. "What made you go to Joe's? I'd imagine it was all the
same reason."

I thought of the kitchen counter that night and colored slightly. I
glanced over to see her smirking.

"On that note, I don't think I'll come in."

She winked at me and returned the compact to her purse, unhooked
her seatbelt, and climbed carefully out of the car. Then she leaned back
in the window. "We leave Monday morning."

It was Friday.

And the reality hit me with the force of a truck that I didn't want
to go.

"Monday—but—can't we just—"

"Monday." Her voice was empathetic, but firm.

"Why?"

"Because I have business at home on Tuesday."

"What business? What could you possibly have left to do after this trip?"

"Darling, I mind my own; you should mind yours." She straightened, calling to Tony, and walked slowly toward the cottage stairs.

Monday.

She opened the screen door, leaning down to kiss Tony's forehead before going into the house. He rose to follow her.

Monday.

I pulled out my phone and checked the time, then drove down toward the end of the road. But instead of going to Joe's, I turned to go back into town.

I parked my car at the top of the hill on Main Street, got out, and crossed the street to stand on the sidewalk in front of the bank. Closing my eyes, I imagined the house from the pictures in my grandmother's album, its walls rising in front of me. My grandmother running up the steps with my grandfather, dashing back down them to chase after Tony.

Life is complicated and messy for everyone.

I opened my eyes, the house evaporating.

Then a flash of red caught my eye. A cardinal. It flitted from the roof of the bank down in front of me, then swooped around the side of the building and out of sight.

I glanced around to see if anyone was watching, then left the sidewalk to follow it. As I rounded the building, my lips spread into a smile. There, at the back of the bank, stood my grandmother's pear tree, the bird perched on a low branch, his head tilted as he studied me. I approached the tree and placed a hand on its trunk, the wood familiar beneath my hand, realizing what my grandmother meant when she said this place was in my blood.

"Thank you," I whispered to the cardinal, who nodded as if he understood, before returning to the car.

Monday, I thought as I sat behind the wheel, not ready to put the car in gear. *Monday.*

I took a deep breath. The safe thing to do was to end it. There was an expiration date on this relationship—or whatever it was—now.

You have to make a choice, my grandmother whispered in my head. *Do you let fear win?*

I pulled away from the curb. And like my mother before me, at my grandmother's prodding, I decided to jump.

We should have gone to sleep early Sunday night. I had a long drive ahead of me with no licensed driver to take a shift. But by the time we tried to fall asleep, neither of us could.

"I've got more than a month before school starts. I could come back."

"I can go down there too."

"People do this, right?"

He nodded, which I couldn't see in the darkness of the room, but I felt the movement of his head near mine. He put a hand to my face. "We take it one day at a time, and we'll figure it out."

We dozed off eventually, both of us sleeping fitfully, until Joe woke and looked at his phone screen. "Are you awake?" he asked quietly.

"Kinda."

"Do you want to see the sun rise over the water?"

I sat up. "We forgot to do that all weekend."

"Let's go out."

He pulled on shorts from next to the bed, and I grabbed his shirt. He took a blanket from the back of the sofa on our way out to the deck, Jax lifting her head at us as we walked by, then going back to sleep.

The sky was just lightening, and we sat together on the outdoor sofa, snuggled up against each other, the blanket protecting us from the chill of the night air off the water. I yawned. I would need a lot of coffee to get us home. But it was worth it.

A pinprick of brilliant light appeared on the horizon, growing slowly larger by the second, reflected in perfect symmetry against the water. I had seen the sun set against the ocean in California and that trip to Greece, but I had never seen a day dawn over it.

I turned my face up to Joe's, only to find he was looking at me. "I don't want to leave."

He hugged me tightly, kissing the top of my head. "I don't want you to, either. But I'm glad I found you."

"I am too."

We stayed like that for a long time, the sun climbing higher and higher over the waves before I rose to take a shower.

As the water washed over me, I leaned my forehead against the tile wall, wondering how I was going to go back to my childhood bedroom now. Then the glass door opened behind me and Joe stepped in, pressing a kiss to the nape of my neck.

I looked at him over my shoulder as he ran a gentle hand down my side and around my stomach, pulling me close against him. "It's the one place Jax won't interrupt us," he said.

Then a black nose appeared against the fogged glass.

I laughed and turned in his arms, kissing him under the spray.

~

After we said goodbye and I promised to call him when I got home, I returned to the cottage, my hair still damp, to pack the rest of my things. Tony wasn't there.

Bringing my bag down the stairs, I found my grandmother sitting in the living room. "Ready?"

She nodded, scooting to the edge of the seat, then leaning heavily on the arm of the sofa to rise.

"Let me just put my bags in the car and I'll go get yours."

"Tony brought them to the front hall."

"Neither of you should be lifting those heavy things."

She pinched my cheek. "May you live long enough for your bossy grandchildren to treat you like a child."

With all the bags in the car, my grandmother stumped slowly down the stairs, clinging tightly to the railing. Then she stopped to look at the cottage one last time, as did I.

"Maybe the color isn't so terrible," she said.

"It's not."

She stared a moment longer, ghosts running up and down the stairs. Then she shook her head and turned toward the car.

"Come on. It's time to go home."

I took another look at this house that was, in many ways, all she had left of her parents, her brothers and sisters, her childhood, committing it to memory, before joining her in the car.

As I put it into gear and started down the road, I saw the empty lot where the Gardner house had stood reflected in the rearview mirror.

"Do you know who owns that land? Where the big house was?"

"Of course."

She didn't elaborate.

"So who owns it?"

"Why, Tony does."

"Tony?"

"And me, I suppose. Although I told him I didn't want it."

"What?"

"Old Mrs. Gardner left it to the two of us. She died right before I married your grandfather. She thought Papa would come around. Or that we'd run off if we had the money. But there was no way to explain that one to anyone, so I told Tony it was all his."

"And he never sold it?"

"No. The old fool could have a fortune, but instead he throws away the property taxes every year just so they don't put up condos."

"That's—wow. And you swear you never cheated on Grandpa?"

"No, darling. I might lie and steal, but never that."

I thought for a moment. "You could have bought the cottage with your share."

"No, I couldn't have."

"What do you mean?"

She closed her eyes. "That was the fight at Helen's funeral, you see."

CHAPTER
SIXTY-ONE

June 1991
Hereford, Massachusetts

Evelyn no longer flinched at the sound of earth hitting a coffin. After Vivie, Miriam, Joseph, Gertie, and Sam, by Helen's funeral, a mere seven months after Sam's, she could shovel in her spade of dirt, hand it to the next mourner, and be done.

But now it was just Bernie, Margaret, and her. Fewer than half of the Bergman children. She looked at Bernie, who showed every one of his seventy-one years and resembled Joseph more and more by the day. Margaret was closer to her age, which wasn't so bad. Losing Sam had been a blow, but she still had Bernie and Margaret. For now at least.

And it was easier with Anna there. Joan hadn't come, but Anna had brought the children. And there was nothing like slipping one hand into Jenna's and the other into Beth's to take the sting out of a situation. She glanced at her daughter, who was trying so hard to hide the morning sickness of a third pregnancy. *She'll tell me when she's ready,* she thought. *There's no rush.*

Fred drove them back to Bernie's house, where they would sit shiva. Only three days instead of the seven they used to observe. The world had moved on, and if you weren't Orthodox, most people didn't want to give up a whole week to mourn the dead anymore.

Evelyn had assumed they would stay at the cottage, because why wouldn't they? But it had passed to Sam when Joseph died, and with Sam gone, Louise was the owner. She was cryptic on the phone, saying it was occupied, so they rented rooms at the Inn, where the children could play on the beach in the mornings before going to Bernie's house.

It was a shock to see that Bernie's and Helen's children were now in their late forties, and their grandchildren who used to toddle around the beach were now young adults.

She picked at the deli plate on her lap, uninterested, looking around the room with the watchful eyes of a cat.

Then Louise entered.

And Evelyn pounced.

"Darling," she said, kissing her sister-in-law on the cheek. "How are you?"

The question was a formality. She looked terrible even before Sam died, and his recent death had not helped.

"Not so good." Louise dabbed at her eyes. "This feels like Sam's all over again."

"Well, it's the same people, after all." Evelyn took her by the arm and led her to a chair. She let her get settled and brought her a drink of water before sitting next to her. "Now, be honest with me—are you renting out the cottage?"

Louise twitched guiltily.

"I figured out your little secret. I understand, of course, but you still should have told us. I don't mind paying you to use it when we want to, but I do expect you'll make it available for us."

"I—"

"I understand it's legally yours, but it's all of ours still. You know that."

"Evelyn, I sold it."

Evelyn stared at her sister-in-law.

"It wasn't fair; you all expected it to be yours whenever you needed, and Lord knows Sam didn't leave so much money, and I—"

"You *sold* my cottage?" Evelyn's voice was loud, and everyone looked over.

"It wasn't yours. It was Sam's."

"It was ours! It wasn't yours to sell!"

Bernie appeared at Evelyn's side, Fred following quickly, Jenna peeking around the door frame, having followed her grandfather. "Outside, now," Bernie ordered his sister, but Evelyn wasn't budging.

"Is it done? Or still happening?" Evelyn's eyes were flashing. Margaret came into the room and crossed her arms.

"I—it's not final, but it will be next week."

"Over my dead body it will." She gestured to Bernie and Margaret. "We'll buy it instead."

"Evelyn," Bernie said calmly. "Outside."

She looked at her brother. "Don't you talk to me like I'm a child."

"Evelyn," Margaret said, putting a gentle hand on her sister's arm. "Come out on the porch."

"I already talked to them," Louise said shrilly.

Evelyn turned to her siblings, looking carefully at their faces, then marched out the front door, Bernie and Margaret following.

"What did you do?"

"We let her do what was right for her."

"And what about what was right for us?"

Bernie sat in a chair on the porch. "I live here. Most of my kids are here. I don't need a cottage at the beach. And when's the last time you came for the whole summer? Ten years ago? More?"

"I was here last year!"

"For a week," Margaret said gently. "It wasn't fair to ask her to keep a house so you could spend a week here and there. And I don't want it anymore."

"If it was fifteen years ago, I would have bought it with you," Bernie said. "And we could have kept living out the old days. But it's not. And I don't want to burden my kids with that when I go."

"Why didn't you ask me? I could have pulled the money together."

"Because we knew you would hound her, and she needed to sell it. She's had a rough go since Sam died."

Evelyn looked at her brother sitting in a wooden rocking chair and realized the next time she came to Hereford could be for his funeral. That might be the last time too, with only the few nieces and nephews who remained and the cottage gone. And while she could and would bear a grudge against Louise, she decided not to hold one against her only remaining siblings.

"Okay."

Bernie looked at her askance. "What are you planning now?"

"Nothing. You win."

Margaret placed the back of her hand against her sister's forehead, and Evelyn swatted it away. "She's not warm. She's up to something."

"I've mellowed in my old age."

As her siblings disputed that assertion, a car parked across the street. The door opened, and out stepped a man with graying hair.

Bernie saw him first and began to laugh, a big belly laugh that ended in a fit of wheezing, the souvenir of a lifetime of smoking. "Chief Delgado," he said as the man walked up the steps. "Perfect timing."

Tony stopped in front of the three on the porch. "Bernie. Margaret. Evelyn. My deepest sympathies."

"Go on in," Bernie said. "Half the town is already here. We'll be in directly."

Tony paused a moment, meeting Evelyn's eye. She offered a half smile, which he returned with a nod before entering the house.

"Mellowed, my foot," Bernie said.

"Hush." Evelyn ruffled the little bit of hair he had left, then went in the house.

CHAPTER
SIXTY-TWO

My mother wanted to know everything about the trip, but by the time I got back from bringing my grandmother home, carrying her bags in, and helping her to unpack, I was exhausted. I mumbled something about it being great and started up the stairs.

"Was she okay? Did she take her pills? How crazy did she drive you?"

I turned around on the third step. "She—" I stopped for a second. "She's something else."

She started to ask another question, but I couldn't rehash the whole trip right then. "Mom, I need some sleep. I'll give you details tomorrow, I promise." I took two more steps, then stopped again. "You should go back sometime. Sofia wants to see you."

"You met Sofia?"

I smiled at her. "I met everyone."

~

I slept fourteen hours, texted Joe good morning, and took a shower. Then I sat at the desk where I did my homework as a teenager and pulled out the envelope I had been avoiding for the last few weeks. I signed my name at the Post-it arrows, then slid the documents back inside before going downstairs, the manilla envelope under my arm.

"Jenna?" my mom called from the kitchen.

"Hey, Mom."

"Can I make you some breakfast?" I smiled. She hadn't offered me breakfast since the first week I was home. She must have missed me.

"I'll just have some coffee and cereal."

"I don't mind."

"It's okay. I need to go drop this off."

She looked at the package under my arm. "Is that—?" I nodded, and she looked at me in wonder. "What happened in Hereford?"

I set the envelope on the counter and went to the coffee machine. "A lot." As the coffee brewed, I turned to face her. "I'm going to start looking at apartment listings today too. You were right. I need to get out."

"I didn't mean—"

I wrapped my arms around her. "I know, Mom. But sometimes you've just got to say you're not going to let fear win and then jump."

She pulled her head back to look at me, then nodded slowly. "Let me know how I can help."

I said I would, then answered her questions about the cottage, the town, Sofia, and Joe as I ate my cereal.

~

I still had a key, but I knocked on the door anyway.

There was the sound of footsteps before the door opened, then I was face-to-face with Brad for the first time in months.

Neither of us spoke for a long moment. It was a little surreal. We shared a life for six years, and now he was practically a stranger in a body I knew. "Hey," I said finally.

"Hey." His tone was guarded, despite the fact that I had texted him before I went over—I didn't think Taylor would appreciate me just showing up, even with the paperwork that simplified her life.

"I brought the settlement agreement. And your key. And this." I pulled my engagement ring from a small felt bag. I knew full well that my grandmother would have said I was a fool to return it, but it had been his grandmother's, and keeping it didn't feel right, whether he planned to give it to Taylor or not.

He studied the ring, surprised—he hadn't asked for it in the settlement—then looked back at me, and his shoulders slumped. "Do you want to come in?" He hadn't taken anything from me yet.

I hesitated. "Is Taylor here?"

"No."

I didn't really want to go back in there. But there were things that probably needed to be said, so I nodded, and he stood back to allow me to walk past him.

Not much had changed. I hadn't taken the furniture, as most of it had been Brad's before I moved in, and I had no place to put anything. It was like a strange little time capsule, familiar yet from another life.

I set the envelope, key, and ring on the table where he had left his ring six months earlier and followed Brad to the living room, where I sat in the same spot I had been in when he announced he was leaving.

"Jenna, I—"

I held up a hand. "Hang on." He stopped, and I paused to collect myself. "You should have talked to me sooner. Before anything happened with Taylor. Even if you weren't willing to try to work things out, you should have told me. I know neither of us was happy. But that wasn't fair."

For a few seconds, he didn't respond, then he nodded.

"Don't do that to Taylor too." He started to protest, but I cut him off. "Look, you didn't think you'd do that to me at the beginning either. Don't be that guy again."

"Can I say something now?" I nodded. "I *am* sorry."

I looked at him for a long moment. "I know that. And I'm sorry for not signing the papers earlier."

"What changed?"

"Me. Everything. I'm ready to move on." He was staring, and I wondered if the shift in me was actually visible. It felt like it must be.

But I was also ready to leave. I stood up and looked at him one last time. "Be happy, Brad."

I didn't take a final glance around. I didn't need to. The weight was lifted. I had no idea what my future held, but I didn't need to look back.

~

The following morning I was scrolling through Zillow listings, broadening my search criteria to try to find the best place for my money. It didn't have to be perfect—but it did have to be big enough to accommodate Jax when Joe came to visit. Now that Brad had the paperwork, he'd be starting the sales proceedings on the condo, which would leave me much more financially stable. And I had plans that night with two friends whom I hadn't seen in way too long.

I heard a car door shut outside, followed by my grandmother's voice in the hall. She never knocked unless the door was locked. "Jenna?" she called loudly.

"In the kitchen." I rose to greet her. I didn't want her trying to go up the stairs to find me. "Did you drive here?"

"Of course I drove."

"I'm gonna tell Mom you don't have a license."

"I have a license. Whoever said I didn't have a license?"

"Let me see it, then."

"I don't have it *with* me, darling. Then people might know how old I am."

I shook my head. I would probably never know whether she was legally allowed to drive unless I called the police. And I wasn't positive they could make her produce a license even if she had one.

"What are you doing here?"

"Maybe I missed you."

"Did you?"

"No. But we have business to discuss." She took a seat at the kitchen table, and I sat back down as well.

"Business again?"

"This time it's your business." She reached into her purse and pulled out a manilla envelope that, for a brief moment, I thought was the very one I had brought to Brad the day before. She held it tightly for a second, then passed it to me.

"What's this?"

"Open it."

I undid the clasp and pulled out a stack of documents, then looked at her, my eyes wide. "This—what? How?"

It was the deed to the cottage.

"I signed it over to you yesterday."

"But how did you get it?"

She waved her hand dismissively. "I've owned it for years now."

"But—Louise sold it. And Bernie and Margaret wouldn't—I don't understand."

"She did. And your grandfather offered the woman who bought it a lot more than she paid, but she said no. So he told her if she ever decided to sell to let us know first. And about ten years ago, she called us."

Ten years ago.

"I told Fred it was silly. We were traveling so much and wouldn't be spending enough time there to make it worth it. But he said we could rent it out and that it was a wonderful investment. The whole town has turned into such a tourist destination. So we bought it." She reached across the table and took my hand. "And it's the perfect place for you to get a fresh start."

I squeezed her hand, my chest constricting at the magnitude of the gift she was giving me. What it meant to her. What it could mean for me. But—

"I don't want to leave you." It sounded so foolish when I said it, but it was true. She was a few weeks shy of eighty-nine. And after this week, I couldn't imagine losing the last few years we would have.

She patted my hand and smiled that wicked Evelyn Bergman Gold smile that still held so many secrets I hadn't uncovered yet. "Maybe you don't have to. I own the cottage next door too."

EPILOGUE

I opened my eyes, looking around at the now-familiar room, but still needing a few seconds to orient myself. Sunlight crept around the edges of the drawn curtains, which fluttered softly in the breeze from the open window.

Inhaling deeply, I could smell the salt of the ocean and the crisp odor of the pitch pines. The air had the hint of a chill in it, a whisper of what was to come from a Massachusetts winter.

Home, I thought drowsily. *I'm home.*

I had taken over the downstairs bedroom, claiming the antique dresser and desk from upstairs as mine when I learned they had come from the Main Street house.

Rolling over, I nestled in to go back to sleep, but a creaking sound caught my attention. It came again. Then a laugh, and my grandmother's voice saying Tony's name, followed by more creaking.

"We have *got* to start shutting that window," Joe murmured, rolling over to wrap his arms around me. "That's just gross."

"It's sweet too." The creaking intensified, and I got up to shut the window quickly. "Okay, it's gross."

I crawled back under the covers and snuggled up against Joe. But something was off. "Why are you so hairy?" I asked.

"Why are *you* so hairy?"

We looked at each other, then pulled the blanket back.

"Jax!"

She grinned up at us, perfectly content where she was. And for the first time in my life, so was I.

ACKNOWLEDGMENTS

I honestly have no idea how I wrote this book because it somehow happened over fourteen weeks in the hour and a half after my kids went to bed—after I spent all day teaching from home with a baby, in a pandemic. But I do know it wouldn't exist without the help of so many people who kept me sane during this whole crazy process.

First and foremost, I have to thank my amazing editor, Alicia Clancy, and the whole team at Lake Union. You believed in me enough to buy this book before I even wrote it, and there are no words to express how much that confidence helped bring this to fruition. Thank you for your insightful edits and for letting me add "published author" to my bio.

My agent, Rachel Beck, is seriously one of my favorite people on the planet. I love being able to bounce ideas off you, and you're one of the only people I'm comfortable asking for help (which, for a perfectionist with social anxiety, is REALLY saying something!). Thank you for being in my corner and for being the most amazing agent and friend in the world.

Thank you to my husband, Nick, for taking over sitting in Jacob's chair while he fell asleep so I could write. For cleaning the kitchen, taking the dogs out, watching the kids, and the million other responsibilities I shirked to write this book. Thank you for listening when

I needed to work a chapter out and for supporting my passion even before it helped pay the bills. I love you.

Thank you to Jacob and Max (and Rosie and Sandy) for being my reason for everything. Mommy loves you more than anything in the world.

To my mom, Carole Goodman: I could write a whole separate book thanking you. (I'm not doing it, so don't ask!) Thank you for talking this story through with me from the very beginning, for watching the kids, for answering Cape Ann questions, and for being my permanent first reader.

To my dad, Jordan Goodman: Thank you for the lifetime of support, the pictures that helped me create this town, the instilled love of photography that crafted some key scenes, and the idea to make Hereford fictional instead of trying to use Gloucester. I can always count on you for the practical answers that make my life easier every day, and I appreciate you so very much!

To my grandmother, Charlotte Chansky: Evelyn may not be you, but she wouldn't exist without you either. Thank you for the million stories, the utter disdain for rules, and the lesson that a good tale is much better than the truth. Also, I want everyone to know that the Sweet'N Low rest stop scene one hundred percent happened, even if the rest of the book didn't.

To my brother, Adam Goodman; my sister-in-law, Nicole; and my nephews, Cam and Luke: Thank you for believing in me—and for buying enough copies of *For the Love of Friends* for your whole neighborhood. That was both insane and the best gift ever.

To my aunt and uncle, Dolly and Marvin Band: Thank you for kvelling every time you talk about my writing. You always make me feel so much more accomplished than I actually am!

To my uncle Michael Chansky and aunt Stephanie Abbuhl: Thank you for your generosity—the epilogue was written entirely from my favorite chair in the downstairs den of the Avalon house. (And no,

Mike, that doesn't mean you get royalties!) Thank you to my cousins Andrew, Peter, and Ben Chansky for your excitement over all of my publishing news.

To my cousins Allison Band, Andy Levine, Ian and Kim Band, and Mindy and Alan Nagler: Thank you for loving me, encouraging me, and always being there for me.

To Mark Kamins: Thank you for helping me navigate how to actually manage my money now that I'm getting paid for my passion (still so weird that that's a thing!) and for being my number one Canadian fan (I'd give you the American title too, but then Mom would fight you!).

To Kevin Keegan—my life changed the day you walked into Doc Goodwin's ninth grade English class and said, "A future editor-in-chief could be sitting in this room right now." Thank you for absolutely everything.

To Jennifer Lucina: Thank you for being the best friend I could ever ask for. I am better at everything I do because of you.

To Rachel Friedman: Thank you for always grounding me and making me feel like I'm not crazy (even when I might be acting a little crazy).

To Sonya Shpilyuk: Thank you for being you and for loving me for the ridiculous human being that I am.

To Sarah Elbeshbishi and Jennifer Bardsley: Thank you for being my beta readers and friends. Your insight and belief in me mean the world.

To Jessica Markham: Thank you for providing free legal counsel and for taking the time to make sure I knew what I was talking about.

To my Apub debut siblings, Eden Appiah-Kubi, Jennifer Bardsley, Elissa Dickey, Paulette Kennedy, Kate Myles, and Mansi Shah: Thank you for helping me navigate this all. You're the best, and I can't wait to see what our futures hold.

To Katie Stutzman, Georgia Zucker, Jan Guttman, Sarah McKinley, Reka Montfort, Kerrin Torres, Laura Davis Vaughan, Joye Young Saxon,

Christen Dimmick, Amy Shellabarger, Shelley Miller, and Christine Wilson: Thank you for being my friends, my cheerleaders, and my people.

To the Confino family: Thank you for your support.

To my students, past and present: Thank you for being so excited about this wild, wild ride.

And finally, to my readers: Thank you for making my dreams come true.

ABOUT THE AUTHOR

Photo © 2021 Gina Psallidas

Sara Goodman Confino is the author of *For the Love of Friends*. She teaches high school English and journalism in Montgomery County, Maryland, where she lives with her husband, two sons, and miniature schnauzer Sandy. When she's not writing or working out, she can be found on the beach or at a Bruce Springsteen show, sometimes even dancing onstage. For more information visit www.saraconfino.com.